Andrew Holmes

Andrew Holmes's first novel, *Sleb*, was published in 2002 to critical acclaim and was shortlisted for the WHSmith New Talent Award. *All Fur Coat* is his second novel.

ALSO BY ANDREW HOLMES

Sleb

ANDREW HOLMES

All Fur Coat

SCEPTRE

Copyright © 2004 by Andrew Holmes

First published in Great Britain in 2004 by Hodder and Stoughton
A division of Hodder Headline

The right of Andrew Holmes to be identified as the Author
of the Work has been asserted by him in accordance with the
Copyright, Designs and Patents Act 1988.

A Sceptre paperback

1 3 5 7 9 10 8 6 4 2

A CIP catalogue record for this title is
available from the British Library

ISBN 0 340 82363 1

Typeset in Sabon by Palimpsest Book Production Limited,
Polmont, Stirlingshire

Printed and bound by
Mackays of Chatham Ltd, Chatham, Kent

Hodder Headline's policy is to use papers that are natural,
renewable and recyclable products and made from wood grown in
sustainable forests. The logging and manufacturing processes
are expected to conform to the environmental regulations
of the country of origin.

Hodder and Stoughton Ltd
A division of Hodder Headline
338 Euston Road
London NW1 3BH

For my wife and best friend, Claire

Acknowledgements

Thank you so much for all your support, love and encouragement: Mum and Dad; Granny; Dave, Nat and Georgina; Tobs, Sarah and Daniel. For early read-throughs and thoughts: Dave and Lucy (may the Fawce be with them); Andrew Gordon, Joanna Anderson, David and Maria; Nick Taylor; Rob Waugh; Alex Simmons; Steve O'Hagan; David Roberts; Matt Thorne and Jenny Eclair. For making it a team sport: Antony Topping; Katy Follain; Juliet Van Oss and all at Hodder. And for technical support: Dr James Le Fanu; Sunset at Browns, and Katia at Spearmint Rhino.

THE FIRST DAY

CHAPTER ONE

Standing here, scared, it occurs to me that I've known Cooper for too long. In one way or another he's been in the background of my life since I was barely out of my teens – a shadow. Only, a small shadow, because he's not a big guy. And I guess you could say that my relationship with him has changed over the years. Once upon a time I thought he was a funny little man with a floppy tongue which was too big for his mouth. One of God's throwaway gags. Now it comes to this: him, holding court in the front room of his terraced house in Plaistow; me, standing before him like a nervous courtier.

For the moment he's ignoring me, more interested in his two council estate cronies, the pair of them installing a huge television set while he bleats moist-sounding orders from the safety of his perch. It's a good-sized front room as front rooms go; still, it's not quite big enough for three and a half men and a telly as big as a car windscreen.

'No, not that shelf,' he barks at one of the cronies, who straightens and gives me the benefit of a well-honed hard stare before looking testily at Cooper. 'Put the DVD on the top shelf and the video on the bottom.'

Cooper's command centre is a huge armchair, a recliner that lifts his little leggies off the floor so he can watch his new home entertainment set-up in perfect comfort.

'Mind out the way a minute, Greil,' he says. He pronounces my name the way I like, to rhyme with 'real'. He has that much respect for me, at least. I take a step to the side. I wish he wasn't getting the goons so riled up, I think, trying to project an aura of relaxed calm into the room. The heat doesn't help. It's early but the sun already has his hat on, and I can feel droplets of sweat tickling at my underarms. I feel hungover sick and adjust the waistband of my trousers with a thumb that comes away wet with perspiration and probably, if I was to sniff it, smelling slightly of dry-cleaning. I swallow dry and try to remember that I'm among friends here; that I've known Cooper for years, certainly for longer than his cronies – from a time before he even needed cronies, in fact – when together we were like a little starter pack to the music industry. Him, the bright-eyed and big-tongued club owner. Me, the guitarist with an equally bright-eyed band helping to put his venue on the map.

'Not seen you in the *NME* for a while, Greil,' he says. He means writing for it, not appearing in it. 'You given that up altogether?'

'That's right,' I say, just about my first words since entering the house. 'Nationals now,' and I flap my suit jacket for extra emphasis, creating a breeze that disturbs the room's fetid air: fag smoke, BO, fried food.

''Course,' he remembers. 'I've seen your name in one of the Sundays. You do them little album reviews.'

'And other things,' I say, ignoring the way his tongue seemed to shift over the word 'little'. 'Interviews. Theatre reviews and stuff.'

'Theatre reviews? Fuckin' hell, an art critic. Do you get free tickets and that?'

His eyes gleam but I'm spared by one of the cronies who straightens from the back of the telly and says to Cooper, 'We need a Scart lead, Craig.'

Craig Cooper. What a name. Picture poor Cooper's parents, looking lovingly into their newborn's cot – 'Let's call him Craig' – no doubt unaware that within his infant mouth lurked an outsize tongue; sentencing their offspring to a glottal future of working it around his own name.

'A what lead?' he says now.

'A Scart lead.'

He sighs. 'Mind out the way a minute, Greil. Why do we need one of them? What's wrong with the lead that came with

4

it?' I move over more and feel the emptine... hoping this Scart lead business doesn't turn...

'The lead that came with it is an RGB c... the first crony. He wears a white baseball cap th... the general direction of the ceiling. This season's lo... accessorising it with a gold earring, tracky bottoms and a ... T-shirt available from J.D. Sports. Acne, model's own.

'The RGB will be fine,' says the second one from the other side of the TV, glaring hazard warning lights at his mate. He's bigger. Indistinct prison tats. Looks like he supports Arsenal, but you can't be sure.

'No it won't,' says the first.

'Yeah it will,' says the second.

'No it won't,' says the first.

'Tenner says it will,' says the second, and I perk up at the smell of a wager in the air.

'It'll work, yeah,' says the first, ignoring the bet, 'but the signal won't be digital. See, the DVD is a Digital Versatile Disc, but the RGB is an analogue connector. In order to preserve the integrity of the signal we need to use a digital connector, which is why we need a Scart lead.'

Cooper looks impressed. He looks to see if I'm equally impressed by his intellectually nubile cronies. In turn, I look impressed.

The second crony just looks exasperated. Maybe he's having trouble settling into his new role as part-time electrical installation engineer. 'Yeah,' he insists. 'But it won't make any *difference*.'

'Yeah, it will,' says the first, and if they have a fight, which seems likely, my money's on the second crony. Of course, I don't actually have any money, which is why I'm praying they won't have a fight.

'It's not going to make any difference to him,' says the second, jerking his thumb at Cooper.

'Woah,' jumps in Cooper. 'What am I, the cat's muvver?' He addresses the second crony. 'Will there be a difference or not?'

'...so you'll notice,' he replies, sulky.

'But there *will* be a difference,' says the first, the pair of them daggers across the top of the TV.

'That settles it, then,' says Cooper from his throne. 'We need a Scart lead. Have we got one at the store?'

The store. The fabled store. Where things are kept. Where things happen. In my pockets, my fists clench.

'Don't think so,' says crony one. 'Pretty certain not.'

'Jesus,' says Cooper, his tongue coming out for air. 'Then we'll just have to buy one, won't we? One of you's going to have to go out and get it. Come on, hands up.'

Neither of them wants to go and they end up tossing a coin, which flips through the volatile air to land in favour of the Scart lead supporter. He does a fine job of hiding his look of triumph.

'I'll need some money,' says the RGB apologist, his jaw set. I sense trouble clearing its throat.

Cooper looks my way. 'That's all right. Greil's got some money for us, haven't you, Greil? We'll take it out of that . . .'

*

Sonia Jewel sits at her desk in a carefully arranged job interview pose. She thinks she looks forbidding, like people should call her ma'am in a BBC costume drama. But it's an act, you can tell. Sonia's one of those people who's decided they're a character. Chances are she used to be a model herself, before she started the agency, and now she sits in judgement on girls like me, calling us all 'darling', purring it poshly at us in between posh drags on a posh cigarette.

She regards me silently over the desk, which is supposed to give me the willies. So in return I do my bit, meeting her stare all sweetness and light, with just the right trace of nerves, which is what she's looking for after all. I bite my lip a little. Model? I should get an Oscar just for this. Best performance of an awestruck wide-eyed innocent in a supporting role.

The wall behind her is tiled with what seems like hundreds of framed pictures: newspaper cuttings, dozens of Page Threes, spreads from glossy magazines, all with one thing in common – two things in common – boobs. All of them girls like me, who no doubt sat in this very seat, only wide-eyed for real, waiting for her to say, Sorry, our books are full, or, Your hips are too wide, or, You're too small, or whatever women like her tell the failures.

In front of her on the desk is my portfolio ('They're good pictures, Heidi. Professional. Must have cost you a pretty penny.' *Thanks, they did. Simper*). She's taken a good look. I've stood up for her, given her a twirl, felt her eyes assessing me and wondered if she's a lesbian. And now she breaks the never-ending stare, convinced she's got me quivering like a plate of birthday jelly, bless her, and snaps shut my portfolio. 'Well . . .' she says, pausing the kind of pause you'd expect at the final of *Pop Idol*, 'I think we can probably make a model out of you, Heidi.'

'That's wonderful,' I say breathlessly. 'Thank you.' And I think the right thing to do in this instance is to close my eyes, so I do. And I find myself thinking of my ex, Mark, who spent the last three months of our relationship going, 'Should you be eating that, what with you wanting to be a famous model an' all?', and the girls at school who always talked about being models, and one who even went so far as to do topless for a local photographer and then went strangely quiet, and the ones who entered Carnival Queen, or enrolled in classes, or went and did those soft-focus makeover pictures. Bitchy girls – all tattoos and single-parent families now. I think about them, and I'm giving them the finger.

When I open my eyes Sonia's smiling at me, and for a second I forget that she's spent the last twenty minutes shamelessly trying to manipulate my emotions, and instead I envy her job making people's dreams come true. I've got to admit, it feels good.

For the first time I notice that she has a bit of stuff, mayonnaise or something like that, stuck to the side of her mouth. Maybe now we're friends I should tell her. Maybe not.

'So,' she says, 'you're a dancer. Where do you work?'

'All Fur Coat.'

'Oh. Really?'

'Do you know it?'

She laughs. 'No, darling, not know it. Heard of it, naturally. And what about modelling. Ever done any?'

'No, not apart from the portfolio.'

'You're sure? Nothing in the past? Best to tell me now . . . Never been in the papers? No kiss-and-tell?'

I shake my head no.

She looks at me doubtfully, as though I'm lying. 'You must be the only dancer in the West End who hasn't.'

'Not me,' I say. Then, 'Should I, do you think? Does it help with the modelling?' I smile at her like butter wouldn't melt.

'It can, yes. Plenty of girls do it. And providing you don't become known just for kiss-and-tell, it can be useful. Beware, though. If you're tempted it helps to get a bit of modelling under your belt first. Bookers get a bit sniffy if the only print work you've got to show them is "Spurs Star Lifted My C-Cups". Why do you ask?'

'Oh,' I say, 'no reason.' Then, 'When can I start, do you think – the modelling I mean?'

'Well, there's good and bad news. The good news is that a lot of the girls are on holiday. The bad news is that they're on holiday because work is a bit thin on the ground at the moment.'

'Oh,' I say.

'But don't worry. There's the odd exhibition coming up, and there's always work for girls on the stands. Stand is about right. You'll spend a lot of time handing out leaflets and looking pretty. Nothing too demanding, darling. Plus it's very hot, so the papers will be looking for girls they can put in picture spreads. A shot of you cooling down beside the seaside, eating an ice lolly, things like that. I'll put you forward if anything comes up, talk you up to the people I meet. Your picture will go on the website.'

She pauses to leaf through a large diary on the desk in front of her.

'Tell you what,' she says at last, 'I can't guarantee anything, but there's a job here I could put you forward for, casting soon. How's about that?'

'That's brilliant.'

*

In Egypt there lives a species of bird formally known as *Pluvianus aegyptius*, more commonly referred to as the Egyptian plover. A vagrant species, the bird feeds by picking food from the mouth of a gaping crocodile, which, whether hungry or not, will never eat the plover, recognising the important function it plays. The alliance between the two – rare, but not unique in nature – is symbiotic. Their relationship is conducted on the banks of the river Nile.

On a poster in London, a man in a pinstriped suit stands behind a goddess. The man is indistinct. He stands shrouded by shadows and smoke, nothing more than an impression, a sinister presence. The only part of his body not obscured is his hand, which rests on the shoulder of the goddess sitting in front of him, lounging really. Dressed as a Thirties showgirl, she is a bright centre of colour and focus amid the gloom. Hers is a careless, capricious sexuality. Her legs are crossed – a glimpse of strappy shoes – and she holds a cigarette in a manner that appears confrontational, despite the long holder resting between two fingers.

On close scrutiny of the poster one can see tiny traces of lipstick tipping the end of the holder. Her lips are *profondo rosso*. Carmine red. Parted, moist and almost scornful. Her eyes, though. Her eyes betray the truth her body strives to hide. She wishes to appear hard but her eyes suggest a softness, a vulnerability. A pain. The pain of captivity, perhaps. Of dreams destroyed by powers beyond her control.

She wears little more than a slip, a showgirl's dress decorated with beads around the neck. The outline of one nipple can be seen through the fabric. The other nipple should be

9

correspondingly visible but it is obscured by something. It is covered by a piece of chewing gum.

I reach for it now, the gum. I reach and my fingers pinch it from the poster. It comes away trailing a thin rope, and I dab the gum back to collect it so that when I peer closely at the poster there is just the tiniest remnant left, almost invisible. She is perfect again. Tonight is her big night. She opens tonight. She needs to look her best. I flick the chewing gum to the pavement.

'Thank God. For one horrible moment there, I thought you were going to put that in your mouth.'

I turn – reluctantly, unwilling to be drawn away from her image – to see two men standing behind me. Both wear sunglasses. Something about one of them is familiar. He has his hands in his pockets, smart suit – a wealthy man's suit – and he's pushing his chest and stomach out like a man whose life is meeting his expectations. His companion is standing slightly back and looking hot. He has his arms folded across his chest. An assistant. Or a bodyguard. A person paid to stand back and bear the temperature.

The rich man moves his sunglasses on to his head, which is odd because even though he's not old, he's too old for this to be an acceptable thing to do with his sunglasses. Beneath his shades he has a rich man's tan that nevertheless fails to penetrate his crow's feet, which look like cracks in a dried puddle.

He laughs: 'You've saved the cleaners a job, anyway. Nice one. I'd shake your hand, but . . .' I look at my hand where I see the gum hasn't flicked to the pavement as I'd intended. It clings to the end of my finger still, like a wart. 'Tell you what, we'll leave the handshaking, eh?' He seems amused. He glows beneath the sun. 'What's your name?'

'Simon.'

'Simon.' He pats one hand to his jacket. 'Are you homeless, Simon?'

'No,' I say, 'I'm an artist.' And I find I'm pleased he's made this mistake, pleased he's caught me off guard, in a reverie. An *artistic* reverie. His suit and easy manner tell me all I need to know about him; in return, I'm an enigma.

Still, his faux pas amuses him, his puddle cracks close up. 'Then it all makes sense,' he says. 'You're an artist. You appreciate beautiful things. And she,' he points at the poster over my shoulder, 'she is bee-yoo-tee-full.' I flick my finger but the wart clings on. 'What's your line of work then, Simon?'

'I just said. I'm an artist.' I can never quite omit the damning note of pride in my voice when I say this, and it seems to produce another smile in him now.

'Yeah, but what do you do, art-wise? You draw? You sculpt? Bricks, cut-up cows and that? What?'

'I paint.'

'And decorate?'

I ignore him.

'Just pulling your lariat, mate. What sort of stuff do you paint?'

I think of the goddess on the poster behind me, my daily pilgrimages to gaze at her image. *Her*, I think suddenly, the idea seeming to fill my skull with sunshine. I paint her.

But to him I say, 'All sorts.'

'You paint liquorice?'

I ignore him.

'S'all right, mate, don't mind me. And this all-sorts painting, does it pay the rent? You'll pardon me, I'm sure, if I say that your artistic status notwithstanding, you don't *look* that prosperous.'

'I do all right,' I lie.

The rich man smiles up at the sun, which smiles back. He indicates the poster. 'She's a work of art, isn't she, Simon? You know her name?'

Her name is not on the poster, which simply advertises the show's title, *Moll*, the venue, dates and booking details. But elsewhere, at the front of the theatre, is a separate notice displaying cast information, and from here I learned her name

11

– Emily. Emily Benstead – and that *Moll* is her debut West End show.

'She's my wife,' he says (his wife, I think), 'and this,' he spreads his arms to embrace the theatre before him, 'is my show. You see, Si, we're both artists after a fashion. We both appreciate beauty, ain't that right?'

'Yes,' I say.

'Mr B, we're going to be late,' says the other man.

'Yeah, yeah. Wait up. I've got something I want to ask Simon.'

I flick the wart, which remains on my finger. Mr Benstead drapes a hand across my shoulder. He towers over me. I feel the cotton of his suit against my cheek.

'Simon, mate,' he says. 'How would you like to get paid for doing something you've just done for free?'

'I'm sorry?' I say, concentrating on keeping my wart away from his suit.

'I'm saying, you see this poster, it's everywhere, mate. Blanket promotion all over town, and it's not cheap. It is *not* cheap, mate. You use the tube at all?'

'Not really.'

'Then you might not have seen it, but it's all over. Those little framed adverts up and down the escalators, you know the ones I mean?'

'Yes.' I do know the ones he means. About A3 – perhaps a bastard size. I'm suddenly electrified by the thought of this poster's identical twin existing all over the underground system, just below my feet. Emily everywhere.

'I used to be a footballer, Si, did you know?' he says, hooking me out of my daydream.

'I thought I recognised you,' I reply truthfully, because I *have* seen him. On television, giving his opinion after football matches; in old newspaper photographs, kissing his shirt after a goal, beaming teammates hanging off him like Siamese twins.

'Yeah, maybe from the papers. I'd guess you're too young

to remember my playing days. I tell you one thing I've never forgotten from those days, though, mate. Psychology. And now I'm thinking how that psychology applies to my show, because I tell you what, if I was a punter, and I saw one of my posters and it had stuff on it like that, I'd think, whether I wanted to or not – because it's all psychology – I'd think, "There's something up with that show. It's a bit tatty". You know what I mean, Si?'

'I think.'

'So what about this? In honour of the opening night tonight, I give you a hundred quid to spend the day buzzing round the tube stations in Central London. Not everywhere – you've no need to go to bleedin' Neasden – just the ones in town, where the tourists gather, you know? Go round and make sure all those posters are doing their job, right? You make sure that nothing obscures that work of art right there. You become her protector . . .'

'Mr B?' From behind us comes the questioning voice of his assistant.

'Don't worry,' says Mr Benstead. 'Simon's a trustworthy lad, aren't you, Si? And anyway, we'll be checking a couple of stations later, random ones.' He thinks I don't see him wink at his assistant. 'We'll check this afternoon, and later – no, not later, we're busy later – okay, tomorrow, if that's all right by you, Si, Simon can pick up his money. What about that, mate? You doing anything today? Easiest hundred quid you ever earned. What about it?'

('*You become her protector.*') 'Yes,' I say. 'Yes, I'll do it.' And Mr Benstead slaps me on the back, sending me stumbling forward, which I combine with a flick to finally rid myself of the wart.

'Excellent,' he barks. 'Give him the Liaisons card,' he says to his assistant, then to me, 'If you come to that address tomorrow, you can pick up the hundred, which I'll give you with my thanks. Sound all right?'

'Yes.'

He pulls his sunglasses from his head and replaces them on his face, goes to shake my hand but thinks better of it. 'Then let's not delay,' he adds. 'Big day ahead. I'll see you tomorrow, Si. Good luck, eh? Oh, and ask at the box office inside. Tell them I said to give you a spare poster. Souvenir of your day.' And he bounds up the short steps to the theatre door, leaving me with the assistant who gives me a long, appraising look before handing me a card bearing the name of a nightclub, Liaisons.

'Just ring the doorbell,' says the assistant, and he, too, is gone.

I stare at the card a moment, take my rucksack from my shoulder, open my notebook and place the card inside.

CHAPTER TWO

Well, I've learnt a couple of things today, at least. I've found out that Cooper's fuse has shortened considerably since the last time I looked. And I've found out – not that it's something I've ever wanted to know, but I've found out – that my hand, my whole hand, fits quite comfortably into the slot of Cooper's kitchen toaster, which one of his goons has fetched from the kitchen and set up on the arm of his chair. Cooper hasn't even moved. And now the toaster's plugged in and I'm standing with one hand in my pocket, the other in Cooper's toaster. I'm sweating a little.

It's a thick-slice toaster, naturally. A big, silver, thick-slice toaster. The kind you see in cafés, with a little caddy handle for ejecting the bread.

'Eh, boss, shall I fetch the toasted-sandwich maker?' says the RGB crony. The three of them crack up laughing.

'Yeah, yeah,' cackles Cooper, 'then we could have a toasted *hand*wich.' The three of them crack up laughing again.

The Scart lead fan stands by the socket. He's smoking a cigarette from the inside of his hand, the way you'd expect, his eyes narrowed to slits. The toaster's plugged in and the caddy handle's down, but the socket's turned off. RGB, whose mood has brightened considerably since I revealed that I had no money to pay for the lead he didn't even want to fetch anyway, stands at my side, the non-appliance side, just in case I try to make a break for it. Looking more closely, I can see that he does support Arsenal after all.

Meanwhile Cooper sits fiddling with the timer control in a vaguely sinister fashion, like Inspector Gadget's evil dwarf twin. He winds it all the way round to Defrost.

'See that, Greil? You've got some bread out of the freezer, you need it defrosting, you use this setting. I always find the Defrost setting ends up slightly toasting the bread, though.' He twiddles the knob back a few notches. 'My opinion, here is where you want it if you just want defrosted bread without the toast element, even though the shading, here, seems to suggest it's for people who like their toast well done. Course, you end up having to make adjustments after the first toasting session anyway, because the toaster's in its stride by then, so what's lightly toasted on the first go ends up being well done by the third slice. I don't know if they mention that in the manual, but I'm sure I'm not alone in saying that I've never once read a toaster manual. I wonder, though, what would happen if you set it here?' Now he moves the timer right back to the beginning of the cycle. 'It hardly seems worth bothering with, does it? Or maybe it's for people who want their butter to melt, but don't actually want the full toast experience.' He indicates to Scart, who pushes the socket button. The timer starts clicking. *Tick-a-tick-a-tick-a-tick-a*. The toaster makes a barely perceptible sound as it crackles into life. RGB moves that bit closer.

'Craig,' I say. 'See, I'm perspiring quite heavily. I could break the toaster. You know, short it out or something.'

'No worries, Greil. We got plenty of toasters in the store.'

I feel warmth begin to tickle my palm. 'You know, Craig, it is sort of starting to get hot,' I say, watching the timer tick round. Then, just as the heat becomes uncomfortable, it pings finished.

Cooper looks at me, smiles; indicates to Scart, who turns off the power. 'So it gets hot then?' he says to me.

'Yeah,' I say, feeling the toaster cool around my hand. 'Yeah, it gets hot, okay?'

'Enough to melt the butter?'

'I'd say so, yes.'

'Well, that solves that, then,' and he turns up the timer to halfway, about the same setting I use on my toaster at home.

'Come on, Craig. Come on, mate,' I say. 'Please don't do this, eh?'

'Because why?' he says.

'Because I can get you the money. I just came to ask for an extension, that's all.'

Cooper splutters. 'What, the dog ate your money? This isn't homework, Greil. It's not a fucking theatre review. It's three months is what it is. Three months of you saying, "Ooh, Craig, I ain't got your money," and me seeing your name in the paper and thinking, "that's funny, he's telling me he's broke but there's his name in the paper—"'

'Those things pay fuck all.'

'Oh yeah? And what about all that sniffing when you came in, eh? Summer cold, is it? Don't make me laugh. You're stuffing my money up your fucking nose.' He pokes a finger up his own nose, making a mad sniffing face at the same time. 'I ought to burn you, Greil. I ought to burn you because you always were a piss-takey bastard and you're still taking the piss now.'

'Craig, I'm not taking the—'

'You are. You still are. The only difference is that you're a sad loser now, and I'm sick to the back teeth of you losing on my time.' He waits for me to tell him I'm not a sad loser, but I don't. I'd be lying. Instead I regard my hand, up to the wrist in his toaster, saying nothing.

'You've got two days,' he says at last. 'Two days to pay what you owe me or I'll turn you all the way up to Defrost.' He pushes the caddy arm and the toaster ejects my hand. 'And don't get crumbs all over my carpet.'

They're probably watching me from behind the net curtains as I make my way to the car. I make sure I'm the picture of contrition as I get in and start up. Once I'm round the corner I stop again, and for a moment or so I study my palm.

And then I close my eyes, and I pray that when I open them

again my life will have fucked off and left me alone. But I open them again, and it hasn't. It's still there.

I never said sorry. Sorry, Cooper, for taking and not giving. For taking the piss. He was right, we did, and me worst of all. As a band we were politically correct before anybody had even heard of the term, but all the time we were laying into the me-culture – musical highlights: 'Spazz Sick' (Mitchell/Sharkey); 'He-Rape' (Mitchell/Sharkey) – we somehow forgot about Cooper.

It goes without saying that we called him Mini Cooper, and worse. And we conveniently, accidentally-on-purpose misheard his overtures to become our manager. It was okay to give us rehearsal space, to loan us the money for gear, to give us no end of support slots, and headline gigs whenever he could, and free beer (in exchange for which we called him the Mini-Bar), but when it came to managing us? Well, we never actually said why we didn't want the big-tongued dwarf tagging along behind us, being our ambassador. That would have been plain rude.

When everything fell apart it was me that ended up paying off the loan – still am now – and topping it up too. And maybe I kept going to him because of the guilt. Guilt over the piss-take; guilt because he helped us and we ignored him in return. I wanted to make him feel good about himself, like a mack daddy instead of the runt he always used to be. Only, somewhere along the line he really has become the mack daddy. A tiny, vicious alderman, the toast master. He was right. I always took the piss. If I was him I'd have put me up to Defrost and left me there.

So, what am I bid for an old, tan-coloured Mercedes? A classic, but only in the loosest sense – in the sense that drug dealers openly guffaw when I chunter by. But it's mine. I've had sex in it, I've slept in it three times, lost it twice, accidentally let it roll down a hill near Chichester and once spilt a packet of chocolate raisins in it. Three years ago that happened, and rogue raisins have been turning up ever since. And when, at the third attempt, I manage to find a dodgy dealer willing to take a tan Mercedes off my hands, and I leave the lot with a grand and some change – enough to make my peace with Cooper – I know that I'm going to miss the car, and I'm going to miss finding those raisins.

At home I get to work. I write and file a theatre review and then I write a review of the new Cornershop album, and despite the album being brilliant, I compare Cornershop unfavourably with the 'now sadly defunct' Systemitis, 'from whom a retrospective is long overdue (ahem)'.

It strikes me that nobody will know the review's author was lead guitarist with Systemitis, so I take out the '(ahem)'. Anybody who does remember me will get the joke. So I add 'surely' in, so it reads '. . . from whom a retrospective is *surely* long overdue'. Because it is a joke. And I file that review, which means it's the end of my working day, so I have a drink and a line of coke, and then another drink, and then I do a bit of air guitaring to 'Li'l Devil' by The Cult.

In my playing days I used to wear my guitar really low, only just above my knees. I was semi-famous for my low-slung guitar look; I did it way before it was fashionable. The thing about low-slung guitar is that to look good you either have to lean right forward, the shoegazer way, which makes you look as wet as Manchester, or right back, which is what I did. I looked the business: bare-chested and sweating cobs; hips thrust forward, head back and mouth open like I was about to receive libations from the righteous rock gods. Or like I was trying to catch a sweet in my mouth. Either way, it was a look.

But now – distressingly – I find that I've forgotten how to air guitar even. I'm holding the neck of my air guitar up by my elbow, the gay way, like that wanker out of Level 42, and after a while I give it up, put on my jacket which swings heavily with the weight of the money, which

I don't take out and put in a safe place, and I leave the flat.

*

Today is foot day. Della doesn't know that. She thinks we happen to be doing our feet by chance, or maybe that it's symbolic because she leaves tomorrow. What she doesn't know is whether she was here or not, I'd be doing the same thing. I'd be doing my pedicure and watching TV. Sorry, Della, mate. Business is business.

It would count as a girl's night in, if it was night. I'm working later so we make the afternoon our night. Della brings a bottle of wine and we close the curtains against the baking sun, so apart from the sounds of the kids playing football, and apart from the fact that we're watching a kids' programme called *My Parents Are Aliens* and not *EastEnders*, it's night.

We slip into our respective roles easily. Della plays the part of good-humoured sceptic ('All this trouble for feet?' she says, kicking up a grotty trainer. 'These little walky things at the ends of your legs that no one ever sees?') while I play half older sister and half enthusiastic-girl-at-make-up-counter. We've saturated our cotton-wool balls with nail polish remover, and I've shown Della the best way to get nails clean. You have to hold the cotton-wool ball on the nail for a moment before you start wiping, using a circular motion. Then we get the wine open, pour a glass each, and soak our feet. Della has my washing-up bowl, I have to squish my feet into a salad bowl. We do it twice. Once for twenty minutes with bath beads in the water to help soften the feet, and then a second time for ten minutes using sea salt tablets that help get rid of dead skin. Della takes the piss, in a good-humoured, sceptical way. In return I compare my big toe, which looks like a big toe should look, with her big toe, which looks like a mouldy pink mushroom. She gives me a look which says she couldn't give a stuff about the way her big toe looks. I show her my Gucci watch. The points are shared.

I'm in full teacher mode when I go on to filing then moisturising our feet, and not with a hand moisturiser either. They don't contain enough moisturiser, especially for hot-weather feet. I get my feet-formula cream from the Body Shop.

Della is – or was – a waitress at the club. Was, because tomorrow she returns to Australia. We waitressed together for a while, only she never had the 'if-they're-going-to-stare-at-my-tits, I-might-as-well-charge-them-for-it' moment that I did. Or maybe nobody was staring at her tits. Either way.

Della and I, we're about as different as two girls can be, but I'm gutted to see her leave. I don't make friends easily – at the club, not at all. This is partly because I can't be bothered to make friends with the girls at the club – most of them are straitjackets waiting to happen – and partly because I used to be a waitress, same as Della. Thing is, there's a bit of a waitress/dancer divide at the club. Always has been as far as I know. The waitresses wear little outfits with waistcoats and bow ties, and the dancers . . . well, we don't. The waitresses reckon we're letting the side down – the side being the whole female side – by taking our clothes off for men. They never say so, but you can tell. And obviously they envy us the money and probably the attention too if they're honest. Like I say, they never come out with any of this, but I used to be one, so I know.

On the other side of the fence, which isn't really a fence, more like a wall, the dancers think the waitresses have it easy and don't like the fact that they get tips. They – or should I say we? – say the dancing's the main attraction, and dancers are self-employed so they should get all the tips going, not the waitresses. Maybe it's because she's Australian, but Della never seemed to notice the undercurrents of resentment that pull and push us all at the club. And maybe because she's Australian they never seemed to apply to her anyway. Hence, me and Della: friends. Me and everybody else: hmm, the jury's out.

Once our feet are scrubbed and free of dead skin we clean under nails, file and clip, and then use cuticle sticks before we apply a base coat polish. I pass Della a packet of toe dividers and she holds them up in astonishment. 'Jesus, Hide. You ever thought that perhaps you take this kind of thing a bit *too* seriously?' And then she notices the back of the door where I keep my rota. 'And what the fuck is all that about?'

She hobbles over on the balls of her feet, me cringing because I think she's going to get bits of carpet on her polish, or polish on my carpet. Also because she's about to discover that today is foot day.

'Okay,' she says, peering at the calendar, glass of wine in one hand. 'Explain. What is *S/B K. off*?'

'Sunbed. Knickers off.'

'Right. So *S/B K. on* is knickers on, right?'

'Yes.'

'Sorry if it sounds like a dumb question, but, like, *why*?'

'You have one sunbed with knickers on, and one with knickers off. It's so you're brown down there, but not as brown as the rest of you.' She still looks gone out. 'It's for the punters. So it's not totally white and pikey, but they still feel like they're seeing something no one else ever does, see?'

'Does everybody do that?'

'I don't know about everybody. I do it. Makes sense to me.'

'I've got to admit, there's a kind of perverse logic to it,' she says, indicating the rota, 'and the Heidi thing to do is to write it down so you know whether it's S/B K. off or on. Gotcha. And *Wax*, that means wax, right? Ouch. Every fortnight? Christ.'

''Fraid so. Till I get laser hair removal.'

'And what's this? What does *F* mean?'

'Facial.'

'*M*?'

'Manicure.'

'*DL*?'

'Driving lesson.'

'Still with the same guy – Doctor Octopus?'

'Last time we were talking about what car I should buy, and

he said he thought I should get something small and sporty, like me.'

'He never!'

'He did.'

'And what's today? Today is *P*. Let me guess . . . Oh no. Pedicure?'

In reply I look sheepish.

'See, this is what you get when you cross Monica from *Friends* with a lap dancer. You get a Heidi – a control freak who takes her gear off for money.'

Della hobbles back and I wince again at the thought of the possible meeting of damp Chanel nail polish with my carpet. 'I'm not a control freak,' I say.

'Are.'

'Am not.'

'Hide, where's the TV remote?'

'Over on top of the TV.'

'Next to the stereo remote and the video remote. I rest my case.'

She arrives back at the sofa miraculously having failed to spill wine or wreck the carpet. 'And don't give me those little-girl eyes,' she says. 'They might work on the punters; they don't work on me. Shit, Hide. I don't know if you're a traitor to women or an example to us all.'

I laugh the right laugh, which in the circumstances is a kind of embarrassed, sorry-can't-help-myself laugh, because I know that Della doesn't mind, not really. She hasn't got a bitchy bone in her body.

She sits down and we apply two coats of the nail colour and then a final coat, and I tell Della her pedicure should last two weeks – even though I'll do mine again next week – and that the next time she does it, sitting in a beach house perhaps, she should think of me. We sit waiting for the coats to dry and Della moans, Why can't we use a hairdryer, and I say, No, the polish will crack, and then the phone rings and I know before I answer that it's Sonia. I just know.

'Darling,' she purrs, poshly. 'Sonia. Listen, are you busy tomorrow?'

I'd promised Della I'd see her off from her flat. A final glass of wine. 'No,' I say, reaching out an excited hand to grab her arm.

'Excellent. You know this job I told you about, casting soon?'

'Yes.' Beside me Della squeals as I squeeze her arm too hard.

'Well the casting's tomorrow. They want to see you.'

THE NEXT DAY

And now here we are. Heidi Mark Two. Heidi the model on her way to her first ever casting. It's for a lads' mag, said Sonia, and I recognised the name because ex-boyfriend Mark used to read it. 'It'll be topless, but there's no problem with that, is there, darling?' she asked. No, I told her. No problem with that at all.

Heidi the lap dancer has prepared for this like it's a military operation, much to Della's delight. After the Sonia call, I forced her to sit through endless outfit combinations before badgering her into doing a 'mock casting'. 'Hopefully they won't be pissed, though,' I said as she glugged back a third glass of wine on an empty stomach.

'You're joking. It's a lads' mag isn't it? They'll all be pissed as farts. You don't know what you're letting yourself in for. Go stand outside and I'll summon you in.'

I walked in and she invited me to sit down, so I knelt on the carpet opposite her. 'Right,' she said. 'Thank you very much for coming in at such short notice. Your name is?'

'Heidi Charlton.'

She pretended to make a little note. 'Isn't that a dance, the Charlton?'

'That's the Charleston.'

'Very good, Ms Charlton. Brains as well as beauty. Now . . . um, tell us . . . um . . . Okay, what sort of things do they ask you at a casting, then? Like, show us your boobs or something?'

'They won't ask to see my boobs.'

'Well, go on, then. What sort of things will they ask?'

I didn't know, not having been to a casting before. 'A

meeting thing' was what Sonia had said. But she didn't expand. Her other line was going and she rang off leaving me with just the date, time, place – and the fact that it was 'a meeting thing'.

'I don't know. It'll probably be like a job interview. What sort of things do they ask at job interviews?'

'Fuck knows. I can't remember the last time I went to one. What about you?'

'I had a kind-of interview when I started dancing.'

'All right. And what did they ask you?'

'They wanted to see my boobs.'

'Oh God. Look, try this, they always ask this at job interviews. Okay, Ms Charlton. Why do you want the job?'

'I don't quite know what the job is yet.'

'Jesus, it's standing there with your tits out while people take your picture, Hide, what do you think it is? Let's try it another way. Okay, Ms Charlton, why do you want to model? After all, dancing: it's bloody good pay . . .'

Respect, I thought then, thinking of the club: of the beery, bloated faces and schizo eyes, like little brats at a birthday party greedily eyeing up each other's gifts. But being a model means respect. If you tell a man you're a lap dancer, his eyes light up as though he's just spotted an empty parking space, and he'll check to see if his wife or girlfriend is nearby, and go, 'Really?' And it's as if you've said, 'I'm a lap dancer,' but he's heard, 'I want to sleep with you.' But tell him you're a model and it's different. You say, 'I'm a model.' He hears, 'You can look but don't touch; I'm out of your league.' Don't ask me why it should be that way, but it is. Maybe if you're a man it's something to do with distance. A model's on the page, out of your reach, but in the club she's there with a hand on your arm, telling you how much she loves your aftershave, buttering you up. Maybe it's because a lap dancer gives you what you want. A model tells you what you want.

'I don't know,' I said. 'It's every girl's dream, isn't it?'

'It is if they look like you, babe.'

Later we kissed goodbye and she tottered off, laughing at how pissed she was, and it still being bright sunshine outside. I poured the rest of my half-glass down the sink and didn't even touch a drop later, at work. I left the club as early as I could to get as much sleep as possible. This morning I had a five-minute facial followed by a mini-manicure, and I was still ready a good twenty minutes before I needed to leave for the tube. Not a bad job, I think, catching sight of my reflection in the window of the tube train. Tight black spaghetti-strap top to show off my hair (blonde, ponytail), and boobs (real); black boot-cut trousers and pink heels that are high, but not too high, and go with my pink bag. Perfect feet, of course. I'm clutching my portfolio to my chest with one hand, holding on to the handrail with the other. Good nails (pink); the polish matches my toes.

I'm running through my mental checklist when I stick my fingers in my back pocket for my ticket and can't feel it there. Me being so organised there's no way I'll have lost my ticket, I reason, as I fumble around in my other pockets and find it's not there; check my bag, not there either. No way I'll have lost my ticket, not with me being so in control . . .

*

I hate famous people.

This one, for example. Three-quarters of an hour late and she's left me sitting in the conservatory area of the bar with the sun baking the glass which passes on the effect with its compliments. A single colonial-style ceiling fan wobbles uselessly above me spanking the thick air with all the enthusiasm of a Westminster madam – three hundred pounds a night and they can't even air-condition the fucking conservatory. And since I am wearing not only an open-necked shirt and suit, but also last night's booze marathon, my skin has started weeping with the sheer misery of it all. I lean forward and button up the jacket. Have to, my shirt's started spotting. Should have ordered a water, not a coffee. Might have cooled me down. As it is, I can't work myself up into hailing the waiter for a bottle of mineral water. I'm concentrating on keeping still, keeping cool. Keeping my cool.

Her name is Vegas (actually, her name is Sally Tompkins, but she no longer answers to it). She was once in a semi-successful girl band but went solo. Her first album sold bucketloads thanks to enormous promotion. But she got above herself and stopped doing press. Now she has a new album 'waiting in the wings', as I will probably write later on, and she's decided to give a couple of interviews, but only the good ones. One of them is with a Sunday supplement, which gave me a call, perhaps because of my background in music journalism so I have at least heard of her, but more likely because their usual writers are off sunning themselves in France – as any sensible person would be. It's hardly going to win me the Nobel Prize for journalism, and I've done a million interviews like it, but not for this Sunday, where I've finally been granted a chance to escape the world of 'little reviews', as read by Craig Cooper. I prepared for my big break in characteristic fashion. I went out and got pissed.

At last she walks in. She's of-course gorgeous, brown-skinned, stepping into reception from the heat outside, oven fresh. Standing at the foot of her celebrity is another woman I take to be her PR, about my age, a fighting-dog type.

The reception area checks its motion then rearranges its orbit to suit her. A middle-aged woman blurts a gasp that tells the sleb everything she needs to know: she's been spotted. Middle-aged woman's husband smiles at his wife. Probably brought her to London for a long and expensive weekend; see a show, trawl the sights, spot a star or two. Their cases are at their feet and she'll go home happy now.

I half rise from my seat, finding the fighting dog's eye and raising a here-I-am hand. People in the conservatory swivel to check me out, joining mental dots between me and the sleb, drawing their own conclusions. None, I bet, think boyfriend or fellow famous person, not waiting and sweating like this.

I curse her again. They do this deliberately, I swear. Always having to prove who's boss.

The fighting dog touches her client's elbow and points in my direction, saying something into her ear at the same time. Vegas stops warming herself in the limelight and trots towards the conservatory, which shuffles expectantly. I reach and deposit my chewing gum in the ashtray, waiting until she's almost with me, rising and holding out my hand.

'Hi,' I say, deploying the biggest smile in my armoury. 'Greil Sharkey. It's really good to meet you, Vegas.'

Vegas does perfect teeth back at me, and she really is stunning. Pure star all the way through. 'Hi,' she says. She makes it sound like she's been waiting all her life to meet me, but her eyes are hunting the room and the teeth are doing all four corners even as she gives me the briefest of handshakes. She tries her best to hide it, but I spot her surreptitiously wiping her hand as she sits.

Fighting dog turns out to be a kitten after all. 'Hello, Greil,' she says, breaking her serious face with a surprising smile. 'Nice to meet you, and I'm really sorry we're late. We had a shoot that overran.'

She's into me. And maybe if she were younger, and she didn't have a face like a bulldog licking piss off a nettle, and she wasn't wearing half of Boots on her face, and she didn't have absolutely nothing in life to offer me apart from a cock sore from her cack-handed, desperate attempts at masturbation and self-pitying tears afterwards when I fail to unload over her hand, well, then, maybe I'd be into her too.

'That's all right,' I say.

'I'm Jenny, by the way,' she adds, but I prioritise that information downwards. Instead I find myself looking at Vegas – her lips, actually – idly wondering if she's had them done, and what they'd look like around my cock. Despite myself, I entertain occasional thoughts of sex with my interviewees, and it's not unknown, especially with the low-level stars, the ones who think a leg-over means a leg-up – I've done a couple

31

of indie-pop *chanteuses* you might have heard of. But this one's too big, too famous, so why bother trying? I'll have to wait a bit. After all, today she's wreathed in fame. Hotel receptions stop to gawp at her. She's got pain-in-the-arse PR twats at her beck and call and a second album 'waiting in the wings'. But she's only one flop single away from the day receptions don't stop to gawp, and her PR twats ring me asking for interviews, rather than vice versa; when keeping me waiting won't be an option because I might not hang around; and when you only ever see her on one of those nostalgia programmes, cringing in mock embarrassment at the clothes she used to wear, transparently hungry for another taste of what she once had. Maybe when she's launching her comeback bid and I'm doing a favour-for-a-favour interview – then she won't keep me waiting. And maybe then I'll get a blow job off her.

Vegas smiles again (she's had the lips done, I reckon). I smile back but I can't be bothered to prostrate myself at the altar of celebrity today, so I don't do the full works. Briefly I wonder whether she'll smell yesterday's alcohol on my breath but find that I don't care either way. I lean over and put down my dictaphone, a shabby old thing with a cracked lid that looks vaguely incongruous on the hotel table. Jenny shuffles in her seat. 'Would anyone like a coffee?' she says.

'Not me,' I reply. 'I've just put one out. I could handle a water, though.'

'*Sin gas?*' she says.

'What?'

'Sorry,' she laughs. 'I've just got back from Spain. That's what they say when you order a mineral water. *Sin gas*. It means uncarbonated.'

'Right.' Thinking, Christ, she's trying too hard. Earth to Jenny.

'Oh, how was it?' pipes up Vegas, as if Jenny's just arrived back from the airport. I shoot Jenny a look of evil, polished up especially for the occasion. She takes the hint:

'Good, thanks, Vegas. Can I get you a coffee?'

32

'Mint tea, please,' says Vegas. Her bit of socialising with the staff is over for the day, thank God. Jenny signals for the waiter, who hurries over like he's got a firework taped to his arse and a box of matches coming up behind him. The celebrity effect. Quick service and satisfaction guaranteed. Jenny orders tea then asks if anybody would mind if she goes to the loo, and not to start without her, and something about her manner suggests to me that she isn't going to the loo for a wee, but for the same reason I often go to the loo without needing a wee, and I file that intelligence away for later use. With Jenny gone, Vegas and I settle into an uncomfortable silence during which I'm supposed to tell her how great she looks, or how great I think the new album is, but don't. One thing you have to remember about beautiful women: if you pay them a compliment, you belong to them. If you pick a fault, they belong to you.

That priceless nugget of wisdom belongs not to me, but to Terry, the manager of All Fur Coat, the venue for last night's . . . fun.

All Fur Coat is a gentleman's club I sometimes go to. It's not a club for gentlemen, because people like me go there and I'm no gentleman by any stretch of the imagination. Neither is it a club run by gentlemen, because Terry manages it, and he's about as morally upstanding as I am, which is to say, not very ethical at all. He *knows* people, as he's constantly reminding me, or threatening me, one of the two. Still, he's not a bad bloke. I wrote a lot of his advertising blurb for him when he started out. He's always on at me to get him more publicity, gives me drinks on the house and pays for the occasional dance in return for some tenuous promise of a free plug in the future. I tell him I'm a freelance, and that people commission me to write stuff and I write it, and that plugs for mates don't really fall under my mandate. But the drinks and dances keep coming gratis, and I keep going. Who could blame me?

Last night was the same, but different. Having failed to

impress my front room with my air guitar skills, I headed for town, ready for a bit more action. Shooting the moon – that was me last night. A couple of drinks, a pocketful of money and I felt like Jack the Lad. A Jack the Lad who fancied a little flutter on the horses. Still early – that twilight time between the end of the afternoon and the beginning of the evening – I made a beeline for Ladbrokes, where I took up residence on a swivel stool and trained my eyes on the screens above. A man with betting on his mind can always find something to gamble on, and it's just as easy to lose on the dogs as it is the football and the horses, or who's going to pick up the MTV award for best album, or whether or not there'll be snow for Christmas. Believe me, I know.

Two hours into my swivel stool residency and I was £100 down, but feeling optimistic, the kind of optimism you buy from barmen or from drug dealers. So optimistic that my fingers strayed to the envelope of money weighing ever more heavily in my inside pocket . . .

What possessed me? Christ only knows. I was either trying to forget Cooper or thumbing a fuck-you in his direction. Whatever, the outcome was the same. It's not easy to blow a grand on a single bet. It takes a certain kind of man, a certain kind of guts. The kind of man who buys his guts from barmen and drug dealers. No, it's not easy, but I'm happy to report that I managed it, and when the race was running I bellowed loud enough to drown out the sound of my heart breaking. But not loud enough as it turned out. By squeezing my eyes tightly shut I was able to prevent the tears, but only just. And I waved goodbye to the grand, and headed out into the night, going . . . Where?

Somewhere I could forget.

I hadn't been there in months, not in the evening, anyway, but suddenly the idea of sitting at the bar with women stripping just above my head seemed like the perfect way to continue the evening. The ideal way to bury the guilt. Weird, that.

So I headed for All Fur Coat, where stripping's not stripping, but dancing – pole or lap; where the bouncers are not bouncers but doormen – or even 'colleagues' for all I know – wearing suits, unclipping a velvet rope to let you through (providing you're suitably dressed – no jeans or trainers); and punters are guests – and gentlemen, like I say; where money's money and flesh is currency. It's like a Harvester for the female body. You half expect a girl to greet you with, 'Have you ever been to an All Fur Coat before?'

In I sauntered, basking in the doorman's greeting, flashing teeth at Karen behind the desk who smiled and motioned me down the stairs, knowing that behind me she'd be speaking to Terry on the walkie-talkie. And sure enough, there he was, waiting for me at the bottom of the stairs.

'Mister Sharkey,' he growled, using two hands to shake my one, then clapping me on the back. 'I can't remember the last time we saw you in here of an evening.' Neither could I. He steered me into the main room, still chatting. 'Always good to see you. Will you be sitting at the bar, or can I tempt you with a table?'

Have you been to an All Fur Coat before? Bar or table. The eternal conundrum. You sit at a table and you get at least one girl to keep you company, usually two, if you're me, which I am. At the table you get conversation. The girls treat you like you're a combination of Tom Cruise and Jim Carrey. They laugh like a hyena stuck down a drain at every comment you make. They say things like, 'You're quite toned. Do you work out?' Perhaps brush a hand across your chest as they do so. A gossamer promise in that touch, a fictional intimacy that masks the reality of their purpose. They don't think you're funny, or toned, they probably don't even like you very much. What they want you to do is give them money in exchange for a dance that you can have topless at your table, or top and tail in the back room. How far the top and tail dance goes depends on the girl, or on how much money you're willing to give her, or whether security are watching or not.

The bar's the place for the gentleman who can't be bothered

with the subterfuge; who's not telling himself he's here for female company-and-why-not; who's admitted the truth: he wants to see women naked. You can sit with your drink at the bar, which travels around the outside of a stage where the girls pole-dance, one after the other, all day from 11 a.m. opening right up until closing time. The principle's the same: you leave tips for the dancers on the bar. You just don't get your ego massaged is all. You sit, you drink, you crick your neck feeling like a carpet bug in Pamela Anderson's bath mat. And you can look out over the club, see the sad bastards getting their heads swelled and their bank balances reduced by the girls who strut around in evening gowns slashed to the waist, plunging back and front, not drowning but waving in a sea of testosterone that you can actually smell as you walk into the club.

Harvester or not, I like the way the place works. The way it lifts the bonnet on love to expose the greasy engine beneath. As though all that *Men Are from Pluto, Woman Are from Uranus*, women's-magazine, agony-aunt relationship bollocks has been reduced to a simple commercial sexual transaction. There's a purity to it, a truth the journalist in me can admire. That, and the girls. No wonder I'm drawn to them. Hustlers, every one: smiling, glamourpussy con women skilled in the chameleon arts, each one the living fantasy of the man they sit beside, marketed as cleverly as Coca-Cola, hot-wired to our hard-ons and wallets.

Last night Terry rolled his eyes at my decision to sit at my usual spot – the bar. 'Go on, Mister Sharkey, have a table. I'll get one of the girls to come and make a fuss of you. We don't often see you in the evenings, might as well make a night of it, eh?'

'Honest, Tel. I'm a barman. I mean, I'm a bar man.' And anyway, over at the bar a brunette with great tits was just starting her act. I hadn't seen her before. One of the advantages of coming at night, I thought: you get to see the evening shift. He probably keeps the best ones for the evening. I would if I were him. Save the best babes for when you get the proper paying crowd in, not the afternoon layabouts like me.

A doorman I recognised called Bruno walked past and Terry stopped him. 'Bruno,' he said, jerking his thumb back towards the private booths. 'I saw touching back there earlier. I don't want to see any touching. And I don't want to see any of the girls grinding, neither. We're a gentleman's club. And if the filth are in they'll close us down.'

'I'm always telling them, Boss,' said Bruno with the air of an older brother being unfairly reprimanded. 'They never listen.'

'That's because they've got pound signs where their ethics should be,' said Terry, giving Bruno a conversation-over slap on the back. Off Bruno went, his slumped shoulders suggesting the dilemma of a person whose job it is to prevent men touching naked women writhing in their laps.

Terry relaxed and turned back to me, tutting: 'A "bar man"? Lord save me from bar men. Take a seat, then. I'll get Paul to sort you out with a drink.'

We shook hands and I turned away before I let my face register his words. Two words in particular – 'a drink'. Not, 'a tab', which has been known, or 'some drinks', which is more usual, and which we both know means three. But 'a drink', in the solitary, lonely singular. It could be because it's night-time, but I can't see what difference that would make. More likely, Terry's sussed me. Not that I've ever tried to pull the wool over his eyes or anything, but perhaps he's finally come round to the opinion that I'm a less useful contact than he'd assumed. Shit. The free drinks had been an undisputed highlight of my All Fur Coat visits. I ordered a double vodka and tonic from Paul the barman and turned to look out into the club.

Over the way a girl in a minuscule black dress was half turned towards her customer, one leg hooked up on the velour-covered seat. Always velour in places like this – the pubs, clubs and bookies that count me as a customer, anyway – I've forgotten what it feels like to sit on anything else. As I watched, she laughed at her customer's joke, reached a hand to brush his hair and said something that made him blush. Nobody compliments a man on his hair, I mused; nobody but lap dancers. From a larger table came a cheer and a dancer stood, offering her hand to a seated punter who took it, stood, and allowed himself to be led to the back room.

'There you go, Mr Sharkey,' I heard Paul say behind me, my drink arriving, and I swivelled on my seat to face the bar.

Which is when I saw the girl. Between taking my seat and ordering my drink the brunette with the great tits had come and gone. And no doubt her mum loves her, and maybe somewhere there's a man who will love and cherish her, and she'll don gardening gloves to prune rose bushes in a picket-fence future. But history won't remember the brunette with the great tits, because, like me, history shifted its gaze to the girl who came on next.

She'd walked across the stage before I laid eyes on her; taken up position just as the MC was saying something I didn't hear, but which must have been her name. I didn't hear because I was too busy staring at her, frozen like an escaping prisoner caught in the glare of the searchlight – rendered immovable by the girl who swished to the central pole and stood, smiling, waiting for her music to begin.

Kylie Minogue, I thought.

The track they're playing, it's definitely Kylie Minogue. The 'diminutive pop princess', which is what I referred to her as when I interviewed her. On that day the diminutive pop princess had kept me waiting for at least three-quarters of an hour (they all do; they think it's their God-given right) and I'd whiled away the time getting drunk. It was that track the DPP was promoting, I remembered. The signature thump-thump-thump of the bass – 'subterranean bass' according to the press release, which I dutifully regurgitated in the write-up. 'It goes down brilliantly in the clubs,' the DPP had said to me, and I regurgitated that, too.

But watching the girl, seeing her body begin to move, from the hips first, then up and down against the pole to the thump-thump-thump of Kylie Minogue, I saw that Kylie was right. It was going down brilliantly in this club. The music seemed to fill the space, rolling out across the club, drawing your eye to the girl on the stage who closed her eyes as she shimmied down almost to the floor and back up again, using one hand to unhook the shoulder strap of her black evening dress. That movement, a delicate aperitif. I caught my mouth hanging open and closed it with a snap that might have been audible but for Kylie's thump. My hands wanted to light a cigarette but my eyes resented the movement, and instead I watched as strap two was teased away from her other shoulder and she dropped her arms to allow the dress to fall away. For a moment it pooled on the bar, a silk rampart around her feet, then she kicked it away, gift-wrapping discarded, and I forced myself to look at her body, hardly daring to, unable not to.

Nothing could be that perfect, surely? From her blonde hair, to the bra which cupped and pushed, to the tiny V of her G-string, nothing could annexe perfection like her body on that stage.

She whirled on the pole. My breath caught in my throat as her hand reached to the clip of her bra and she brought her arms forward to shrug it off. Then she was spinning to the other side of the pole, facing forward again to a muted cheer which bubbled beneath the thump of the bass and seemed to me not to congratulate, but to insult the appearance of her breasts – as though nothing but a gasp of awe would do.

She clasped the pole and worked her body against it. She moved to the other side, turned her back and bent low, running her hands up her calves and higher, brushing her G-string. She pivoted to the front and her eyes closed as her back arched, the pole behind her, her hands playing up the front of her body, the illusion of self-absorption allowing me to study her face. Her face . . .

She opened her eyes, and they were on mine, and a smile appeared as the waves of bass broke, the song faded and her dance ended.

That final smile (meant for me, surely) was a goodbye kiss as she bent to scoop up her bra and evening gown in one graceful movement, taking a quick running step across me and to the side of the stage, where she descended the steps and was gone.

With hands that trembled I reached for my Marlboro, grabbing the vodka and draining it at the same time. The DJ said something I didn't hear and there was another set of legs walking along the stage in front of me. Another girl assuming her position at the pole. I looked at her, wanting to feel as imprisoned as I had moments ago. As though the effect of the last girl could be explained by my own chemistry – too much booze, too many lines – and not hers. I discarded that theory when I found myself leaving the stool and heading for the men's. I was hoping the cubicle would be free. It was.

'Terry,' I called. He was passing the door of the men's as I came out. Hurrying, like he needed to use it himself

'Can't stop, Mr Sharkey, the owner's in,' he said over his shoulder, heading for his office.

I caught up with him. 'Just a quickie,' I said, sniffing. 'That girl—'

'The one on now?' He fidgeted, looked around me, sneaking a look at his office door.

'No, the one before.'

'Wait a tic,' he hailed an older woman on her way past. 'Sandy, will you have a word with Cherry about her tan? She looks like a fucking milk bottle under these lights.' The woman simply tutted and went on. 'Right, Mr Sharkey, got to go. Catch up with you in a minute, eh?'

'No. Terry. The girl.'

'The one on now?'

Christ, it's *Groundhog Day*: 'No, the one before.'

'Heidi?' he said.

'That her name?'

'Yeah. Gorgeous. Look, I've got to shoot, really. Did you want a dance with her, is that it?'

His question thudded home and I suddenly felt job-interview nerves. Any other night, I would. Any other girl, I would. But, 'No,' I said, confusing myself. 'No. I just wanted to know her name, that was all. She was great. Do tell her. From me. Tell her she was great.'

'She's got a lot of fans,' he said with a strange smile. 'I'll be sure to tell her. Laters, mate. All right?' And he clapped me goodbye on the shoulder.

'*A lot of fans*,' I thought, suddenly scared. But she was beautiful. Her body perfect. Of course she had a lot of fans. The kind of suited-up scum who came in here. The sort who'd never get past her tits; who could look for a million years and never see what I'd just seen.

About ten minutes later I caught sight of her again. Just a glimpse, and it was only by chance that I had my head turned away from the bar. Enough to see her and to double-take at the vision of her gliding across the balcony at the side of the club towards the office, knock-knock on Terry's door. Who's there? Heidi. I let the name marinade in my head.

Heidi.

Heidi who?

Heidi really like to see you again.

I got back to the flat late. And drunk. Too late and drunk to be taking a bottle of Smirnoff from the freezer and settling down in front of my computer, but that's what I did anyway. Call it a compulsion. I poured a shot of vodka and laid out a line on a Stone Roses CD while my Mac booted up, putting the line to one side – 'for Ron' – and sipping on the vodka. I clicked 'browse the Internet', listening to the Mac creak like a ghost ship as it connected me to the web. Sipping the vodka, I typed 'allfurcoat.com' and sat back as the page loaded.

There it was. It had changed since the last time I'd seen it. Correction. Since when I'd *written* it. Because at one time it was indeed a Greil Sharkey composition – that and some other promotional gumpf I wrote for Terry. Things had changed in the meantime, though. Where once the site had been a holding page, little more than a photo of the interior, an address and my nebulous blurb about All Fur Coat offering 'intimate entertainment for the discerning gentleman', like it was something more than a glorified titty bar, there was now a plethora of options: 'events', 'contact us', 'the girls', 'links', 'webcam'.

I clicked on 'the girls' and she appeared, a tiny thumbnail picture of her. One of many on the page: 'meet Jetta', or 'meet Lindsey', or 'meet Joy'. I wanted to 'meet Heidi', so I clicked on her picture. The next page was devoted solely to her, and it was here I discovered her surname: Charlton. Heidi Charlton. It might have been made up, of course. Her real name could be Sharon Donkey for all I know. But I liked Heidi Charlton all the same. To me, it fitted. It accorded with my memory of her, the moment our eyes locked.

Heidi, I read, is 25. She has a 34–24–34 figure, she loves dancing and good conversation, her favourite word is 'serendipity', the first record she ever bought was 'Always On My Mind' by the Pet Shop Boys, her perfect evening is a romantic night in 'with a bottle of wine and good company!', and the man of her dreams is the young Paul Newman ('it's in the eyes!').

Above her details was a photograph, obviously taken in the club. She wore an evening gown and leaned on the bar, smiling, a pose oddly reminiscent of a Martini advert, like you half expected Catalogue Man to make an appearance stage-left, wearing an Aran sweater and pointing at something in the middle distance. Still, it couldn't mask her beauty; did nothing to diminish the effect she had on me, and I looked at her for a moment, sipping at the ice-cold vodka and tasting the fire in my throat while somewhere, deep in the disused part of me, long-burnt-out feelings began to spark and collide, exotic and indecipherable.

Then I lifted the Stone Roses CD and reached for my straw. As I did so I caught Heidi's eye and I stopped pre-snort, a man with a Burger King straw at his nose and a CD held in front of him. A stupid man.

'Why don't you leave it for the night, Greil?' she whispered. 'Get some sleep. Maybe have a spliff to take the edge off, then go to bed. Even *you* need rest, you know.'

I hovered, a diaphanous membrane between me and a few hours' sleep, or me and this line and no sleep at all. Then I lowered the straw and CD to the desk. Repulsion beat compulsion in a photo finish. 'You're right,' I said, tasting the self-disgust the coke would have chased away. 'You're right, Heidi. You're right.' It had been a long time since anyone had cared enough to ask me to stop.

I clicked on 'webcams' and went to another page.

'See last night's club webcam!' shouted one icon. Whoever had taken over editorial control of the site was fond of their exclamation marks. Another advertised, 'New! Backstage at All Fur Coat,' and I moved my mouse to it, clicked, barely able to control my excitement.

Only, instead of a fly-on-the-wall view of All Fur Coat's dressing rooms, I got a page asking me either to log in or register. Shit.

'Log in here!' 'Not A Member! Register Here!'

I clicked to register, where a bewildering form asked me to leave my credit card details, verify I was eighteen, go back and fill in the form again because I missed one of the fields, and then wait to see my card details being refused by the issuer. 'Please Try Again Another Time!' yelled the website above the sound of my gnashing teeth. Back at the first page I clicked on 'Log in here!' which wanted me to input a user name and password. I paused, thought about it a second, leaned forward and typed in user name, 'guest'; then password, 'guest'.

Enter.

'Backstage at All Fur Coat, last night!' said a new page. Fucking great. 'Camera refreshes every thirty seconds.' And there in a tiny window about the size of a matchbox was every *Porky's* schoolboy wank fantasy, mine included: a room full of lap dancers, dressing. Undressing.

Lockers, dressing tables, hanging clothes, girls everywhere. The webcam, obviously fixed into a high position on the near wall, looked down upon them, a silent voyeur. The screen was static, but as I watched the picture renewed itself thirty seconds into the future, like flicking a picture book really slowly.

Frozen into the centre of the image was a girl who seemed to be adjusting her shoes. She held on to another girl for support. This one was laughing at something, her head thrown back.

The view refreshed and it was much the same as before: one girl halfway out of the door, the support girl laughing, her head in a different position this time. Shoes girl was still struggling with an errant strap, a difficult buckle perhaps, wobbling on one leg. Other girls around the edges of the frame seemed to be laughing as well, their eyes on the two women centre stage, some sitting, some standing. Oh for sound as well.

The page refreshed, and another girl was entering the room in this picture. It was Heidi, a new presence, peripheral but radiant all the same, to me anyway. Meanwhile the support girl seemed to have left shoes girl to her own devices, stranding her in a comical totter as she took a step forward, looking up at the camera. Her hands were reaching to behind her neck.

The page refreshed once more and support girl was standing directly in front of the webcam now, her dress untied and her breasts bared – a girl's moony at the camera. I recognised her – called Fortune or something. She wore an Amazonian expression familiar from the covers of a thousand lads' mags, her mouth wide in a battle cry. To me it looked like defiance. This camera, I thought, was not a welcome presence in the girls' dressing rooms. Of course not, it undermined their brand. The aloof and implacable sexual hustler was open to exposure as a scratching, zit-popping, farting mortal. Having the camera there meant they could never relax, they never knew who might be watching. Me, in this case. But my eyes were drawn past the Amazonian girl and her admittedly fantastic breasts to the far corner of the room where Heidi had taken a seat in front of a dressing table. The girls around her were laughing to beat the band, watching either the Amazonian girl or the shoes girl, still hopping precariously in her original position. Not Heidi, though. She sat looking into a mirror, excluded, or excluding herself, I couldn't be sure. Either way, she took no notice of the pantomime behind her; she seemed lost in her own world. What, I wondered, went on in that world.

Before I left the All Fur Coat website I downloaded its screen saver, which turned out to be a mini-dancer who walks around the screen striking various poses. Then I went to the search engine Google.com, where I typed in her name, took a slug of Smirnoff, a deep breath and pressed return. The machine groaned for a second, then the screen filled with links. Links for Charlton Heston, Charlton Athletic, Bobby Charlton and Heidi Klum, and one – just one – for a model agency, with the name Heidi Charlton helpfully highlighted in a list of others. Thank you Internet, I thought. Thank you for being the electronic repository for all human knowledge. And I clicked on the link, willing the Internet on like a trailing horse as the page slowly, almost painfully, loaded.

There she was. Heidi. Not a name's-the-same as it could so easily have been, but actually her. This time the pose was less casino cheese, proper model-like. She lay on her front, facing the camera. She wore a bikini but the photographer had sensibly decided it was the face that made the girl, so it was this, not her body, that provided the picture's focus. She stared out of the photo, her head tilted slightly to one side, almost as if curious, as though she was lying in bed listening to a lover's sad story, his tales of woe – mine, perhaps.

Below the picture was a line of text. 'Heidi Charlton. Details to follow. For enquiries please call.' And it told me more than her star sign or her favourite word or how she liked to spend the evening. It told me that she was a new addition to the agency's books, and it gave me an idea.

I stared at the picture for some moments more until I swam to the surface of her gaze and finally clicked off the site. I downed the last of my vodka, then, without Heidi to watch over me, I was suddenly struck by the urge to listen to The Stone Roses. Needless to say, I had to snort the charlie to get in the CD box.

'Greil? . . . *Greil?*'

'Sorry, yes?'

Jenny, having returned from her journey to the toilet, looks inquisitively at me. A scent of mint tea rises from the table between us. Vegas is looking somewhere else, a vacant sign where her face should be. She's temporarily unplugged herself from the dreary mainframe the rest of us call life, dreaming, probably, of picking up an Oscar in some never-to-be-realised future. Must ask her that, I think: *have you ever considered a move into films?* That would be original. Bet nobody's ever asked her that before . . .

'Are we ready, Greil?' says Jenny with a hint of testiness. I snap back to professional mode, discreetly sniff, hoping I'll dislodge some granules of coke hiding in my nasal passage. I get a couple of refugees; I normally do.

I reach into my inside pocket and pull out my little pick-up mic, bringing a tube ticket and some random cellophane with it. They watch politely as I spend what seems like a week attempting to untangle it. 'Ready,' I say at last, and plug the mic into the dictaphone, offering the business end to Vegas. 'Vegas, could you clip this to your collar?'

She looks at me as if I've just requested anal sex, then leans to Jenny, whispering something I'm not supposed to hear, but do: '*This is fucking Matthew Williamson.*'

'My client would prefer not to,' says Jenny to me. 'It's a very expensive item of clothing, and it might mark.'

I let that comment salt the wounds of last night's excess. Yet another drop of sweat falls smartly from my armpit, strangely cold against my skin. I take a gulp of the water – *sin gas* – that the waiter's brought to the table.

'Fine,' I say. 'We'll leave it on the table here, where it can pick up all the background noise,' and I clunk my glass back to the table, the conductor tapping his lectern.

'I'm sure it'll be all right,' says Jenny, then, 'I tell you what. We'll see how this one copes.' She rummages in her bag and produces her own dictaphone, which she plonks down next to mine. I regard the two of them on the table together. Notwithstanding the cracked lid, mine is the Bradford council estate of dictaphones next to the shiny, high-tech, New York loft apartment of hers. She hasn't even bothered with a pick-up mic, nothing to spoil the clean, designer lines. I feel sorry for my old dictaphone, it's been a good and faithful servant to me, it's hugged many a C90 to its bosom. Until yesterday it lived in the glove compartment of my Merc, so it's recently been made homeless, and to add insult to injury it's now being mocked by a younger, sleeker, sexier model.

'What's that doing there?' I say, waggling my pen at her dictaphone.

'I'm taping the interview,' she says.

'Well you don't need to, I'm taping it.'

'I know, but I'm making my own copy for our records,' she says, smiling at my indignant face. 'It's fairly standard procedure, Greil, it's just in case of verification.'

'Verification of what?'

'Your finished text with the content of the recorded interview – in case there are any issues arising.'

'There won't *be* any issues arising,' I say, stranded someplace between hurt and downright angry.

'Then hopefully I won't need to refer to it,' she says evenly.

I clear my throat and cast a look at Vegas, who considers us with an expression that's only a notch above mildly interested.

'Look,' I say to Jenny, 'this isn't that type of interview. It's not Prime Minister's Question Time. We're here to talk about the new album and stuff.'

'That's exactly it,' says Jenny, reaching to switch on the machine. 'Let's talk about the new album.'

In a just and righteous world I'd be big and powerful enough to threaten to terminate the interview, and they'd put the dictaphone away. If my integrity wasn't index-linked to my debts, maybe I'd say fuck it and walk out anyway. But I'm not and it is. God, I hate PR people.

'You wouldn't do this to Norman Mailer,' I say.

'No,' says Jenny, smiling, 'we wouldn't do it to Norman Mailer.'

I give her a sarcastic smile, bring my pad on to my knee, click open my pen, and begin.

'Right. Okay, Vegas, before we talk about the music – the really serious questions [the ones you've insisted on being asked because you're desperate to court a more mature audience] – perhaps we could start off with a quick Q&A for a sidebar. Nothing too taxing. Just a few likes and dislikes. Let's start with your favourite film . . .'

Vegas seems to consider this while I think of a list of possible films it might be: *Pretty Woman*, or 'anything starring Julia Roberts', *Moulin Rouge*, *Ghost*, *The Bridges of Madison County*, *Romeo and Juliet*, *Titanic*, or, 'anything starring Leonardo DiCaprio . . .'

'Um,' says Vegas, still considering. Then, to Jenny: 'What did I see the other night on DVD that I really liked?' and Jenny goes into considering gear, while I think of a list of films it definitely won't be: *Driller Killer*, *I Spit on Your Grave*, *Anal Snow Bunnies*, *The Texas Chainsaw Massacre*, 'anything starring Steven Seagal', *Cannibal Ferox* . . .

They seem to give up. 'Oh,' sighs Vegas. 'Just put "anything starring Brad Pitt."'

The pair of them laugh like they've just invented comedy. I write a number one on my pad, followed by the shorthand outline for *Anal Snow Bunnies*.

'Okay, next,' I say, hoping I sound as if I'm enjoying myself. 'Favourite song?'

In a thinly veiled application to work with some big-name American R&B producers, she starts wittering on about the current music she's into while I begin to compose a list of possible songs that starts and ends with 'anything by Destiny's Child'. And I write a number two on my pad, followed by the shorthand outline for 'Gunpowder Plot' by Systemitis.

I don't think I ever realised what a difficult outline Systemitis is. Pity the poor journalists who used to interview us. Then again, they probably just shortened it to a capital S. That's what I'd do.

Finally Vegas narrows the field down and says something that I don't catch, so I double-check the tape recorder's still working and move on, asking her favourite holiday destination, which prompts another round of umming and ahhing, probably with freebies on her mind. Like I say, I hate famous people.

I write the number three on my pad, and beside it the shorthand for Afghanistan – another difficult outline. Then I write the word Heidi at the top. Below it I write the shorthand outline for Heidi. It's simple. Two straight lines and a tiny submerged accent.

Last night, I went to All Fur Coat seeking something in my oblivion, like a blind man patting at the wall. Looking for redemption. She made me forget, I think. She made me forget about Cooper, the money, and my stupid, shoddy, fucked-up life. She had beautiful feet.

And when at last the interview's over, and Jenny's put the fighting dog back in its kennel and returned to being friendly, and Vegas has disengaged herself from the room, mentally, if not physically, and I've asked all of my questions, the identical twin of which she will no doubt be asked by some other trained parrot today, we shake hands and say goodbye, and I wander out into the street and reach for my mobile phone.

'Terry,' I say, to Terry, who answers his direct line. Answers it by abbreviating, 'Fur Coat.' In his mouth it sounds like a swear word.

'Yeah. Who's that?' he says.

'It's Greil. How's it going?' Standing on the pavement a silver Lexus cruises past, Vegas and Jenny in the back. If they see me, they don't wave.

'Well, I'm doing good, Mr Sharkey. More's the point, how are you?'

'Nothing a hair of the dog won't fix,' I say, full of bluff. 'Listen, I've got a proposition for you.'

'Yeah?'

'Yeah. I'm putting together a feature idea. It's on lap dancers really, but I think I can wangle it so it centres just on All Fur Coat. Would you be interested? Bit of a glamour piece, you know?' Needless to say, this feature idea is news to me. As much news to me as it will be to the magazines I can think of, all of whom have either done lap dancers to death, or wouldn't touch lap dancers with a bargepole, or a pole-dancing pole.

'I'm up for that. I can't stop now, though. The boss is on his way. Do you want to swing by in an hour and talk about it. Where are you now?'

'Out of town,' I lie. 'I won't be around until the evening, but I can come in then, yeah? Perhaps we could have a chat. Maybe I could talk to a couple of the girls, get a feel for the piece.' I curse my choice of words, certain Terry won't allow any innuendo to go unpunished.

Instead he says, 'Talk to a couple of the girls, eh? And who would you be wanting to talk to, then?' If it's possible for someone to be gimlet-eyed on the phone, then that's what Terry is.

Big side-swerve or little side-swerve? I opt for little. 'Gah, rumbled,' I laugh. 'No, honest mate, I thought that Heidi girl had something that might translate really well in the feature, you know? To be honest, the mags are always on the lookout for new models, mate. I don't know if she's ever thought about doing any modelling, but from what I saw she'd be a natural.

We'd get her in the mag and we could use All Fur Coat as the hook to hang it on, you know? So, um, yeah, I would like to speak to her if that's okay with you . . .'

Pedestrians in the street observe a slightly moist man in a suit, one hand holding a mobile phone to his ear, his face screwed up and his fingers crossed. They assume he's waiting for the result of a crucial horse race.

'Tell you what, swing by tonight,' he says, after a pause. 'We'll see what we can do.'

Placed, but not first. Good for an each-way bet.

'I will,' I say, hurrying to the finish. 'See you later.'

I end the call, look at my still-crossed fingers as though they belong to someone else. The mobile in my hand bleeps. A text message.

All it says is, 'Toast?', but it's enough to send a current of dread through me; enough for me to touch at my jacket as if I might have dreamt throwing down a grand in the bookies last night; enough for guilt to churn at my insides like feeding fish. I press delete. Switch off the mobile and pocket it.

I walk into Soho, which used to smell of sin but these days smells of photography, and find somewhere for a drink. In the pub I get settled in a corner seat and phone Deano. Now the editor of a low-rent men's mag, we used to be at the *NME* together, when we were still idealistic young bucks. Me, fresh from Systemitis's near-brush with fame; him, fresh from the University of East Anglia. He went the way of magazines, I went freelance. He's now an editor, I now ask Fuzzy-Felt questions of self-absorbed pop stars on the odd occasion anyone sees fit to employ me. Back then, when we thought we were the *NME*'s new Burchill and Parsons, Deano held me in high regard. This was purely because I'd done the band thing – the flag-burning politics, the touring, the record deals, the lone *Top of the Pops* experience, the explosive fall-out – while he'd been beavering away at his media studies degree. Turned out he'd even seen us live, supporting The Fall, when we played East Anglia. I asked him if he remembered the drunken lead guitarist, and his look almost convinced me that was something to be proud of.

Times change though, and now it's me who accepts the scraps from his table. He hasn't commissioned me for a while, even rejected my last three pitches. Nothing suggests this time will be any different, but with a glass of optimism and almost a full packet of fags in front of me, I decide to give it a go anyway.

'Greil,' he says, and the picture that goes with his voice is of someone rolling their eyes.

'All right, Deano,' I say, and in a pathetic attempt to recapture some of my bygone hold over him, add, 'How's it going, lad? Still flogging Jordan to confused 13-year-olds?'

'Yesterday's news, mate. Keep up with the times,' he says, still phone-eye-rolling. 'Just a sec.'

There's the sound of phone being held to shirt. He hardly need bother, I can hear every word. Him, saying, '*Look, I'll be with you in two seconds.*' Pause. '*No, her, I thought she was great. Definitely her. We'll get letters about her. Right, two seconds, okay?*'

A couple sitting by the bar are having an argument. With a low, urgent voice, he appeals to her, holding her gaze. His eyes, imploring; hers, waterlogged. For a moment she holds her arm out of reach of his conciliatory touch, as if she's raising a hand to answer a question. His eyes meet mine as they roam the pub in search of witnesses to his shame.

'Greil.' Deano comes back on.

'Two seconds. Is that all I get?' I say breezily, insipidly.

'It's just that I'm knocked off my feet, Greil.'

'Busy day choosing models? Poor poppet,' I say, breezy enough for him to feel the chill.

'Something like that. Now, look, what can I do for you?'

'It's what I can do for you this sunny day,' I reply, wondering if I could risk a quick gulp of my pint between sentences. 'You say Jordan's old news, right? Well, how about some new faces. Some girls you'll "get letters about"?'

'Go on.'

'I was thinking a feature on lap dancers . . .'

He sighs. 'Done 'em. We have lap dancers in the mag almost every month. Greil, do you ever actually bother to *read* the mag before you ring me? How long have you been a fucking freelance?'

He's caught me mid-gulp, so I don't answer. I hear laughter in the background and I lower my eyes. The wise man would assume the laughter is directed at something amusing that has just happened in the office, a work experience girl falling over. Me, I assume that Deano is making a dickhead sign at me as he continues, 'A while, yes? You've been freelance for a while. Certainly long enough to know that the first rule of freelancing is to *read* the mag before you pick up the phone. You can't expect me to commission you because you need to repay some favour, or if you're a bit short this month. I need ideas. When you've got one, give me a shout.'

I don't say anything.

There's a pause during which he regrets his harsh words and commissions me for a cover feature at 75p a word. Not quite, but at least he seems to regret his words.

'Look, sorry, mate,' he says. 'Sorry. It's carnage here. I'm on deadline. Bit frazzled. Why don't we go out for a drink soon, yes? I've got to shoot. I'll give you a call when things have calmed down a bit, all right? Take care, Greil.'

That could have gone better.

To be fair, I was expecting a no. Done to death, that's what I thought. But there are no's and no's, and that was a no. Not only that, but it was a no-no from Deano. Presumably I must have pitched him more than the three unsuitable ideas I remembered. A lot more, by the sound of things. It was fortunate for him he went, really. I would have put the phone down on him otherwise. He had a lucky escape there.

I buy another pint and make another call. This time to Graham, my Sunday supplement contact, and currently my only saviour.

You'd have to be Forrest Gump to be stupid or optimistic enough to think you can beat the system, but I plan to give it a try. It'll mean having to beg, but I'm used to that, because the way the system – the freelance journalism system – operates is this: you beg for the work, and then you beg for the money afterwards.

Now, if you're a standard beggar, sitting on Oxford Street on bits of cardboard, then roughly half the people who pass you by each day will be cunts. If you're a freelance journalist, however, you don't have the luxury of the other fifty per cent who aren't cunts, because every single newspaper and magazine in the country is one. So say you're me: a not-very-successful freelance journalist in the begging mould. You probably wish you were one of those just-out-of-uni girls who write columns in the *Guardian*, but you're stuck with being you, which in this case is me. So you roll up and you pitch an idea at a bored commissioning editor who, ideally, you'll know. Let's say, Graham, or Deano.

Deano might actually think your idea is a good one, or more likely you're a mate and you sorted him out with some charlie, so he gives you the work. You're given a deadline for the work, which you do to a high standard, and – crucially – meeting your deadline. Remember those last three words. Now, having done the work, the commissioning editor loses all interest in you. You could be on fire and, unless he wants a rewrite (which he will demand often and at extremely short notice and without any regard whatsoever for what else you might be doing, tending to a sick relative, say), he won't cross the street to pour the dregs of his Starbucks over you.

Now comes getting paid. Most places you submit an invoice. Some places do a magazine mark-up where they get a dozy editiorial assistant to plough through the issue working out what each contributor is owed. When you consider that editorial assistants are usually people who want to be writers on the magazine, but aren't good enough, you get an idea of just how stupid they are. These are the kinds of people who can't spell 'tits', yet they're entrusted with the job of putting food into their contributors' mouths. Clearly, then, a flawed system. Occasionally it works in your favour. Once, for example, I was paid for an interview with the Dalai Lama I never did; more often, it works against you. Your cheque arrives and you've been paid for your 100-word review of the new Herbie Hancock album, but not for your 2,500-word feature in the same issue. Never, note, the other way around.

If you submit an invoice you might ask the commissioning editor, more in hope than expectation, when you'll be paid, but the editor has, remember, lost all interest in you – you might as well be dead – so you say, 'Any idea when the money'll come through for this, mate?' and they hear, 'blah, blah, blah, blah.' Before replying, 'Dunno, probably about a month after publication or something. Ring accounts.' You've met their deadline, you see; they couldn't give a flying fuck about yours.

'On publication'. Remember that. Because if a magazine decides to hold your piece over for a while, tough shit. If they decide to bin it completely, well, you may be able to negotiate a kill fee, but still, at the end of the day, tough shit. Your only chance of getting the money is to wait until it's been published, wait a month after it's been published, have the blah, blah, blah conversation with the commissioning editor, and then ring accounts.

Now I'm not saying accounts don't have a hard job. There is, for example, a con where individuals send bogus invoices to companies in the hope of seeping through the system and being paid. This happens a lot, and accounts departments have to weed out the bogus invoices from the real ones. It can be hard sitting around listening to Capital Gold all day. But, hey, accounts departments. Heads up. How come people send you bogus invoices in the hope of seeping through the system and being paid? Because they know you're shit, that's why. They know that all you do is lounge around talking about your pets and admiring each other's hair. Fact: accounts departments are the only people in the world who play solitaire on their computers. They play it *with each other* – 'Ooh, you made a bad mistake there. How is Trojan, by the way?'

And, of course, they're rude to freelance journalists. For all I know accounts departments have a system like WWI fighter planes, where they mark up the number of contributors they've fucked off during the day. Different marks for 'offhandedness', or 'unreturned phone call', or 'downright ignorance', where Valerie, who's been at the company for so long she has her own seat in the canteen, always wins. So, yeah, you can ring accounts. If, say, you've just had a lottery win and Nicole Kidman's called desperate for sex and you need hauling back to your former earthworm status. Go ahead, make their day.

The upshot is: you do your work, you submit your work to a back-breaking deadline, then wait a minimum of a month to get paid; you ring accounts departments and endure their contempt while '99 Red Balloons' plays in the background.

Unless.

(And this is what I think, fingers crossed, as Graham's phone rings out.)

Unless you can swing an advance, which is usually for about half what the story's worth. Clearly you won't get an advance on things like album and theatre reviews, because they pay so badly anyway. But you do have a fighting chance of getting an advance on a bigger job, an interview with a major pop star – Vegas, say. To do this, you have to know the commissioning editor, like, for example, the way I know Deano. Or in this instance, the way I know Graham . . .

'Greil,' says Graham, and as usual his Belfast accent makes me think of Stiff Little Fingers, but as usual he's hurried, like he hasn't got time to take a breath. 'Weren't you supposed to be doing something for us this morning?'

'I was,' I say. 'I mean, I did. The Vegas interview. Two and a half thousand words, right?' I steel myself against him saying, 'No, sorry, Greil, we've had to cut it right back,' or, 'Sorry, Greil, we've had to ditch it altogether.'

But he doesn't, thank God. Instead he says, 'That's right. How did it go?'

'Very well, thanks,' I say. 'I got some good stuff. Listen, um, Graham . . . ?'

'Yes . . .' he says, wary. He's right to be.

'Do you think I could get the money, like, super-super quick. I mean, could you rush it through accounts. Maybe even get it to me *before* publication. Like, an advance.'

'Before? Greil, I don't know . . .'

'Come on, Graham. It's *Vegas*, for fuck's sakes. That's got to be worth something, right?

'Christ, it's not . . . Look, I'll see what I can do, okay? I'll have a word with the bloke in accounts, but, you know, there's not a whole lot of difference between "account" and "a cunt", so don't go getting your hopes up. In the meantime just make sure it's a good piece.'

I say it will be. I thank him more than is entirely manly and hang up before he can change his mind. When I've rung a couple of accounts departments to chase cheques that will hardly keep me in tea-bags anyway – and listened to 'Take My Breath Away' in the background of at least one – I down the rest of my second pint, fish out a stick of chewing gum and head for the tube and home. It's only midday – might as well make a start on this Vegas feature.

CHAPTER FOUR

It's 9.45 a.m. Just fifteen minutes to go, and what stands between me and my casting is a smirking tube worker with bad teeth who looks as if I've made his day by losing my ticket.

'Well I don't know about that, love,' he says, except he says it to my boobs. 'I've only got your word you bought one, haven't I? I should rightly charge you a tenner. Everyone else has to pay, you know.'

The tube station thunders around us. Well, I think, I should rightly charge *you* a tenner for staring at my breasts. Everyone else has to pay. But I don't say anything because I'm trying to figure out whether he's for real or if he's having his 'little joke', and I'm thinking about the minutes ticking away, and how pissed off Sonia will be if the magazine reports that I was late for the casting. Not a good start. So instead I smile at him – not that he'll notice – and do a sort of embarrassed wiggle, banking on the fact that he's pulling my leg.

'Honest,' I say in my best little-girl-lost voice. 'I bought the ticket at Manor House. If I hadn't bought it I wouldn't have been able to get down to the platform, would I?'

At last, he is joking. 'All right,' he says, pulling the luggage gate open for me. 'Just this once. I believe you, thousands wouldn't.' And in return I give him a grateful face. The kind of face I reserve especially for acts of kindness from lecherous old men at tube stations.

'Thank you, thank you,' I say, slipping through the gate before he decides to pull my leg some more, making for the steps and suddenly realising that I'm chomping furiously on a mouthful of chewing gum, which isn't a good look. And right there before me – like it's meant – is a poster. Not just any poster, but a poster with *her* on it. It's too tempting to resist, so I don't. I have a quick look to see that no one's watching and I mash the gum right in her face. And then I move off, sharpish, feeling a bit guilty, a bit loutish. All the same, when I leave the station I'm smiling. Della sometimes says to me, she says, 'You've got the devil in you, Heidi Charlton.'

Now, let's see. Hair and make-up. I pull a little heart-shaped mirror from my handbag and do a quick check on the street. Not bad considering the heat. Still, there's not too much to take care of. Sonia told me to keep the make-up to a minimum. 'Let your natural beauty shine through, dear,' she said. 'They want to see a blank canvas, someone they can look at and imagine what their stylists will do.' Presumably, I thought, their stylists would simply ask me to remove my clothes, but I've taken her at her word and kept my make-up to a minimum, and what a wrench that was. Next, I switch off my phone – don't want that going off in the middle of my 'meeting thing' – and with a last straighten of my clothes I take a deep, deep breath and set off.

I've got just over five minutes, and I can see the building from where I am. But parked in front is a car I recognise, a Jaguar. I stop short. It's Peter. And how he knows I'm here, I've no idea, but there he is, parked in the road like he owns it. Probably does, for all I know. Why he's here, that's a different matter. But if I was to spread out my mental tarot cards I'd say it's because he's come to talk me out of going to this casting. He and I have different interests: like Sonia said, I need to get some modelling under my belt; he'd prefer it if I remained a dancer for the time being. And if I'd hoped to quietly assemble a body of work without him noticing, then it looks like I've failed at the first hurdle.

'Hello, Angel,' he calls out as I walk past, me acting like I haven't seen the huge Jag with the smoked windows parked at the pavement. A guy I went out with at school, a Scottish guy, he used to call injections 'jags'. He was terrified of them

– hated going to the dentist. Now I think of it, his teeth were as bad as the tube worker's just now.

Peter's looking at me from the back seat of his injection. He's got the window down a touch, just the right amount you leave to give a dog air on a sunny day. All I see are his eyes. Twinkly eyes, like Michael Parkinson.

I stop. 'What are you doing here?' I say, even though, like I say, I know exactly what he's doing here.

His eyes dance like he thinks it's funny I'm pissed off. 'Hop in,' he says. 'Just for a moment.'

'I can't. I'll be late,' I say.

'Come on, it's only a bleedin' casting. They'll keep you waiting for ages anyway. Just for a second, I've got something to show you. Come in out of the heat.' And he unlatches the door. With him, it's like an offer you can't refuse, so I don't even bother trying. I step inside, settling down into the farty leather of the back seat and suddenly wishing I could stay here all day: it's quiet and cool and comfortable, and the electric window to my side glides closed, the way expensive things do.

I catch the eye of his driver, John, in the rear-view mirror. 'Hello, John,' I say, embarrassed.

'Hello, miss,' he replies, lowering his eyes.

I look back to Peter. 'You. How did you know I'd be here?'

He does the puppy-dog face again. 'I called Sonia.'

'I didn't know you knew Sonia.' Stupid, Heidi. *Of course* he knows Sonia. Who doesn't he know? His expression says as much. I frown at him. 'What have you got to show me, then?' I ask.

He reaches into the inside pocket of his jacket and produces a squared-up piece of paper, unfolding it carefully like an ancient treasure map. 'This,' he says, passing it to me. It's a menu. He points at the restaurant's logo and widens his eyes. I've heard of the restaurant. It's the kind of place where people like him get special tables and visits from the chef, and where people like me go once in a lifetime, hoping to be seen.

'What do you reckon?' he says, beaming.

I stare at the menu, letting the logo seduce me, trying to place myself in the restaurant, looking around at the other diners and being looked at. 'Very nice,' I say. 'What you showing me for?'

'Look again. It's the brunch menu, innit? Table for two already booked.' He blows on his fingernails and polishes them on his jacket.

I get it. 'For when?' I say.

'Now. Say the word and John'll spin us round there. Chaffeur-driven to the door. Madam, your carriage awaits.'

For a moment or so I imagine myself walking into the restaurant, my portfolio under my arm. I look good today. Heads would turn, I'm sure. And perhaps someone might indicate for the waiter: *'Can you tell me, who is that young lady over there?'*

Only, of course: 'You can't be seen with me,' I say.

'Don't you worry about that, discretion is guaranteed.'

'Oh, I see. Tucked away in a corner, where no one can see us?'

'*Private*, Angel.'

'Well I can't, anyway, I've got this casting, as you seem to know.'

'Ah, well,' his smile never wavers, 'that's the trade-off, innit? You blow out the casting and in return I take you for brunch at one of London's top restaurants. Sounds all right to me.'

'Not to me it doesn't.' I refold the menu and plop it on to the car seat.

A touch of exasperation pokes its head above his cheery surface. 'Come on, Angel, what's the big deal here?' he says, 'It's a casting, that's all.'

'Yeah,' I say. 'Yeah, so what? What's it to you?'

He rubs his hand over his forehead, suddenly seeming tired. 'Fact is, Angel,' he says, 'I just don't want you to go.'

'Yeah, well, I can see that. Why?'

'Because I don't want you modelling. Not yet.'

'When, then?'

His eyes become flinty. He's used to getting his own way; doesn't like having to explain himself.

'I don't know yet. We have to wait and see. All I'm saying now is blow out this one, just for the time being. One poxy job at one poxy magazine. A lads' mag for God's sakes. What you going in there for anyway? To illustrate some feature on sex aids or something? No. Look, I'm sorry, but it's not what I want.'

It's not what he wants, me to go to this casting. And Peter usually gets what he wants, offers you can't refuse and all that. But as he's talking I get that feeling I sometimes get with him, where I think that if I reached out a hand towards him, my perfect nails would tap, not on the flesh of his chin, covered in thousands of little holes where the stubble comes through, but on glass. The curved glass of a television screen, with him on one side and me on the other. And as he talks his eyes land on my chest, like a fly, resting there a moment before buzzing off back to the window. And I wonder about those eyes, and about him turning up here, and I wonder if I'm more important to him than I thought; maybe even more important to him than he is to me. And I decide to gamble.

'Well, tough, because I'm doing it anyway,' I say, reaching for the door handle. The door unlatches and a blast of warm air fills the car.

'Heidi,' he warns, the kindly uncle routine dropping for good.

'I'll see you, Peter,' I say.

'Don't mess me around on this, Heidi,' he's saying to my back as I clamber out of the car. 'There are plenty more girls where you came from.'

But I'm banking on him bluffing, and I call it. 'Find one then,' I snap. And I slam the door shut, not giving a damn if anyone's seen me get out of the Jag, which draws slowly away from the kerb behind me.

The magazine reception is grottier than I imagined it would be. In my mind's eye I'd pictured marble floors, security guards in smart suits, and a reception desk like you see in American films, maybe with a frosty receptionist wearing a headset to answer her calls. I'd imagined hustle and bustle. Glamorous people walking to and fro, perhaps a couple of stars waiting to be interviewed. I'd expected to be greeted and ushered into a plush waiting room, offered a cup of tea while I waited – I could do with one, I'm parched.

In the end it's only the frosty receptionist I'm right about. She sits all straight-backed at a really average-looking desk, alone in the front office with a tatty-looking photocopier behind her and not much else. On the walls are framed front covers of the magazine, but they don't disguise the fact that the room badly needs decorating.

The receptionist gives me the evil eye when I walk in. It's enough of a dirty look to make me feel ashamed of my appearance, but it's not enough to make me turn tail and run, even though the thought crosses my mind.

'Model, is it?' says the receptionist, like she's trying to fart at the same time. I imagine that's the case, trying to put myself at ease. What is it you're supposed to do with people like this? Picture them on the toilet, isn't it? Well, I can picture this one on the toilet all right. Straight-backed, mouth like a cat's arse. For all I know she could be sitting on it now.

'Yes,' I say, smiling, partly because that's another thing you're supposed to do, and partly because it's the first time in my life anybody's actually called me a model in anger. Even though she does say it, literally, in anger. 'My name's Heidi Charlton. I have an appointment.'

'Just as well,' says the receptionist, picking up the phone. 'Hello,' she says, her voice instantly all sing-song. 'Got another one here for you.' There's a pause, and then, 'Right-ho.'

She puts down the phone and returns to something she's doing on her computer. 'They'll be with you in a minute. Take a seat,' she sighs without looking at me, and I do, laying my portfolio across my knees, trying to imagine how a model should look when she's sitting waiting for a casting.

As I'm sitting there, a young man in jeans and T-shirt strolls down the corridor holding a piece of paper. I straighten a touch, but he walks past and to the photocopier, not without giving me a good look up and down. Mostly down. I can see from his back, as he uses the copier, that he's smiling to himself. He leaves with his photocopy, heading back down the corridor, and moments later I hear the faint sound of cheers and applause.

The receptionist looks over to me from her computer, a nasty smile on her lips.

Another bloke comes sauntering down the corridor towards me, wearing a huge grin and a fading T-shirt that says, 'Will Work For Bandwidth'. He's even less secretive about looking me up and down than the first, makes even less effort to appear busy. Instead, he says to the receptionist, 'Cynthia, has second post arrived yet?' casting another look my way as he does so.

'You know it hasn't, Jonty,' says the receptionist, not even looking at him. And off goes Jonty. Seconds later, more cheers and applause. Cynthia looks over at me with her nasty smile turned up to full volume. I sigh, look out of the window, bite my lip.

Peter's right about one thing, at least. They keep me waiting another ten minutes. Another ten minutes and two more visits from men wearing jeans and T-shirts, more cheers and applause.

Then, at last, comes a girl. About my age, she strides towards me holding my gaze and smiling, her hand outstretched. I get up, resisting the urge to hug her.

'Hello, Heidi,' she says, with warmth. 'I'm Helen, the picture editor. Do you want to follow me? We'll go and meet the editor.'

'Okay,' I say, falling into step behind her as we troop up the dreaded corridor and into what I assume is the editorial office. Sure enough, the four reception visitors are there, no doubt pleased to find their floor show has turned into a travelling circus. There's a mild titter as we enter the room, and it's not lost on Helen.

'Ignore these animals,' she says, not unkindly. 'They don't get to see many real women.'

'No, we don't, do we, Helen?' says one of the animals, to sudden, boisterous laughter, which is just as abruptly cut off as we step into an office and Helen closes the door behind us. A piece of card taped to the inside of the door window comes adrift and Helen sticks it back, motioning me to a seat at the same time. I sit, my portfolio on my lap, and smile at the man behind the desk.

'Heidi, this is Dean, the editor,' says Helen, taking a seat next to him. 'I see you've got your portfolio. Can we have a look?'

'Yes,' I say, 'yes, of course.' And I slide it over, biting my lip, then remember not to bite my lip.

The room falls silent as they leaf through the portfolio. The piece of card at the window unsticks itself again with a noise that sounds too loud in the room. I feel like they can hear my breathing, try to take steady breaths. Thankfully there's not much of a portfolio to look at. It doesn't take them long.

'These are nice pictures,' says Dean.

'Thank you.'

'But they're just portfolio pictures.'

'Um, yes . . .' I don't quite follow him.

'Sorry, what I mean is, you haven't got any published work with you.'

'Sorry, Deano, sorry Heidi,' says Helen, suddenly. 'Deano, this is – or this *would be* – Heidi's first job. She's one of Sonia's new girls. Should have mentioned it before. Sorry 'bout that.'

'No worries,' says Dean, nicely. 'She's got you doing lots of castings then, has she, Sonia?'

'That's about the size of it,' I laugh, thinking, only if you count this one as 'lots of castings', which Dean probably doesn't, so I slightly revise my lie, adding, 'But this is my first.'

That was obviously the right thing to say. Dean's face lights up. 'Is it? Well, that's cool, then, because this is for a section of the magazine we're calling Debutarts, so it's fresh talent we're looking for. No doubt why Sonia sent you.'

I smile, wondering if I really heard him say 'Debutarts'.

Then he says, 'There are no topless in here,' pointing at the portfolio.

'No, that's right,' I say, 'but I am aware this shoot calls for topless and this isn't a problem for me.' Something Sonia told me to say. I repeat it almost parrot-fashion.

'We'll need to see you topless, then, Heidi,' says Helen, sparing Dean. She says it like she's sympathising with my hideous period pains.

'Okay,' I say, uncertainly. 'Um, when?'

'Now, please.'

'Just here?' I cast a look at the door window, where the unsticked card has let a triangle of light through. Somebody passes outside. Helen and Dean are either oblivious to the fact that the card has unstuck or they don't care. More likely, they think what I should be thinking: that if I'm okay to get them out for a national magazine then what's the problem? It shouldn't be difficult, but it is.

Especially with this top on. Too tight. Sonia should have warned me to wear a blouse.

With a final glance at the window – which still fails to move Helen or Dean – I pull at the hem of my top. Up and over my breasts and for a moment I consider leaving it there, but suspect that's not what they're looking for. Instead I hook my hands under the neck and try to pull it off without sandpapering my make-up and destroying my hair. After what seems like centuries of struggle I emerge feeling red-faced and flustered, unable to look to the other side of the desk where Dean and Helen sit, probably embarrassed for me.

I place the top on the table and reach to unclick my bra, dropping my shoulders and letting it slide off, an action that seems so familiar, but shamefully alien at the same time. And then I push back my shoulders and raise my eyes to look at Dean and Helen. With dignity. With what I hope is dignity. *Cop a look at that, then.*

'That's great, Heidi,' says Helen. Dean's eyes slide away. 'Sorry to put you through that. That's great. If you'd like to stick your clothes back on, we won't waste any more of your time. We'll be in touch through Sonia, okay?'

'Thanks,' I say, feeling cold even though it's baking in here. 'Thank you very much.'

'That wasn't too much of a trial, was it?' says Helen as we walk back through the office and into the corridor.

'No, not too much,' I fib.

'You did very well for a first casting,' adds Helen, then, 'Between you and me, I reckon you've got it. It's up to Dean in the final analysis, but I can tell. He was very impressed. Keep it up.'

And on that note, we shake hands, and I swish into reception and out the door, without so much as a glance at bitch-face Cynthia and the next model, sitting in my place, her portfolio laid across her lap. I did my best, I think, as I reach for the mobile in my handbag. I did my best.

There's a message from Sonia, darling: 'Could you give me a call back, darling, just as soon as you're able?'

'Heidi,' she says, when I ring back. 'How did it go in the land of lads' mags? Were they beastly?'

'Not really,' I reply. 'They made me take my top off though.' She tuts at her end. 'But,' I continue, 'the girl there, Helen, she told me she thought I was in with a good chance. She said she reckoned the editor was really impressed with me.'

'Well, that's great news, darling,' says Sonia. 'I had a feeling they'd adore you. I'll give them a call later, find out what their decision is. Now, listen. Something's come up and I need a girl at Docklands in about an hour for a job. Not a casting, a proper job. Can you do it? It would get me out of a bit of a hole if you could.'

I allow the words to sink in, like the back of my head's being tickled. For a crazy second I think I might say no, as if I've used up all my nerves during the casting ordeal and can't summon any more, not today. Then I snap back to reality.

'Of course!' I almost shout. A man passing on the pavement jumps and smiles at me. I hold a 'sorry' hand to my mouth. 'Of course,' I say more quietly. 'What is it? I mean, what do I have to do?'

'Well, darling,' says Sonia. 'Do you know what a seedoo is?'

I make my way down the escalator of the tube station and count the posters as I go, all of them bastard sizes, like *Moll*. Chewing gum appears on a poster for *Chicago*. On an advertisement for a bookshop's two-for-one deal is a sticker promoting an event where demonstrators are asked to turn up in the nude. None of the *Moll* posters are defaced.

In my rucksack I carry my tools, my weapons. My notebook is there, along with my pens, but to them I've added other items . . .

After I left Mr Benstead yesterday, the implications of the job queued up in my head, shoving and shouting. This task, I thought, was like no other – the kind of job from which legacies are made. Without knowing it, Mr Benstead had given me an opportunity to stand away from the crowd and help define myself as an artist. So it was to my notebook that I turned. A notebook which evolved from mere 'notebook' – a place for idle sketches and the odd half-formed thought or idea – to 'journal', where I resolved to record my activities. The job would become an artistic endeavour in its own right, itself a work of art, myself as the artist and the Underground my oversized canvas. And though I had already decided to paint Emily, I now realised how prosaic that ambition was, certainly when I compared it to my new inspiration, more ambitious than a mere portrait. A series; perhaps even an entire show. All this thanks to Mr Benstead, who in one chance meeting had freed me from the humdrum confines of my own mind, had set me on a different path, never trodden. Evidently he considered it all a joke, and probably thought me a gullible fool. But isn't that what we do as artists? We elevate flights of fancy to the level of reality; we operate on the borders of normality; we're the guardians of the ridiculous – the only thing separating us from clowns is the straight face we always maintain. But I smiled as I left Mr Benstead then, because I knew that the joke wasn't on me, not by any means.

But, still, the job. I found a bench to rest and put my head in my hands, massaging my temples as I marshalled my thoughts, trying to place them in some kind of order. The tube map spread itself out in my head, a growing cobweb that threatened to suffocate me until I could no longer breathe and I hurried for the nearest station to purloin a map. Back at the bench the layout in my hands seemed less daunting in reality, and I let its connections and logic coax and calm me into ordered thought. I traced my fingers along the lines, watched the tendrils of tube track meet then part, relaxed into its chaotic order. I counted the black circles of its stations; some, like Bank, or King's Cross, with their connections producing a bulb of liquid on the page that had formed, moved and formed again. The lines with their strange and exacting bends. The Circle Line, an on-its-side bottle, paperclipped by the Northern, spliced by the Central, resting on the cracked pavement of the District. It was into this bottle that I directed my thoughts, again the task before me threatening my ability to breathe, to comprehend and delineate until I did the only thing possible: I went back to the beginning. My beginning: Manor House, outside the bottle, where I could relax and think again.

During the journey there, I cast aside thoughts of stations and routes, and planned instead how I might keep the posters clean, forming a list of items I needed. At Manor House I left the station and from a corner shop stole a duster, a roll of freezer bags and a pair of Marigold washing-up gloves. There are other brands of rubber glove available besides Marigold: Shield and GeeBees. All offer safe, non-slip grips, easy on-easy off designs, and Shield's innovative size guide allowed me to determine that my hand size is Large. But in the end it was Marigold that I pressed to my chest beneath my T-shirt, one eye on the shop assistant. Marigold because that's the brand my mother wore. Because it's a brand I trust. Having taken the items I needed I went to the counter and bought a tin of lighter fluid.

And then I stepped back on to the escalator at Manor House, and I went to work.

On that inaugural occasion I travelled the down escalator and described a loop back up again, counting the bastard posters at the same time. With a feeling like a ligature loosening around my neck, I discovered the figure up was the same as the figure down, and that, at Manor House at least, I could see across the entire well of the escalator, necessitating just one journey up or down in order to see both sets. To this first figure I added the number of posters advertising *Moll*, and I recorded their position in my notebook, noting their exact placings so that if necessary I could find them as a blind man might, running my Marigold hand along the wall, counting the posters – 'one-two-three-four-five . . . *Moll*.'

I searched out the image of Emily Benstead as the production-line posters passed me by on the escalator. The *Chicago* advert, with the actress's groin subject to the indignity of a gum daubing – and not a pyramid either, but a smear – I ignored, and instead cast my eyes forward, looking out for Emily. From the second I first stepped on to the down escalator at Manor House, I became her guardian.

Nobody had defaced a *Moll* poster at Manor House that day, and I recorded that fact in my journal as I took the Piccadilly Line into the bottle, disembarking at all the stations along the way to note down their escalators, the numbers, the figures that began untangling in my head as I took the tube map apart piece by laborious piece, settling into a soothing rhythm of journeys, counting and checking.

My station, Manor House, has 50 posters lining the down

escalator, the same number up. A total of 100 posters. A soothing, round, landmark number. Of these 100 posters, 20 are for *Moll*. Ten on the down, 10 on the up, but at irregular spacings, so they do not face one another across the escalators, and nor do they occur at regular intervals on their individual rows. They are simply scattered there, jostling for the eye of the passenger with adverts for *Les Miserables*, or *Chicago* or one of the other new shows. One stop further on the Piccadilly Line is Finsbury Park station, a cross-platform interchange with the Victoria Line. Being a shallow station, Finsbury Park does not have escalators and therefore none of the smaller bastard adverts, but a single *Moll* advert does still appear at a platform site, an upright single-sheet poster which sits next to one for the Royal Ballet on the southbound Victoria Line. These single-sheet adverts are rarer, much rarer, than the escalator placements.

At Covent Garden I left the system to visit the London Underground Museum where I took a book on the tube network, a guide to it, hoping to make sense of its secrets. That, too, I pushed beneath my T-shirt, like it was armour, before I left the museum shop.

There is a cross-track single sheet at Covent Garden platform, but because Covent Garden, like Russell Square or Hampstead, doesn't have escalators but lifts (Hampstead's, at 55 metres, are the tube's deepest. Indeed the station is the system's deepest, at 192 feet below ground level), there are no bastard adverts, and the bill-poster sites tend to be taken up by retailers or for film advertising. The cross-track posters are of little concern to me. Of *less* concern anyway, because although they can't be reached by the public I've seen them defaced in the past, perhaps by night-time workmen, passing by with hard hats and picks and shovels like the seven dwarfs. And what if they should see their Snow White? So I check them anyway, when I can.

One stop on from Covent Garden is Leicester Square. It's the shortest distance between stations on any line, just 0.16

miles, but the difference between the two in *Moll* poster terms couldn't be more dramatic. In the heart of theatreland, Leicester Square has a cross-track single-sheet on the northbound Piccadilly Line and a staggering 138 bastards on one stretch of escalator. Twelve are *Moll*s. Not only that, but it's busy, one of the busiest on the Underground, even more so in summer, the tourist season, as it is now.

One stop on to Piccadilly Circus and there's an interchange with the Bakerloo, allowing passengers to see north and southbound of a line at the same time, which can take you either south to Charing Cross, with its ornate platform decorations, or north to Oxford Circus, which has 23 escalator ads from the Bakerloo line to the level above alone, making 56 up and down, of which 6 are *Moll*s, irregularly spaced. From this level to street level are another 22 each side, so 44 in total, again 6 of which are *Moll*s, and from the Victoria Line southbound to street level are 42 each side, making 84 on that one escalator alone. Of these 11 are *Moll*s, irregularly spaced. North on the Victoria Line to Warren Street, which has a total of 64 bastards from the Northern Line to the level above, then 112 from that level to the street, and a further 92 from the interchange level to the Victoria Line. In all, Warren Street has a total of 268 framed bastard posters, and 42 of these are *Moll*s.

There are numbers and routes and stations and at first the combination lock seems to click, but not – frustratingly – all of the time. Take Angel. The Northern Line not only has the tube's deepest station, its deepest single point at 221 feet below Hampstead Heath, its longest continuous stretch of tunnel, 17 miles 528 yards between Morden and East Finchley (via Bank), and was the origin of the world-famous 'Mind the Gap' announcement first used at Embankment and then extended to other lines and stations using curved platforms, but, at Angel, it has the longest stretch of escalators on the Underground. From the street to the first level of Angel station, the escalators have a vertical rise of 90 feet. They are an awesome set of escalators, easily the most impressive on the Underground, but their dignity is undermined by the relatively low figure of 44 framed bastards each side, a total of 88, of which 10 are *Moll*s. They appear to be twice as high as the escalators at Manor House (100 feet), but have fewer posters. From this level to platform level, there's a second escalator with a total of 42 posters, 4 of which are *Moll*s, making a total of 130 at the station. At Holborn, 134 bastards, 12 *Moll*s. At Highbury & Islington, just 42 . . .

It soon dawned on me that gum appeared on *Moll* posters less frequently than I had feared. Its first instance was at King's Cross, the escalator down to the north and southbound Northern Line from the Victoria, where somebody had left a piece of gum on Emily's left breast. Stuck hard with age, I picked it off in one clean go from the poster, dropped it into the freezer bag, my first piece of gum. Then I took the Northern south to Angel, and then to Old Street and Moorgate and the heart of the bottleneck at Bank. When I sat on the train, I held up the freezer bag and studied the piece of gum. What I saw was a tiny mound, like mashed potato, fine lines sculpted into its rising sides, pinched and fingerprinted with the identity of its previous owner, as individual as a snowflake.

But with none of the beauty. And I when I plucked it, plover-like, from Emily's portrait I found myself in harness to a sense of outrage that spurred me forwards, the symbiosis in effect.

With it came a rising alarm, a feeling of panic I tried to quell without success. How was I to know if seconds behind my patrol, somebody else left their mark upon Emily, another piece of gum, a marker pen's swoosh, a sticker advertising a left-wing march? I found myself constantly retracing my steps to check – just one more time – that the path I left behind me was clear.

Even keeping solely to the bottle described by the Circle

Line, the idea of checking every station was laughable, and it soon became clear that a single day was not long enough to carry out my task. I had no choice but to continue long into the night, prowling the black spots of Oxford Circus, Leicester Square and Piccadilly Circus; those stations that were filled nightly with people returning home, their bellies full of drink, their heads full of unkind thoughts and their mouths, it seemed to me, full of gum.

I collected the pyramids, easy if they had been in place for some time, hardened with age. Easy to flip off with a single Marigold finger and drop in the bag. I collected the smears, which occasionally chained one of Emily's breasts to the other, and these were more difficult. I found myself treading the steps of the escalator like a swimmer treading water, turning a deaf ear to the protests of other passengers as I pulled stringy gum from the posters with gloved fingers that began to turn black with filth.

I experimented with using the freezer bags as both glove and receptacle, but returned to the Marigold, only ever using the left. Always the left. I encountered two stickers yesterday, and on these I used the lighter fluid and duster, treading the escalator, ignoring the irate travellers around me.

Last night I stopped in the early hours, the gates of the tube station clanging closed behind me, and I began painting as soon as I arrived home, painting from the memory of Emily, burned into my retina, imprinted on my mind. At last I dropped exhausted to the floor of my studio, already scrubbed shiny-bright by the morning sun, where I slept for a couple of hours, waking to images of Emily with gum on her breasts, thoughts of the stations I'd reluctantly left unchecked and knowing the job was not yet finished.

Knowing it never would be.

And so I find myself on the platform equipped with my tools, ready for another day. As I go to take a seat and double-check the contents of my rucksack, I find an all-day travelcard on one of the benches, valid for today. I already have one, but even so, I turn it over in my fingers before pushing it into the back pocket of my jeans. And then, to signal the beginning of the working day, I put on my Marigold.

CHAPTER SIX

A Sea Doo is a water bike, like you see in James Bond films.

It seats two. I know that because me and another model are sitting on it wearing bikini bottoms, life jackets and nothing more – unless you count slightly queasy expressions. We're supposed to look as though we're having a great time, and not as though we're scared stiff of falling into the Thames.

A cab took me from town to the shoot. 'Hi,' said a young man who greeted me when I stepped out of the taxi to face a huge boat moored at the dock. He'd been sunning himself, the boat creaking gently behind him. After all the manic noise and bustle of the city, everything was quiet, peaceful. This, I thought, is a bit more like it.

'I'm Richard,' he said, pushing his glasses up his nose. 'I'm doing the PR for the game.'

'Hello,' I replied brightly, trying to draw his eyes away from my chest with a smile. 'Is Sea Doo a game, then?' I left him staring at my boobs while I looked over the boat, wishing Sonia had told me what I was doing here.

'Not quite,' said Richard, raising his eyes at last. 'Has nobody told you what we're up to?'

'Sorry, no. All I know is that I had to come at short notice because another girl was taken ill.'

'Right, never mind. Okay, we're here doing promotion for a PlayStation 2 game called *Sea Doo Extreme Four*. Do you play PlayStation?'

And despite the fact that he'd no doubt love to meet the first blonde model who shared his passion for computer games, I said, 'No, sorry.'

'S'okay. Know what a Sea Doo is?'

I managed not to laugh and shook my head no.

'No, sorry. Of course. Well, you'll see one in a minute, but it's basically a water bike thing, like you see in James Bond films. We've got another girl here who you'll meet in a minute, Chantelle. She'll be on the bike with you. The idea is that we'll get some shots of you on the bike stationary, and a load of shots of the two of you riding on the water with it. You do know it's topless, don't you?'

He was trying to be professional but he turned slightly pink as he said it. Bless him. I nodded and smiled.

'It's basically a promotional thing,' continued Richard, pushing his glasses up his nose. 'We've got some games journos out there already, they're all having a go on the bikes at the moment, but when everyone's ready we'll do the shoot, okay?'

'Okay,' I said, hopefully sounding more confident than I felt. 'That sounds great.'

'Cool,' he said. 'Follow me and we'll go aboard.'

We walked the plank, me feeling like a pirate, and then to the top deck where, it seemed, everything was happening.

On one side was a group of men I took to be the journalists. They stood laughing and pointing out to the water where two men in wetsuits were speeding around on a noisy Sea Doo. One of the group came waddling on to the deck behind us, freshly togged up in a wetsuit. More laughter from the journalists, who were looking me up and down at the same time. From the corner of my eye I saw Richard do a secretive thumbs-up to the group. Like him they all wore glasses.

To the other side was a man I assumed was the photographer – in deep conversation with a girl as we approached.

'Well, when do you think?' the girl was saying. She shielded her eyes, her hair was pulled back in a pink scrunchy. On another part of the deck I caught sight of the other model, Chantelle, sitting in the sun wearing a bikini, sunglasses and a Walkman. Beside her was a second Sea Doo.

'It's up to you,' said the photographer to the girl with the pink scrunchy. 'But look, it strikes me that it would be better to do the make-up now. Do the make-up, we'll do the shots "on land" as it were and then we can get the girls on the water.'

'Fair enough,' she said, obviously a make-up girl. 'But the water's going to play havoc with the make-up. It'll run.'

'To be honest,' said the photographer, 'I'm not sure if I'd even pick that up. And if they fall in, you're going to have hell's own job getting them decent for the stationary shots. They'll look like a couple of drowned kittens.'

He caught sight of me and clicked that I was one of the kittens. 'Not that you'll fall in, of course.' He laughed. 'Just trying to think of everything.' With a grimace he turned back to what he was doing, sharing a look with his assistant who busied himself with a huge silver reflective thing, like a fabric satellite dish.

Chantelle removed her headphones as I walked over. 'Awright?' she said. 'You Sonia's new girl?' Her accent made 'girl' sound like 'gull'.

'That's right,' I replied. 'I'm the replacement for the girl who's ill.'

'Ill?' drawled Chantelle. 'Who?'

'I don't know,' I said. 'Sonia said another girl had been taken ill?' I joined Chantelle in the sun.

'Fuck knows,' said Chantelle. 'Probably turned it down. Not exactly the world's best job. Fuck knows why they call it glamour modelling.' She indicated the shuffling journalists, pushing their glasses up their noses. 'Ogled by that lot followed by a spin on the Thames. Whoop-de-fuckin-do.'

It didn't seem so bad to me, but I said nothing.

'So what you been up to then?' she said after a while.

'Sorry?'

'You had much work?'

'Um, not really.' Chantelle looked as though she had a lot of work. She fitted in on the deck like a photo shoot was her second home. I felt like I was about to be exposed for the fraud

I thought I was. 'In fact,' I said, before she could interrogate me further, 'this is my first proper assignment.' *Assignment*? Do models say assignment?

'Oh yeah?' she said kindly. 'Nice one, gull. What were you doing before then?'

I steeled myself. 'Dancing. Lap-dancing.'

She looked over at me with new interest, even dipped her sunglasses to get a better look – maybe to check for ankle bracelets, lipliner and fake tan. More likely to get a good look at the competition muscling in on her territory.

'It's good money, innit?' she said, and though she said it with genuine interest, there was a trace of scorn in her voice. Like, the way bin men are supposed to be really well paid.

I tried to think of myself as her equal, chasing away the paranoia. 'It's all right, yeah,' I replied.

'So what you want to be a model for then?'

I could have gestured at her, at the sun beating down on us, the photographer and his assistant busying themselves for our benefit, the make-up girl I could hear complaining about the heat. 'Oh, I don't know,' I said. 'If you've got it, flaunt it, right?'

'You got that right, babe,' she laughed. Then, 'So you won't have done one of these before?'

'Well, no. Have you?'

'Uh-huh,' she said. 'I did *Sea Doo Extreme Two*, and it wasn't in no shonky London neither. They flew us out to St Tropez.'

'St Tropez? Really?'

'Too right. They had us zooming around the sea on that thing,' she pointed at the Sea Doo next to her. 'Boobs out. No life jackets. It was wicked.'

'So you've been on one before?'

'Yeah. You worried?' I nodded sheepishly. 'Well, don't be. You can leave the driving to me, but it's a piece of piss, right. And dead safe. The key's attached to your wrist, so if you do come off the engine stops. And there'll be a guy following us about. Bet you're used to that though, eh?'

I laughed. 'Are we likely to fall off, then?'

'Nah, they're really difficult to tip up. Really wide base, see?' she bashed at the bottom of the Sea Doo like a proud mechanic.

I smiled, feeling reassured, just as the make-up girl strolled over to do our faces.

We did the shoot, the group of journalists now holding bottles of beer and pushing their glasses up their noses, trying to look as if they'd seen it all before but not making a very good job of it.

Just another audience, they're all the same. And if at first I felt odd, standing and posing at the Sea Doo, after a while I relaxed. The assistant, angling his satellite dish to catch the light; the photographer with his easy banter; Chantelle joining in; the shutter clicking, like a cat's purr. *This is* much *more like it.*

'A bit more smiley and a bit less sexy, Heidi,' said the photographer, and I cringed, wondering if I looked as inexperienced as I felt. 'Think more Page Three than top shelf, okay?' he added. I forced a smile.

'Wait a sec.' Richard bounded forward brandishing two copies of the game which he gave to us. 'Could you hold these for a couple of shots?' So we did, looking like a couple of school prizewinners, only topless ones leaning against a water bike.

And then we put life jackets on and got on the Sea Doo – in the water, where I sit scared, no, actually, petrified, wobbling and feeling a lot less like a model and more like an idiot, and hanging on to Chantelle for dear life as she revs the throttle and we wait for an instructor to take his Sea Doo out into the water. I'm chewing my lip and not caring that I shouldn't. The journalists lean over the side of the deck, looking down on us, beer bottles in hands. Now we're that bit further away they've started talking among themselves

81

again, laughing loudly, but we ignore them, listening to the photographer.

'Try and get out to the middle of the water,' he tells us, shouting over the noise of the revving engine. 'Do a couple of passes back and forth in front of the boat and *keep smiling*. Watch the hair, get it flying right back if you can. I'll be shooting all the time, but you won't hear my cues, so *keep smiling*. When you've done a few passes, go out to the middle again and drive towards the boat so I can get some shots of you head-on. Heidi, you'll need to be looking at the camera if you can, and when you're head-on try and look over Chantelle's shoulder so we can see you, okay?'

I smile a weak affirmative, watching the water where the instructor does a neat turn and stands in the seat of his own Sea Doo, giving us the thumbs-up ready.

'Ready?' says another instructor.

Chantelle yells yes and I hug her tighter. She blips the throttle and we draw cautiously away from the boat. One of the journalists shouts, 'Open her up!' to a chorus of guffaws from his mates.

'Hey,' shouts Chantelle over her shoulder. 'You know I said I'd been on one of these in St Tropez?'

'Yes,' I yell back.

'I wasn't driving. The other girl drove.'

'Fuck,' I shout.

'Don't worry about it,' she shouts back, obviously enjoying herself. 'It's a piece of cake. Ready?'

I cling harder in response. She takes the journalist at his word. She 'opens her up'.

I come off first. I'm thrown right off the back and I think I drag Chantelle with me. Perhaps if I'd been hanging on tighter, I might not have. Or maybe she wasn't holding on tight enough so the bike took her by surprise. More likely, Chantelle shouldn't really have opened her up, and the sudden lurch forward took us both by surprise. Either way, one minute we're sitting on the Sea Doo in the sun, the next we're in the freezing cold water.

The first thing I hear when I come to the surface is myself, gasping for breath. The second thing I hear is the laughter coming from the journalists on the deck. A little part of me that isn't trying to stop drowning thinks, That's strange, I've never had an audience laugh before. The other thing I think – slightly bizarrely, considering – is that I've forgotten about Della.

I suppose it's lucky I'm so wet when I eventually get out. That way nobody can tell I'm crying.

CHAPTER SEVEN

At Oxford Circus I encounter the travelcard's previous owner. I'm at the ticket barriers, about to reach for my ticket, when I become aware of a conversation immediately to my left, hardly audible above the gates, thunderclapping open and closed. A member of staff is talking to a nervous blonde girl wearing a tight black top and a sickly smile. It's the kind of smile people use when they stop you in the street to ask for charity donations.

'Well I don't know about that, love,' says the member of staff. He towers over her. 'I've only got your word you bought one, haven't I? I should rightly charge you a tenner. Everyone else has to pay, you know.'

At his words I stop, and someone piles into my back, tuts loudly and moves to the barrier next door. There's more tutting behind me as the flow of passengers redirects itself to other gates, a river to my dam. I hear a 'for fuck's sake', an 'idiot', but don't care. Instead I watch the blonde girl and think of the travelcard in my back pocket, how the fact of it there has started to needle me suddenly.

'Honest,' she says, still simpering at the man. 'I bought the ticket at Manor House. If I hadn't bought it I wouldn't have been able to get down to the platform, would I?'

'All right,' he says, opening the gate for the girl. 'Just this once. I believe you, thousands wouldn't.'

Thinking of the travelcard I found at Manor House, I do believe her. The thousands who wouldn't swarm around me, their protests going unheard as I let the information settle in my head, try to think. On the one hand, I know that the travelcard in my pocket is an answer, but I'm too timid to raise my hand

and give it. By the same token, I know that if I don't, I'll be tortured by question marks. I'll know that I had it within my grasp to return it, to create a symmetry within the day, and that I failed.

That last thought is enough to propel me through the barriers – the waters flowing freely again – and I go to follow the blonde girl—

Who stops suddenly, looks quickly left and right, takes chewing gum from her mouth and squashes it on to a poster in front of her.

She is gone, smiling, and I stand in front of the poster seeing lights dance in front of my eyes, refusing to believe what they see. It's a one-sheet upright poster advertising *Moll*. I didn't know of its existence. Emily sits, the hand on her shoulder, the smouldering cigarette. And where her nose should be is a blob of chewing gum left by the simpering, smiling blonde girl whose travelcard I have in the back pocket of my jeans.

As if of its own accord, my Marigold hand shoots out to pluck off the gum, but I stop and reach into my back pocket instead, taking out the girl's travelcard which I use to pinch off the mess from Emily's nose. I deal with the tiny strands that follow it. I wipe her nose as best I can with my Marigold hand, but her nose still bears the mark of the gum. Not thinking, I reach for my duster, but little yellow fibres of duster stick to the gum, so I give up, hating it, and head for street level, leaving the mark of gum behind. Getting it off the larger posters cleanly is almost impossible. They lack the shiny coating that the escalator adverts have. It's not a failing on my part, but I can't help but feel that it is.

Outside the tube I nearly bump into two policemen who are patronising a homeless man by being nice to his dog. 'Woah there,' says one as I swerve past, and he directs a quizzical look at the Marigold. I hurry on, not breaking the law.

That bitch, I think, blinking in the sunshine. That bitter, resentful bitch. I look this way, that, trying to find her on the street, holding the travelcard which I fully intend to return.

Then I see her, crossing Oxford Street. I begin to jog in her direction. A man in overalls sings, 'hands that do dishes can be soft as your face . . .' at me, but I ignore him, keeping the blonde in sight, watching as she reaches the other side of the road and begins to make her way down a side street. I cross, a bicycle courier curses. I make it to the traffic island and stop, seeing her reach a car, lean down and speak into the window. Then she looks left and right and gets in.

My anger filters into disgust. I fold the travelcard carefully and put it back into my jeans. I know what you are, I think. I've got your number. And I turn and head back towards Broadwick Street and for the art shop.

My mind broils as I make my way there. Not just at the blonde bitch and a residual image of Emily's nose, flecked with the last remnants of the gum and yellow duster, but once again at the enormity of my task. Sitting on the train earlier I opened my journal to satisfy myself which stations remained to be counted and checked. I had allowed the routine of it to massage my mind, bathed in the knowledge that I had it within my power to prevail as Emily's guardian.

But now I feel it like a hollow pain in the pit of my stomach: the nagging, familiar sense of futility. Even restricting my rounds to the bottle, making and consulting methodical notes, it's clear that I can't possibly police every single *Moll* poster on the underground system, not if I don't know where they all are. How many other *Moll* posters are located near ground, outside my journal's catalogue? How many other blonde bitches have left a champed, beige disclosure of their jealousy on Emily's nose?

I need to speak to Mr Benstead.

I go to Liaisons, the address on the card. Outside are gaudy advertisements, abstract representations of the club's treasures, colours used to suggest disco lights and promises fulfilled. A silhouetted female body fills one of them, neon-bright lights emanating from her centre, as though her insides are exploding with music.

'Yes,' says a voice when I ring a bell by the door.

'Hello,' I say. 'My name is Simon. I'm an artist. I'm here to collect something from Mr Benstead. He's expecting me.'

'Wait there, I'll come and get you.'

Inside, the nightclub is warehouse-big, empty and silent. It seems as though inhabited by the ghosts of nights gone by: the smell of stale cigarettes and booze, a hint of dry ice. As I'm led through the entrance hall and then through double doors into the main room, I look up to see lights and balconies rising way above me, a planet-sized mirrorball hanging from the ceiling. Along one side of the ground floor lies a huge bar, almost the length of the room, the dim lights of the club reflected from the mirrored tiles and rows of optics. From somewhere there is the sound of clinking, a noise which echoes around the room, and I see a barman refilling a refrigerator with bottles of beer.

'Mr B's not here,' says my guide over his shoulder. 'You'll need to speak to the manager.'

I count twenty-three optics before we reach the foot of some stairs and make our way up, across a balcony with a bird's-eye view of the football pitch-sized dance floor below. There, at a table, is a man in a suit, a calculator spewing paper on the table before him, pen in hand. He looks up.

'Bloke here says he's collecting something from Mr B,' says my guide, leaving me standing in front of the manager, who stares.

'Yeah? Your name is?'

'Simon.'

'Oh, right. I've got something for you. Follow me.'

We walk to the edge of the bar where he leans over and plucks an envelope from behind it, handing it over. 'Simon, the liquorice artist' it says on the front in pen. I can feel the weight of notes inside.

'I need to speak to Mr Benstead,' I say.

'No can do, *Simone*. Just been told to give you this envelope,' he says, firm.

I pick up the envelope and hold it meaningfully. I meet his eye and become another person. Very slowly I say, 'I need to speak to Mr Benstead about an extremely important matter.'

'Nope.'

I hold his eye. 'It's . . . *very* . . . important.'

'Like I say mate – no.'

I tap the envelope mysteriously, and without relinquishing his gaze, say, 'It's a matter concerning his wife, Emily—'

'Look, I—'

'*And her breasts.*'

He raises his eyes to the mirrorballed heavens and says something under his breath I don't catch, then shouts in the general direction of the balcony, 'Des! Is Mr B at the Arsenal tonight?'

'S'right, boss,' comes a disembodied voice.

He snatches the envelope out of my hand and scribbles an address on it. 'There,' he says. He'll be there later on tonight. You go there and tell the people on the door that you need to speak to Mr Benstead, but, um, if I was you I'd leave out the part about his wife's breasts, all right?'

I take the envelope and leave, making my way to the tube to resume my morning's work. I start where I left off, at Oxford Circus tube. On the escalator between the ground and first level on my way down to the Central Line, I remove a piece of gum from Emily's chin, and the act of taking it calms me slightly. It helps me to focus my mind on the work ahead.

CHAPTER EIGHT

It happens because I'm not concentrating. Or maybe because I've had a couple of lunchtime pints and I'm carrying a sizeable hangover from last night and – oh, go on, then – I've had a cheeky line for the way home, just to keep me upright, you understand. Or maybe just because I could do with a good night's sleep.

I bowl into the tube station and get a child's ticket because funds are running seriously low and I need every penny I can get, even if that means pretending to be the world's largest twelve-year-old. Going through the gates and cringing at the little green light and tell-tale beep that advertises my crime, I go through to the escalators, and there I see the kid. You can hardly miss him. He's wearing a single yellow washing-up glove for one thing. I catch sight of him at the bottom of the escalators, going like the clappers. He's not quite sprinting, but he's walking the way we used to at school, when we were in a rush and the teacher told us not to run.

But then he's gone, he disappears off my register, and I'm hurrying, deep in thought, mentally assessing and discarding money-raising schemes. Then I'm clattering down the second set of escalators, and vaguely I see the kid also on the escalators, but I don't realise he seems to have stopped. Not until it's too late.

And suddenly he's in my way. I'm plunging down the steps, aware of him there, but in the accepted order of events he's so far ahead of me that he's already stepped off at the bottom. Only he hasn't. I look up to find myself almost on top of him, and at the very last second, with no hope of stopping, do a nifty swerve around him.

And I would have done it, too, if it hadn't been for that pesky kid. If, when I whip my head around to spit venom at him, I don't see what I see: the kid stopped – not slowed down, but actually stopped – his legs calmly treading the moving steps below his feet.

And that's a move right there. Already that makes him the John Travolta of the stairways. But combine that with what his top half is doing. He's using his hand – the hand with the washing-up glove – to carefully pick a piece of chewing gum from a show poster. On his face is an expression of almost total serenity.

So I don't spit venom. But nor do I turn my head forwards to see the end of the escalator approach. I'm half-turned, feet on different steps, off balance, and the next thing I know I've landed in an undignified and painful heap of man and suit at the bottom, while he shoots past and makes straight for a waiting tube train.

As falls go it's no Colt Seevers and I land badly, elbows pushed into my chest and instantly feeling a pain in my heart, like it's being gripped by a fist. Please let me live through this and I'll never do drugs again, I think, even as my hand goes to my chest and I realise the culprit is my dictaphone.

I stand and thank an old woman who stops to see if I'm okay, letting her hobble away before I brush myself down and reach into my pocket for the tape recorder. It's broken, of course. Its lid has come off at the hinges, the tape naked and shivering beneath. I put the lid in my pocket because some hopelessly optimistic part of me imagines a future where I sit down and mend my dictaphone's lid, having eaten a sensible meal, done the hoovering, and watched an unusually thrilling episode of *University Challenge*. Then I try the tape. My heart's in my mouth but I rewind a little, press Play and hear myself say, 'That about wraps it up, Vegas, unless there's anything you'd like to add? No? Then I won't keep you any longer.' And I don't say Phew, but I think it, and replace my dictaphone in my pocket, only in the other side, away from what I can already tell will be an interesting bruise.

*

For a second I almost feel sympathy for him as he retires gracelessly to the ground, a recalcitrant penny-for-the-guy on the tube station floor. Only for a second, though. Too many other things to concentrate on: stations to inspect. There's a cross-track *Moll* poster at Leicester Square, and I feel compelled to check it now . . .

I get to my studio with a few precious moments to spare. In time to rearrange my canvases, putting a couple out of sight, taking one to another room away from prying eyes, unwilling, for the moment, to allow Jill to see my latest piece. I want to keep my powder dry. I hear a car, look out of the window and there she is, getting out of her Golf, struggling with a handbag and a mobile phone clamped to her ear.

Before she knocks on the door I remove the yellow Marigold and hide it, studying my left hand as if it belongs to someone else. It feels wet and dry at the same time. Clean but grimy. And I run the fingers of my right hand over it, rolling bits of something into my palm. Moist and dead skin perhaps; maybe particles of the Marigold's luxury soft-flock lining.

I open the door and Jill walks in, her handbag slung over her shoulder. I find myself resenting her visit, the first time I can remember feeling that way.

'Hi, Si,' she says, striding into the studio, only stopping when she walks across some newspaper taped to the floor. It amuses her to greet me that way – 'Hi, Si'. She always has.

'Isn't something missing from here?' she says, studying the newspaper beneath her trainers. 'Don't you usually have your thing here?'

'My easel.'

'S'right. Where's it gone?'

'Through in the other room.'

'Makes a bit of space, I suppose. Jesus, but it's hot in here, mate.' I notice that her cheeks are red and strands of dark hair stick to her forehead. She makes a theatrical fanning motion with her hand.

'Is it?' I say.

'Too right. Do you mind if we open a window? It's stifling.'

'Yes. I can open a window,' I say, moving over to struggle with its catch.

'I can't believe you haven't noticed it. You must be boiling in here.'

'A third of the world's population lives in houses made of mud,' I say.

'Come again?'

'Mud. It's a cooler material.' I walk back from the open window and Jill moves to stand in the draught. I should offer her a cup of tea or a drink of water, but I don't want her to stay. I'm being rude and I know it. If you're happy and you know it, you're supposed to clap your hands. So what do you do if you're sad and you know it, or if you're being rude and you know it? You're only supposed to clap your hands when you're happy and you know it if you really want to show it, but if you're being rude then you're showing it anyway, so perhaps if you're rude and you know it, and you really want to show it, then you should refuse to offer someone a cup of tea. That's what I do.

'Mud. Okay. I believe you, thousands wouldn't. Where you been?' She indicates the rucksack I'm still wearing. I remembered the Marigold; forgot about the rucksack. 'Anywhere nice?'

'I have a sort of job,' I reply. Because I'm being rude, I can't look at her.

'Oh, do you? S'good.' My refusal to offer her a cup of tea still hangs in the air. 'Well?' she says after a moment. 'What sort of "sort-of" job?'

I try to imagine telling Jill everything, but find that I can't. 'It's not really a job,' I say, 'it's more like research.'

'Something to do with your painting?'

'Sort of. I'm pursuing a new direction.'

'Ooh. Sounds exciting. When do we get to see?'

'Not yet.'

'Don't be shy, get 'em out for the girls.'

'I'm using colours now.'

'Cool. But why can't I see? Come on, Si.'

'I'm sorry, Jill. I just don't feel ready to show you anything yet. That's all right, isn't it?'

'Well, let's see. I drag myself over here to see how you are all the time, and you keep a load of secrets from me. Yeah, sounds all right to me.'

'Sorry.'

'Never mind, I'm used to it. That reminds me, do you remember Garry?'

'Garry, yes.'

'He's got a job. Not a "sort-of" job, either. A job-job. He works making futons now, really good ones. All handmade.'

'Great.'

'I could have a word with him. See if there's anything else there. Something for you, maybe.'

'I'm fine, thank you. I've got my art.'

'Yeah, but a bit of extra money would come in—'

But her phone goes and she fishes around in her bag for it, barely gone cold from earlier. 'Oh, fucking thing. Look, I'm going to have to take this. Busy-busy. Why don't I escape into the kitchen, take the call and make us a nice cup of tea? You give a second thought to showing me this new direction of yours.'

I nod and she moves through to the kitchen, closing the door behind her. I put my head against the door, but hear nothing apart from a low hum. Some minutes later she reappears with two cups of tea, handing one to me and resuming her place by the window.

She blows on the tea, takes a sip, says, 'Ah,' then places her mug on the windowsill behind her. 'Are you eating?' she says.

'Um . . .'

She tuts. 'Si, mate. Have you been eating?'

'A bit.'

'You don't *look* as if you have. You look like an advertisement for famine relief. Christ, what are we going to do with you? Vitamins?'

'I've been taking them. I have, Jill, I promise.'

'Good. Last thing we want is you getting unwell, right?'

'Yes.'

'Cool.' Something on the floor catches her eye. 'What's this here?'

'That? Nothing. Some papier mâché, that's all.'

'Looks interesting.'

'Thanks.' I stand with my back to the radiator, running my hands along its uniform ridges, feeling the cold metal with my fingers. Jill watches me, slowly moving her face in the cool draught from the window. For some moments we stand while we drink our tea.

'When are you next doing your "sort-of" job. The research?'

'Tomorrow.'

'Just "tomorrow"? Si, that was your cue to tell me what you're doing. Jesus you're hard work today.'

'Sorry.'

'All right, I can tell when I'm not wanted.' She puts her empty mug back on the windowsill. 'I'll bugger off, then. Tell you what, I'm round this way tomorrow. Will you be in about the same time? I'll pop back, see if you've got your talking head on. Oh, and I'd get some more milk if I was you. That stuff's on the turn.'

'Okay,' I say. 'That would be fine. Sorry. I'll look forward to it.'

'Yeah, right. Looks like it.'

I close the door behind her, then stand on tiptoes to see

94

through the window and watch her go. She walks to where her car is parked at the pavement and lets herself in, already talking on her phone. Not until she's started the engine and driven away do I remove myself from the window and so back to the studio, where I retrieve my latest piece from its hiding place.

*

I make it just in time. Della answers the door, saying, 'God, I thought you weren't coming,' but I'm pushing past her, dimly aware that she's holding her tickets and passport, almost tripping over the suitcases arranged in her hallway and making it to the toilet where I fling up the lid, inhale bleach in one great whooping breath, and throw up.

'Hide?' Della comes in behind me and drops to her knees. 'You all right, girl?'

'BLECH,' I reply, spraying the bowl a second time, my insides fighting up to my chest, dropping, then rising again as I heave a third time. I'm sobbing and the toilet bowl's echoing my sobs as I heave again, but dry this time.

'Christ,' says Della, pulling my hair away from the toilet. 'What happened to you?'

'Fell in the water,' I manage, my words sounding as if I'm talking in a cave. 'I fell off a fucking Sea Doo.'

'A what?'

'It's a water bike thing, like you see in James Bond films,' I groan. But then the sight of my own vomit floating on top of the toilet water sets me off again.

'Better out than in,' I hear Della saying from behind me, and it sounds like she's trying not to giggle.

'Are you laughing at me?' I gasp, between dry heaves. 'I suppose you think I bloody des-BLEURGH-erve this.'

'No, Hide, no, darling. It's just . . . It's just kind of weird seeing you like this, y'know? Sorry . . .'

'BLECH.'

'Oops – you all right there? What on earth were you doing

on a water bike anyway? I thought it was just a casting you were going to?'

I spit. 'I did go to the casting,' I croak, feeling my stomach rise again. 'It was good. They're going to make me a Debutart. BLECH.'

'A "debutart", eh? Rock 'n' roll, Hide, you must be made up.'

'Della?'

'Yes.'

'Stop taking the fucking piss out of me.'

Della's bathroom is empty, everything packed. Even without my head in the toilet her flat seems to echo our words. All that's left of Della is the odd bit of Blu-Tack still stuck to the walls, the occasional potted plant she's left for the next occupants. Her front room is bare apart from a bottle of wine, a corkscrew and two glasses left on the table.

'I guess we won't be wanting that,' she says after she's rooted some toothpaste out of her bag and I've sluiced the sick taste from my mouth, feeling not much better, but a bit.

'I'm so sorry,' I say. 'I'm so sorry I'm late.'

'Jeez, you've got a good excuse. How did you end up in the river?'

Insides still churning, I tell her about my day and how I ended up in shit creek without a paddle, literally. Just a mouthful of river water and a gang of journalists laughing so hard, so cruelly, unforgivingly hard. They all forgot to be gentlemen: the journalists, the PR guy, even the instructors. They were laughing too much to remember their manners, and it was work I thought about when I eventually got out of the water. All Fur Coat, the gentleman's club where the men aren't really gentlemen but at least they have to pretend, which is a lot better than the alternative.

Della checks her watch. 'You gonna be okay to get home, honey? You won't have me to look after you.'

'I'll be fine,' I say, but I feel wrung out and my hands are shaking as I raise a glass of water to my lips. 'I'm feeling a lot better,' I add, deciding to stay off work anyway. 'Can I use your phone?' and Della waves a yes, giving me a concerned look before moving to the window and peering out.

'Hello, darling,' says Terry when I call. 'How's the famous model?'

I freeze. *How could he know?* 'What?' I say. 'What did you say?'

Terry laughs. 'Thought that would get your attention. There's a journalist coming in tonight, wants to talk to you.'

'A journalist?' I get a sudden sensation of panic, a thumping in my chest, thinking of Peter. I bite my lip, then remember not to bite my lip.

'Yeah, he's doing something for a magazine.' I relax slightly. 'He's looking for new models for a feature on the club. Wants to speak to you tonight. Dunno why, I told him what a dog you were and everything but he didn't seem to mind. Hey, are you all right, darling? Not ill or nothing are you?'

'No,' I almost shout. 'No. I was just calling to say I might be a bit late. I'm, um, I'm seeing Della off.'

'Nice one. Well you be sure to give her our love. Don't matter if you're a bit late, love.'

'Thanks,' and I put down the phone, my head in as much turmoil as my stomach. 'I'm going in,' I announce to Della, who spins around from the window.

'Oh no you're not,' she says. 'You're either going to a doctor or you're going home. You're not going anywhere like that. Look at the state of you. You're white as Christmas.'

Slap a bit of warpaint on and I'll be as good as new. 'I've got to,' I say. 'Terry says they're short-staffed, and you know how much I lose by staying away.'

'But Hide, you've swallowed half the Thames, girl. Don't be an arse.'

'I had my mouth shut,' I lie. 'I didn't swallow any water.'

From outside a car beeps and Della tweaks the net curtain. 'Shit, there's my taxi. I've got to go. But listen, I don't care what you say. You don't fall in the river then go off to work, you'll do yourself a mischief. You're not going in, okay?' I stand. 'Promise me you won't go in, Hide.' But she's already glancing about for her tickets, moving around the flat and doing last-minute checks as we head for the front door, dragging out her suitcases and closing the door as the driver loads them into the car.

I think of the wine bottle and two glasses left on the table. Della's going-away drink. She takes me by the shoulders and looks into my eyes. 'Promise.'

'I promise,' I say.

'Good. Now give me a goodbye hug, and without vomming all over me, please.'

I'm laughing and crying as we hug and say goodbye, and then the driver's beeping and Della's cursing at him, climbing into the back of the taxi which pulls away with her twisting to wave farewell from the back window. I wave back until she's out of sight, then I tuck my portfolio under my arm and head for the club.

It's bright, sunny and warm. A beautiful day, even if you've spent it half-drowned and throwing up into someone's toilet. People have finished work and are either making their way home thinking of barbecues, or meeting friends for drinks, standing on the pavements outside pubs, making use of the tables and chairs that come out at this time of year. Me, I step into the no-weather zone of All Fur Coat, where there are no clocks or windows and where it's always dark whatever the time of day, and I'm wondering who on earth would want to forego the charms of the warm evening outside to spend it here.

Quite a few, by the looks of things. The club's about a quarter full. The punters in here all have that familiar look of men who have been drinking for hours. Slouched at tables, grins splashed sloppily across their faces, ties at half mast. By now they're probably drunk and spent-out and they'll soon be replaced by the evening crowd, a fresh load of bulging wallets we'll spend our evening trying to empty. Walking across the floor I take a deep breath against a queasy feeling in my stomach and wish it would go away. Tonight I hope that the men I meet will be sober and polite, keep their hands to themselves, pay for a dance or two and ask for nothing more. I hope my pole-dances go well and I'll get generously tipped. Tonight, I want the impossible.

A man at a table touches my arm as I pass. 'Hello, sweetheart,' he says, huffing lager fumes all over me.

'Sorry,' I say, with a smile, trying not to wince away from his breath. 'I'm not on just yet.'

'That's all right, darling,' he grins, 'I'll wait.' But as I shrug a friendly shrug and walk away, another girl approaches him. She leans and puts her hand on his shoulder, whispers something into his ear and takes a seat. He'll buy her a drink. They'll sit and chat and she'll suss out what kind of customer he is. Whether he's drunk or rich enough to buy a dance straight off, or if he needs a little coaxing. The first thing she'll look at will be his hands, and if he has a wedding ring, she'll ask about his wife. If not she'll ask about his girlfriend. 'Does she know you're here?' And she's aware how much the answer no is worth. In return he'll ask her if she has a boyfriend and she'll say yes, whether it's true or not. She'll tell him that her boyfriend doesn't know what she does for a living, whether it's true or not, because she knows how much that's worth, too. A man will pay to think he's getting one over on another man. She won't mention the child she probably has, but she'll definitely mention the daytime job she probably doesn't – make-up artist, actress or singer. She'll tell him she doesn't work here often, that it's just a way of earning a bit of money on the side. Like she's not on tap. Like he should get her while he can. I know all this because it's what I do. It's what we all do. And most of the time, it works. You might think a girl was a feminist if she told you that blokes are all the same. She's probably a lap-dancer.

I drop in on Terry to pay him for the evening. It costs me £90 a night to work here. If I worked afternoons it would be cheaper and less stressy, but there aren't as many punters in the afternoons; they tend not to spend as much. The ones who come in the afternoon are usually content to sit at the bar and watch the floor show. The ones in the evening want the full works. As Terry says, 'You pays your money, you takes your choice.' More to the point, I want the days to concentrate on my modelling.

'Hello, babe,' he says when I knock, walk in and start fiddling around in my purse.

'Hi, Terry,' I say. 'Been a good day?'

'For ice-cream salesmen, perhaps,' he says, reaching for his receipt book and cash box. 'For a club, not so. How was Della?'

Della in the taxi. The wine bottle and glasses. My promise. 'She sends her love.' I pull out some notes and coins and plop them on the desk in front of him. In they go to the cash box and he starts writing out my receipt. 'Who's this journalist, then?' I add as breezily as I can, like I'm not really bothered one way or another.

'Greil?' he says, concentrating on his writing. 'Nice enough bloke. Hangs around a bit. Delusions of grandeur, but he reckons he's going to do a feature on the club. About bloody time.' He looks up and studies my face for a moment.

'Are Liverpool playing at home, love?' he says, concerned.

'How would I know?' I snap, too sharply.

'No, I mean, have you got the painters and decorators in? You're looking peaky, girl.'

'Sorry, Terry,' I reply, a little more composed. 'I must've overheated a bit on the tube on the way in. Feeling a bit dehydrated, I think. I'll get a drink of water in a minute.'

'Go easy on the vino tonight if you're feeling dried-out,' says Terry, still looking concerned. 'Alcohol's the worst thing in this kind of weather. Not that you lot'll ever take any notice.' Then: 'And you'll want to be looking your best for Greil, eh?'

'Of course.'

'You ever thought of doing any modelling, babe?'

'Modelling? Well, I don't know, I've never thought I'd be—'

'Good enough? Nah, you're probably right. Ugly boat race, body like a burst tyre. I'd best tell him not to bother, eh?'

'No,' I snap, again. 'No, of course I'll speak to him. Can't hurt, can it?' And I put the receipt he gives me in my handbag and leave his office on jelly legs that only just carry me to the dressing rooms, where I walk in on a crowd of dancers admiring a girl's new clit ring.

The girl's called Paris. She's telling her audience it didn't hurt. *Of course it didn't hurt, having a piece of metal rammed through your clitoris, of course not.*

'Heidi, isn't it?'

A dancer I don't really know, called Fortuna or something, a loud girl, always going on about her kids and the rich punters she's supposed to be going out with, even though it's against the rules. She nobbles me almost as soon as I walk into the changing rooms and open my locker. The other girls stop oohing and ahhing over the clit ring and fall into a kind of uneasy silence behind her. They do that because she's like the tough girl at school, only instead of smoking behind the bike sheds and stealing people's dinner money, she gets implants to prove who's boss. Three sets of implants, I heard. She used the same surgeon as Jordan, which practically makes them designer implants. And because she's got enormous tits and an almost-as-enormous mouth, and because there's a hush that falls over the changing rooms, I immediately assume I've done something to upset her – accidentally nicked one of her punters perhaps – and that I'm about to get beaten up for it.

'You're Heidi, right?' she says. She looks like a drag queen. Her lips are like two little hot dog sausages: botox, or collagen, or rat's vein or whatever it is she's got in there; her black eyebrows are painted on, halfway up her forehead, arched like the McDonald's logo; and she smells strongly of baby oil. Someone who smells of baby oil can't beat you up. That would be like being beaten up by a baby. If Fortuna beats me up now I might never be able to face motherhood. This and all kinds of other crazy stuff goes through my mind.

'Yes,' I say, my voice a timid mouse-squeak in the room, and I hate that mouse-squeak; hate myself for feeling ill, unable to meet Fortuna's stare and say fuck off back to whatever skank-hole you crawled out of.

She looks behind her as if gathering support from her audience. 'We've got something to ask you,' she says, looking back at me.

'Ask', I think, is better than 'tell'. I think of those prisoner films, *The Shawshank Redemption*, where one brainy prisoner gets roped into writing letters for the others. Maybe they think I'm brainy, or posh. They think that because I don't shout like they do, or swear about the punters and waitresses, or because I haven't got children and a history of bad relationships, or implants or tattoos or a belly piercing. Even though I'm not brainy or posh and I did have my eyebrow pierced once, only it went septic because we did it in my bedroom with a hot needle. Me and my friend Laura, who's now married, I think.

The radio in the changing room is on. It's playing 'Who's That Girl?' by Eve. All I can smell is baby oil, smoke and perfume, and together they make me feel nauseous. I feel my peripheral vision go out of focus and lean on the locker for support, hoping I don't appear arrogant. Fortuna's face dissolves for a second then comes back, twice as mean as before.

'Yes?' I say at last.

'It's about that,' says Fortuna, pointing at the wall behind her. I vainly try to focus on what she's pointing at.

'What?' I say.

'The camera, darlin',' says Fortuna firmly. 'The Internet camera thing. We was hoping you could have a word for us.'

'What do you want me to say?' I reply, unsure what she means.

Fortuna looks behind her again. One of the girls shrugs. It's very hot in here, I think. 'It's an invasion of privacy innit? For a start. I mean, that's just the tip of the iceberg.' Fortuna folds her arms across her massive breasts and I catch myself staring at them, thinking of airships and suspension bridges. I shift position slightly and the locker makes a dull clunky sound as I lean back against it.

'The camera,' she continues. 'I mean, it's giving them for free what they have to pay for out there, innit?' There's a murmur of agreement behind her. 'It's takin' the money out of our pockets.' There are more murmurs. I feel like I'm on the set of *Jerry Springer*. 'The food out of our babies' mouths,' continues Fortuna. One girl says, 'That's right, Heidi,' a kinder voice than Fortuna's, but still, it adds to the wave of pressure I can feel coming my way.

Somewhere inside, a part of me not concerned with falling over or fighting Fortuna remembers the webcam and the problems it's caused in the dressing room. The other night Fortuna flashed her tits at it, screaming at it like it was a peeping Tom. The girls hate it, obviously, and now they want me to do something about it. They want me to 'have a word'. But the fact that they've asked me – asked *me* – means what? That they think I'm Terry's favourite. Or, worse, do they know something about Peter?

'What about Sandy?' I say without conviction. Sandy, the club's 'house mum'. Hard-faced and permanently weary she stalks the dressing room more like an ugly sister than a fairy godmother. She's supposed to be there to help us with feminine issues, the kind of stuff that makes Terry and the rest go red and cough, but she's developed some kind of emotional immunity to all our problems. Talking to her about periods and child-minding and problems of the heart is like feeding garlic to a vampire, so no one ever does. 'House Cow' we call her, on the rare occasions she creeps through, issuing orders to empty ashtrays, or clearing us out on slow nights.

Fortuna answers my Sandy suggestion with the contempt it deserves, with a botox-injected sneer.

'Of course,' I say at last. Finally, after a lifetime cowering in front of Fortuna, regaining some semblance of composure. 'Of course.'

She seems to relax. The girls behind her seem to relax.

'Of course,' I say, settling into my role. 'I'll do whatever I can.'

The door to the changing room bangs open and a girl – Pleasure I think she's called – comes into the room, her voice raised. 'Fuck! He came,' she shouts, holding her hand away from her body as if she's put it in dog mess. 'I fucking hate it when they do that. How fucking pikey is that?'

'Did he have his cock out?' says someone else. Fortuna seems diverted by the outburst, enough to advise: 'Tell Bruno. If he had his cock out, tell Bruno. They could shut the club down for that.'

'He didn't have his cock out,' says Pleasure, placing her hand on her backside and dabbing for more come. 'Ah, Jesus, he's got it on my G-string.'

It's frightening how quickly you get used to all this: people comparing clit rings and getting spunked on as a hazard of the job. I guess there comes a time when it no longer bothers you how quickly you adapted. 'Quick, get it wiped off – it'll go all flakey and dry out the skin,' says another girl.

'You were grinding!' chime two of the girls together.

'I had a punter got it in my hair once, made me feel sick,' says someone else.

'I was *not* grinding,' says Pleasure angrily, but now the room's attention has moved away from me and Fortuna, the heat is off me at last. 'He just *came*. He must have a fucking hair trigger. Feel sorry for his fucking wife . . .'

'Cheers, Heidi,' says Fortuna, turning back to me, her voice softer within the hubbub of conversation, 'we're counting on you.' And then, with a hint of threat – or is it? Maybe I imagine it – she adds, 'Don't let us down, eh?'

before whisking the scent of baby oil into the air as she turns away.

I mumble something and turn back to my open locker, trying to focus on the picture of George Clooney that's stuck to the inside of the door. Not mine, it was left there by the previous owner of the locker. That and a Calvin Klein vest, which I threw in the bin. For some reason I left the picture of George, though, and I stare at him now, trying to bring him into focus. It's no good, his grey hair looks like an accident with Tippex and I squeeze my eyes shut, trying to get rid of the feeling in my head and gut, wishing that I could open my eyes and George would look like George again, instead of just a blob.

He does, and I feel better. Better enough to deposit my portfolio, thank God I've got a clean gown hanging in my locker and climb into it.

'You all right, girl?' says a girl called Chance, looking at my reflection in the mirror.

Her face is kind, so I say, 'I'm feeling a bit sick, actually.'

'Time of the month? Up the duff?'

'No. Just feel sick.'

'Wait there, then,' and she returns a second later. 'Take one of these.' She has her fingernail pierced and the ring brushes my palm as she drops a pill into my hand.

'What is it?' I say, not sure about accepting a pill from someone called Chance who pierces their fingernails, however kind she looks.

'Doctor gave it me for nerves, for my driving test,' she says. 'It'll settle your stomach.'

And just then my stomach moves, like it's waking up from a deep sleep, so I pop the pill into my mouth with a thank-you. Then I do my make-up and, with a final look in the full-length mirror and a peek up at the webcam, walk out into the club – into the heat and noise and the fog of cigarette smoke which already hangs over the place. Time for work.

CHAPTER NINE

'She'll be out in a minute, Mr Sharkey,' says Terry into my ear. He says it into my ear, not because he's a tender and intimate kind of guy, but because the bar seat I've chosen is beside a speaker, and he's got Madonna to compete with. She's singing 'Put your hands all over my body' into one ear, and Terry's setting up my meeting with Heidi in the other. It should be an intoxicating combination of sensory data. It would be if I hadn't just spotted a familiar-looking figure walking across the club. Familiar and not-familiar. It's one of those I-know-him-or-do-I moments. The sort of feeling you get when you see a TV actor in the street.

'Fucking hell, Terry,' I say to Terry, who turns, 'is that who I think it is?' His hands are in his pockets; he kind of jabs his stomach at where I'm pointing.

'Him?' he says, his belly aiming at the man who seems – oh no, can't be – to be making his way across the floor in our general direction.

'Yeah, him,' I say, turning smartly on my stool to give the club my back and resting my elbows on the bar. A girl's dancing above me, the man still the length of the room away from us.

'I reckon it is, Mr Sharkey,' says Terry, clearly amused. 'Why do you ask?'

'What's he doing here?' I say, grabbing for my cigarettes, like maybe a cloud of smoke will keep the approaching figure away, obscure me from his eyes.

'Famous innee? Didn't he used to be a footballer?' says Terry, leaning back into the bar, sharing some private joke with himself.

'Yes, he's fucking famous. I know exactly who he is,' I snap. 'What's he doing here?'

'You what, Mr Sharkey?'

'Never mind,' I say, glancing back over my shoulder. He seems to have stopped. He's talking to someone seated at one of the tables. A customer. Or one of the girls perhaps. He's not talking to me, that's the important thing.

'You know him, do you?' says Terry.

'God, no,' I say. 'Know *of* him, obviously. But I don't *know* him.'

'He know you?'

'No.' I reply. 'No. Not yet.'

'He comes here a lot, matter of fact,' smiles Terry. 'He might well be coming over to say hello. You want me to introduce you if he does?'

'Fuck no,' I almost yell. 'Look, Terry, if he does come over, whatever you do, don't introduce me. Don't tell him what I do. Please.'

Terry looks quizzical and amused at the same time, clearly enjoying my discomfort, watching me squirm. 'What's the problem?' he says.

'Because,' I say.

Because yesterday, prior to writing a fairly glowing review of the new Cornershop album, I wrote another, less glowing review . . .

Moll

Nicole Kidman's UK stage debut in The Blue Room *was unforgettably described by one critic as 'pure theatrical Viagra'. Ever since, it seems, producers have been struggling to produce a similar degree of tumescence among audiences, with* Moll *the most recent – and oh-so worst – attempt. Trust me, whatever the opposite of Viagra is – suet, perhaps? – Moll is it.*

In a debt to Chicago *the former show won't be demanding*

in a hurry, Moll *concerns the activities of Windy City criminals and their ladyfriends. The* Moll *of the title is a luckless dancer who becomes romantically involved with a big-time gangster-cum-club owner. Songs are sung, hearts are broken and lives are lost in more or less that order. For two and a half hours a cast of pinstriped boys and barely clothed girls throw themselves energetically around the stage for no perceptible benefit, certainly not to the audience. The funny bits are not nearly as funny as the sad bits and the sad bits not nearly so sad as the funny bits. Which is not to say you should make the mistake of thinking this is a so-bad-it's-good laff-fest. It's not. In fact, it seems to exist purely to showcase the talents (as in, breasts) of its star, Emily Benstead, wife of the legendary England player-cum-club owner who is – good God, what a coincidence – the producer of the show . . .*

. . . who is now walking towards me. I should say 'us'. Benstead is walking towards Terry, but since I'm sitting beside Terry that makes him walking towards me as well. And now he's eyeballing Terry and his hand is outstretched ready to greet him, and I just have time to say, from the side of my mouth, 'don't introduce me'. To which Terry just has time to smirk in reply.

True, I'm being a bit on the paranoid side. For a start, the review hasn't even been published. Benstead, therefore, does not yet know that he hates me. Presently, he will hate me. He will hate me a lot. You'd hate anyone who wrote this about your wife . . .

Emily Benstead looks great, and no doubt looked great on the dance floor at Liaisons from where she was picked for a life of celebrity wifedom. But she's no performer. She can't sing, for a start. Her co-stars visibly cringe whenever she opens her mouth and this is far, far too often. Tellingly she is given just one – presumably unavoidable – solo and even this is clearly the victim of an attempted drowning by orchestra.

Elsewhere, the cast do their best to sing above her vocal deficiencies, but cannot. Sadly for them, indeed for us, her glaring lack of anything approaching ability shines through each time.

Neither can she act. Despite taking on the presumably tailor-made title role, Emily Benstead has all the charisma of a stagnant pond with none of its hidden depths. And if she was something of a nifty mover on the aforementioned Liaisons dance floor, then precious little of that grace has translated to the West End stage. Think of Elizabeth Berkley in Showgirls *then times it by Mariah Carey in* Glitter *to the power of Patsy Kensit in* Absolute Beginners *and you're still a million decimal points away from the disaster that is Emily Benstead's performance in* Moll.

I take a calming slug from my beer and light another fag with nervous fingers as he reaches us, slaps Terry's shoulder and takes his hand in a vigorous shake.

'Terry,' he says. Shake, shake. 'How's things?'

I try to look interested, but not interested. As if I'm here, but not quite here. And as they embark on a round of double-barrelled hand-shaking and back-thumping I deliberately disengage myself, looking out over the club. Two brunettes catch my eye, expertly working a table of four banker types. The conversation seems to focus on the quality of the men's suits, and one of the girls puts a theatrical hand over her eyes to fondle the lapels of each banker in turn, announcing the winner to cheers from the group. A waitress brings champagne. A third girl joins the table, her spender-sense tingling. Over in the far corner of the club a fat man who seems to have fallen asleep gets a rough wake-up from security. Another bouncer walks to admonish a pissed-looking punter who seems in danger of taking a picture with his mobile phone. In fact he's in danger of getting his head kicked in if he tries to take so much as a napkin, let alone a picture. In All Fur Coat-world photography ranks with child murder. A girl flashes one of her tits for a customer – an appetiser. Another girl stands and begins a slow dance for a shiny, grinning punter. And then I see Heidi.

She's appeared from somewhere, from the dressing room most likely. She's walked out of a side door and reaches to brush some blonde strands away from her face, leans on the balcony rail for a moment and looks over the room, seeming to look in my direction. I should say our direction. Either way, she straightens and she too begins to make her way over, descending a set of stairs, beginning to weave her way between the tables, waitresses, customers, other girls.

For a moment there is only her. Heidi. Her dress could be made of navy cling film for all it hides. It undulates to the rhythm of her body as she walks; ridges of fabric rise and fall.

And now Terry is saying, 'Very well, thank you, Mr B, very well. What about yourself? How's the show?'

I cringe next to him, smile at Benstead. I hope a just-interested-enough smile, to reinforce my here-but-not-here status. Ironic, really – I've cast myself as moll to Terry's gangster. My eyes slide back to Heidi.

'We've had the press night,' says Benstead. I wince inwardly, remembering the press night, tramping out in disgust before the cast even took their bow. 'Went down a storm, it did,' he continues. 'All the hacks I spoke to loved it. Bloke from the *News of the World* said it was a triumph.'

Triumph Dolomite, I think, as Benstead goes on: 'Got the opening night to come. Should be a good do. You want to see it, Tel? I'll get you a seat, mate.'

'Nah, don't think it's my scene,' says Terry. 'Never been the arty type.'

'Come on, Tel, broaden your mind. Bring Mrs Tel along, make a night of it,' insists Benstead.

'Well, she has been on at me to take her out . . .' says Terry.

'All sorted, then,' says Benstead, and awards Terry a hearty clap on the shoulder. The two of them lapse into a silence that I barely notice as I follow Heidi's progress towards us.

Then Benstead's eyes are on me. Or I become aware of Benstead's eyes on me, and Terry must become aware also, because, after what seems like a week, he says, 'Sorry, Mr B, where are my manners? This is a mate of mine,' he waves towards me, never losing his cool, and then indicates Benstead. 'And this is Mr Benstead. He's the owner of the club.'

Benstead locks on to me and out comes his hand, ready to shake.

'Please,' he says, as I smile and shake, still processing the information. *He's the owner of All Fur Coat.* Bloody hell, you dark horse. 'Please,' he says. 'Call me Peter.'

*

I'm making my way over to Terry and the man at his side who must be Greil the magazine man, when I suddenly realise Peter is standing with them, his back to me, shaking the stranger's hand. So I do an about-face before I reach them. It's a very catwalk-like move, if I do say so myself. I kind of shift direction, as if that was what I intended all along.

I circle, return to the back of the club and cast a look at where Terry and the other man are. Peter's moved away, thank God, so at last I make my way back, getting a good look at the other man as I go. He's quite handsome, but sort of arrogant-looking. As I walk towards them he's looking at me, staring at me, almost like he's never seen a woman before. Then, as I get nearer, he seems to remember himself and he gives me a big smile. He stands, and Terry says—

*

'Heidi, this is Mr Sharkey.'

Christ, she's here. And at last I pull myself together, flash her a Shark-smile and stand, my hand outstretched for what feels like the millionth handshake of the day.

'Greil,' I say, gulping, a strange imitation of my introduction to the club's owner. 'Please. Call me Greil.'

We touch.

Her hand is trembling slightly as I take it in mine and hold her gaze, return her smile, which is weak, forced. She's just wary, of course. Who wouldn't be? After all, I'm a journalist. She's probably wondering what she's let herself in for. I feel a sharp squib of guilt which I try to douse, not wholly successfully. The shame of studying her on the Internet, of fabricating this meeting, remains and intensifies when I look into her questioning eyes. I'm shaking her hand, but really I'm dragging her into the lion's den.

'Here,' says Terry, guiding Heidi by the elbow. 'Why don't you take Mr Sharkey to a table. I'll get a couple of drinks sent over.'

Heidi smiles, and turns with a swish of fabric that I don't hear, but feel, and leads the way, folding herself into a booth, laying her hands demurely on the table in front of her. Taking a seat opposite, I put my cigarettes on the table, then reach into my jacket for my dictaphone which I place beside them. I don't turn it on. There's no point, it would never pick up anything above the music anyway. It's there for show. Partly to prove I'm genuine, partly to impress her, make her feel like a real star. She looks down at it pointedly.

'The last person to speak into that thing was the pop star Vegas,' I say, hating my own ooze.

She smiles, but it's the smile of the terminally polite, like someone forced to endure a civil servant at a dinner party. I run a hand through my hair and lay an arm across the back of the seat, pointing in her direction. There's a pause, during which I reach into my jacket again and take out one of my cards.

'Here,' I say, holding it across the table to her. 'Have my card.'

'I can't,' she says, almost as though hypnotised. 'We're not allowed to take customers' numbers.'

Of course. But that throws me. 'Well,' I say, 'I'm not strictly a customer in this instance. Um, Terry has told you what I want to speak to you about?'

'Sorry,' she replies, as if gathering herself slightly, and she takes the card and puts it into a small purse she's carrying. 'Sorry. Yes. I wasn't thinking.' Irritatingly, she doesn't seem to look at the card, which is a nice card – Greil Sharkey. Freelance Journalist – so she doesn't ask me about myself, like, who I work for. She doesn't probe. Again, it throws me.

'That's a beautiful frock,' I say. I'm being disingenuous, sick fuck that I am. I'm trying to charm her with my quaint use of language. *Frock*, for Christ's sake. She smiles still. A waxwork, or a rabbit in my headlights. Hardly set to dazzle, but there you go. I sigh and reach for my cigarettes, taking one and holding out the packet towards her, thinking: she's looking a bit on the green side all of a sudden, as if she's about to puke.

She does. A great whooping spew all over my arm, which is holding out the cigarettes towards her. And as my hand jerks instinctively away, spraying sick and cigarettes over the next table, she pukes again, this time on my dictaphone, where her corrosive gastric juices immediately get to work on the tape of my interview with Vegas.

THE DAY AFTER

CHAPTER TEN

'Hello.'

'Yeah, hello.'

'Is that Mr Sharkey?'

'Yes. Who's this?'

'You don't know me.'

'You're right, I don't. Which is why I just asked who you are.'

'You're a journalist, aren't you?'

'Again, you're right. Now would you mind telling me who you are, and what you want. Especially since— What the fuck time is it?'

'It's early.'

'Christ. Specialist subject stating the bleeding obvious. I'm putting the phone down in three seconds unless you stop wasting my time, got it?'

'You're a freelance journalist.'

'One.'

'So you sell stories to newspapers.'

'Two.'

'Well, I've got a story for you to sell. A big one.'

'Okay, spit it out.'

'No. We'll meet. I'll tell you when we meet.'

'Listen, mate. You've been watching too much television if you think I'm going to meet someone I don't know for some bollocks promise of a story. Either tell me now or I'm putting down the phone, okay? If it sounds like it's worth my while, then I'll meet you.'

'You do know me.'

'How?'

'We met.'

'Where?'

'On an escalator.'

*

A washing-up bowl is the last thing you should see when you wake up. On your bedroom floor, anyway. But here it is – hello, washing-up bowl – staring up at me in a grey plastic yawn, a scrunched-up ball of tissue and a tiny puddle of sick in the bottom. As sick goes, it's that end-of-stomach stuff, like off-colour egg-white. The sort of throw-up your stomach produces when it's empty, and all it can do is regurgitate foul-tasting gunk that burns your mouth. A girl at school was a bulimic. They said the constant puking rotted her teeth. Tasting my mouth, I can well believe it.

It's almost certainly not, but I imagine that at the centre of my little blob of egg-white I can see the tiny pill Chance gave me in the club last night, as if the last thing my stomach rejected was the very thing supposed to make it better. I must have had a fever. Or, rather, I must still have a fever. My forehead burns and I can't seem to remember much about the events of last night. With a groan I recall being sick over the journalist, suddenly losing it when he offered me the cigarette. He gave me his card – I should call to apologise. But what happened after that? Lots of people fussing around, one of the girls helping me to— where? Either the dressing rooms or Terry's office, one of the two. And then me coming home, somebody keeping me company in the taxi but I can't remember who. And the taxi dropping me off outside my flat and the driver saying, 'You all right, love?' and my companion going, 'She's fine. Leave her.' And them driving away and me being sick some more.

I pull my head up on to the mattress and it's like lugging the rubbish outside. I'm shivering now – gone from hot to cold – and I try to curl up into a ball beneath the duvet, even though doing that hurts my stomach, bruised from puking so much. I drag a pillow over my head and go back to sleep.

When I wake up it's to the sound of my mobile ringing from somewhere deep inside my handbag. Since my face is squished into the bed and I wake up feeling not better, but worse, I let it ring, let it go to voicemail, before I claw my way to the edge of the bed and focus on my bedside clock.

It's 11.58 a.m.

No, it's 11.59 a.m.

The flat is quiet. Judging from the light pouring through the gap in my bedroom curtains, it's another beautiful day outside. Bits of dust are dancing in the shaft of light and the room feels warm, but in a moment or so I'll be freezing again. Slowly I feel for my bag and bring my phone into bed where I access the message, burrowing beneath the duvet like a mole. A mole with a mobile phone.

I'd hoped the message might be from my mum, ringing because she's had some mum-like premonition that her daughter's ill. But it's from Sonia, sucking on a cigarette her end and sounding as though nothing's wrong with the world.

'Hello, darling,' she drawls into my voicemail. 'Hope all's well. Heard about your little mishap with the Sea Doo yesterday. No broken bones, I hope . . .' I snort derisively. 'Well, listen, I've got a bit of news for you. Remember your casting yesterday? I had a call about you and they absolutely loved you . . .'

I catch my breath.

'. . . but they're going to use another girl.'

I let my breath go in a sigh that nearly blows off the duvet. 'Now, darling, don't be *too* despondent. It was only your first casting, after all. And I'm sure I'll have plenty more for you in the near future, although I don't have any for you right at this moment in time, I'm afraid. Tell you what, darling. Leave it with me and I'll try and sort you something out very soon, okay?' And with that she goes, taking another little piece of me with her. I resist the temptation to throw my phone against the wall – it doesn't seem to be bringing me anything but bad luck lately – and instead I close my eyes, try to sleep again.

The next time I awake it's to the sound of the phone ringing for the second time, on the pillow beside me now, and again I pick it up and hope it'll be my mum, but the phone tells me 'Petermob', and I frown, thinking, What now?

'Angel,' he says. It's like yesterday never happened; there's a question to his voice, maybe even a concern.

'Yes?' I reply, disgusted to find my voice is shaking.

'How's the poorly soldier? You had us worried there last night.'

'I'm all right now, thanks. A bit sick, that's all.'

'Anything I can do?'

'Was it you that brought me home last night?'

'Jesus, you really were out of it, weren't you? I wasn't with you, no. I arranged for you to get home safely.'

'Then thanks, you've done enough.'

'What about a doctor?' he asks. 'I can arrange to have one see you just like that.' I hear the sound of him clicking his fingers. He clicks his fingers and doctors come.

'It'll be a twenty-four-hour thing,' I tell him. 'Upset stomach, that's all. I'll be all right by tomorrow.'

'You sure?'

'I'm sure.'

'As long as you are.'

'I am.'

'I can't help you in any other way?'

'No, I'm fine, thank you.'

'You're certain about that? Nothing I can do to help cheer you up? Not a big bunch of flowers?'

The doorbell goes.

'Is that you?' I say, smiling despite myself.

'Nah,' he says, 'just a florist, innit?'

But of course, when I answer the door looking yucky in my

dressing gown and slippers, with hair like wet straw, and the first thing I see is a huge bunch of flowers, one of the biggest I've ever seen in real life, it's Peter, not a florist, who's standing behind it somewhere.

'Hello,' he says, craning around the flowers. 'I came as soon as I could.'

I give him a sceptical smile. 'Do you do this for all your dancers who get ill?'

'You're joking, aren't you? 'Course I do,' he replies.

'You'd better come in then,' I say, catching sight of his injection and John at the wheel, wondering how comfortable they both feel outside of central London. The estate outside seems quiet. Somebody's walking their dog. Across the road a kid sits on a wall. I close the door behind Peter as he steps inside, immediately filling my small flat with his presence. He comes in and towers over everything. Even the smell of my flat is immediately replaced by his smell, which is cigar smoke and leather car interiors and aftershave.

'Point me the way to the kitchen,' he says, shooing me into the hallway, 'I'll put these in some water. You go and put your feet up.'

I go through to the lounge, and in a moment or so he appears from the kitchen holding the earthenware pot I use to keep cooking utensils in, flowers replacing the usual spatulas, spoons and little whisks it holds.

'There's a vase,' I say from the sofa.

'This is a vase,' he says, smiling.

'No it's not, it's . . . oh, never mind.'

'It's very tidy in here,' he says, setting down my utensils pot and folding himself into an armchair.

But he's pissed me off, because I know that when I next go into the kitchen I'm going to find a counter covered in my cooking utensils. And he probably thinks he's been unbearably cute by 'mistaking' my utensils jar for a flower vase, like he's Hugh Grant or something, when in fact he's just been a pain in the arse.

'Look, Peter, the flowers are very nice, thanks, but do you mind telling me what it's all in aid of?' I feel grouchy about the impending mess he's made in the kitchen; about being ill. But most of all about sitting here with no make-up on.

'It's an apology,' he says.

'For what?' I say. 'For trying to bribe me?'

'Well, yeah, that. And for what I said – about there being plenty of other girls where you come from.'

'Oh? There aren't, then?'

'None like you.'

He's too big for the armchair. He sits forward looking like a fish out of water – part real, part an act he's putting on for my benefit. Looking at him I get that TV feeling again.

I put my feet up on to the coffee table and watch his eyes dart up my legs. 'Apology accepted, then,' I say, feeling better for those eyes. 'And I can go to whatever casting I want?'

He shrugs. 'You want to go to castings, not much I can do to stop you.'

'Good.'

I study him for a moment. His eyes rove around my lounge, seeming to admire the coving. Hanging between his legs his hands clap together softly.

'While you're here,' I say eventually, 'something weird happened at the club last night, something that made me wonder if the other girls know what's going on.'

His head jerks my way. Fear flicks across his face. 'Why? What did they say?'

I tell him about the webcam conversation and watch him absorb the information, his face now creased with concern. 'They said that, did they?' he says. 'To ask me? They specifically asked you to ask me?'

'No, but something obviously makes them think I've got some kind of influence. Either with Terry, or with you. You can't blame them. How many times do you think I can disappear into the office without them wondering what's going on?'

He stands and shoves his hands in his pockets. He's not bothering to act now; any attempts at being cute are forgotten. 'It wouldn't do for it to come out,' he says.

'Not yet,' I say pointedly.

He glances at me, trying to read my face. 'No, not yet.' The silence throws a shadow into the room. My flat suddenly feels too small for the both of us. He reaches into his coat pocket and out comes his mobile, which he flicks open and raises to his ear in one suave movement. 'John,' he says. 'Come round.' Then, to me, 'I must go, Angel. I'm needed at the club.'

'Making a tour of your investments, are you?' I sneer, hating the words as they leave my mouth. The way I use them like little stones to throw at his conscience.

'If you want to look at it like that,' he says, 'yes. I am.'

When he's gone it occurs to me that he didn't ask why I was ill at the club last night. Or how the casting went.

CHAPTER ELEVEN

'FUCK!'

I don't even bother to inspect the dent my dictaphone's just made in the wall. Nor do I bother to clear up its plastic guts from my floor. On one level I think I needed a new dictaphone anyway, and as for the wall, I'll use a bit of filler on the dent and slap on a coat of paint while I'm at it, because I haven't done any decorating since George left and quite frankly the whole flat needs a lick of paint. On another level I think it'll probably stay the way it is, like the busted towel rail I haven't got round to fixing, or the bulb that needs replacing in the spare room, the one I nicked because the bulb in the bedroom had gone and I couldn't be arsed to go down the shops for a spare bulb. Or the lid of my dictaphone that, if I'd fixed it, might have stopped Heidi's sick ruining my tape.

On another level entirely, I think:

'FUCK!'

Because where yesterday I had a recording of Vegas – after all that, a perfect recording even in the din of the hotel – answering my oh-so-fucking probing questions, today all I have is a hangover.

Waking up, my first thought was for the tape, and I staggered to the lounge to confront horrific scenes of drunken tape-mending gone wrong. At some point, deep in my cups, I'd decided that despite the machine being doused in sick, I could save my interview. The evidence is scattered over the coffee table: one of those tiny little screwdrivers, the kind you'd use to unscrew the casing of a TDK FE Ferric 90-minute cassette; a pair of scissors; a roll of Sellotape, bits of Sellotape all over the place; and, of course, yards and yards of unsuccessfully spliced cassette tape. Everywhere. Unspooled and coiled spaghetti-like on the table, on the floor, on the sofa. Shiny, creased, crunched and useless. So to make myself feel better, I heaved my redundant dictaphone at the wall. And for the third time now, I say:

'FUCK!'

Because I need that Vegas interview. It's currently the only chance I have to pay the money I owe. I'm already a text message into final demands. This is not good. This is the bit in the film where the hero takes desperate measures.

I find my notebook and look at the lovely shorthand outlines I've made for *Anal Snow Bunnies*, Systemitis and our big hit, 'Gunpowder Plot'.

You clown, Greil. You fucking clown.

For a moment or so I stand in my lounge, wearing only my pants and with a dictaphone-sized bruise on my chest, like the mark of a broken heart. Then I look to see if the post's arrived, hoping against hope for a freelance cheque in there, something I've forgotten about, perhaps. But there's no cheque, just Jiffy bags holding CDs I've been sent, a water bill, a demand for ground rent from the freeholder, and a postcard addressed to 'Mrs H. Sharkey'.

The postcard is from Lancôme, details of some offer or another. I turn it over in my hand for a moment or so, staring at the name before my mind drags itself away from its photo album and returns to the problem in hand.

Back inside the flat I dig out my emergency wrap of coke, which has enough for one line in it, have a tiny dab, knock back a slug of vodka and dial fighting-dog PR girl Jenny.

'Jenny, hi, it's Greil Sharkey, from yesterday, how's it going?' I feel the voddy light a fire under my hangover. Feels good. Catching sight of my face in the lounge mirror, I give myself an encouraging wink.

'Oh, hi, Greil, I was going to give you a call some time today, find out if you got everything you needed from Vegas. Was everything okay?'

If this works, I'll happily eat a tramp's hat.

'Well, not quite, Jenny. In fact, I was wondering if you could schedule me a little more time with her. Say, today sometime. I could do it on the phone if that would be easier.'

When Jenny's stopped laughing at what I then pass off as a joke, I try a different tack. 'Jenny, the reason I called was, I've been transcribing my tape and— look, I'm not just being awkward about the whole microphone thing, it's just that there's something I can't catch off the tape and I was thinking . . . Well, you know how you were doing your own recording . . . ?'

'Hmm, was I? What, you mean the recording you got all radge about?'

Through gritted teeth I say, 'Yeah, that's the one.'

'What about it?'

'Well, I was wondering, er, I mean I'm sure it was a clearer copy than mine . . .'

'It was, thanks. Crystal.'

'Yeah, good, well, then, um . . . I was wondering if I could perhaps get a borrow of it?'

The silence is broken only by the click-clack of knitting needles as the gathered peasantry cranes to stare up at the apparatus of the guillotine.

'I see. And why would you need to borrow it, exactly?' she says. Which isn't a No. In other words, the blade falls but sticks before it reaches my neck.

'Because . . . Like I say, I'm not being arsey about the whole microphone-on-the-Matthew-Williamson-top and everything, but there were a couple of things I didn't pick up, the odd turn of phrase, things like that.'

'Even so, it's a bit irregular. I'm not sure where the firm stands on—'

'Jenny, come on, this is a soft piece to go with egg and bacon on a Sunday morning. I'm telling you, it'll be the least controversial interview you've ever read, I fucking promise you . . . Sorry. Excuse my French . . .'

'*C'est pas grave*,' she says.

'Sorry?'

'It was a joke. It was French.'

'Er, okay . . . Anyway, the thing is, to get the essence of Vegas, to fully encapsulate the whole feel of the phenomenon that is Vegas, I really need to catch the rhythm and timbre of her voice. Not only do I want to capture what she says, but the *way* she says it. Surely it's in the interest of your client to allow me to do the best interview I can.'

There's a pause, during which I sniff my armpit and curse myself for using bad language with her.

'God, Greil,' she says at last, 'you must have the world's worst dictaphone. Mine picked up everything.' Yeah, so did mine, I think, only a lap dancer puked on it.

'Great,' I say, 'but *can I borrow it*?'

Jenny sighs heavily. 'Well, no. I can't let you have the tape. But I tell you what, you tell me what you're missing, and I'll have a listen and email the relevant quotes to you.'

'Listen, it really would be easier if I just borrowed the tape.' She's going to lose her patience if I keep pushing but I need that tape – need it like a leg needs its kneecap.

'Greil!' she says, exasperated. 'Don't take the piss here. I'm already sticking my neck out.' And I consider confessing, I really do. A come-clean thought has been ringing my mental doorbell persistently since the conversation began. But I don't know her well enough to trust her. How could I be sure that she wouldn't use my incompetence against me? Or, worse, against the magazine, bartering for better, more flattering coverage of her client?

In the end, I do something I shouldn't, but in the circumstances it'll have to do.

I say, 'Okay, Jenny, lend me the tape and I'll let you see the piece before I submit it.'

People who aren't journalists or PR people would think, big deal; those who are know that seeing the piece before it goes in is the Holy Grail for the PR person. It's when they know they've made the journalist their bitch. Who gets to see copy before it goes in? Hardly anyone. A sleb whose presence will add an extra 25–50,000 copy sales, perhaps, and even then . . . And Vegas, bless her doe eyes, she's a big star all right, but only in a parochial kind of way, and does she shift 50,000 extra copies? She wishes.

So when I drag my integrity to the altar, Jenny snatches for the sacrificial dagger with barely a second's thought. 'All right,' she says with a sigh, and I wish I could bet that she has a big fuck-off grin on her face.

'Today?' I say, my heart leaping for joy, fun, Arsenal on the run.

'On one other condition.'

'What?'

'You take me for lunch when we do the handover, and you give me the tape straight back. But I'll be making a copy in the meantime, okay?'

'Fine.'

'Great. I take my lunch at one.'

One o'clock's not good. It'll only leave me about half an hour to get to her after my appointment with Mystery Guy who phoned earlier. But hopefully Mystery Guy will turn out to be the waste of time my better instincts tell me he will be. So I say yes, we make our arrangements and I'm gone before she can change her mind.

Does she fancy me or does she just want the novelty of being bought lunch by a journalist, to complete her feeling of utter mack daddydom? I want to believe it's the former, but I know it's the latter when I catch sight of myself in the mirror and see the surrender in my eyes. See what isn't really me, but a shadow. A dissatisfied, malevolent poltergeist laying waste to everything I once was. I close my eyes against the shame.

I've still got the postcard in my hand, the one addressed to Mrs H. Sharkey. Another reminder of the fall. Of course, there never was a Mrs H. Sharkey, it's one of those idiosyncrasies of junk mail. She was never my wife, and even seeing the name feels unfamiliar. She was known as George.

I met her at one of our gigs. We were all sitting in the dressing room, which was hardly a dressing room at all. Rather it was a glorified toilet that had once been spray-painted black. Since then the hundreds, maybe thousands, of bands who'd played there had left their mark, and every available space was covered in graffiti, the silver marker pen the favoured weapon of choice. Graffiti was layered on graffiti, words on words, like a giant DNA code, until the individual words lost their identity and became absorbed into the writhing mass. Karl, our dancer, was shaking a tin of red spray paint, halfway through a large Systemitis logo he was spraying across the back wall, only its sheer size rendering it readable.

He shook the can – *tuk-a-tuk-a-tuk-a-tuk-a* – taking an immense pride in his work. But his industry was embarrassing the rest of us. We were planning to sack him the following day. There he was, proudly crafting the band's logo when in a scant twenty-four hours he'd be wanting to add 'are a bunch of cunts' to it.

Karl was just a dancer, that was all he did. He stood front stage right and danced while making bug-eyes at the audience. For a while we thought it was only us and the Happy Mondays who had a dedicated dancer, but then we realised The Blue Aeroplanes had one, and then Flowered Up had that guy Barry Mooncult, who wore a set of petals around his neck. And those three bands were all more famous than us, so we'd collectively decided that having a dancer was a backward step, and Karl had to go. Poor old Karl, he later became a landscape gardener and once did Teddy Sheringham's house.

I was sitting next to our singer, Midge, who'd been my best friend since school. Anyone who knows anything about music knows that the best way to lose a best friend is to form a band with him, and that's what happened to me and Midge, but it hadn't happened then. At point we were still a united front, the band's guiding lights, and any animosities tended to develop between us and the rhythm section, bass and drums, Eric and Jonny, a pair of moaning gits from day one, and when the band split a couple of years later it was almost worth it just to get away from those two. As a band we were halfway between the gutter and the stars, and beginning to tire of the view. We had 'next big thing' following us around, our live shows were frequently described as 'awe-inspiring' and 'incendiary', but nothing seemed to be happening. At first the glowing reviews were enough, but we'd reached the point where we wanted to exchange the plaudits for sales, and dressing rooms like this one for ones with huge riders and security posted outside, keeping away the hordes of pert female fans. As it was, the fans could just walk straight in if they wanted to; we even had a few who did.

We'd ambled on stage full of the arrogance of our potential.

'Hello,' drawled Midge. 'We're Systemitis and the *Melody Maker* says we're relevant as fuck.'

And on that I knocked out a chord: KUH-RUNG!

And Jonny might have been a miserable flid, but he knew how to hit the drums, which in this case were a pair of steel dustbins turned on their side and supported by breeze blocks. He followed my chord with a double bash on the bins: CHOK-CHOK!

Again, that chord, feeding the anticipation, Midge staring out into the crowd wearing a look he'd nicked from Johnny Rotten.

KUH-RUNG!
CHOK-CHOK!
KUH-RUNG!
CHOK-CHOK!

And then I played the chord again, but this time I sustained it, digging at the foot pedal, leaning into the sound then offering it to the monitor, feeding it back until the girls were putting their hands over their ears and the boys couldn't wait for it all to go off.

Then, go-Jonny-go, he's pounding out an intro and – BOK! – we go straight into 'Paracetamol Paradise' which is a song about the mollification of the masses that me and Midge wrote one night when we were pissed. It took me a few years to see the irony, but we meant it at the time, and we played it like we meant it, like our lives depended on it, in fact. If it was proto-political industrial agit-punk rock 'n' roll you were after, there was no better show in town.

Later we were drunk and arguing about our name. We'd been together two years and we still argued over the name. As usual, the rhythm section didn't like it.

'It's shit,' whined Eric. 'It's just crap. It's got no . . . Do you know what I mean?'

'The problem . . .' said Jonny, but his words evaporated. Midge was already shouting above Eric.

'Every fuckin' time! We all agreed on the fucking name. *You* agreed on the fuckin' name!'

True. It was Midge's suggestion, but we all took a vote, being the democratic, anarcho-Marxist unit that we were.

'Well, I think it's shit,' spat Eric.

'The problem . . .' started Jonny to no avail. Only I heard him.

'The problem,' said a new voice, and we all turned to look at the door of our toilet-cum-dressing room, where a brunette was standing with a friend peering over her shoulder. She held a pint of lager in a plastic beaker. It was the first time I ever saw her, Mrs H. Sharkey, as she'd erroneously come to be called by cosmetic firms; Ms H. Foreman, as she should have been addressed; George, as we ended up calling her. George, you see? As in George Foreman? Maybe you had to be there.

It was like a moment out of a film. She knew that, and I resented it immediately, the way she tried to engineer her entrance for maximum effect. I was waiting for the rest of the band to see through her too, but the effect it had on them seemed to be the desired one. 'The problem,' she said, having successfully commandeered the attention of the room, 'is that it sounds too much like cystitis.'

Bear in mind we were hardly out of our teens.

'What's cystitis?' said Eric.

She slept with Midge before she got round to me.

We might have stayed together if she hadn't slept with Midge. When I say 'we', I mean both – we: the band, and we: me and George. Basically it all got fucked up because George slept with Midge before she slept with me. Everything got fucked up. It meant things were never right between me and George. The spectre of Midge hanging over us the whole time, it poisoned us as effectively as the alcohol we became addicted to. It hung in the space between us; in arguments it existed between the lines we spoke.

And as for the band.

George became our manager, just as she no doubt intended all along, though she never said so. And if the spectre of Midge haunted our relationship, then the spectre of Cooper also haunted her relationship with the band. I don't know if it's my memory playing tricks on me, but in the image I have of her, in the doorway that first meeting, Cooper is somewhere in the background, reproachfully watching events unfold.

Despite the fact that Cooper had given us everything, and despite the fact that George's only qualification for management was presidency of her student union, it was she who got the job. Her talk of optimising our merchandise sales – the promise of more money in our pockets – impressed us more than Cooper's tongue and awkward manner.

At least they weren't empty promises. Not only did she mysteriously increase T-shirt, tape and CD revenue (her over-the-shoulder friend, Maxine, stayed on as chief salesperson in this capacity), but she proved to be just as efficient at booking us gigs, at persuading the right journalists to appear, at then hiring the right PR firm to do a bit of pit-bulling on her behalf. Not that she really needed the help – she was a ferocious and shrewd operator, and it was near enough down to her that we had our one and only Top Forty-scraping hit, 'Gunpowder Plot', a singy-shouty proto rap/rock anthem that was years ahead of its time, decades before Limp Bizkit and Linkin Park turned the formula into platinum sales. I haven't spoken to Midge, Jonny, Eric or Karl for years, but I bet like me they watched *Top of the Pops*, Limp Bizkit and Linkin Park, wondering exactly what it was they were doing right that we did so wrong.

In the end it was rave music that smashed the Systemitis. People began losing interest in being upbraided over their apathy; they decided they'd rather dance in a field instead, and when I took my first E, some three or four years after the demise of the band, I could see why. Ecstasy made everything all right; we were insisting it was all wrong. My Ecstasy experience didn't stop me hating dance music, though. There was no epiphany there. That wouldn't come until I discovered the benefits of cocaine. Cut me I bleed punk.

So journalists stopped liking us. Indeed, they started taking an active dislike to us. Our buzz turned into a fart and people stopped coming. Six months earlier we'd been waiting for it to happen, we'd been holding discussions, seriously talking about 'breaking' America. Next thing we knew we were tottering drunkenly on stage at some tiny arts centre or the other, and Midge is grabbing the mic, saying, 'Hello, we're Systemitis and the *NME* says our brand of political hectoring is about as effective as the Maginot Line.'

We played on. I played with my head down, letting my hair hide my shame, but I did look up at one point to see George and Maxine at the bar. Maxine had her head in her hands; George looked like a woman trapped in a burning car. It was bad. Really bad. During the course of our slow downward spiral our performances had gradually moved from 'incendiary' to 'room temperature' and next to 'damp', but that night, following Midge's Maginot Line comment, we fell apart. We were so drunk that we accidentally played 'Gunpowder Plot' twice, but if anyone noticed they were too kind to say.

Eric played most of the gig with a broken string (and the bass only has four), Jonny was so pissed he couldn't keep time, and Midge slurred drunkenly through lyrics he could barely remember. Even the DAT machine retired a song early, leaving us thrashing around with no keyboard effects, watching the last of our audience slowly desert us.

After the show had finished we began arguing again. This time I turned on Midge.

'What the fuck was that?'

'What?'

'You know what. That fucking business at the beginning of the gig. Why didn't you just tell them we're shit? Why didn't you just tell them to fuck off? Least then we wouldn't have had to go through the fucking business of playing for them.'

'Did the *NME* really say that?' said Eric.

'Yes they did, man,' rounded Midge. 'All I was doing was repeating what they said.'

'So fuck what they said,' I shouted. 'Don't go fucking repeating it.'

'You're just fucking frightened of the fucking truth,' shouted Midge, the two of us breathing lager fumes in each other's faces. The door to the dressing room opened and George was witness to the pair of us squaring up to each other, an explosion in an expletives factory.

'Fuck am I frightened of fucking anything. I just don't want you slagging off the fucking band before we're about to fucking play.'

'Oh, fuck off. What band? It's fucking falling a-fucking part anyway.'

'Yeah? Yeah? Is it? Well, thank you very much for letting me know, Mitchell. I'm free to go form a proper band, am I?'

'You? You couldn't form a piss-up in a brewery. You form a band? Don't make me fucking laugh. What you going to call it?' He threw a look at George: '*Sloppy Seconds*?'

Like I say, Midge and I grew up together. We got into music, girls and drugs together. We got into early punk, The

Pistols, The Damned, The Clash, then the revival stuff, The Exploited, Anti-Nowhere League. But those bands were kind of missing the point, so then we got into the Kennedys and Crass, especially Crass – we used to follow Crass around. I gave him the name Midge, he called me Greil Sharkey after our favourite music writer, Greil Marcus (except we mispronounced it: his name rhymes with rail). We believed in stuff. We had principles. We campaigned against vivisection and joined CND, we marched against apartheid and the poll tax and the Criminal Justice Bill together.

But believe me, if I could have killed Midge then, I would have.

In the event, I had a pretty good try. We'd had punch-ups before, of course. Never serious, but testing enough, just so we knew who'd come out on top if it ever went to the wire. If you'd asked us before that moment, we'd have had to say that things were even-Stevens. We were the same strength, both of us the same age and pretty fit after spending a couple of years bouncing around on stages. But I won that one – quite convincingly as it turned out.

It was the very definition of a pyrrhic victory, though. That punch-up was the last time we were all together in one room. Midge and I saw each other on one other occasion: a sullen quarrel over the ownership of an amp. It was mine, I was sure of it, but Midge's smashed nose and hurt eyes convinced me to let it go to a more suitable home.

So then George and I settled down to a life together. Systemitis was good for one thing, at least: I got a job at the *NME* (and I wasn't too proud to turn down what was obviously a gesture of part-sympathy, part-guilt on the editor's behalf), and George landed a job with the PR company that had done our press. The upshot was that we stayed in the industry we still loved. We got to hear music and go to the same places and mingle with the same people. For a while, all was cool.

The flaw was that we both had a drink problem by then.

I'm not sure whether the description was floating around in those days, but today you'd call us high-functioning alcoholics. Basically it meant we could be alcoholics and still have jobs and family and friends. We were clever alcoholics, in other words.

We carried on being clever, high-functioning alcoholics for—

I was going to say for longer than is strictly healthy, but that goes without saying. We carried on for a while, and our respective jobs allowed us to continue for longer than most people would have managed it. The music world's so much more tolerant of the kind of aberrant behaviour that accompanies the committed binger. Not as tolerant as it would like to believe, but more tolerant nonetheless.

For a long time things were really great between us. The alcohol was a mostly welcome, occasionally unruly house guest. There's never a dull moment with two clever, high-functioning alkies, so we fought more than normal people, but we fucked more than normal people too, and our gestures were always grander than most, our lows lower and highs higher. Occasionally, one of us, and it would normally be George, would have a hungover panic attack, suddenly, horrifically, reassessing her life, reaching the most coruscating conclusions, which would be even worse if she was approaching her period.

'Look at us! We live like students!' Even if she didn't say anything, I'd know. She'd don washing-up gloves and begin stalking the house carrying dusters, J-cloths and bottles of Mr Muscle or Windowlene. 'Leave me! I'm nest-building!' The vacuum cleaner would go on; once she even began painting the kitchen wall – it's still half-painted now. The trouble was, we'd always be on another guest list that night, or maybe the following night if it was a slow week: a band I had to review, a gig she was PRing, a friend's club, an opening night, a must-see band, an unmissable gig, a launch party, an awards ceremony, a must-see band playing an unmissable gig at the launch party for a new awards ceremony. And the next day we'd be waking up groaning and giggling at whatever had happened the previous night, and the lid stayed off the paint pot and the brush which laid across it dried to uselessness, the vacuum cleaner was forgotten and life-auditing resolutions were put away until the next time.

One morning I woke up to George climbing out of bed. She dragged a bottle of Jack Daniels behind her, just like a sleepy little girl and her teddy bear. For a moment or so I let the image warm the cockles of my heart until the reality barged in and I saw it for what it was: we'd just had a threesome with a bottle of JD.

I pulled the duvet up over my hurting head and tried to block out the sounds of weeping coming from the lounge of our flat. They were followed by other sounds, the familiar notes of bottles being noisily discarded, their contents emptied down the sink. There was more crashing and banging, George, going positively tonto, galvanised by the shame of her bedroom companion or, should I say, *both* of her bedroom companions. In lieu of my girlfriend's arms, I pulled the duvet more tightly around me. That's where she differs from me, I thought: I would have turned to her, we could have looked for absolution in each other's arms. As it was, she saw me as part of the problem. She was right, of course – I was; but then so was she. She may have been shutting me out, but she was also trying to shut out that side to her.

A little while later I heard her thumping down the hallway towards the bedroom and I braced myself for her entrance.

She looked terrible. She'd slept in her make-up and cried since, so she'd not only woken up with a large spot on her chin, but she had panda eyes to complete the set. On top of that she wore last night's drinking. Her eyes were closed to red-rimmed slits. There wasn't a refuge in the world that would have refused her.

Not that I looked any better. In fact, what did she see when she looked at me? That was the problem between us – I was a mirror she didn't want to look into.

And that was the moment she decided she wanted to be able to look in the mirror. I didn't know it then, but she was serious when she said, 'That's it. That's it. I'm finished with this.' Words I had heard a thousand times before. Like I say, normally accompanied by the sound of the vacuum cleaner and always turning out to be in vain.

This time, though. This time she really meant it.

I held out my arms to her: 'Come to bed.' My need to be with her was as real and physical as my need to have another drink, but I knew she'd poured all the bottles into the sink.

But no. As well as the drink she denied me the closeness, sitting on the edge of the bed instead; edging away whenever I tried to hold her to me.

'No, Greil,' she said, blocking my needy hand. 'You're either with me or you're against me. I'm not drinking again. Never. I don't want to wake up feeling like this ever again, do you hear?'

I said yes. I wasn't really listening because I'd heard the same words, or variations, so many times before. A long time ago I decided it was our combined destiny to live our lives this way, lurching from one drunken episode to another, functioning just highly and cleverly enough to keep us going, so I thought of the tears and recriminations as all part of the package, a small storm to be endured before the next outbreak of good weather.

But this time she really meant it.

And it ended up tearing us apart because I didn't give up. At first I admired what she was doing, and certainly my own drinking began to decrease, but after a while, I suppose when she really got the bit between her teeth, she became evangelical about it. She no longer put up with my drunken episodes; instead they began to remind her of her own. She frowned on drinking at home. If I came home armed with a bottle of wine, the corners of her mouth would turn down. All the time she was trying to convert me to sobriety and she'd do it in increasingly inventive and touching ways. One Saturday afternoon we bought a liquidiser and a juicer and went home via the supermarket where we stocked up on fruit. Then we spent the afternoon making juices, and we juiced so much fruit it made our stomachs ache. Not to be deterred, the next day she invented her own juice. It was her way of saying she cared enough to ask me to stop; I didn't, or couldn't, or didn't care enough to try. The juice was made up of strawberry, banana and orange, and she called it a Sharkey Sensation. It was thick, and she served it cold.

In the meantime my job at the *NME* had begun to crush me. Writing about other people's rock 'n' roll ideals didn't seem the same as living them, especially since the advent of dance music had rendered them almost extinct anyway. I wanted to use my contacts to make the move into hard news, hoping to touch people at a more profound level than persuading them not to buy the new Orbital album. Trouble was, news journalists don't have much respect for the traditional free-loading, PR-puppet music writer. Reporters are the fourth estate; the free press the first indication of a working democracy. Music journos? Well, they know a pretty song when they hear it. So the world of current affairs didn't exactly swoon at the sound of my freelance overtures. The odd titbits courtesy of Deano and Graham was as close as it got. Typical Greil Sharkey – always knocking on the door; never any answer.

The beginning of the end for me and George was after some incident or other, and I forget exactly what it was, but it was something the new and sober George ruled was intolerable. Whatever it was, it was enough to provoke a give-up-drinking-or-I-leave ultimatum which she didn't immediately act upon – a minor stay of execution.

'I'm a man! It's my psychological imperative to have no willpower,' I roared, drunk.

I couldn't keep to my diet, not like she had.

Have you ever tried to give up drinking? Like I say, it's all about peaks and troughs, and when you give up drinking you miss the troughs as much as the peaks; you realise that we don't drink just to feel better, we drink to feel worse too; that way we know we're alive.

'Fucking hell, that man can drink,' I'd bray, arriving back from another interview where my subject drank only mineral water. And George never knew it, but I developed a sudden interest in cookery, nose in Jamie Oliver every night, purely to justify my daily bottles of wine. 'I've cooked us something special tonight,' I'd say, and I could hardly be expected to drink water with the special meal, could I? Not when I'd gone to so much effort.

And eventually her support and love gave way to disgust, and what she saw beside her in bed each morning was the ghost of her old banished self, the exiled mirror image, until she got so sick of it she decided to act upon that threat of leaving. She took it out of the bank, as it were. And, always canny, she waited until I was hunched up with self-disgust after the latest episode before she left me; when I was desperate for punishment and more than happy to disappear into a stagnating pool of self-pity after she'd gone. Clever, that . . .

So I tear up the postcard. Even if I wanted to forward it to George, even if I thought that she might want news of a special deal being offered by Lancôme, or even if I wanted to remind her: hey, remember me? I'm sorry, George, for what happened to us, I'm sorry for what I did and let's give it another try, please . . . Even if I wanted to I couldn't, because I have no idea where she is. I know she's still in PR, and daily I wonder whether work will cause our paths to cross, but so far it hasn't. Maybe one day it will.

Thinking about her reminds me of Heidi. It's inevitable, like a road that begins one place and ends another. And thinking of Heidi I reach out to my Mac, switch it on and wait for it to boot up so I can visit the All Fur Coat website. I feel something like guilt as I do so. Something like guilt that could be mistaken for hope.

CHAPTER TWELVE

After Peter's gone I go through to the kitchen, tidy up the utensils and put the flowers into proper vases, one of which I place on my bedroom windowsill. Then I drag my duvet through to the lounge, planning to curl up on the sofa with my knees pulled up to my chest, watch daytime TV and feel sorry for myself. My stomach's still wondering whether or not it wants to be sick again, but with any luck I'll feel a bit better later on, when I plan to do my eyebrows and make some calls: Helen at the lads' mag ('Hey, Hel, good to meet you, don't forget about me!'); Sonia ('Hey, Son, get me more castings!'); the journalist ('Please forgive me for being sick all over your suit, and about that magazine feature . . .')

Before I settle down in front of the TV, I go for my handbag by the side of the bed. In it is the small purse I carry with me at the club, for punter's money, a lippy and a compact, and where the journalist's card will be.

But I never get as far as the handbag. I hear the letterbox click and go to the front door to investigate. It's too late for second post: it'll be a flyer for a pizza delivery company, or a clutch of taxi cards, or something telling me to think about God. It turns out to be none of those things. What I see as I round the corner of the hall is a handful of what looks like white blobs on my hallway carpet.

*

I'm beginning to see everything now.

I see Mr Benstead enter the blonde bitch's home, her ground-floor flat. From across the road I see him stand at the door with a bunch of flowers, and register the look on her face: arrogant, venal. Before he steps inside, his eyes jigger this way and that.

He scans the area for signs he may be spotted, his deception discovered. For him, Lady Luck grants her blessing – those residents of the estate in full-time employment have gone to work; the majority who aren't have yet to wake up. Lady Luck always looks kindly upon the Mr Bensteads of this world.

As her door closes behind him his car pulls away and disappears from the mouth of the estate. I recognise it as the car I saw her approach yesterday, when I took her for a prostitute. It turns out I was right, after a fashion.

I have a cleverly chosen location. From my place on the wall I can keep her flat in view while being camouflaged by the shrub behind me. Its overhanging branches hug my body. The occasional person walking a dog gives a start to see my dangling feet – odd but not illegal. At my back is a church where black people go; when they go they're dressed up in colourful, gold-trimmed clothes and hats, but not now. The church is empty. Now I'm left to watch in peace; the road is mine.

I resent being here and watching from the wall. Either I should be on the tubes and checking posters, or I should be painting, putting the finishing touches to the triptych I intend to use as the centrepiece for my first show, when Emily herself will be invited to see my work. And the fact that I'm currently unable to continue, that I'm here instead, does nothing to decrease my—

My what exactly? My *loathing*, I decide, letting the word settle in my head, surprised at it there, luxuriating in its doughy texture regardless. My loathing for the blonde bitch, growing as the evidence mounts up before me.

It began last night when I visited the club. Not Liaisons, but All Fur Coat – Mr Benstead's *other* club, as it transpired – where I needed to speak to him, worker to employer.

A bouncer on the door stopped me with a hand on my chest and I felt a bubble of anger within me rise, suppressed mainly by the sheer size of the Cerberus. 'Where do you think you're going?' he said, not looking at me. Instead he directed his gaze over my shoulder as though I was intended as a diversion for some other infraction.

'Into the club,' I replied, trying to ignore both the pressure on my chest and my own irritation.

He laughed. 'No, you're not. Not dressed like that, you're not.' I'd taken off the Marigold to be on the safe side – it was in my pocket, a comforting rubber presence – but even so. 'No jeans,' he continued. 'No trainers. This is a gentleman's club.'

'You don't understand,' I said evenly. 'I work for Mr Benstead. I've come to collect something from him.'

If anything he became more wary and the hand on my chest even firmer, but at least he looked at me now. 'He expecting you?'

'No.'

'Then you have no business being here.'

'But I do. Could you at least tell him I'm here. Tell him Simon's here, the artist. Tell him it's important, to do with Emily. Tell him; he won't mind. If I didn't have business being here, how would I know this is where he is? I know he's here because they told me at Liaisons he would be.'

The indignity of pleading to enter a place I instinctively hated nagged at me. Here, I thought, beauty ended. Not that I could see anything, but I could smell it: smoke, booze, people, underpinned by something heavier, muskier and more primal.

Behind us night had not yet fallen and people were passing to and fro in the street. They no doubt registered the over-developed bouncer intimidating the artist half his size. I wasn't drunk, I was no threat, but still, he had to do his job. Two men walked past us and the bouncer welcomed them into the club with a wave of his free hand, saying, 'Evening, gents,' and then turned back to me. His hand became a finger that he held before my face. 'Stay there. It's Simon, you say? An artist?' he said, the last word sounding like an insult from behind his teeth. Anything less from him and I would have

143

been disappointed. Why not just say it? I thought. Why not just say: 'A *piss-artist*?'

'Yes,' I replied, holding his gaze, hating him: a bully.

'Wait.'

A moment later he returned; his expression said 'I've got my eye on you' even as he waved me to the stairs leading down into the club.

I counted the stairs. Eight down to a dog-leg, then six to the floor below, darker; the stairs no doubt angled that way to keep the curious even more curious; the club seeming to close in on me, trapping me. Along the suffocating walls were framed pictures of topless women in black and white. I counted those, too: six. Each of them, it seemed to me, a grotesque parody of Emily in *Moll*.

At the bottom was a second bouncer, less aggressive than the first. He was saying, 'a skinny geezer?' into a walkie-talkie as I came to the foot of the stairway. The volume of the music had increased as I made my way downstairs, but even here at the mouth of the club it was dulled, as if heard from beneath a pillow.

'You Simon?' said the bouncer to me, and I agreed I was.

'Follow me.' He led me from the bottom of the stairs past a cloakroom to a door, vibrating from the music behind it, which he opened without ceremony, as though entrance was as much an everyday occurrence for me as it was for him, and the music escaped from the room and assaulted us both.

I wasn't shocked by them, the gaudy women, as I passed through. Their existence at one end of a scale only confirmed the reality of a polar opposite: to my mind, Emily. I found myself thinking of her as I walked through the club, using her like holy water to ward off the evil spirits around me. Outside the club I was her guardian; inside, she was mine. Here on the church wall the thought warms me as surely as the sun filtering through the shrub.

Things seemed to happen quite quickly then. Walking behind

the bouncer along a balcony area, with the bar just below us, we passed three men in conversation. One of them was Mr Benstead, but I was surprised to recognise another. It was the man on the tube, the one who fell on the escalator at Oxford Circus. I knew him immediately, even half turned away, and I found the sensation disquieting – a coincidence that drummed irritating listen-to-me fingers against the inside of my skull. Like the half-remembered tube map, fuzzy connections semi-formed in my mind, only ideas then, but as I say, I see more clearly now.

And the next person I recognised, with fresh surprise, was the blonde bitch, outside whose home I now sit. Last night she was an unpleasant memory from earlier in the day, a girl I saw deliberately deface Emily's picture but nothing more. Seeing her again in the club I felt a renewed sense of things slotting into place. Clues I couldn't ignore were being placed before me. Assembling, almost, as the blonde bitch wandered across my field of vision wearing an evening gown, moving towards Mr Benstead and the strange escalator man, and then . . .

She diverted swiftly to her left, her hand suddenly up to her forehead, looking unsteady on her feet. I felt like I was walking across a giant cinema screen, watching the movie as I passed. Or like I was a backstage guest at a play I'd just seen, suddenly realising that the leading lady was . . .

She was drunk.

The blonde bitch was drunk.

But still – interestingly – she was sober enough to want to avoid Mr Benstead and the escalator man. Something there she did not want to confront. But what?

Abruptly the show ceased as the bouncer stopped in front of a door, which he opened, motioning me inside. 'In there,' he said. 'He'll be with you in a minute.'

I stepped inside, sat down and waited. Ticking, it felt like. Ticking as the cast of players lined up in my head.

After some time Mr Benstead entered, then still the object of my respect. But he looked flustered, the same man but in a different frame of mind than at our previous meeting. 'Simon,' he said, and I stood from my chair to greet him.

'I need to speak to you about something,' I said in return, my words tumbling out. The wait had made me nervous. I'd counted all there was to count in the office, formed all the patterns I could. My mind had played around the outskirts of what I'd seen outside: the escalator man and the blonde bitch. I considered mentioning them to Mr Benstead but opted against. Some instinct, perhaps, but what luck it was that I kept silent. Unwittingly he set me on the path that led to this wall, this vigil. I felt like a sponge soaking up information as the night passed.

His mind seemed elsewhere as I began to explain how I had removed the gum from the posters the first day then returned to complete my task on the second day, and how I'd realised that—

'Simon,' he said suddenly, interrupting me. 'I can't thank you enough, mate. You've done us proud, but listen, where do you live, mate?'

I told him; he considered. 'Then I need you to do me a little favour, mate. In return, I'll give you a hundred quid. A hundred quid to sit in a car. What do you think?'

I nodded a yes.

'One of the girls has been taken ill,' he said. 'She's been sick. I'm putting her in a taxi with instructions to take her home, but I want you to go with them. Now listen, between you and the driver I want to see her home safely. You're to drop her off at the door to her flat, see she goes inside and closes the door and then you fuck off. You and the driver. On no account are either of you to go inside her flat, you understand? If you do, I'll find out and bad things will happen. The taxi driver will be told the same. Do I make myself clear?'

I said yes, my stomach in anticipatory knots.

And then I was in the back of the taxi and beside me was the blonde bitch, a development which had lost the power to surprise, given what I'd already seen. As we left the club I saw the escalator man with another man. Together they stood beside a table being mopped by staff. The escalator man held a packet of soggy cigarettes, his arm dappled with something that looked like Farley's rusks but that I knew to be vomit.

'Heidi?' said Mr Benstead, his operation about to begin. He leaned in the window and spoke to the blonde bitch, who wore the same dress I'd seen her in earlier. She lolled drunkenly in the back of the car exuding a faintly unpleasant smell of sick, near-delirious, slurring and mumbling.

'Heidi?' he repeated, reaching in across me to shake at her shoulder. 'Heidi, you're going to be okay. These guys are going to see you home safely.' He shot meaningful glances at me and the taxi driver. Only the taxi driver returned his look with a yes-nod. I absorbed the latest piece of information.

The blonde bitch's name is Heidi.

Mr Benstead looked sick himself. Concern was etched on to his face, the expression ill-fitting on him.

'Heidi?'

She mumbled and raised her head which had sunk to her front. 'Peter?'

'You'll be okay. I'll be in touch tomorrow, okay . . . Angel.'

Then he said 'Go', and he was withdrawing from the window and banging the roof of the car goodbye.

'Be in touch,' slurred the blonde bitch hazily, in a far-off drunken dream. 'Touch . . . Touch the customer's knees or shoulders for balance only.'

Her head dropped forward as the car drew away from the pavement. I caught the driver's eyes in the rear-view mirror. He looked at me with the deliberate indifference of a man who senses a threat and I indulged myself in the luxury of an unreciprocated antipathy. Hate me all you want, I thought. Hate me all you want.

She raised her head to look out of the window, saw the lights of the city speeding past and looked away like she might be sick again. Gradually her eyes focused on me beside her.

'You're a strange fish,' she slurred.

'I'm an artist,' I replied.

Piss-artist, mocked the eyes in the rear-view mirror.

'You don't look like an artist,' she said quietly. She picked her way around her words with lily-pond care.

'Appearances can be deceptive,' I said back, just as softly. The driver's eyes darted to the mirror as he strained to hear.

'Are you all right there, love?' he asked, but he said it to me, really: *Watch your step, Sonny.*

'Fine, thanks. You're very kind,' she managed, but she sounded dislocated, retreating. Her head lolled back to her chest.

Leaning in closer, I asked, 'Who was that man you were sick on?' Nearly whispering now.

'Share list,' she said, sleepy.

'Share list?'

'Is she all right?' called the taxi driver.

'She's fine,' I replied.

'If she looks like she's going to be sick, you say quick-style. If she yaks in my cab you're helping clear the fucker up.'

'Okay, okay,' I said. Then, to the blonde bitch, softly, like the gentlest wake-up kiss: 'Share list? What do you mean?'

She stirred slightly: 'Journalist.'

Journalist.

'A journalist. What was his name?'

Her eyes didn't even open. As if in her sleep, she said, 'Dunno. He gave me his card.'

'Where?'

'In the club,' barely audible. I was losing her quickly.

'Where's the card?' I whispered, silky soft.

'In my purse.'

'Stop,' I called to the front. 'She's going to be sick.' Thinking of damaged upholstery, the driver came to a halt with a minor screech of tyres, leapt from the car and yanked open the back door, just as the blonde bitch was violently – gratifyingly – sick on to the road outside.

She heaved a second time. More sick splattered on to the road.

'Fucking nice one,' said the driver to me, neither of us paying much attention to the blonde bitch as she heaved again, dry this time, and began sobbing between gulps of air.

'Fucking nice one,' he repeated.

Cars passed us. The blonde bitch heaved some more, sobbed some more.

'Pat her on the back or something,' said the driver, smoking, his arms resting across the roof as he stared out over the city. I thumped the blonde bitch on the back like you see mothers do with choking children. One of her hands came back to stop me, batting me weakly away.

As she lay across the seat, her head hanging from the car door, I reached into her bag for her purse and found the journalist's card – Greil Sharkey, freelance journalist – zipped up the purse and replaced it in her bag. Then, as a last-minute thought, I reached into my back pocket to dig out her travelcard, folded over the piece of chewing gum she left on Emily's poster, and dropped that into her bag as well. *I'm watching you.*

We stayed there a few moments more. The driver smoked his cigarette and we let the blonde bitch cry herself quiet before he bundled her into the seat, closed the back door and we continued on our way. Some of his wariness towards me vanished, as though we were comrades in arms.

And I thought: *Angel.* That was what he called her: Angel (the longest stretch of escalators on the Underground, a vertical rise of 90 feet, 44 framed bastards each side, 88 in total, 10 of which are *Moll*s). At first he called her Heidi, then he called her Angel. He called her Angel when she seemed to be drifting away from him. He called her Angel and she came back to him for a moment or so, enough to give him an inebriated smile. A smile of recognition, then. Of warming to the name he called her. Snuggling into it like a winter duvet.

*   *   *

Before, and with Jill's blessing, my work was an aggressive montage of instinctive, angry brush-strokes, large in scope, swift and cathartic in execution. I deliberately limited myself to greys and blacks, the colours of my condition. But that was before Emily, and since finding her, I've expanded my palette, both figuratively and literally. In place of monochrome I've discovered colour, and instead of instinct I've found design. These things soothe and massage me, just as effectively as before.

For the triptych, I took the *Moll* poster Mr Benstead gave me and created a grid into which I sketched the detail of the poster. Using charcoal, and with the grid as my guide, I transferred the detail of the poster to three canvases, each larger in size than the previous one. I had difficulty fitting the largest size through the door of my studio, even more difficulty hiding it from Jill when she visited, but as I say, I want her to see the entire work, almost finished now. The piece will be complete after painting the colours in oil and adding the four huge pyramids of gum I'm currently constructing from papier mâché in my studio. These I will place on all but one piece of the triptych: the third element, to symbolise my own place in the poster's creation. Deliberately, and inevitably, this third section will be the boldest and brightest statement of the three – a rebirth.

I feel myself adapting to the structure of the work well. From idea to grid to outline and finally to colour. This way, I create connections within my work. I form patterns, very important to me.

From an outline, a sketch, I colour in.

He called her Angel.

And now his car returns from wherever it has been and pulls to the kerb opposite her flat. I wipe a hand across my forehead, sweating, then remember not to wipe the Marigold hand across my forehead – it's dirty. Exhaust fumes hang lazily in the heat.

Across the road a group of youths have gathered and they're

playing with a dangerous dog, a bull terrier of some kind, a generic estate trophy dog. It wears a studded collar and the boys tease it with a branch, making it leap to take the stick in its jaws. When the dog catches the branch the boys can lift the dog bodily off the ground, although it takes two of them to do so.

They momentarily forget about playing with the dog when the Jaguar pulls into the road, watching the car instead, but maintaining a respectful distance, wisely – only the drug dealers have cars like that around here.

Their attention is drawn to the car, but I watch the blonde bitch's front door, and sure enough it opens and out he steps, pulling the door gently closed behind him, sure not to make too much noise, not wanting to upset his poor, hungover . . .

Mistress.

He turns away from the door and the man I used to respect wears the look of a dizzied fool, the confused but happy expression of a boy unsure how he's just made the adults laugh. Now he surreptitiously adjusts his trousers as he comes across – it takes him five steps – but the youths have recognised the famous England footballer and they call across, ignoring the dog which still bounds to grab the stick one of them holds.

For a second he seems alarmed, appears about to ignore the boys. Then he looks over, smiles and waves: a queasy smile, a hesitant wave. They give him a cheer in return, looking to see where he's appeared from with no success. I wonder how he feels, being spotted. I wonder if he feels a fear that drives crampons into his testicles and ascends to his stomach. I hope so.

And then, as quickly as he's appeared, he steps into the back of the car which pulls smoothly away from the kerb, a low engine hum barely intruding upon the sunny serenity of the day.

I wait a number of moments, watch the boys as they go back to playing with the dog. I hang around until they drift off, then jump from the wall and, shoving my Marigold hand into my pocket, wander casually over to the front door of the blonde bitch's flat. There I reach into my other pocket for a plastic freezer bag half full of chewed, dried-up chewing gum, which I upend through her letterbox, most of it falling in clumps smartly on to her carpet, some sticking in the bag, which I push through for good measure before turning on my heel and walking casually, but swiftly, away.

And with that, I leave, head for the tube, where I'll consult my journal and do a little work on my rounds, check the cross-platform poster at Leicester Square, then go to meet the journalist: Greil Sharkey.

CHAPTER THIRTEEN

I check the post. Two more Jiffy bags containing CDs, both from bands I've never heard of and will instantly forget, bands with names like The Greenfly Debacle. I ask you. Even so, I transfer the contents of at least three days' worth of CDs into one Jiffy bag and leave it ready to collect on the way out. I may not have heard of The Greenfly Debacle; the bloke at Reckless Records certainly will have.

I dress in a hurry, and badly. Is it wise to wear the same suit that Heidi Charlton was sick on last night? I attack it with a damp J-cloth but, even so, probably not. Especially not since it's a fiendishly hot summer's day, possibly the hottest day since records began – aren't they all? – and perfect sick-baking weather. Please don't mind my forearm, madam, I had a fight with some parmesan – you should see how the cheese looks, ha-ha. To paraphrase Morrissey, if I smell a little sick, well, that's because I am sick.

Bastard. How come Morrissey lives in LA and I'm having to illegally buy a child's tube ticket just to afford the journey across town to meet the nutter who'll waste my time before I go and buy Jenny a lunch with money I don't even have? That, I think, depressed, is pretty much the size of it. That and the fact that I don't have any gak, which is irritating. Sustainable, but irritating. Somehow I think that a couple of lines before I set out might have made the journey easier to bear. Certainly it would have helped anaesthetise the pain of the message which arrived, ooh, just before I left; just as I closed down the All Fur Coat website. I'd hit the 'shut down' command on my Mac at exactly the same time as my mobile began ringing. One of those weird, unsettling micro-moments when you think an action has somehow caused something entirely unrelated to happen.

I let it ring then dialled the voicemail. 'You have – one – new message, and – no – saved messages.' It was Cooper.

'Greil, Greil, Orange Peel,' he began. That was what he used to call me in the old days, when he mounted a doomed rearguard action against the torrent of piss-take from the band. Like, if we made up nicknames for him then he was going to do the same to us. Greil, Greil, Orange Peel. He thought it nettled me, but any exasperation I showed was at the sheer crapness of his name-calling.

'Well, it seems I've missed you,' his message continued, 'and there I was, just calling up for a friendly chat. I was hoping we could get together, maybe over breakfast. Never mind, I'll give you a call later in the day, find out how you're going. See you later, Greil.'

It could have gone worse. You've got to count the absence of overt threats and raised voices as something of a bonus. Maybe it's bought time, maybe it's not.

So I call Graham, curator of the Sunday supp and currently my only hope of raising the necessary. I ask Graham whether he's had any luck with an advance on my Vegas interview money. He tells me no, and how am I getting on with the copy for the Vegas interview? Deadline tomorrow, don't forget. And I pretend he's breaking up and ring off. So much for the advance.

Even with my financial woe I'm not forgetting about Heidi. How could I with the contents of her stomach at war with my Ozwald Boateng? And as I scoot to the tube I phone Terry at the club, loosening my tie at the same time. It's a hot day, but Terry's cool; actually, cold. I wasn't expecting outright contrition, but at least some small recognition of the fact that one of his employees puked over me. Apart from carrying bits of Heidi around on my sleeve, the only other silver lining had been the free drinks I'd expected in compensation, a series of reparations I was hoping would stretch over a couple of weeks at least. As it is, Terry can hardly wait to get rid of me, and when I ask him for Heidi's number I have to check that the line hasn't gone dead.

'No can do, Mr Sharkey. Your feature idea's been nixed, I'm afraid.'

'Why? I thought you were into the idea.'

'I was. But I mentioned it to Mr B last night, and he wasn't. He *very* wasn't, actually. You sure you've never crossed swords with him?'

Last night. My *Moll* review comes out today, but Benstead blocked my feature last night. How come? For a second I wonder if he somehow accessed the review before it was printed, but then realise that's impossible. Okay, not impossible. Highly unlikely – conspiracy-theory levels of unlikely. But if not the review, then what other reason would he have for stopping the feature?

'But why? It's good publicity . . .' I let the words die on my lips. Indignation's not a country I want to visit since the feature's a big fat lie anyway. No good getting all outraged about it.

'No worries,' I say instead. *Hey, shit happens, what-ho.* 'I'll leave it then. Tell you, though, any chance of Heidi's number anyway, I'd like to check she's okay, know what I mean?'

'Nah, best not. Tell you what, I'll pass on your thoughts, how's about that?'

'Fuckin' hell, Terry, what am I? Some kind of threat to women?'

'Boss doesn't want you talking to any of the girls, Mr Sharkey, especially not Heidi. You're welcome to come in, of course you are, but I can't have you talking to the girls, not like that. It's a how-do-you-say? An edict from on high.'

'Why?' I say, indignant. A group of lads walking a pit bull saunter past, close enough to deliberately nudge me a reminder of how tough they are. I pay them no attention.

'It's no big deal,' says Terry. 'He just doesn't want any features on the club, that's all.'

But I'm not listening any more. I've already had enough excitement for one morning. In a nutshell: no phone number for Heidi – Plan A, abort-abort. Time to reach for Plan B, which is.

There is no Plan B.

Instead I grab a paper and, aw, shucks, there's my review – that thrill of seeing your byline never quite goes away – and then I catch the train into town and go to Reckless Records, where the bloke goes, 'Who the fuck are The Greenfly Debacle?' before giving me a begrudging fiver for a Transglobal Underground compilation, and he takes The Greenfly Debacle and friends off my hands for three quid, but only after I threaten to throw them away anyway. Next I go along Oxford Street, where I pay by cheque for a new dictaphone, which comes with the free gift of a pick-up mic that I don't need but take anyway. And in the shop I stand in silent awe of the assistant, whose spots all seem to have decided to club together and form one gigantic spot, to which his fingers stray at least twice during our lightning-brief encounter, and after that I make my way over to Covent Garden, where I immediately recognise the little turd who made me fall over on the tube yesterday.

He has a table all to himself – surprise, surprise – and he's sitting squinting up at me in the sun, looking like a cat about to torture a vole to death. Little punk.

'No washing-up glove today?' I pull out a chair with a rattle of metal on pavement and sit down, trying and failing to catch the eye of a waitress.

'Thought I'd leave it off in your honour,' he says evenly, meeting my scorn. Where does he get off with this amazing self-confidence trip? I think. Clearly the watching world sees a well-dressed – and handsome, if I do say so myself – journalist sitting opposite a grubby little dork whose one saving grace is a *very* passing resemblance to Iggy Pop, and even that's not always a compliment. Yet this kid acts as though the roles were reversed, like he's the one at the controls. Wrong, I want to say. I'm the cool one; I get to act like the mack daddy in this conversation, okay? But I don't, and instead I find myself unable to decide if I find his self-assurance very irritating, mildly spooky, or somewhere in between . . .

I motion for the waitress, who doesn't see me. I'm not even sure I want to waste precious pennies on a double latte frappuccino or whatever the coffee *du jour* is; a coffee would just about triple today's cumulative outlay. On the other hand, Freak Boy here obviously hasn't ordered coffee and I want to assert some kind of authority over him. Easier said than done, though – myopic waitress from hell seems immune to my ever-so-rakish smile.

I straighten and adjust my jacket. 'I haven't got long,' I say, not lying because I really don't have long. Jenny will be waiting, hopefully with salvation in her handbag. 'So why don't you start by telling me why you called. You've got something to tell me, yes? Something to do with yesterday on the tube, is it?'

He ignores my question, and as if I haven't spoken, says, 'What's in the bag?'

In lieu of coffee he has a notebook and a pen lying on the table in front of him. They're placed carefully, like silver service settings, and one hand is resting on the notebook even while the other's dangling a question mark over the bag with my dictaphone in it. If I'm honest, the kid's weirding me out. Experience tells me he's merely a catalyst for my various psychic deficiencies to kick in, but still – he's horny for a head fuck, as Midge used to say.

'It's a dictaphone,' I reply, suddenly very, very tired.

'Can I see?'

'Knock yourself out,' I reply, and wouldn't it be good if he took me at my word? The waitress might even pay our table some attention if one of its occupants suddenly bashed his own head across the edge of it: '*Don't worry, he's just knocking himself unconscious, but could I get a double espresso, please?*'

No such luck. Instead, he removes the dictaphone with inordinate care, even folding the bag neatly before he inspects the box.

'What's VOR?' he says, reading from the packaging.

'It stands for Voice Activated Recording,' I say, feeling oddly proud of my new dictaphone.

'That would be VAR,' he states.

'Good God, Sherlock, you must be right.' He looks gone out. Memo to self: alien life form is impervious to sarcasm. 'Okay, then, it must be Voice *Operated* Recording. But look, so what? Can we cut to the chase, please?'

'What does it mean, then? Voice Operated Recording?'

'Fuck's sake, it's just a function of the machine,' I say. 'It means it can start recording when it hears voices.'

'Just voices. Or any sounds?'

'Look, to be honest I've never used that particular mode, but at a guess I'd say it probably doesn't recognise voices as such; it's just a noise thing, you know?'

'What would you use it for?'

I stare over the table at him, and not for the first time today, well, this week actually, I wonder just what I've done to deserve the train derailment I call my daily existence. I take a big sigh, the sigh of the defeated man, and take off my sunglasses to meet his eye across the table.

'Dream much, Smudge?' I say.

'What?'

'Do you dream much?'

'What did you call me?'

'It doesn't matter. Do you dream much?'

'Yes. I'm an artist, of course I dream.'

'A dreamer. An artist. Very good. Do you talk in your sleep, Smudge?'

'My name's Simon. Why do you keep calling me that?'

'Doesn't matter. Do you talk in your sleep?'

'I don't know, do I? How would I know?'

'Most of us get told at one time or another. Not you

158

though, eh? No Mrs Smudge to fill you in on your nocturnal emissions?'

'I don't understand . . .'

'Well, if you had one of these, perhaps by the side of the bed, set to VOR mode, then you could wake up in the morning and you could hear what you were saying in the night, do you see? It would hear your cries, and it would faithfully record your every utterance. Would that be a help, do you think?'

*

'Maybe not in that particular instance, but I'm sure I could find a use for a machine with those capabilities, yes.'

'What are you writing?'

'The model number down.'

'Listen, mate. I don't mean to be rude, but can we get to the reason why you called me. It's something to do with the tube yesterday, right? How did you get my number?'

'It was on your card.'

'Right. And how did you come by my card?'

'I took it from a girl.'

'Who?'

'A girl I think you know.'

'Fucking *who*?'

'What's this?'

Storm clouds form on Greil Sharkey's face as I place my hand on his newspaper. He is leaning forward, his body straining to reach the information as soon as it leaves my mouth. He wants me to say a name; he doesn't want me to enquire about his paper.

'It's a fucking newspaper,' he snaps, wiping sweat from his top lip and replacing his sunglasses, pouting almost. Pathetic, vainglorious.

'Fucking heat,' he says under his breath.

*

The sun leaps from behind a cloud and surprises me, scorching my hurty eyes. I put my sunglasses back on.

'Fucking freak,' I mutter, but if Freak Boy hears me he doesn't care. He's pointing at the paper, taking power tools to my nerve-endings, which are severely in need of some R&R. 'It's just a newspaper,' I say, sighing. Nearby a mobile phone playing the theme tune from *The A-Team* goes unanswered. 'Answer the phone,' I growl under my breath, before it becomes apparent that it's not a call but a demonstration, and the next theme tune in the owner's library is *The Good, the Bad and the Ugly*. It strikes me that people who use novelty rings on their phones should be destroyed.

*

Opposite him, I am cool. Literally and metaphorically. I think of the figure I saw in the club last night, one arm soaking with the blonde bitch's puke, the other reaching for a drink with trembling fingers. The same, sad man, only sadder, who sits before me today; who's here at my bidding, come to do my work for me. I think again: pathetic, and wonder what he was like at school. One of *them*, without doubt. I imagine they're all like this one now, shrivelled and reduced, their sense of self-importance undiminished. It's not that I hate Greil Sharkey as such. What I feel is more like contempt for him as a type. And if I would normally take steps to avoid meeting him and his like, it just so happens that today he's the right tool for the job.

'Is it today's?' I say, picking up his paper. He seems to squirm with irritation as I do so. 'I do a lot of travelling on the tube. I like to read the paper.'

'Have it,' he snaps. 'But on one condition – you stop pissing about and tell me what I'm doing here. What girl? And what's the deal with the glove and the chewing gum?'

On the table his mobile phone rings an interruption and he lifts his sunglasses in a jerky, nervous movement to see who's calling. His face wears a look I can't decipher as the glasses fall back over his eyes and he lets the phone ring some more before snatching it from the table and dropping it into a pocket of his jacket. It continues ringing, muffled now. Somewhere beneath a sunbed tan he goes pale. Quite a pantomime.

'Who's that?' I say.

Ring-ring.

'Someone I don't want to speak to,' he replies as levelly as possible, sunlight dancing on a sheen of sweat above his eyes.

Ring-ring.

From somewhere there's the sound of a crowd applauding a performer. He swallows. The phone stops ringing.

'When *you* dream, Greil, do telephones ring in your dreams?'

He sweeps his packet of cigarettes from the table and stands up, bristling and angry, a nerve touched if not scalded. Even behind his sunglasses I can sense his eyes, seething lava pits. 'Fuck you,' he spits.

But I almost pity him his transparency. He no more wants to leave than I do. So calling his bluff is as easy as remaining quiet and pretending to scan the front page of his newspaper, leaving him dangling furiously in the air above our table.

'If you don't tell me now, I'm leaving,' he hisses uselessly, his clumsy gambit hanging out to dry for all to see. I look at him and wait for him to sit down when, with great magnanimity, I hand him his dignity back: I tell him what he's come to hear.

It doesn't take me long; a short enough speech: 'Peter Benstead is having an affair with a lap dancer at the club he owns, the drunk girl you were talking to last night. Her name is Heidi.'

He takes off his sunglasses to squeeze the bridge of his nose and I can see his eyes gleaming with greedy excitement. Controlling a slight trembling at the sides of his mouth he leans forward across the table, all trace of anger gone; my instincts were correct. 'She wasn't . . .' he starts, then stops. 'How do you know?'

'I know.'

'All right. How long?'

'Long enough.'

'Where and when do they meet?'

'I don't know. You can catch them.'

At this he looks doubtful. Nevertheless he cannot disguise his glee at the news. As I'd expected, the information itself is what is important to him; he can fill in the blanks himself, despite his protestations to the contrary.

'You're not telling me much,' he says. 'How can I be sure you're not just making it up?'

'I've told you everything you need to know. And you can't be sure.'

'Well, then, how did you find out?'

'It doesn't matter.'

In one sense he's agitated because I've only given him half the story, a teasing entrée, and I'd be just as frustrated myself having to deal with such incomplete data. Even so, he's visibly more relaxed now he has his information.

'Okay,' he says, 'as tips go, it's not bad. A little light on facts, but it's worth checking out. To be honest, I'm not sure what the tip-off fee for something like this is . . .'

I feel offended but don't let it show. 'I don't want a tip-off fee. I want the affair to be made public.'

He looks surprised. 'And why would you want to do that?'

'Because of Emily.'

'Who? His wife? Emily Benstead?'

'Yes.' I tell him about Emily, and he laughs and looks across the courtyard at people strolling in the summer sun. His composure is returning; I've given it to him like a gift, but he's too stupid to realise.

'Jesus,' he says, 'he pays you to do that? God, Benstead, you drongo. That's what he pays you to do, is it? Ride on the tubes – what is it? – "protecting" her?'

'Yes,' I say.

He laughs. 'Jesus. Talk about fucking hubris.'

So I do. I tell him about my system, about the bottle, the notes I keep, the counting. I tell him as though he is interviewing me and my task is to convince him of my suitability for the job. I talk and I can't help it, and even feel myself going red at one point, describing the escalators at Angel – a 90-foot rise – and the distance between Covent Garden and Leicester Square of 0.16 miles and the fact that it takes just forty seconds from the time the doors close at Covent Garden to the time they open at Leicester Square. He laughs again. 'I've heard that one.' And I regret my boasting suddenly. It's undermined the depth of my purpose. So I restrain myself from adding that the £1 fare from Covent Garden to Leicester Square in relation to the length of the journey makes it more expensive than space travel, although this is true.

We sit in silence for a minute or so. Nearby an old lady is feeding pigeons with breadcrumbs from a bag similar to my freezer bags, and a connection between me and her seems about to form in my mind, but drifts away like smoke before it can take shape. A kid with his fingers in his mouth watches the old woman. Greil Sharkey chuckles at the absurdity of the world. 'You're protecting Emily Benstead,' he says at last. And he laughs again, but with a jagged, scabrous edge this time, as though he knows something I don't, which he doesn't. As though he has the bitter experience I lack but I'll learn soon enough, which he doesn't. As though my ideals are hopelessly out of step with those of the world around him, which is the absolute truth . . .

As we both stand to say goodbye a man approaches the table, looking sheepishly at the journalist. 'Sorry,' he says, and he screws his face up with embarrassment. 'Are you Greil Surreal?'

He looks surprised, happy though; casts me a look from behind his sunglasses. 'Well, once I was, yes.'

'You've lost your dreads.'

He looks even more embarrassed. 'Yeah, you know, it was a wrench, but . . .'

'I had to cut mine off when I left uni,' says the kid, running an apologetic hand over his crop. 'Listen, I didn't want to hassle you. I just saw you here and I . . . Well, I just wanted to say that me and my mates thought you were the dog's bollocks, man. Fucking Systemitis, you know? You were just saying shit that needed saying, you know? For me, there was you, Disposable Heroes, Public Enemy, fucking Manics sold out when Richie disappeared . . . We needed more bands like you, not less. Sorry. It's just . . . you know, I thought you were great.'

'Thank you.' He's flattered but slightly embarrassed at the same time. Ironically, so is his fan. Their two heads seem to bob up and down as they talk. I feel like an anthropologist watching species mate.

'So, what are you doing now?'

'Freelance journalist.'

'Music?'

'Mostly.'

'The rest of the band?'

'Various things, really. We haven't kept in touch.'

'Oh . . . Okay, well, listen, it was great to meet you. Thanks for the memories, man.' Then they shake hands and I nearly feel sorry for Greil Sharkey when the fan – unintentionally, I'm sure – wipes his hand on the back of his trousers as he walks away. Greil sees, and forlornly inspects his own palm for a moment or so.

'That could have been worse,' he says to me, but to himself really. 'I expected him to call me a sell-out or something. The suit, you know?'

'Greil Surreal?' I say in reply.

He laughs: 'That's nothing. Our drummer's name was Jonny Skins-Slapper. We had a sound engineer called Dee Fenestration. We all thought it was hilarious at the time. Actually, it *was* hilarious at the time.' He's almost happy.

'Why surreal?'

'No, not surreal,' he says. 'We weren't trying to escape reality, we were confronting it. It was So Real. Greil So Real. Don't worry, you're not exactly the first person to make that mistake.'

'Why did you split up?'

He looks away, over the square. 'I dunno. I guess because we asked questions. And people don't want questions, they want answers.'

He looks sad, and for a moment or so I feel a genuine pity for him, wanting to comfort him almost.

'Do you know what they used to call me?' I say.

When I take my leave of the journalist I breathe in deep, then go underground, heading towards Oxford Circus. There I make my way to a branch of a well-known electrical retailer, which I won't name, where I push a waist-high barrier to enter. Like at the supermarket, it's a one-way barrier that encourages customers to leave by the checkout – so they feel they have to buy something. Shops do this kind of thing nowadays.

Over to my left are the checkouts, where people with blank expressions queue to buy blank tapes, handing over cards to pay. Next to these is an exit barrier through which the dissidents who choose not to purchase items must leave. They are watched by a security guard, a Cerberus like the bouncer at All Fur Coat, who glares meaningfully at their bags, as though he is equipped with X-ray vision. He isn't though. Not unless this is an advance in the field of retail security I'm unaware of. Nor does he physically check the bags, so an item stowed away might pass him by undetected.

Assuming an indifferent air, I find the tape recorders I'm looking for. In the middle of the shop, surrounded by a buzzing ocean of televisions, videos, DVDs, printers and computers, there's an island. Here it seems is where they keep the small but valuable items, safe from thieving hands. On one side of the island are MP3 players, Walkmans, MiniDiscs, radios and other tiny electronic goods, while the other seems dominated mainly by photographic equipment. The island is inhabited by two, maybe three, natives – assistants who serve from behind counters with display cabinets at their backs.

I don't need to consult my journal to see that they have Greil So Real's in stock. It is a Sony TCM-20DV cassette-corder, price £29.99. There is a model on display, next to an Olympus, one in a line of other, similar cassette-corders, and as I watch, an assistant with oily hair and a large boil on his face turns and reaches for one to show a customer.

I hover for a moment, feigning interest in a display of MiniDisc players. The assistant shrugs when he's asked about the functions of the cassette-corder. He touches his boil and looks surreptitiously at his watch – nearly lunchtime – stifling a yawn. Meanwhile the customer turns the cassette-corder over in his hand, frowning slightly before returning it to the assistant with a thank-you and turning to leave.

From the counter I pick up a catalogue of video game consoles, pretending to leaf through while I watch the assistant. For a moment or so he stands with nothing to do, but instead of leaving to help his colleagues on the other side, both of whom are busy with more customers waiting, he stays there, looking at his watch again, willing lunch to arrive more quickly. They must need to stagger lunch. One o'clock approaches, so it seems fair to assume that at least one of the island staff will shortly disappear for a break, opening a zone of probability I might advantageously exploit. Perhaps. By the same token, lunchtime must also be their busiest period, when potential customers are on their own breaks. If anything, more staff are likely to appear in the next few minutes in order to optimise the efficiency of the store's lunchtime service.

As I'm considering this I also note the distance across the island's moat – the space between the counter and the display unit. It's impossible to reach from this side of the counter, not if I want to keep both feet on the floor. A swift grab is therefore out of the question. Nor does there seem to be any way of timing the assistants to find a window of opportunity. Bored as they are, they seem to respect their meagre duties and continue to remain vigilant. Assessing my options, it appears I need to create some kind of a diversion.

But not yet.

Lunchtime is coming; more staff will arrive and the island will be busy with customers purchasing Walkmen. In addition to that, the security guard has seen me loitering; I'm sure of it. In the circumstances, it appears the best course of action is to leave and return at a later date armed with a suitable plan of action.

So I exit through the browser's barrier, and I take my journal from my rucksack to verify where I need to begin the day's rounds before joining the tube at Tottenham Court Road.

Tottenham Court Road – 'TCR' as it appears in my journal – has a long set of escalators leading from street level to the Northern Line, and lots of bastards, but surprisingly few *Moll*s – just four: two up, two down – since most of the slots are permanently taken up by advertisements for independent electrical retailers. Even so, the station is an essential stop-off point as there are a total of seven posters pasted up in platform-connecting tunnels, and although my records show just one incidence of chewing gum removed from this site, it's a major station and needs to be regularly checked; its proximity to the borders of theatreland sees to that. I shudder at the thought of the defaced *Chicago* poster on the westbound Central Line platform which has a drawing of a penis pointing at the actress's mouth, and a speech bubble with her saying, 'Yum!'

I breathe deeply and with satisfaction. I feel in control. Things are *ordered*. They are as I have arranged them. And as I descend the elevator I put on the Marigold, symbolically continuing my work for the day, and I plan my route which begins here, then dissects the middle of the bottle to Leicester Square, Charing Cross, then as far as Embankment before I go along to Victoria, then up to Green Park and then Bond

Street from where I'll walk along Oxford Street and back to the well-known electrical retailers, by which time it will be the middle of the afternoon.

When I step on to the tube I remember Greil Sharkey's newspaper and take it out of my rucksack to read. I read it quite thoroughly and I'm just leaving Charing Cross when I get to the Arts section and my breath catches as I see a picture of Emily. Beside it is a review of *Moll*, which begins: '*Nicole Kidman's UK stage debut in* The Blue Room *was unforgettably described by one critic as "pure theatrical Viagra" . . .*'

*

From outside I hear the sounds of kids playing football and I wonder whether they're the same lot who pushed chewing gum through my letterbox. At least it wasn't dog shit, I think, dropping to the sofa and pulling the phone to my lap. It could have been worse.

'Terry,' I say when the phone answers. 'Terry, hello, it's Heidi.'

The voice that barked 'Yes' down the phone instantly softens when I say hello. 'My little wounded soldier,' he growls, like a dog having its belly rubbed. 'How are you feeling?' I tell him not bad, feeling better, sore insides from being sick so much. I say I feel a bit better than I did last night and thanks for taking care of me, and he starts to say something about it being 'all Mr B's work, darlin',' so I act surprised, like you would be if you worked for Virgin and Richard Branson made you a cup of tea.

'Make sure you don't come to work until you're feeling better,' he says. 'Don't want you being sick on any more punters.'

'God, sorry. Was he pissed off?'

'Greil? Nah, he's a journalist, innee? He's used to the smell of vomit. No doubt he'll try and sting me for the cost of the dry-cleaning, but I'll chuck him a few drinks on the house; he'll be sound.'

'Okay,' I say. Then, 'Listen, could I get his number off you? I'd like to give him a call, just to say sorry. And maybe to arrange another meeting with him.' I cradle the phone on my shoulder and fiddle through my purse for the thousandth time, but there's still no sign of the card I could have sworn he gave me.

'No need to apologise, darlin', he's as good as gold, I'm telling you. A friend of the club, as they say.'

'Still, I'm going to need to see him again, aren't I? You know what you were saying about the modelling? Sounded interesting.'

'Ah, babe, look, I don't know how to say this, so I'll just tell you straight – the feature's been cancelled.'

'Oh,' I say. 'God. Why?'

He pauses a little. 'Not sure, doll. Greil just said it had been canned, at least for the time being. He's a freelance, you know. I reckon his magazine's pulled out, something like that. Bit of a sore point with him, I suppose. I wouldn't be at all surprised if the poor geezer was a bit sensitive about it. Best not pursue it, know what I mean?'

'Not because of me, then? I didn't piss him off last night?'

'No, darlin', no. Nothing like that. It's just the way it goes. You know what these magazines are like, don'cha, babe?'

Actually, not really. And every chance I get to find out turns into a dead end.

'Yeah, I s'pose. Still, though, can I have his number? I'd really like to ring and apologise . . .' Because it would be good to have his number, wouldn't it? He seemed friendly enough, nice. And it's all about contacts. There's a long pause at the other end of the line. 'Terry?'

'Sorry. Sorry, babe. Listen, don't worry about it. I'm sure to see him in due course. He mainly comes in for an afternoon drink. I'll pass on your thoughts when I next see him, how about that?'

'I can't ring him myself?'

'No, not saying that. Ha! Well, kind of. It's just that I

can't . . . I don't reckon I can lay my hands on the number, you know. And anyway . . . You know what these journalists are like.'

'Um, I suppose so,' I say, puzzled. 'Maybe I'll see him at the club, then?'

'I'm sure you will. Whether he'll want to talk about it, I don't know, but I'm sure you'll see him.'

'Is there something wrong with him?' I say, and want to add: *or you*, but don't.

'Nothing wrong with him a couple of drinks won't fix. No, really, don't you worry your gorgeous little head about it. I'll smooth things over for you, yeah? You go and get yourself a snuggly buggly day in bed and hopefully we'll see you tomorrow. 'Kay, babe?'

'Okay,' I say, sounding as uncertain as I feel, and we say goodbye. I put down the phone and sigh a big sigh. Blown out again. What is it? Do I have 'reject' tattooed in special ink across my forehead or something, invisible to all but those who consider me for modelling jobs?

Or is it something else?

Maybe I'm being paranoid. I pick up my mobile and scroll through to the letter H. Hairdressers. Health Club. Holly. My finger hovers over the green call button.

I think it must have been Della who told Holly I wanted to be a model. Must have been. Della was the only person there who knew. And I don't know what came first for Holly, assuming it was her idea: did I fit a profile she had in mind, or did she look at me and a little lightbulb go off in her head?

The lightbulb, I think. God, it's not that difficult to find a model in a lap-dancing club. Throw a bouncy ball into the dressing room at All Fur Coat and you'll hit five or six girls who say they're models just for the hell of it, and four or five who've actually done some – top shelf, maybe a video – because the work's always there if you want it, if you don't mind showing it all and then some. But you'd be hitting damaged goods. Girls who've fallen for the wrong lines and done the wrong work. Or girls with too much baggage in tow: kids and bad husbands and violent boyfriends. Or maybe girls who are just too much girl, the Fortuna types, all boobs and make-up, like some kind of scientific sex experiment.

But throw your bouncy ball and you'd only hit one Heidi. I didn't realise it then, but I was my own biggest commodity. I still am. Not long in the job, not twisted out of shape by it. No visible work, tattoos or piercings. No significant others or childminders always on the phone. No stupid made-up name like Sunset or Cherry. No dodgy porn history or everyone-knows-she's-got-a-drug-problem. Just me. Not popular, not hated. Good at my job, but hungry to get on. Quietly earning the money to get my portfolio together, but otherwise a blank canvas. And most importantly, I have never kissed and told.

Plenty of the girls have. Journalists come to All Fur Coat a lot. What they see inside the club is a room full of stories, and they usually get them. Cards are handed out, surreptitiously, below the tables, so the girls know that if they end up going home with a footballer or a soap star or a *Pop Idol* judge or TV presenter, there's always money to be made. Not much – those kinds of stories are exaggerated. And especially not much to a lap dancer used to pocketing hundreds of pounds for a few hours' work. It's pin money really. Most of the girls do it for the exposure: for the photo shoot and the chance to add 'model' to their mental CV, the hope that their Sunday morning revelations will lead to something more, a career outside the club.

It never does, though. For those same bouncy ball reasons, it never does, and they're still there, week after week, still scanning the room for new slebs to snare. Some of them get a taste for it, are on first-name terms with the guy from the *News of the World* or the woman from the *Sport*. But if there is a route out of the club for them, it's never up. Because underneath the Impulse they smell of desperation. Because they get their tits out for the paparazzi outside China White. Because they sit at their dressing tables applying lipliner, going, 'I wanna be fay-muss.' Because they're not me.

So, yes, it was vitally important to Holly that I've never been a kiss-and-tell. Not that I haven't had offers for the kiss (and the tell bit's a given) – I just never have.

Not until Holly spotted me. Too right Peter better apologise for saying there are plenty more where I came from. He knows there aren't; Holly knew it, too.

She handed me her card one night in the club. Not under-hand, the way the punters and the journalists do, just gave it to me under the doormen's noses. Public Nuisance PR, it said. 'I do Peter Benstead's publicity,' she added. Then I'd only met him a couple of times. An introduction by Terry the first time, 'Ah, Peter, let me introduce our new girl, Heidi,' and he'd taken the trouble to remember my name for the second brief encounter. 'Heidi, isn't it? Everything all right, Angel?' He calls us all Angel. It's his version of those names we all hear a thousand times a day – darling, love, honey or babe. Only Peter ever calls you Angel. If it's deliberate, it works.

'I was wondering if you could give me a call in the next couple of days,' Holly said next. 'I'd like to meet up with you. I've got something to discuss with you, something you might be interested in.'

And now my finger hovers over the button to call her, and I'm wondering whether I should. Because if I call her, I'll be answering a nagging feeling I have, a little wormy piece of paranoia, and it's not a good look.

So in the end, I don't call.

*

'Do you know what they used to call me?' says Freak Boy.

'No,' I say. I put my sunglasses on. 'What did they used to call you?'

'Dog Shit,' he says.

I look at him.

'Right,' I say. 'Um . . . sorry?'

'That's okay,' he says, and he goes. He walks away with that same half-walk-half-run that's dorky but somehow still conceals an almost menacing self-assurance. Despite the heat a minor shudder runs through my body. I'm not sorry to see the back of him, not at all.

Myopic Waitress from Hell saunters over blowing hair from her face and fishing for her notepad. 'What can I get you?' she says, as though I haven't been sitting here for, oh, twenty minutes trying to catch her eye the whole time.

'Ah,' I consider. 'Do you do banana splits?'

'No.'

'Okay, um, what's your pie like?'

'We don't have pie.'

'Right. In that case, have you got a cheesy wedge?'

'Fuck off, I'm getting the manager,' and she whisks off between the tables.

'Spit roast?' I call after her, and promptly leave the table.

Okay, let's appraise the situation.

The situation is: Fucking *Hell*. As situations go, it's the good shit. It's laugh and run and hello trees, rivers and mountain goat. I can hardly contain myself. Covent Garden or not, I laugh and click my heels, and an American tugs at his wife's sleeve. 'Whaddaya know?' he says, a walking national characteristic.

Good one. What do I know? I know that Peter Benstead is an insecure egomaniac who pays someone to take chewing gum off his wife's tits. And that he's unwittingly employed London's biggest nutjob for the task. Him doing this puts him squarely into the 'hapless' category as it is, but no, the cream in the already tasty coffee is that Peter Benstead is shortly to be exposed for having an affair, and he's going to be exposed by me at great expense to a tabloid paper of my choosing, thus solving my debt problem and lighting a fire beneath my career. I promise myself a pint for this excellent piece of thinking.

And then there's Heidi.

I'm not daft. I'm aware that it's fairly usual for the besotted to believe that the object of their affections is 'Too Good For . . .' Otherwise, what's the point of having an object of your affections? And, of course, at some level I vaguely believe that Heidi is 'too good for' the company she keeps: too good for lap dancing, too good for spinning naked on poles being leered at by the likes of me, too good for glamour modelling. But if these are kind of abstract, not-fully-formed TGFs, well, I *know* she's too good for Peter Benstead. I *know* it. Benstead, his crap show and trophy wife; Benstead who celebrated every goal like he'd just found a cure for cancer; who will use Heidi and spit her out like an overheated Pop Tart as soon as he gets bored.

So, Heidi. I get to save her from the clutches of the evil Benstead. Naturally I'm aware that exposing her affair in a newspaper isn't the most romantic way to go about winning a lady's hand, but first things first, I'll worry about that later.

I'm walking on sunshine, so I don't notice the crowd of pigeons until they suddenly erupt from around my feet, their wings sounding like machine-gun fire. Or like a drum roll, which in my head becomes the opening to 'Lust For Life' by Iggy Pop, dirty, unwashed and thrilling. One of the five best bass lines ever committed to vinyl. Round and round my head it goes as I hurry off through the piazza: 'La-la-la-la-Lust for life.'

I check to see there are no cleaver-wielding kitchen staff on my tail before I slow down and fish for the wretched mobile in my jacket. Sure enough there's a message on there – two, in fact – but I don't listen to them because I know what they'll be about. Instead I ignore a nagging feeling that I've forgotten something and dial Graham's number with the trembling fingers of a man about to collect a lottery win.

'Graham!' I say.

He greets me like an old friend, his voice full of Northern Irish warmth.

'Greil? What the fuck? If you spent as much time at your fucking computer as you do on the fucking phone.'

Christ, he sounds like he wants to kill me. 'Graham,' I interrupt. 'Shut up.'

He splutters. Good story or not, I kind of regret telling him to shut up; you don't shit in the zookeeper's Ready Brek if you can help it. 'Sorry.' I say. 'Look, sorry. I'm a bit hyped. I've got a story for you.'

'So you should have . . .'

'No, no. I mean a story. A *news* story.'

See, I do little music bits in Graham's supplement. The odd interview. The supplement comes with the newspaper, and though you get one free with the other, the supplement is where my relationship with the paper ends. I could try ringing the newsdesk to sell them my story, let them know I write for Graham, but I hardly think my witty drubbing of the last David Gray album will have them keening like oversexed sirens to hire me. So I'm hoping Graham will broker the deal. I tell him as much.

'Well before we stop the press,' he says, 'why don't you start by telling me what it is, this story of yours.'

'It's . . .' and I suddenly stop, feeling as though I'm about to let the grinning man in the wonky dog collar value my family heirlooms.

'Erm, listen,' I say, squinting at the sky in search of inspiration. 'The story I've got, well, once I've told you, that's it. That's the story. How do I know you won't just use it anyway, without me?'

Graham sighs. A young girl thwacks me with her rucksack as she turns to talk to her friend, almost knocking my sunglasses off. I resist aiming a kick at her backside. Drops of sweat run from my armpits to my waistband. Winnie the Pooh and Christopher Robin take bets on which one will reach my belt first.

Graham sighs again. 'We use an old journalistic technique called trust, Greil. It's all around us. You can't feel it, or touch it, but it's there. Close your eyes and feel the trust, and give it to me straight.'

'It's just that I can't afford to get stuffed on this one,

Graham. It's a good story. And ... Well, I don't know if you've been picking up my vibes over the last couple of days, but I could really do with some fast cash, and I'm looking for an advance on this, and . . .'

I'm gabbling. I think of Heidi, and it's a sedative, healing thought. Her favourite word is serendipity, her top hunk the young Paul Newman ('it's in the eyes!'). She can save me from myself.

'Greil, calm down,' says Graham, milk into my thoughts. 'What *kind* of a story are we talking about?'

'Good. Probably a front page.'

'A splash, eh?'

'Oh yeah, it'll make quite a splash.'

'No, Greil, a splash is what we call the front-page story. I guess they don't have front pages where you come from.'

'Not with stories on, no.'

'Jesus. Well, look, if it sounds okay the news editor is a pal. I can give him a call. But not until you give me a bit more to go on.'

'It's an affair.'

'Er, right. Well, for a start, they're going to want to know if you have proof, or if you can prove it. Who are we talking about?'

'One of the parties is Peter Benstead.'

'Ex-England player, failed spell as Spurs manager, now man-about-town club owner? Husband of Emily?'

'Yeah.'

'Okay. Who's he shagging?'

'That's giving you the whole caboodle, isn't it, mate?' I say.

Graham puts on a Darth Vader voice. Sounds like he's speaking into his mug to get the right effect: 'The trust is weak in this one,' he says. Then, in normal voice, 'Okay, is he shagging a man or a woman?'

'Woman.'

'Shame. Famous?'

'No.'

'Under age?'

'No.'

'Are there drugs involved?'

'Dunno. Doubt it. He's not the type, is he?'

'Is there a type? Okay, you're probably right. What sort of girl are we talking about here?'

'How do you mean?'

'I mean are we talking star-crossed lover, or slapper? I mean is this a full-on love affair with a social equal, or has he just got a bit of fluff in tow?'

'She's – *[I'm so sorry, Heidi]* – she's a slapper.'

'And has she come to you with this?'

'No.'

'Then how do you know?'

'A good source. Bang on.'

'I see. So you're sure about it?'

'Oh yeah, absolutely.'

'Okay, do you want to hang on? I'll see if I can raise my mate.'

'Graham,' I almost shout before he can put me on hold.

'Yeah?'

'Before you do, this is my story, right? I want this story. It's *my* story, yeah?'

'Leave it with me, Greil.'

'And . . . Graham?'

'Yes, Greil.'

'I'll need some cash up front. I'm going to need an advance on this one. Half up front.'

A beat, he sighs. 'Leave it with me.'

The line goes quiet. I wipe a grimy film of sweat from my face, waiting . . .

'Greil?'

'Yes!'

'Have you got a brown paper bag there, pal? You sound like you're about to hyperventilate.'

'Don't dick me about. What did he say?'

'Yeah, not bad. Nice little yarn. And good timing, apparently his wife's in a show or something. There's a problem as far as you're concerned, though.'

'What?'

'He's going to put some of his own news people on it. Your music credentials didn't exactly lift his trousers. I put in a good word and that, but he was fairly adamant.'

'No,' I say, almost shouting.

'You'll get a good tip-off fee, and if it's hard news you want to get into, a solid tip-off is a good place to start . . .'

'No.'

'Greil. Don't shoot yourself in the foot here. These guys do stories like this for breakfast.'

'I can fucking do it.'

'Look, if it was just a case of writing it up you'd be more than capable. But it's more delicate than that. We've got to have something concrete, which'll mean getting pictures, and once we've done that, we'll have to go to Benstead, and his missus, and the girl, and depending on who wants to say what, there's a lot of horse trading that goes on. And that's all before a single word gets written. It's just not the sort of job they give to guys fresh off the boat. It's no reflection on you, mate, it's common sense.'

I clench the mobile at my ear. They want to cut me out of the loop, I think, frantically. Then, 'What if I could persuade the girl to open up?' I say, seeing in an instant how I can play it both ways: get the story *and* win Heidi's trust into the bargain. I award myself a pint. Another if I can successfully pull it off.

'Come again?'

'I mean, what if I can get her interview in the bag straight away, as though she'd come to us? Then it'd be my interview, right? Your news boys can do all the Benstead stuff, and I'll take care of the girl.'

'So now you're telling me you can get the girl to talk?'

'I think so, yes.'

'Even though she hasn't come to you with the story?'

'Yes.'

'So here's this girl, and she's bowling along, having it away with Peter Benstead, who's probably treating her like a princess, but one word from you and she's going to turn into Alicia Douval?'

'Who?'

'It doesn't matter. She's a kiss-and-tell girl. The point is, how are you going to persuade this girl to talk?'

By lying to her, I think. By giving her no choice but to talk. And by making it seem as if I'm doing her a favour at the same time – the nice man from the magazine protecting her from all those horrid men at the newspaper.

'I reckon I can do it,' I say.

'Why don't you be a bit more certain about it before I get back to my mate . . . ?'

Hint hint. 'Yeah, yeah. I'm certain,' I say. 'She'll trust me. Let me do this, Graham. I *need* this.'

He sighs again. 'I really hope you're not thinking of jeopardising the story, Greil. Because if you go jumping the gun and scare the girl off it's not going to look good, is it? You'll look like a chump, and, more importantly, I'll look like a chump. You know that would officially be a stupid thing to do.'

'Would I be that dumb?'

'Okay, wait there.'

I do. The phone goes quiet and I wait, Covent Garden buzzing around me, sweat poppling my forehead. At last, Graham returns. 'Okay, Greil, if you get an interview in the bag, then, like you say, it's your interview. They'll hold off for the time being.'

'Fantastic.'

'But listen, don't rush things. Speak to the girl, establish her trust. If she's willing to talk, get in touch with us. It's a good idea if you take her somewhere nobody else can get at her, somewhere neutral. We can point you in the direction of hotels we use. Have you got that, Greil? Greil . . . ? Are you there . . . ?'

CHAPTER FOURTEEN

They called me Dog, although it was they who ran in packs. The Shit came later, when words like 'shit' became common currency. And they didn't hate me because I couldn't kick a ball, although I couldn't, or because my trainers were not the right brand, although they weren't. They hated me because they were frightened of me. Because in me they sensed a lack of what it was that governed their own lives. They hated me because they did not hold the key to my misery, because they didn't understand me.

So their hatred of me was something unique at the school. Universal, it was enjoyed by all, irrespective of their place in the school hierarchy. By the teachers who could only ever have admitted it within the confines of the staff room. By parents who shot me dark looks as they shepherded their children by.

But especially by the other pupils. They hated me with the special loathing people reserve for paedophiles. They screamed at me. Spat at me. Their parents told them why my mother knew all the lorry drivers' names and their incomprehension manifested itself in taunts and beatings. From the corners of their eyes they watched me creep around the edges of their world.

I was thirteen when I escaped them. That night I made my way home across the playing fields of the school. Most pupils left by the front entrance, or gathered in the forecourt to catch buses, but this thirteen-year-old lived uncommonly near the school, he was virtually its neighbour. To get home I needed only to cross the pitches, which were sometimes football and sometimes rugby, and occasionally converted for track sports.

Because it was winter I had to pick my way carefully to avoid the deceptively large puddles which would lie waiting in the grass, or the sometimes vast plains of stippled mud which collected around the goal ends, but even this effort was nothing to what it would have cost me to use the front gate, because it was there that the other kids gathered, and their older brothers gathered there too, and the beatings would start when the final bell had rung and they cravenly watched weary teachers point their Fiats home.

I clutched a carrier bag from Safeways as I gingerly crossed the sodden playing field. In it I carried my school books; the novel I was reading; some bread rolls stolen at lunchtime.

As I crossed the playing field I counted. I counted the number of fence posts to my left, and the fencing panels in between. I looked over to a council block and counted the windows, then counted the windows which had their curtains drawn, then tried to create patterns from the windows with their curtains drawn.

At the bottom of the playing fields I counted the uprights which supported the link-fence. There were four uprights on the left-hand side of the hole in the fence I used for access, and six uprights on the other side. Beyond the fence a short stretch of no-man's-land, an illegal tip where only washing machines, me, and the occasional art class dared to tread; beyond that the pavement, sanctuary and home, where I would find my mother asleep, in bed.

My steps became even more cautious as I approached the embankment which led down to the hole in the chain-link fence. A wrong foot here was slapstick entertainment but could be very messy, so I picked my way down the steep incline with great care, mentally celebrating my steady feet at the bottom as I wriggled through the hole and into the school's hinterland. Here there was a short stretch of undergrowth through which the years had beaten a path, and this led to a patch of wasteland which gradually claimed discarded property as its own: unwanted white goods stood there like gravestones among the pyres of black bin liners, the occasional skeleton of a bike chassis.

It was not unusual to find other people there – this route was an accepted, if unpleasant, shortcut; people often let their dogs do toilet there – so I paid little mind to the voices I heard, even though my senses were sharp enough to register even the faintest murmur carried by the wind. Alert and wary, but not scared. Not at this point, because there was no apparent threat, and not because of what I had in the carrier bag that dangled from my hand. The voices grew louder as I made my way across the wasteland and I thought I located their source from the copse, the undergrowth away to my left. At the same time I smelled cigarette smoke. The voices, I guessed, belonged to some other pupils from the school who had found a new place to hang out and smoke, and they would most likely allow me to pass unhindered, although the temptation to shout something at me from their hidey-hole would be too much to bear. I steeled myself against the inevitable taunts from the copse, but expected nothing more.

Perhaps they had finished their cigarettes, ground out the Peter Stuyvesant they'd probably stolen from Jason Saul's mum, blown out the final lungfuls of smoke. For as I drew level (and I crept past, conditioned by years of bullying to restrain my presence, keep it to the bare minimum) the bullies stepped out of the copse and into my path. They were led by Jason Saul, stinking of his mum's cigarettes. Later she would cradle his head in hospital and tell the police and papers that his attacker was an animal.

Which, of course, I was. A trapped and terrified animal, I felt my breathing go heavy, like the bullies might hear it. To me it seemed to fog the air between us and for a moment or so there was nothing but that sound, of me struggling to control the fear billowing from my nostrils.

'Yeah?' said Jason Saul, who was the leader, a vicious thirteen-year-old thug who would later be painted in court as, 'mischievous, perhaps, like any other boy his age experimenting with social rules, but hardly the malicious hooligan the defence would have you believe'.

'Yeah?' he said again, not, it seemed to me, in the playful spirit of experimenting with social rules, not even for the love of polemics, but in the malicious spirit of being about to beat up Dog Shit for the pure hell of it. Because it pleased him to do so, like a little king.

So I said nothing; nothing I could say would change the course of my immediate future, not in the common scheme of things.

Today was different, though, and I hugged my carrier bag to my chest as if in defence, but in fact to grip the comforting shape of the Philips screwdriver I had there.

At what point I had decided to arm myself, I wasn't sure. There was no epiphany; no single moment when, in a blur of fists and feet, I made my decision. It was true, my mother did listen to 'Coward Of The County' by Kenny Rogers an almost obsessive amount, and I often wonder whether or not those words (I can still remember them now) had an adhesive quality, had somehow formed a symbiotic attachment to the passage of my future. My temperament, I reason, welcomes the kind of cyclical resolution represented by the song. Had it seeped in at a primal level, conjoined the counting and pattern-forming inside? These outside influences had a habit of doing that. A mere ten years later Emily Benstead would join my compulsions in much the same way.

'You want to go past,' said Jason Saul, unaware of the effect country and western music was about to have on his eyesight, 'you have to pay a toll.' He was flanked by his two friends who sniggered. Grubby faces and dirty shoes.

I ducked my head and made to move around the trio, but they stood in my way. I looked behind me, to where the path led back to the school, and there was no salvation there, nothing but the shame of having to retrace my steps, running the gauntlet of the gates.

'What you got in yer bag?' said Jason Saul, changing tack. 'Vaseline?' The others sniggered.

I knew then that I was about to use my Philips screwdriver. My sympathetic nervous system, a branch of my autonomic nervous system, kicked into life, preparing my body for action. I felt for the screwdriver and I looked at Jason Saul, making an instinctive but nevertheless conscious decision to go for the leader . . .

That was the decision I made when I arranged to meet Greil So Real. Not because he is the leader; in fact my rationale was to use him as a conduit to hurt, firstly the blonde bitch, but second and, more particularly, Mr Benstead. *He* is the leader. It is he who has betrayed me. Together I thought we had begun a journey to protect Emily, to keep her image clean of vandalism, that harsh reminder of a society that has forgotten its manners. I believed we were the same that way. Yet his intentions were simply to protect his investment.

My idea had been to use Greil So Real against Mr Benstead, but something has changed. I take the paper and reread it.

'Emily Benstead has all the charisma of a stagnant pond with none of its hidden depths.'

And I've no idea who Elizabeth Berkley or Mariah Carey are, but I've heard of Patsy Kensit, and I'm certain that being compared to all three is a grave insult, the kind of insult over which men duelled in the old days.

'. . . the disaster that is Emily Benstead's performance in Moll,' he wrote. He compares her to suet, a primary ingredient of inedible puddings. Greil So Real is not to be trusted. He is no longer our friend.

After my rounds, and on the way back to Oxford Street, I go into a twenty-four-hour shop – a convenience store – and find a shelf of tinned food towards the back: soup, beans, spaghetti hoops. I look in the mirror, put there to help shoplifters check the coast is clear, and the coast is clear, so I put a tin of beans into the pocket of my jeans, untuck my T-shirt to hide the bulge and wander out. I have never bought a tin of beans before, so I don't know how much the tin costs, but I'm willing to bet that the price increases in relation to the tin's proximity to the West End of London, and that by carrying it further into the centre of town, I am in fact adding value to it.

I walk into the well-known electrical retailer and on entering see something that pleases me. The guard has moved. He's now standing by the entrance, leaving the exit – the tiny, begrudging barrier – unguarded. Good. I have the Marigold in one trouser pocket, the tin of beans in the other.

The shop is less busy than at lunchtime and I wander through the aisles, keeping an eye on the central island as I do so. There is the assistant with the boil; he is attempting to help a customer, so I wander closer and pick up a copy of the well-known electrical retailer's Game Guide for the second time today. 'First for new technology' it says. There are pictures on the front, and I recognise Mario. There is also a spaceman and a man who wears a bandanna and carries a pistol. The catalogue has all you need to get 'the expert edge', or so it says, and I ponder whether it will give me the expert edge I require as I walk to the opposite side of the island, reach into my pocket and open the tin of beans without taking it out.

To do this I have to use both hands and pretend to be interested in some printers as I do so. I hold my jeans with one hand, yank the tin's ring pull with the other. The lid comes off in my hand and I feel a little bean juice slop into my pocket, but hardly enough to worry me. Then, leaving the lid by the side of a printer, I turn and walk towards the island – the camera side now – and I give a quick look left and right as I do so, because now comes the tricky part.

Bringing the Game Guide to my trouser pocket I jam it over the top of the tin which I pull out of my jeans, tip over, and leave on the counter, walking quickly away.

Behind me is a copy of the Game Guide with a tin of beans standing on it. Besides the fact that the tin is upside down, there is nothing to suggest that it is open. In a moment or so, one of the island's guardians will spot the tin and he'll assume a customer has left it behind and pick it up, thus spilling beans all over the counter. His surprise will alert other members of staff and the assistant with the boil will go to investigate, thus leaving the cassette-corder side of the island unmanned. In his absence I will be able to duck down, make my way into the island, take the machine I need, place it in my rucksack and simply walk out of the shop without arousing the guard's suspicion.

I go back to the cassette-corder side and wait. Just a matter of waiting now – until the beans are spotted by one of the two assistants on the beans side.

But nothing happens and the assistant with the boil stares at me with obvious antipathy, which is based on the fact that we are both the same age, but he's on one side of the counter and I am on the other. He touches his boil. I wait for excited cries accompanying spilled beans, but there is only silence.

Then one of the assistants from the other side walks around and grabs the assistant with the boil, speaking in a low voice I only just catch.

'Oi,' he says, 'we're on a wind-up. Look at this.' They both hunker down and stare through the display to the other side, going silent for a moment or so, giggling to themselves.

'What am I looking at?' sniggers the assistant with the boil.

'Tin of beans there,' says the second, pointing. 'It's open, look. Only Vadge hasn't seen it. He'll go over in a minute, you watch. He's gonna get beans everywhere.'

They both chuckle, like those two Muppets who used to sit in the balcony and make fun of Kermit.

'Did you put it there?' says the assistant with the boil.

I'm outraged as the second assistant doesn't quite claim full responsibility for the beans, but doesn't deny it either. Instead he gives his colleague a conspiratorial wink. The kind of wink you'd give someone if you wanted them to think that you'd rigged up a tin of beans to spill over a colleague – without fully implicating yourself.

They stay hunkered down, watching, doing their Muppet laugh at the same time.

'Here we go, game on,' says the second. 'He's just flogged that guy an Olympus. Any second now . . .'

There's a startled sound from the other side of the island and the two assistants near me have their hands over their mouths to contain their laughs as a third man rounds the side of the island, the tin of beans in his hand.

'What the fuck is this?' he says, furious. His trousers are liberally coated in bean juice above the knee. 'Is this you?' he shrieks at the assistant, 'because there's fucking beans everywhere round there. Look at me,' he indicates his trousers. 'I've got beans all over me. If this is your idea of a fucking joke . . .'

It occurs to me that if my plan was to get one side of the island unmanned, then it has, in part, worked. It's possible that the camera side is at this very moment being pillaged by opportunist thieves. The cassette-corder side, meanwhile, is more heavily guarded than ever as a fourth man approaches the island: older, managerial.

'What's going on here?'

'Vadge has spilt some beans over Photographic, boss,' says the second assistant.

'No I have not,' says Vadge. 'One of these twats left an open tin of beans on the counter.'

'So you tipped it all over yourself, did you?' says the manager.

'No, it was—'

'Look, I don't give a shit about your bean fetish. Get it cleared up, get yourself cleaned up. You,' he points at the second assistant, 'get back over to Photographic, and you,' he points at the assistant with the boil, 'stop laughing. Christ, this is a shop, not a playground.'

I've observed the scene from behind a display of headphones, but now, as the sentries return to their posts and Vadge makes his way to the rear of the shop, I try another tack. Approaching the island I try to attract the attention of the assistant with the boil, who ignores me for as long as he can before I might potentially complain. His smirk disappears as he reluctantly moves across to serve me.

'Yes?' he says, his eyes roving over the top of my head.

'I was wondering,' I say. 'That cassette-corder there, the Sony?'

'That what, mate?'

'The Sony.'

'No, what did you say before Sony?'

'Cassette-corder.'

'Cassette-corder?' he says. He seems to find this amusing.

'Yes.'

'You mean the dictaphone?'

'The cassette-corder, yes.'

'I think I know the one you mean, yeah.' He doesn't bother checking behind him.

'Does it have VOR?'

'What, mate?'

'Does it have VOR?'

He frowns and turns. I check to see that the security guard is still beside the entrance. He is. I check that the exit barrier is free of obstructions. It is.

The assistant with the boil picks up the cassette-corder and studies it thoughtfully.

'Don't think so, mate.'

'Could I see?' I say, doing a final guard/till check. All good.

'S'pose,' he says, passing me the cassette-corder.

I hold it for a couple of seconds, then say, 'Thanks. I'll have one,' and he reaches below the counter, bringing out a boxed version, nice and virgin new.

'Pay at the till,' says the assistant with the boil, touching his boil and leaving me to pick up the box.

'Thank you,' and I take a couple of casual steps away from the counter in the direction of the till, checking the guard, ready to make a dash for it.

'Oi,' says the assistant from behind me. I grimace and turn to see him holding out a tiny box to me. 'Forgot,' he says. 'That one comes with a free microphone.'

I thank him and take the microphone, move away from the counter. I feel his eyes on my back, but I'm checking the guard as I move towards the exit barrier, waiting for the right moment.

And perhaps I look suspicious standing in the middle of the shop, stare fixed on the guard, because from behind me the assistant with the boil says, 'You all right, there?' just as the guard's attention is hijacked by an attractive girl in a short skirt. And I take to my heels, the cassette-corder tucked under my arm like a rugby ball. The assistant with the boil shouts. I see the guard's head swivel in my direction. The cashier simply stares with her mouth wide as I race past her into the street. Behind me a security alarm sounds as I take off down Oxford Street, vaguely feeling I made that operation more complicated than it needed to be . . .

CHAPTER FIFTEEN

Lust for life!

La-la-la-la-Lust for life!

One of the five best bass lines committed to vinyl, I said. So what are the other four? Come on, Greil, what are the five definitive bass lines of all time? Amaze us all with your incredible musical knowledge. Or, not your knowledge as such, but your taste, your savoir-faire, your discernment, your – how shall we say – *je ne sais quoi?*

This is the kind of thing I argued, no, debated, with George all the time. This *sort* of thing, anyway. So, in memory of George, I'd say the five best bass lines ever are . . .

'Atmosphere' by Joy Division, 'Walk On The Wild Side' by Lou Reed. 'If There's A Hell Below' by Curtis Mayfield. And we're talking off the top of my head here, and okay, this is a bit of a rogue choice, but 'Justice' by New Model Army, and including 'Lust For Life' by Iggy Pop that makes five.

I know what George would say, of course, because I happen to know what her favourite bass line *ever* is, the cause of more than a few argument/debates *chez* Sharkey. It's 'Bug Powder Dust' by Bomb The Bass, which I can't include in my list because it's a dance record, and, as George was fond of criticising me for, I hate dance music – it killed our band.

'Oh, get away,' she laughed.

'I'm telling you, Gee, fucking dance music, the fuck. What else, then? Go on. One minute we're ready to blow up, we're turning A&R men away at the door, the next minute everyone's dancing in fields and we can't get arrested. Fucking dance music killed us.'

'I seem to remember Systemitis opposing the Criminal Justice Bill,' she said, her tongue in her cheek. One of her favourite facial expressions, that. She used to stick her tongue in her cheek and raise her eyebrows – a bit like Davina McCall except sexier. She was right, too, we had opposed the Criminal Justice Bill, the CJB, just as vigorously as we opposed Clause 28 and the Poll Tax, all tiny glimmers of hope for the Systemitis philosophy, especially the CJB, when it looked like kids might stop boshing pills for just long enough to register the fact that the government was trying to curb their lifestyle. But our anti-Criminal Justice Bill single, 'Right 2 Dance', hardly inspired the masses to revolution, and it had some ill-advised dance mixes by – and it still makes me cringe – ourselves. How hard could it be, right? Take Jonny out of the mix, whack on a 4/4 beat and we're cooking on gas. Clearly not. Our 'Repetitive Beats' mix was an embarrassment; our 'Police Raid' mix just as bad. We were supposed to be proper musicians: how come we couldn't lick dance music? And when it came to the march, a huge affair that began in Hyde Park and very nearly kicked off at Downing Street, what should have been one of our finest hours was, characteristically, one of our worst. Our PA didn't work and everyone was noticeably ignoring us in order to dance around the float in front where – I think – Carl Cox was DJing. Needless to say, 'Right 2 Dance' was our last single; the NME's Maginot Line comparison came shortly afterwards.

The thing is, I could cope with dance music fucking up the band and wrecking my musical career, but my journalism went tits up for the same reason. Dance music. You can't write about dance music. It's impossible to write about dance music. How can you write about a style of music that asks no questions of itself, or of the listener? It facilitates either blankness or deep lateral thought, that's the whole point. And if it doesn't do that then it's not dance music and there's no point in writing about it because no fucker's buying it. So we tried, with our Kingmakers, and Menswears and Top, and any other number of indie no-marks that sank without trace, but we weren't fooling anyone – the closest we got was the Madchester scene. Otherwise it was farewell *Record Mirror*, *Sounds*, *Vox*, *Select*, *Melody Maker*; hello *Mixmag*, *Muzik*, *Ministry* and *Jockey Slut*. Oh, and farewell Greil Sharkey. Seeya, *NME*. Hello to the world of occasional freelance 'pop' journalism, 'little reviews' and doomed attempts to break into news. Typical Greil Sharkey. Always knocking on the door, never any answer. Everything about me: wrong, wrong, wrong. Shouting about injustice when people just wanted to dance; grinding my teeth on amphetamines when everyone else was using acid and Ecstasy. If the revolution was televised, I'd video it.

And that, like the way Phoebe Cates hates Christmas in *Gremlins*, is why I will never choose 'Bug Powder Dust' as one of my five favourite bass lines ever.

But now, for the first time since I don't know when, I feel like I'm on the cusp, like I can reach out and touch what I want. I got me a proper news story to write. The truth, not some 500-word ad feature for someone's latest record. So I'm feeling pretty happy, and to celebrate I make my way to the pub and use the money I've saved on tube fares and frappuccinos to grab a quick pint before I go home. Inside they're playing De La Soul, the first album, one of my favourite hip hop albums of all time. There's something about it, though. Something that seems to remind me. But then I've reached the bottom of my first pint with bewildering speed and, ignoring the demands for cocaine my head is making, I order another, all the time enjoying De La Soul and reading a paper that someone's left behind, paying special attention to the news stories, imagining my byline there.

I can't help myself putting a pound into a fruit machine. I remember a time when a pound would get you ten goes on a fruit, and it wasn't that long ago, either. Me and the rest of Systemitis, helping to smash the state by pouring cash into a fruit machine. These days a pound gets you four goes: go one is hope, two is defiance, three is anger, four is defeat. Still, I put that one minor flaw in the diamond of the afternoon behind me, order a third pint. Be rude not to.

My brain's going gaketty-gak crazy by the time I leave the pub and walk straight into bright sunshine with a three-pint buzz on. My brain's right. The day would be improved immeasurably by a couple of cheeky lines, maybe three. Needless to say, in order to buy coke I need to have money, and I don't have any, none at all. If I had some it's possible I could win some more. In fact, I'm certain I could. To bet, or not to bet, that is the question. Although it's not of course, because the pot is empty. The line of my Ozwald Boateng is agreeably unspoiled by anything so vulgar as cash or coins, and like Britain's aristocracy I have nothing in the bank either.

I check my pockets one last time, trying not to let imminent failure spoil my day. Nothing. So where to get some extra money? The cash machine would bust a digital gut laughing if I tried shoving my coke-encrusted card in there, and the only other option is to borrow some. I could maybe borrow some from Terry, I think, making my way to Leicester Square tube. After all, he sort of owes me for the mess on my sleeve, and while I'm there I could check on the Heidi situation, start building my bridges for a fresh charm offensive.

I bundle up behind a tourist to get through the ticket gates without paying, and although she looks around with a look of Germanic horror, I apologise loudly and gesture at the barrier as though it's faulty. The advantage of wearing a suit is that neither the tourist, the natives or any staff who happen to be watching think I'm up to no good. A man who looks that expensive can't be dodging his fare, right?

On the platform I study a poster on the other side of the tracks which advertises *Moll*, and I wonder how it would look amended with my quote: 'pure theatrical suet'. Pretty good. I bet Benstead would be pleased with that, the two-timing cock. And what of Mrs B? Not only wearing a lacy whalebone corset and fishnet stockings, but the horns to boot. How will she feel when the piece comes out? Rich, probably, when her lawyers tell her just how good her grounds for divorce are. The only victim in this whole affair will be Heidi, and though she doesn't know it, she has me to protect her. As I wait for the tube, that thought gets sampled and looped and played over and over in my head, as comforting and calming as my three pints at lunchtime. Heidi – my salvation, my redemption, my cortisone.

Just as the train pulls in to take me to the secret underground station which serves All Fur Coat, I flick my chewing gum at the poster of *Moll*. It's not a bad shot, but it falls some way short of Emily Benstead's norks and lands on her knee instead. I'd like to see you get that one, you weird fuck, I think, as I board the train . . .

All Fur Coat doesn't have its own secret underground station, sadly. Instead I use the regular tube and walk to the club, turning my face to the sun to get the most of the rays. I feel strangely relaxed. My decision to try and score some coke has given the day a bit of badly needed direction. That and the fact that I'm on the verge of something big, so I can justify doing coke, because my old skool mentality associates coke with being affluent and successful. In reality it's about the scummiest drug I could do, but still I cling to these quaintly outdated notions. The same way I cling to the belief that I got my tan in Cannes, not on the Holloway Road; that my once expensive suit didn't pass its sell-by date two years ago. You can take the man out of the Eighties, but you can't take the Eighties out of the man.

A doorman called Karl stands at the door of All Fur Coat. He looks like St Peter would have if he'd joined the Reservoir Dogs.

'All right, Karl?' I say, checking out my reflection in his sunglasses. With my own shades on I look like his twin. Except an older, slightly weedier twin. Twin-*ish*.

'Not today,' he says, and I'm about to protest when I realise he's not speaking to me, but to a group of lads who have approached him while I've been staring at my reflection.

'Come on, man,' says one, at the head of the group. Despite the heat, all four of them are wearing anoraks. Big, heavy anoraks. If I had to guess I'd say they were on their school holidays, probably the products of broken homes and poor parenting, borderline delinquents. They've spent the morning drinking alcopops and decided to come West for a spot of juvenile hellraising. I wonder if they're drunk enough to take on Karl. Christ, I'd love to run a book on that fight. *Karl v AlcoLads*. You'd have to back Karl, but then, one of the AlcoLads might have a knife. On the other hand, Karl might be packing his little cosh, which they all seem to have, and which for all I know is handed out in a special bouncer's welcome pack and has the All Fur Coat logo stitched into it. *AlcoLads with knife v Karl with cosh*. I'd still back Karl. In fact, I think the only situation in which I wouldn't back Karl would be *AlcoLads with Uzi v Karl with the flu*. Even then . . .

'Come on, man,' says the leader. He's not black, but he's talking and acting like he is. His homeboys shuffle around him like So Solid juniors. Somewhere buried beneath a set of predetermined poses and acts each of them has a real self, but they couldn't find it, not without a torch and an upbringing. The pose is all they know. That and some dimly understood notion of respect and survival. And the necessity of wearing big coats in hot weather. 'It's all fucked up,' says one, spitting. We're in agreement, but they don't notice me, half in and half out of the club entrance. Their attention is focused on Karl. Clever boys.

'We eighteen,' says the leader. You can't tell where Karl is looking, thanks to the shades. His mouth curls up in the hint of a sneer, but there's no derisive laugh, no attempt to belittle the lads. Clever Karl.

'Not today,' he repeats.

'We got money,' says the leader, and from his pocket he

brings a huge roll of money which he waves in front of Karl's face, his lip curled into an arrogant, so-there sneer. It's a big roll of money, the kind of roll of money you expect to see Ray Winstone carrying. I don't like to think how much is there, but the note on the outside is a twenty and the roll is a good two inches thick. You do the math, as they say in America.

Karl remains impassive. Of course. The Sultan of Brunei wouldn't get past Karl if he was under age, and if anything the money-showing simply strengthens his resolve. The gang's leader thinks he's waving a magic wand, when he might as well be brandishing a mouldy pineapple for all the effect it has on Karl. The leader puts the roll back into his pocket.

The pocket of his anorak. A gaping pocket.

'Sorry, gents,' says Karl, a master of irony. They shuffle a bit more, and try to stare down Karl who barely looks in their direction, signalling the end of the encounter, and they decide it's best to leave and the leader says, 'Fuck it, man,' and spits at the pavement and they turn and go.

Hands in my pockets I have one eye on their exit stage left as I move to face St Peter. 'All right, Karl?'

'Mr Sharkey.' We both pretend that he hasn't just been *very* cool.

'Terry in?' The four lads go off down the street, each doing their own gangsta impression. I feel the cloth of my pockets on my wet hands. It feels grubby.

'Sorry, Mr Sharkey. He's gone to the theatre, would you believe?' And no, I can't believe it. Because with Terry out of the picture I have no chance of laying my hands on any cash.

'Oh yeah?' I say, keeping it bright and breezy. 'To see what?' But knowing exactly what. To see *Moll*. Karl confirms and lets a customer into the club as I rock on my heels a moment or so, casting a final look down the street at where the Anorak Squad is moving towards the horizon.

'Okay,' I say. 'Well, it can keep,' and I clap Karl a friendly goodbye on the shoulder and take off, swallowing, trying to locate the group of lads before they disappear completely.

Later, I will bitterly, *bitterly* regret, not only my actions, but the three pints that put the idea in the post. I'll fetch my bottle of vodka from the freezer. At some point I will remember exactly what it is that's been bugging me all day: I've forgotten to meet Jenny.

And all the time I'll be wearing the regret on my face, which hurts when I wince at the memory of what's about to happen.

But not now.

Now I see an opportunity. And my mind sniffs around it as I walk, quickly at first, until I get the lads in my sights and slow down to an amble a short way behind them, watch as they make their way towards the tube station.

They're little thugs who have somehow come into a bundle of cash, and whatever their means of inheritance, it's not legal. They think the cash makes them big men. They believe it's their ticket to places they otherwise would not be allowed to go. They think it provides them with privilege and gives them respect without the need to earn it. Somebody needs to rob them of that illusion. Somebody needs to rob them. And hey, it might as well be me.

One of them has lit a cigarette and is smoking as they enter the tube station. If that doesn't put me on the side of the righteous, what does? I swallow again, aware of it, like a crisp lodged in my gullet, but thinking also of that gaping pocket and how easy it will be to slide a hand in there, undetected – as I brush past on the escalators, perhaps, or bustle by on the platform. I've never pick-pocketed anybody before, and it's not something I plan to take up as a career or even as an intriguing pastime, but it can't be that difficult, certainly not in this case. Not with the victim too arrogant to be wary, his senses insulated by an unseasonal coat. It's all I can do to resist blowing theatrically on my hands as I round the corner and enter the tube station.

I'm in time to witness the Anorak Squad menacing their way to the escalators. They've waited for the right moment, in this case until an old lady was about to pass the barriers, and then nearly bundled her over as they pushed through. It's more grist to my mill, but I still feel more than a twinge of shame as I pull off a similar stunt to get through.

They're shouting and pushing one another at the top of the escalators. Other passengers are moving out of the way, exactly the desired effect. The crowd's heavy but they seem to make their own space, some people tutting loudly, but more often than not passing by, stony-faced, as if nothing untoward is happening. Then, with a last bit of push and shove, they join the top of the escalator and resume posing, still swearing loudly, passengers filing past them in the fast lane.

One of those passengers needs to be me. I locate the leader at the front of the pack, and begin to move down the escalator, keeping my eye on him and on his gaping pocket. In front of me, a woman, moving fast. Behind, a man is keeping pace with me, our feet drumming a machine-gun beat on the stairs.

Now I'm level with the last of the Squad. Two steps more, and I need to time this just right; need to stumble slightly; the merest pause is all it takes, just a tiny bit of contact with the leader and the roll of cash is mine. I expect a fuck-off in return. A watch-where-you're-fuckin-going and maybe a retaliatory shove, but none of that matters, just as long as I get the cash without arousing suspicion.

And why should I? I'm a man in a suit. Men in suits don't arouse suspicion.

My heart hammering, I take another step down, then pretend to stumble and fall across the front of the leader. As I do so my left arm shoots out to grab the rail while my right snakes into his coat, finds the roll, brings it out – perfect – and then I'm saying sorry, I'm regaining my feet and continuing on my way. Don't look back, classic London-style, the roll in my hand . . .

I hear a shout of 'Oi!' A reaction to my stumble. The

adrenalin of the theft is greying out my senses and I feel only my feet taking me away, steeling myself against a second shout, one that will confirm the theft has been discovered.

My shoes loud on the escalator steps: CHOKA-CHOKA-CHOKA, like a drum beat. Then the sound of an electric guitar, some feedback, a chord. For a second there is nothing. No escalator nor passengers, just the feel of the money in my hand and the music in my head which drowns out everything, all sound is gone.

Even my own cry as I lose my footing –
CHOKA-CHOKA . . . *CHUK*
– and stumble for real this time, collapsing on to the escalator which delivers me to the bottom in a breathless bundle of suit and perspiration. For the second time in two days I take a fall on an escalator. And then I'm grabbing at my jacket, scared my clothes will get caught in the escalator and drag me into its metal jaws. I've let go of the money. Not deliberately, but somewhere between falling and landing and yanking at my clothes, the money has gone, and as I take a wild-eyed look around I can see it, as if in slow-motion, like a hand grenade in a film, trundling along the tiles, across the mouth of the escalator. Why shouldn't it? It is a roll, after all. It's simply responding to a set of inherited characteristics.

And it's for much the same reason, I guess, that when the Anorak Squad see the money, then me scrabbling to regain my feet, and put two and two together and come up with four, they immediately set to work on giving me a good kicking. Why shouldn't they, I think, curling into a protective ball and hearing the thud of their trainers against my body, my head. Why shouldn't they? They're simply responding to a set of inherited characteristics.

CHAPTER SIXTEEN

I place the cassette-corder on the floor of my studio and move to open a window.

Next I prop each segment of the triptych against a wall and study them, tilting my head this way, then that. Hoping to see a different perspective; becoming the viewer for once.

I walk to the first two parts of the piece and there examine the papier mâché I've used to represent gum. They each perch on Emily's left breast. The irony is that I have placed them there, using a butter knife to create the whorled ridges of a fingerprint. Some unseen vandal's spoor, which marks the first two sections of the trilogy but is absent from the third and final part. In all, my finest work yet, I think. My finest work by some distance, despite its failure to satisfy the images conjured by my mind. Maybe the first lesson an artist ever learns, certainly the most painful: you can never compete with the person in your head. He will never be appeased by anything below absolute perfection.

'A tripartite cosmetic rendering of a fantasised reality,' I practise to the empty room, indicating each of the elements in turn, my Marigold a yellow pointer that I must remember to remove before Jill arrives.

I go to my bed where I remove my bedclothes, pillowcase, undersheet and duvet cover. I walk back through to the studio, carrying them like a washerwoman; like Toad of Toad Hall when he dressed up as a washerwoman to escape prison.

The pillowcase goes over the smallest of the three, hanging over it ready to be removed with a flourish, to gasps of admiration from Jill, and I do something similar with the undersheet and duvet cover. The triptych stands shrouded, three rectangular spirits, two of which bear the impression of my papier mâché chewing gum.

Then I bend down to the cassette-corder box, open it and remove the instructions, which I read carefully before tutting slightly, collecting my rucksack and heading for the door.

Ten minutes later I return with the batteries, a packet of three blank tapes and the experience of a man in the shop who looked pointedly at my glove and kissed his teeth loudly, in disgust. Fifteen minutes after that, the door buzzer goes and I let Jill in, full of bustle, fanning herself against the heat as she steps inside.

'Hi, Si,' she says, glowing with the late-afternoon heat. Her eyes flick about the studio. 'Hey, you've brought your stand back,' she says, smiling.

'My easel.'

'S'right. Does this mean we get to see the masterpiece, then?'

In answer I walk to the side of the room. In lieu of any mess to divert her eye is the triptych, sheeted and awaiting her verdict.

'Ah,' she exclaims, catching on. 'Wicked.'

I smile in reply, but feeling a tension which seems to radiate from my chest, tightens my shoulders. I notice the original *Moll* picture still taped to the wall and curse myself for not removing it before – a potential reference point when in fact I want my endeavour to be judged alone.

Her phone rings in her bag. 'Do you want to take that?' I ask, hoping the answer's yes.

'It can wait, babe,' she replies, the tone of a parent indulging a child. 'Let's see what you've got to show me first.'

So I do.

I wait until her phone has finished ringing then walk to the first part of the triptych, take a corner of the pillow case and spirit it away from the canvas. There it is, the first movement in the suite. Emily, the shadowy man, the papier mâché mound of gum adorning her breast.

Jill crosses her arms across her chest. She doesn't look at the painting, she looks at me, before – very deliberately – turning her attention to the work.

She makes noises. She studies. I stand behind her, letting her examine the first painting before walking to the second, and, with the flourish from my imaginings, remove the duvet cover.

More noises, and this time she walks closer to inspect the papier mâché. Even though I'd prepared a response should she ask after its significance, she doesn't. So I hide any disappointment and unveil the third, the undersheet falling to the floor at the given tug. Whore's drawers.

Again she looks at me.

Look at the *painting*, I think, working hard not to shout the words in her face.

But she looks at me.

And I'm staring ahead. Not at her, at the painting. With my expression, I'm saying, Look at the *painting*. *Admire* the painting. But her plastic surgery smile is directed at me, the way you might study a child, as though its deployment secures my complicity, my trust and friendship. Like a road sign: *Trustandfriendship Straight On*.

At last she looks towards the work and I feel myself unclench as she appears to scrutinise it for a moment, moving forward for a closer look, then walking along all three to study them in turn.

'It's a tripartite cosmetic rendering of a fantasised reality,' I try to say, but the words come out as, 'It's a cosmic triffid fantasy.' She doesn't notice and I attempt to control my breathing while her back is turned.

'Right,' she says, a strange smile playing across her lips. 'They're very . . . interesting, Si.'

'Interesting?'

'No, you know, *good*. They're really good.'

'Do you think?'

'Yeah, course. Properly good. Aren't you clever?' She turns

and straightens, her head tilted slightly to one side and smiling me that same *Trustandfriendship* smile.

'It's an *it*,' I say through my teeth.

'What's that?'

'It's an it, it's not a they. The whole is the parts. The parts are each an element together forming a whole. A singular whole. It's a triptych. Three parts of a singular whole.' Why has she not enquired about the subject of the painting? The chewing gum cones?

'Then, *it* is very good,' she says. 'What are you going to do with it now?'

'I've considered putting it on the market,' I lie.

'On the market?'

'But I'm not sure I could bear to part with it.'

'Yeah, well, you've obviously put a lot of work into it. How long did it take you?'

'A while.'

She looks around at the studio. Her eyes are scanning the room for signs of other artwork.

'I've devoted myself entirely to this,' I add.

'I can see. You've been a busy boy. Working nights?'

'Oh yes.'

She looks at me. 'And missing meals?'

That last question. Dropped as casually as a sweet wrapper, but with the weight of a tactical napalm strike.

'No,' I reply, sounding as if I'm being strangled.

'That's good,' she says. 'And taking your . . . Taking your vitamins?'

'Absolutely.'

'Then good,' she says. Her phone rings. She blinks. 'Shit,' she says, 'I'm going to take this one, all right? Tell you what, I'll make us a nice cup of tea while I'm at it, how's about that?'

I wave her towards the kitchen even as she's digging into her bag for her mobile. She hurries, her hand struggling to find it. She gives a little laugh. 'God, so much rubbish,' she says, moving away from me to angle her handbag into the light. I crane to see if I can spot her phone. Something she's holding prevents her searching effectively. A bottle of perfume, it looks like.

And then she's found the phone, answering it, still clutching the bottle of perfume in her other hand and moving towards the kitchen, which she enters, closing the door behind her.

THE DAY AFTER THAT

I wake up, and for a cruel fraction of a second – the time it takes me to sit upright and shield my eyes from the shaft of sunlight penetrating the curtains – I feel wonderful. But then it hits with a spiteful sting. The way only memories can. 'You've been beaten up by a bunch of teenagers,' says my regret. 'Touch your face and see if I'm wrong.' I obey, and feel an unfamiliar sensation, as though I've woken up wearing somebody else's face. With it comes a recollection of falling. Of a shout and the smell of money on my hands as they covered my face. My body curled up against trainers which swung vicious metronomic kicks at a body that surely couldn't be mine, but was.

Greil Sharkey, human drum. Roll up, ladies and gentlemen, to see the human drum and his young helpers perform—

'Venus In Furs' by The Velvet Underground.

'They probably like dance music,' jeers my regret.

I sink back to the bed, the memory an internal scream; an evil spirit against which I squeeze my eyes tight shut. So tight the tears can barely escape, but they do, and I feel them roll across the scorched terrain of my face, unaccustomed to the purity of rainfall.

Walking through to my lounge I feel the cowl-eyed menace of a killer, the hatred directed internally. And when I get there I square up to the mirror like a boxer, slowly raising my head to bid good morning to my reflection.

It's bad.

I look like a serving suggestion on a packet of pain. Above my eye the skin's been split and there's untended gunk there, like the stuff you scrape off the lid of a bottle of ketchup.

Everywhere else is mainly bruises and angry discolouration. A bruise around my mouth is a chocolate-bar-kid's smile, my ear is red and damaged, throbbing.

I feel for my ribs, which ache to match the sickening clamp on my testicles. At least I still have all my teeth, I think, inspecting the bruised backs of my hands. They shake slightly, no doubt a delayed reaction to the beating, the onset of shock. For that I need a stiff drink and fortunately I've failed to replace my vodka in the freezer, and fortunately there's still a taste or two left in it.

So I take a swig, to deal with the shock, and I feel the alcohol's consoling hug. Holding the bottle up to the light I check there's another splosh left, which I leave on the mantelpiece then walk over to my Mac and switch it on – that orchestral booting-up sound it makes familiar, like home. Comforting.

I check my watch and look for my mobile phone, which tells me I've missed one call and that one call was from—

Yes, of course it was. But there's no message, not this time. Nothing to deal with apart from an ominous shadow that passes across my mind. My Mac moans and groans as it boots up, like a grumbling old woman, but I wait for her to settle then check my emails, because there's always a hobo of hope employed by that action. Nothing apart from the usual deluge of junk telling me about club nights, record releases, some PR twat's leaving do, and spam with subjects like 'Every Teenage Girl Needs A Good Facial!' and 'Get A Bigger Dick In Three SHORT WEEKS!' So I dial Jenny, walking back to the mantelpiece and grabbing the bottle to my lips as I do so.

I catch sight of myself in the mirror: bruised face, vodka to my mouth, and phone to my ear. Me, Chandler and Hemingway, surfing deadlines. The tough guy in the mirror takes a slug of liquor, and the consoling hug has become a hearty slap on the back. Walking back to my Mac I double-click the Internet icon.

The phone rings out. There's no such thing as a short week, I muse.

The Internet boots up and I go to the Favourites drop-down menu and click on All Fur Coat, the phone still ringing out in my ear.

It answers. Click. Goes to voicemail. The All Fur Coat website loads one image at a time and I hover my mouse over where I know the webcam icon will appear.

'Hi, this is Jenny,' says her voicemail. 'I'm sorry I can't take your call right now, please leave a message and I'll get back to you just as soon as I can.'

I click the webcam icon and the Mac does her old woman groan in response. I find myself feeling remarkably mended thanks to Doctor Vodka and I almost leave Jenny a jaunty message as a result but stop myself just in time. Let's just think about this. Yesterday, you, Greil Sharkey, the Sharkster, left her sitting in a restaurant all alone without the courtesy of a phone call. Compounding the ungallantry of this act, you then failed to call and apologise. You have been a cad of the most unscrupulous kidney. She's therefore likely to be a very unhappy camper indeed, and quite rightly so. If you, Greil Sharkey, the Sharkster, were fucked about like that you'd go postal.

Shit, looks like poor old ma's going to have to be rushed to hospital again. What is it this time? Another heart attack. Touch and go. She's out of the woods now, but I spent most of yesterday by her bedside, just holding her hand and talking to her, trying to find the strength to say the things I always wanted to say. I mean, I would have called you, but you're not supposed to use mobiles in those places, are you. Do you forgive me? What can I do to make it up to you?

Sorted – I need to speak to her, person to person, massage her ego with some *huile de Sharkey*. I cut off her voicemail and try her at the office; voicemail again. Late for work, perhaps. Maybe in the toilet.

I click on 'New! Backstage At All Fur Coat.' And press the

phone off. My money's on her being on a tube late for work, or on the toilet at work, or on another line.

The page loads frustratingly slowly, strips of the picture appearing a bit at a time. I reach for my Marlboros and light one, let it hang Bogart-style from my bottom lip as I stand over the grumbling Mac, watching – wishing Smirnoff made paracetamol-flavoured vodka.

The picture loads and there is the hideaway of angels once again. 'The angels with all the angles,' I drawl. There are perhaps five girls in the room, and I look vainly for Heidi, knowing she won't be there, but looking anyway. And she's not, of course. But I let the screen refresh anyway, because the next image might show her entering the room – the cavalry arriving. I think of the bottle of vodka behind me, knowing there's one more swig there. A third drink I really shouldn't have because I can't get drunk again. I need to 'maintain', as George and I used to say back in our boozing days.

The screen refreshes. The Amazonian girl, the one called Fortune, is at the lockers. She's saying something to one of the other girls, all are watching her. She wears just a bra and panties.

If the next image shows Heidi coming in, I won't take a third swig.

It doesn't. Fortune is opening a locker. The girls are laughing at a joke I will never hear. Returning to the mantelpiece I polish off the vodka and avoid my eyes in the mirror.

Back again and the page refreshes. My hand hovers over clicking off the website, but the next image might show Heidi entering, so I leave it. I press redial on my phone, feeling the hot rush of alcohol to my head and watching the screen at the same time. On the inside of the locker that Fortune opens is an indistinct picture of someone who looks like Father Ted. She's taking something out of the locker, a folder, or a portfolio of some kind . . .

The phone answers. 'Hello?'

Here goes: 'Uh, hello? Is that Jenny?'

'Ah,' she says, 'the wanderer returns,' which is so *not* what I expected to hear from her. So not, that the Marlboro almost falls from my astonished mouth. My senses go to Def Con One. How come she's taken it so well?

'Yeah, the wanderer's back,' I say, wary but playing the part and hoping she'll show her hand. 'How are you?'

'I'm good, thanks. Better than yesterday, anyway. You got my message all right?'

'Yes, I did, thanks,' I lie, the penny dropping with a splash into my vodka pool. 'I was hoping we could reschedule. Today . . .'

The website refreshes and now the girls – all of them – are gathered around Fortune as she shows them something in the folder.

'Today's not good,' she replies. She doesn't say this because she's a booked-up industrious sort of gal, but because she has an arse that wants licking.

'How can I tempt you?' I felch. 'Beautiful day like this . . .'

What I should be saying is that I'm angry you were taping my interview in the first place, and the only reason I need your poxy client's interview is because if I don't get it, Graham will hold me to ransom, delay my tip-off or, worse, nix the Heidi interview and I'll end up with a barbecue manicure, courtesy of evil dwarf Cooper.

The page refreshes: silent but uproarious laugher at whatever it is Fortune is showing them. Still no sign of my pain relief.

'And I still get approval?' says Jenny, sing-song.

'No, not approval,' I reply through gritted teeth. 'You get to *see* the piece, that's all.'

'Yeah, yeah, that's what I meant. I still get to see it?'

'You do.'

'You've twisted my arm. We'll meet for lunch.'

'And you've got the tape?'

'Yes, in my bag. Oh, and Greil? You're paying.'

And I say yes, of course, I look forward to it. And as we

arrange to meet I watch the page refresh. See the dressing-room door open, half showing a figure that turns out not to be Heidi when the page next refreshes. Just another girl, Fortune beckoning her over to look in the folder . . .

By the time I've had a bath, taken a wet flannel to my battered suit and put it on, I'm beginning to wish, no longer that yesterday's botched heist had never occurred, but that it had been successful. A little neon sign in my head, one that says 'Need Coke', has just buzzed into life, flickered on once then gone off.

I splash on some aftershave, which makes me feel a bit more human, probably because it's got alcohol in it. Then I gobble three Nurofen, which should send a SWAT team to the high school massacre going off in my head, and I step out of the door and into the furnace outside, grateful for one thing at least – sunglasses to hide behind, to cry behind, to mask my bruised, bloodshot and half-open eyes behind. What's the betting I'm the geezer who keeps his glasses on in the tube, where there's no sun? I'll give you short odds on that one.

On the way, I call Graham, who says, 'Where's my bloody Vegas copy?'

'Uh, yeah,' I say, 'when did you need that for again?' knowing full well the answer is, Today.

'First thing this morning,' he growls.

'How about first thing *tomorrow* morning?' I say.

'How about lunchtime today?' he snarls.

'How about close of play today?' I plead.

'Five-thirty.'

'Six o'clock.'

'Quarter to.'

'You're on.'

'Not a second later, Greil,' he says. 'And I want a headline on it.' He says this because I usually key in 'headline to come' so he has to write it himself. I tell him I'll come up with a headline, a good one.

'And I want a stand-first,' says Graham. And he says this because I normally leave the little twenty-five-word sell for the feature blank as well, and he has to come up with that, too.

'Don't worry about Vegas,' I say. 'It'll be a beautiful thing. Now, listen, another reason I was calling. This splash.'

'Oh, now he knows the lingo it's a splash all of a sudden,' he says. 'If you mean this Benstead story, it doesn't take priority over Vegas.'

As I come up the road I see a police car at the entrance to a block of flats. Instantly feeling the parrot of paranoia on my shoulder, I do a mental stocktake: no drugs. As if in response the neon 'Need Coke' sign flashes on again.

'I know, I know,' I say. 'But it's in the pipeline. I'm getting the wheels in motion and all that . . .'

'What wheels are these. Wagon Wheels? Weren't you supposed to be speaking to your man or something?'

'My who?

A second police car comes cruising down the road. Its siren screeches a single 'here I am' whoop then falls silent. At the noise a policeman comes jogging from the doorway of a ground-floor flat and up to the second police car as it draws to the kerb. I'm about level to hear the policeman as he leans into the car window. 'You owe me a pint for this, mate,' he says to the driver. Not far away a group of kids have suspended their game of football to watch the police cars. More kids are drifting closer, the way kids do, hoping to give the pigs some lip.

'Your man, the slapper. Have you spoken to her yet?'

'Not yet,' I say. 'But look, I wanted to check on the advance situation.'

'What advance situation?'

'The situation with the advance.'

Having done Darth Vader, Graham now does Yoda, except with a Northern Irish accent. 'Confused we are,' he croaks.

'We were talking about an advance on the Benstead story.'

'Well, yeah, but you've got to speak to her first . . .'

Here's my plan. I waylay Heidi soon. As in, tonight-soon. I lie to her. I tell her the whole of Fleet Street's about to descend on her doorstep. 'You know that bit in *Notting Hill*, when the Welsh geezer goes out in his underpants? Like that. Except worse.' I tell her there's nothing she can do about it; her only chance is to come with me. Then, before she has a chance to check it out, *especially* before she has a chance to speak to lover-boy Benstead, I spirit her off to a hotel and get the interview sorted while simultaneously unleashing Graham's dogs of war on Benstead.

'I'm speaking to her really soon,' I say. 'So I was thinking, maybe I could get the advance, um, *today*?'

'Greil, you haven't got a story yet. How can we advance you money for a story that might not exist?'

Good point. 'Okay,' I say. 'What about when I've spoken to her? Tonight, say.'

'If she speaks, yeah. But Greil, let's not get carried away here, eh? I know you're all hot under the collar about this story, but Vegas feature first, all right? By the end of the day.'

I tell him yeah, yeah, of course, and ask for the number of the duty newsdesk just in case I can speak to Heidi tonight and need a hotel at short notice. He huffs and puffs and lectures me about my priorities but gives me the number anyway, and I tell him he's a sweetheart and end the call with a final rubberneck at the police activity behind me.

As I come up to the tube three derelicts on a bench are swigging from a bottle of fortified wine and serenading an uncomfortable-looking woman letting her dog poo into a hedge.

'*And we'll have fun, fun, fun till our daddy takes the T-bird away-hey-hey*,' they sing, harmonising, the bright sun their conductor.

I smile on my way past and they raise the bottle in a toast, beards twinkling and still singing as I reach the mouth of the tube station and go down: '*Fun, fun, fun, till our daddy takes the T-bird away-hey-hey . . .*'

CHAPTER EIGHTEEN

'Okay, Roger. All right. See you soon. Goodbye.'

Words spoken yesterday boom from the speakers in my studio. I walk to the stereo and press Stop, then Rewind, wait, then press Play again.

The tape begins a second time. From the speakers comes Jill's voice, talking on the phone; the clunk of my kitchen door closing behind her as she lets herself into the room; silence as she listens to the caller, filling the kettle as she does so. She is unaware of the cassette-corder, hidden in an empty box of Sultana Bran on the kitchen windowsill. At the sound of her voice the recorder has begun recording . . .

'Yeah, yeah,' says Jill's voice on the tape, agreeing with something she hears – click – turning the kettle on. Inside the kettle the flakes of scale disturbed by the sudden onrush of tap water will settle to the bottom and the filament will begin to heat up. She listens still; only the drumming of her fingers on my kitchen worktop prevents the VOR mechanism from deactivating.

'That's all good, mate,' she says after a moment. 'But listen, Roger, something else has cropped up. Yeah, I'm here now, actually . . .'

As she continues speaking, I go to the centre of the studio floor and stand near my easel, then move back to the stereo and make a minute adjustment to the balance control. Satisfied, finally, that the sound is equally distributed throughout the studio space, I go about my morning's business.

To the background of her betrayal I walk along the triptych, then fetch my rucksack and check the contents: journal, glove, freezer bags, tube maps. All suitably divided among the rucksack's pockets. I slice open the plastic of a fresh tape which I place into the cassette-corder and add this to the contents of my rucksack along with the microphone.

'Okay, Roger. All right. See you soon. Goodbye.'

On the stereo the conversation ends and I go to rewind it, pressing Play, returning to the centre of the studio to check the sound, then making a tiny adjustment to the balance control.

'But listen, Roger, something else has cropped up. Yeah, I'm here now, actually . . .'

I feel a kind of calm. A serenity I couldn't have expected given the circumstances – given what the tape is telling me. It appears I am running out of people to trust.

'Okay, Roger. All right. See you soon. Goodbye.'

I rewind it and switch off the stereo before shouldering my rucksack, leaving the studio on my way to the blonde bitch's flat.

*

Waking up I realise two things. One, I feel like a proper human being again, and two, every cloud has a silver lining.

I think this as I stand in front of the mirror and regard my stomach. Yesterday, my enemy. Today, my best mate. Tauter than it has been since school it slopes away from my chest and lies obediently flat in the shadow of my newly jutting hip bones. Cool. Overnight I've turned into Calista Flockhart. And as I stand admiring my new figure in the mirror, I remember that little squirmy worm of paranoia that almost had me ringing Holly yesterday. It *was* just paranoia, I decide. That's all it was.

I go to my rota – Della would be laughing at me right now. Two things today: F for facial, and it's time for a sunbed – 'K. on'. It's a time-consuming job being a fantasy. But then we're just like salesmen, got to make the merchandise look its best. A salesman doesn't need to go for waxes and sunbeds, or have pedicures and manicures, or make sure his armpits are never stubbly; he'll probably never shed a tear over a large spot that's appeared on his bottom overnight, and his customers don't get drunk and tell him he's too fat or too thin or his boobs aren't big enough or are too big. Otherwise, though, pretty much the same.

I take a bottle of Evian from the fridge and run the bath. An hour later I spread a deep-pore cleansing mask across my face – feeling like a kid finger-painting – apply some Eight-Hour Cream to my lips, pull on my dressing gown and go through to the bedroom. There I switch on the fan and set it to oscillate, and for a moment or so I stand and enjoy the breeze, which glides across me, feeling cool and weird on the face mask, flutters the curtain and glides back again.

Back and forth. There's a click as it reaches the end of its sweep and starts a new one, whirring, almost like the sound of the camera shutter on the Sea Doo shoot.

I flop on to the bed and dial Peter. The curtains flutter. Maybe a cloud passes across the sun because it goes slightly dark in the room for a moment.

'Hello, Peter,' I say, and, as the fan passes cool air over me, I ask him again about the webcam, because I don't want a reprisal of Fortuna and her menacing baby oil smell, and I'm thinking that Peter needs to keep me sweet – and keeping me sweet means keeping Fortuna out of my hair.

By the time we've finished speaking the mask is dry and I lie on the bed, reluctant to move from the fan's breeze. I move my face slightly beneath the mask, cracking it so when I look in the mirror I'll have an old lady face. What spurs me into action is a tiny spider I see from the corner of my eye, scuttling up behind the curtains, and I roll off the bed and go through to the bathroom to finish cleansing.

And then something strange happens.

It happens just after I've called Helen. After I've cleansed and moisturised and found Helen's number in my diary, called it up and got her voicemail. It went straight through, the way it does when someone's on another line, so I left my name and number and ended the call.

And I'm sitting on the sofa, half watching the TV, hoping Helen will ring straight back, when something catches my eye. It's the light suddenly changing, a momentary darkness in the room, and I look up at the lounge curtains and see a shadow.

'Flash does the hard work so you don't have to!' says the television. I squint at the window, my eyes adjusting as I begin to make out the shadow behind the curtains. A shape, I slowly realise, of a person standing at my window.

I go still, suddenly scared and trying not to think about the chewing gum through my letterbox yesterday. But on another level thinking, It's a trick of the light, a strange shadow thrown by the sun, a person walking their dog, a man cutting the grass – not somebody peering into my window.

And then I hear a shout from outside, a muffled chorus of raised voices followed by an almighty thump at the glass, as though something's been thrown at it.

In an instant the shape has gone, and I sit there for a long moment, startled, my hand at my throat. I sit. Dead, dead still, for at least the length of another advert, but nothing else happens. No more unusual noises or shadows, just the sound of the kids playing outside, and I relax. I actually hear my breath come out of me before I realise I've been holding it, and I go to the curtains to peek through.

There's nothing to see, and I realise the answer to the strange thump lies with the kids. They're playing football, traffic cones for goalposts, and one of them is walking back towards the group with a ball under his arm – obviously the ball that just thwacked into my window. I feel myself untense. Silly blonde. The thump was the sound of the wayward ball, that's all, and I lean in to inspect my window in case they've cracked it.

But what I see on the glass isn't a crack. It's not even the mark of a ball, the way you see sometimes when a ball's been whacked really hard at a window. Instead, there's an imprint of—

Definitely, yes. Because there's the chin, and the nose and forehead, and even a lip-shaped mark, all squished, sort of side-on, on to the glass. It's the definite imprint of a face. Someone's greasy sweat mark. Someone who pressed their face against my window.

I withdraw quickly, my heart hammering. I try to calm down, but the thought which overrides all others just says: *a face at my window*, and I shudder, despite the heat, and despite the fact that I can see the kids; and the boy carrying the ball drops it then miskicks it so badly that the others all start shouting at him, and they're obviously much more interested in swearing at each other than they are in staring through my window. It's like that thing, 'What's wrong with this picture?' Everything seems normal. The kids are playing, the sun is shining. I can hear traffic. Everything's just the way it should be.

Apart from the greasy sweat mark on my window.

I'm startled when the phone I'm holding rings, and I stare at it for a moment or so, gathering myself. 'Hello?' I say. Then hear the sound of the letterbox going and swivel in the direction of the sound, jumpy.

'Hello. Is that Heidi?' says a voice, which must be Helen. 'It's Helen. Just returning your call. I'm sorry you couldn't make the shoot.'

Her words don't sink in at first because I'm half-running from the lounge, trying to juggle the conversation with my sudden need to close my windows, check the door, thinking, A face at my window. *A prowler.* In the hallway I peer around the wall towards the front door, dreading what I'm going to see there. Not chewing gum. Please not chewing gum.

It's not chewing gum. It's a postcard from Ted Baker telling me about their sale. And then Helen's words sink in. *I'm sorry you couldn't make the shoot.*

'How do you mean?' I say, hoping she hasn't noticed the lengthy gap. 'How do you mean "couldn't make it"?'

I pop my head into the bathroom. The window's ajar so I close it one-handed, putting a comforting layer of frosted glass between me and the world.

'Um, I mean the Debutarts shoot for the mag,' replies Helen, maybe slightly irritated, like she's got better things to do. 'We were told you couldn't make it.'

I hurry through to the kitchen and cradle the phone between my head and shoulder so I can twiddle the venetian blind closed.

'Oh. When was it?' I say, feeling confused.

'It's tomorrow. We were told you had a virus and couldn't make it. Look, is there something we should know, Heidi?'

I'm struggling to think, and I go into the bedroom and sink morosely on to the bed, trying to recall my conversation with Sonia the other morning. 'I'm not sure,' I say. 'I mean, Sonia said you'd chosen another girl. I'm sure that's what she told me. I mean, I did have a . . . Well, I was ill, but I'm all right now. I would have been fine to make a shoot tomorrow. I'd love to do it.'

'I'm afraid it's a little too late now, hon. We've booked another of Sonia's girls.'

'Another of Sonia's girls?'

'Yes. Look, Heidi, if there's been some kind of breakdown in communication, then I'm sorry about that, but we were simply told you were ill, so we booked another girl.'

'But why would she lie to me? Why would she say you'd booked another girl?' That paranoia feeling's suddenly woken up again.

'We *did* book another girl, Heidi. *After* we were told you were ill. Listen, I'm sorry, darling, but I really must go. I suggest you have a word with Sonia to clarify things your end. It sounds to me as though there's been some kind of mix-up. Perhaps we could see you in the future, yes?'

'But I would have been fine . . .'

'I really must go.'

'Oh, okay. Thanks. Thank you.'

I sit on the bed, staring at the phone in my hand like it's the phone's fault. The fan whirrs and blows and I suddenly remember the window's open; turn to close it.

Which is when I see something hanging down from behind the curtains.

CHAPTER NINETEEN

'Hello, Greil,' says Jenny, standing politely from her pavement table as I approach. 'I ordered you a beer.'

'Hello, Jenny,' I say, taking it.

Quite frankly, I'd rather get my scrotum tattooed than have to endure this lunch, but I'm not being given the choice: I need the tape. All morning I've had my day's routine running like a sampled loop through my head. Like near the end of *GoodFellas*, when Ray Liotta has to get rid of the guns, make the coke pick-up, get the pasta sauce ready *and* return for the lucky hat, all to the tune of 'Layla' – the last part of the song that you never hear on the radio. That's how I've felt since sun-up: I've got to get the tape, get home, write the feature (all before six, no, a quarter to six) and somehow speak to Heidi (though God knows how) in order to get the advance to pay Cooper tomorrow. And the whole lucky hat in all this, the phlegm in my soup, is the fact that I have no fucking money.

So how the hell, I think, staring into Jenny's hungry maw, am I going to pay for this meal?

I may need to borrow Freak Boy's washing-up glove, I ponder, as Jenny and I do a bit of air-kissing and I take a seat and feel her eyes wander over the ploughed field of my face. 'What the hell happened to you?' she says. An old lady on the table next to us looks up from her Jilly Cooper and cracks crow's feet to study my face.

'Oh fuck,' I say, leaning forward and lowering my sunglasses for more evidence. 'I was mugged. A couple of blokes jumped me on the way home yesterday. Took me by surprise. One minute I've got the road to myself, the next thing I know I'm sprawled on the pavement and these two guys are giving me a kicking. It was all over so quickly I didn't have time to react. Took my wallet, cards and everything. Which means . . .'

But as I've been speaking, Jenny's tongue has poked satirically into her cheek. Her eyebrows have raised, and for a moment or so she reminds me of George, the way she used to look when I tried and failed to lay on the bullshit.

'Which means I'm temporarily embarrassed for cash,' I finish.

But my lie has withered in the heat of her disbelief, so it actually comes out as: '. . . I'm temporarily embarrassed *for cash*?'

Tongue-poke, raised eyebrows. Christ, why didn't she buy that?

'What? It's true . . .'

She shakes her head, bemused. 'God, trust a journalist. And what *really* happened?'

'I fell down the stairs at a tube station.'

'And then got in a fight with a brewery, by the smells of things.'

We're *outside*, for Christ's sake.

'I had a drink to drown my sorrows, yes.'

'And then slept in your suit?'

Jilly Cooper tuts.

'No, *actually*. I just haven't had time to go to the dry-cleaners.'

'Well, you look like you're suffering now.'

Now I remember the last time I met Jenny, her visit to the toilet. And feeling like a village fête organiser who crosses her fingers and prays for sunshine, I lean forward even closer. 'I am a bit, yes. Don't suppose you've got any coke, have you? I could do with a little pick-me-up.'

She looks around in semi-shock. 'God, Greil, cut to the chase, why don't you?'

'Sorry, you know, I'm just wilting a bit. I just thought, if . . .'

'I have, as a matter of fact.'

Wheel out the maypole, mine's a jar of home-made marma-lade. 'Really? You little lifesaver. Tell you, a wee dab of that would be just the ticket.'

'Before a meal?' she asks.

Cocaine's an appetite suppressant, just ask Kate Moss. So that's good: eat less, have less not to pay when the bill arrives. 'If you don't mind. I'm really beginning to spin out here.'

On the table beside her is a small bag, the kind that doubles as a mini rucksack. She tugs open the flap, reaches inside for her purse and fishes out the wrap. Next, under the pretext of 'taking my hand', she takes my hand and turns it over, the wrap dropping into my needy palm like sacrament.

The picture caption that accompanies my trip to the toilet says: '*Coke-a-hoop: Greil Sharkey celebrates finding some free charlie.*'

The toilet's a deep subterranean affair with a tiny cubicle, and even though heat rises it's baking hot and it's like being in the Black Hole of Calcutta, except with no one to speak to. Not that I let any of that stop me. The caption that accompanies my time in the cubicle says: '*Cistern overload: Greil hoovers up more of Jenny's coke than is strictly polite. That'll learn her, eh, readers?*'

'I ordered you another *cerveza*,' she says when I return.

'A what?'

'A *cerveza*. It's Spanish for beer,' and indeed there is a fresh bottle of beer weeping condensation on the table before me.

'Thank you,' I say, taking it and ignoring a nauseating your-secret's-safe-with-me smile she gives me. I smile back, glug on the beer and enjoy the view from the top of the cocaine rollercoaster.

'Feeling better?' she says slyly.

'Much, thanks.' And I take her hand, giving her back the coke with a quick check to see that Jilly Cooper's not watching us. 'Just what the doctor ordered.'

'Talking of which, have you decided what you want?'

'A salad, I think.'

She purses her lips, like 'I told you so'. I return with a shrug.

'Well,' she says, the wrap still in her hand. 'I can hardly sit here and listen to you gabber on, now, can I? If you can't beat them, join them.' And she stands from the table. 'Please excuse me,' she adds, pulling an even tinier bag from her tiny bag, 'I think I need to redo my lippy.' And with a knowing wink she moves off.

Booze and coke fizz inside me. I burp slightly and watch Jenny's backside retreat to the restaurant. Not a bad backside. I wonder what it would look like with me on top of it. From behind would be a good idea with my face looking the way it does. That way she wouldn't have to look at the mantelpiece while she was being poked by the fire.

No, that's not right. It should be: That way the mantelpiece wouldn't have to see the fire while it's being poked.

Neither is that. It's: That way the mantelpiece doesn't have to look at the poker while the poker pokes—

And then I catch sight of Jenny's bag sitting on the table.

I take a slug of beer, trying to ignore a very bad idea that's just sauntered through my head with its hands in its pockets. And now it's sort of hanging around with a 'who, me?' look on its face. The idea has suggested that although we know Jenny's taken a little bag to the toilet, she mentioned redoing her lippy, which means there's every likelihood the little bag she's taken is her make-up bag and not her purse, which is probably sitting in the rucksack thingy in front of me.

If I know women, that purse will have money in it, proper folding money. Men like to use their cards everywhere they go, because we tend not to need cash for the little things you can buy from Boots. Women, on the other hand, they always have cash, and by my reckoning Jenny's should be sitting in front of me.

Being as casual as I can, I reach over and grab Jenny's bag, one eye on the restaurant door, mentally calculating how long it takes a girl to find the toilet, get a cubicle, unwrap a gram of charlie, express silent fury that I took more than my fair share, have a line anyway, maybe go for a slash at the same time, redo her lippy, check she hasn't tucked her skirt in her knickers and return.

Next door Jilly Cooper looks over the top of her novel at me, but fuck her, I delve into the bag like it's the most natural thing, as though it's my bag to delve into. I feel Jilly's eyes boring into my guilty neck.

Shit. No purse.

I plop the bag back down. Perhaps Jenny has a make-up bag/purse combo she uses. Or maybe she just keeps her money in her make-up bag. On the other hand, she wasn't *really* going to redo her lippy. She said that for the benefit of the cameras, so to speak. That probably *was* her purse and inside it she'll have the cards and notes she needs for a successful coke sniff, being the cards-and-notes kind of girl, rather than the rolled-up-tube-ticket kind of guy that I was.

Shit. So dumb. So wrong. No financial salvation lies that way.

Or does it?

The idea, which is dressed in a manner not too dissimilar to Johnny Rotten in his Sex Pistols heyday, has just reminded me what I saw during my quick root through Jenny's bag.

The tape.

Now he wants me to take the tape and do a runner because that, he says, would be the road to financial salvation. Because then I could skip out on the meal *and* save myself precious time in this whole end-of-*GoodFellas* scenario. And who gives a fuck about Jenny anyway? She can take care of herself.

So with a glance at the restaurant door, and figuring I'll have to move quickly because she must be at the knicker-checking stage by now, I reach over and once more pluck Jenny's bag to my side.

It's all too much for Jilly Cooper. 'Young man,' she says. 'I'm sure it's none of my business, but are you sure you should be looking in the young lady's bag like that? A gentleman—'

'Of course I'm fucking sure,' I growl, rooting now for the tape. 'We're married. What's mine is hers. I mean – the other way around.'

'Um. I'm sorry, but are you sure you're married? Not that it's any of my business, but—'

'Of course we're married.' I glance up at the restaurant door. A drop of sweat plops from my forehead and into Jenny's bag. My fingers touch the tape.

'Are you sure?'

I stare in disbelief at Jilly Cooper, who looks slightly scared but Home Counties stoical. Christ, what is this? Jenny 'took my hand'. I 'took' hers. Of course we're married, how much more intimate do you want? On the other hand, it's the air kissing. The dumb, stupid mwah-mwah air kissing.

'Young man?'

I don't shout, 'Fuck you, you dried-up middle-class bitch,' but it takes an effort of will. Instead I palm the tape, drain the last of my lager and stand, moving out from the tables and down the street, heart banging away like Keith Moon on steroids.

'Young man?' she calls. But I don't respond. Tape safe, I'm walking off, half-running. The way we used to at school, when we were in a hurry and the teacher told us not to run.

CHAPTER TWENTY

Outside, the sun is a pulsing blob of egg yolk. The day is stretched out, lazy and breathless, like an obese man after dinner, and I'm sweating before I've taken a step. The heat seems to melt over me, the air like treacle, and my breath snags in my chest as I tread the pavement, dead and rotting in the sun. What drives me on now is Emily: the pledge I have made to protect her. From everyone, it seems. From everyone including Jill.

Before I reach the blonde bitch's flat I sit down on a wall and feel the cool embrace of a tree's shadow. I remain there some moments, calming myself after the exertion of the walk, waiting until my breathing has slowed, until the stench of dog urine becomes unbearable and I have to continue. Now at least I feel collected, able to focus on my destination and purpose more clearly.

Ahead of me is the estate, and I squint in the bouncing sun to see the blonde bitch's flat. In front of her building a group of youths are playing football on some grass, but probably too far away to bother with. Apart from them and the occasional passing car there is little sign of life; the heat has driven people indoors to the sanctuary of closed curtains, air conditioning and fans. From one of the blocks I hear the steady thump of bass, from an open window the tock-tock-applause sound of a tennis match in action, the commentator saying, 'That really is magnificent,' as I pass by and reach the blonde bitch's home, stealthy now.

Her flat is at the end of the block, like a semi-detached Lego brick with other Lego bricks piled on top of it. Little more than a box. Either side of her front door are two windows but I ignore them for the time being and make my way to the rear of the flat. Here I see two more windows and let the symmetry stroke my nerves a moment. Two windows at the front, two at the back. I peer into one now, looking between the slats of a blind to see a kitchen, and as I watch she passes by the doorway, wearing a dressing gown and with something white on her face, like a mask. She's unaware of me, but I duck down again, crabbing across to the second window, a curtain blowing slightly in a breeze created from within. The window open, I move as close as I dare and know immediately that I'm inches away from her. From inside is the sound of a bed creaking and I listen to her hum a song as I slowly, silently, undo the top flap of my rucksack and remove the cassette-corder.

I come as close to the window as I can, hardly daring to breathe. A quick glance behind to see that nobody is watching. I sharpen my ears, trying to establish whether or not she's alone. I saw no sign of Mr Benstead's car but that means nothing. I know from my previous vigil that no car is not a guarantee of his absence. His deceit is profound.

I take a fresh cassette from my bag and feed it into the cassette-corder, each tiny, inaudible sound like a banging gong to my straining ears. Still there is no other noise from the room apart from her movement, and I feel myself grimace with impending disappointment – until I hear her voice.

'Hello, Peter.' She's indistinct from behind the window, but it's unmistakably his name.

I hold my breath. He is there in the bed, I think. In my mind the image forms of a slumbering Mr Benstead awakened by his mistress, white-faced like a geisha, and I'm straining for his reply as I move closer. In one hand is the cassette-corder, and I gently press the Record button, holding it towards the window.

It's no good. Even with my limited experience of the machine, I know its microphone lacks the sensitivity needed to record her conversation – not from inside the bedroom, seemingly miles away, the noise for the day ready to drown out words I can barely hear myself.

But I remember my free gift at the well-known electrical retailer; how I stowed it in a pocket of my bag that I unbuckle now, retrieving the small box. It's a microphone lead. At one end is a socket that plugs into the hole marked 'mic' on the cassette-corder; at the other end is the microphone itself, foam-covered, like a tiny, black bug. Silently I unfurl the lead and plug it into the cassette-corder.

Now, I think. Now. In one hand I have the tape recorder, in my other is the microphone. Holding it like a wedding train I slowly feed it through her open window – with microsurgery care.

I listen, but there's only silence until I hear her voice for the second time, saying, 'Now, listen, have you done anything about this welcome?'

'Welcome'. Is that what she said? Her words are hijacked by the afternoon before they can reach my ears. Even so, it's now obvious what I'm hearing – a telephone call. I crane to see how far the microphone has descended, praying she can't see it, but wanting – no, *needing* – to pick up those parts of her conversation that are lost to me.

'I don't really care what they think,' I hear her say after a pause for his side. 'I just want the welcome removed.'

The microphone is only just over the lip of the windowsill, maybe not enough to pick her up. The lead is at full stretch so I move across to drop it further down. But I move too far. The curtains flutter and for the briefest second I see myself reflected in a mirror in her bedroom; pull back, breathing hard, sweat pouring from me now.

'I'll tell you what,' I hear, faintly, from the room, 'if that fucking drag queen has another go at me, you won't have to worry about the story coming out because there won't *be* any story to come out.'

To give the microphone more play I try holding the cassette-corder to the window at arm's length, but I look behind me and see a woman with shopping bags staring in my direction; see what she sees: a man facing a wall with one arm outstretched like half a scarecrow. I give it up. Baring my teeth against possible noise, I carefully place the machine on the windowsill and for the benefit of the nosy bag woman I turn around and adopt a nonchalant pose. I put innocent hands in my jeans pockets, pretend to be looking for something on the ground. She walks past. I meet her gaze and she looks away.

More mumblings from behind the window and again I hope my microphone will pick it up, the data I need. And then I hear the definite sound of a goodbye and reach for the cassette-corder on the windowsill, reel in the microphone and replace it in my rucksack. I adopt a crabbing walk to scuttle to the side, breathing heavily and wondering whether I will have recorded enough evidence to present to Emily. Moving back to the kitchen window I peer through again but there's no sign of the blonde bitch so I return to the front of the flat.

Here the footballers continue their game, too engrossed, too competitive, to worry about me. I move to one of the two windows, finding it frosted but ajar – a bathroom window. From inside I hear running water, the sound of her singing: 'Let me be your fantasy, woah.'

I dawdle there a moment or so. A man walking his dog passes on the pavement and I pretend to watch the kids like a distant spectator until he's gone. Now there is just me, the far off footballers, and her.

I move along to the second front-facing window, which might or might not be her lounge, and, braving the footballers' gaze, slide up to it, carefully angling my head to try and peer inside. I can see her – just. She sits on her sofa. I move more closely to the window, my nose almost touching the glass.

The two events are simultaneous.

The distant warning: 'Watch it!'

The ball striking the back of my head.

My face pounds into the window. I sprawl, hurt, to the ground.

For a second or so I lie stunned, hearing an echo of the ball's ring retreating to a spot behind my eyes, listening to the sound of laughter which might be coming from the group of footballers – might simply be a recollection conjured by old bruises. A trick of the mind has me lying, not on a sun-baked estate, but on a rain-soaked playing field, pitiless wind delivering derision to my ears. 'Wanker, Dog Shit!' I want to curl up, protect myself against the blows that fall in punishment for a spastic pass, a cruddy tackle, a crucial goal I could have prevented . . .

Self-preservation sends me scrambling to my feet, my face a smiling traitor to my feelings, holding up an I'm-okay hand, darting a look back to the window where the blonde bitch's curtain remains undisturbed.

But now the footballers, their hands on their knees, near breathless with laughter, are motioning for the ball back. The ball which rebounded from my head and landed agonisingly near by. Their arms are making great sweeping motions, 'Kick it back. Kick it back.'

I stare at the ball, paralysed by the sudden presence of my old inquisitor. It mocks me from its resting place. It dares me to pit hope against experience and pray that this kick will be different. That by sheer dumb luck the ball will land neatly back at the feet of its owners, who raise a hand in thanks and go back to their game. That this isn't the kick which flies off at a right angle to my foot, or dribbles fifty yards as my toe embeds itself into the earth, sending me lurching to the dirt once again.

And at my back the blonde bitch is surely moving to investigate the strange noise made by the collision of my soft face with her hard window . . .

The image propels me forward, as much to remove myself from her eyeline as to silence the footballers, calling with their hands cupped over their mouths – the customary impatience of competitors.

I drop my rucksack to the floor ('*What you got in yer bag?*

Vaseline?') and jog towards the ball, reaching for it. But as I do so my leading foot kicks it out of my grasp and I look like a man trying to catch a chicken, chasing after it again, nearly crying with relief as I gather it into my arms, wishing I could be deaf to their taunts.

Carrying the ball, I jog towards them, painfully aware of how I look, like I'm holding jelly, or a bomb, and their impatience grows.

'Kick it!' they bawl until I get close enough to chance that dumb-luck kick, the Dog Shit special.

'Keep your eye on the ball,' they used to shout in PE.

But I don't, of course. I drop the ball, ready myself, and my closed eyes are as squeezed as raisins when I eventually kick it.

I connect, at least. But my foot is hopelessly beneath the ball, and it loops up and off to my right, thankfully nearer them than me, but on the road anyway, bouncing and coming to rest beneath the wheel of a parked car.

As one their arms are outflung, their posture saying, 'What? I'm over here!', each of them an angry crucifix.

'Wanker!' they shout. One of them drops his head and begins the long jog to the ball.

'Girl!'

And again I'm raising a hand, a sorry hand. Raised in hope like the equal I'm so obviously not. A hand wearing a grubby yellow washing-up glove.

'Weirdo!' 'Fucking weirdo!'

I drop my head and turn away from their abuse to see the curtain of the blonde bitch's window fall back into place, and give thanks for that at least.

Gathering my rucksack, I scuttle away from my shame, back to the rear of the building where I slide down the blonde bitch's wall and sit for a moment or so, breathing hard and listening out for the sounds of the game to resume. They do – they will have forgotten me just as surely as I will remember them – and when they do I begin to recover myself and gradually become aware that I'm feet away from the blonde bitch again. She's on the bed – creak creak – and I can hear her voice. Another telephone call.

With my tongue poking from between my lips I reach for the cassette-corder and unfurl the microphone, standing with a near-giveaway crack of my knees to place it on the windowsill. Gently, I press Record; feed the microphone through the window and over the windowsill. Fishing, fishing to hear her.

'But I would have been fine,' she's saying. I ensure the cassette-corder is steady on the windowsill.

'Oh, okay. Thanks. Thank you,' she says from the other side, and I tiptoe to check that the microphone isn't visible beneath her curtains . . .

And see the microphone. See her hand. See it reach for the microphone and pull; react too late to prevent the cassette-corder domino-toppling from the windowsill and falling into her bedroom, my arms reaching for it in a sorry parody of me and a football.

Our eyes meet through the open window and she screams, even as I'm pulling open the window as far as it will go, my arm delving through to grab her hand which still holds the microphone.

She pulls back and I'm yanked forward, still gripping her hand, my shoulder filling the window. A vase of flowers crashes from her windowsill. I tug back and make headway but she's strong – screaming and strong – and shouting now, 'Get off! Get off!', as I'm trying to fit my second hand through the window.

I do. For a split second I grab some hair with the Marigold, but not enough to stop her frenzied yank away, which pulls me back into the window frame with a thud, and I lose my grip on her hair, painfully trapping my arm which I pull free, blonde strands of hair clinging to the sticky glove.

'Get off! Get off!' And I squeeze my eyes tight shut against her screaming, knowing only that I need my cassette-corder back, knowing the moment I let go of her hand I've lost it for good.

She has her feet on the bedroom wall now, pushing to pull. Pulling me as far through the window as I can fit, which isn't far at all. But I use the same trick on the outside wall and make myself more space. Pulling, pulling. Each of us straining. A bizarre tug of war through the bedroom window.

There's a shout behind me – 'Oi!' – that I pay no attention to.

'Get off!' she screams. 'Get off!' And still we pull and strain, and all I have is my grip on her wrist, and all I can concentrate on is that, because if I lose that I have nothing.

'I'm calling the police!' she screams. And of course she can, because she has a phone, but I'm deaf to that, closed to the threat, thinking only of my grip that I cannot lose, my entire arm in her bedroom as she uses all her muscle and all her bodyweight to pull.

From behind comes a second shout: 'Bernard. Kill!' that I take no notice of.

She pulls and I'm jammed into the window frame, my armpit painful on the windowsill, but it's a pain that I ignore, so focused am I on—

And then there's a pain I can't ignore. Not from my armpit, not even from the hand that grips the blonde bitch's wrist, but from my free arm, which I raise almost in disbelief to find a small dog hanging from it.

Somewhere from deep within my pain box I catch a glimpse of a man with colourful arms lumbering towards me. 'Don't you hurt my Bernard,' he bellows as I swing my arm to bash the little dog against the wall. The little dog yelps but somehow keeps its jaws clamped around my now bleeding arm. Vaguely I register the Marigold tearing.

'Let go!' we shout. Me to the dog; the blonde bitch to me.

Despite the pain it doesn't; despite the pain I don't.

'Let go!'

'Get off!'

'Don't you hurt my dog!'

I bash the little dog again and our pain thresholds must be similar, because just as it releases its hold on my arm, dropping, yelping, to the ground, my body makes the decision my mind will not: my grip relaxes. Not by much, but enough for her to finally pull free, and she rolls off the bed with a thump as the force of my pulling dumps me to the ground the other side, the dog swarming all over me, barking and trying to find fresh purchase on my writhing body. I'm on my feet in an instant, warm blood trickling down my arm and into the Marigold, barely noticing her window slamming shut, wanting only to get away from Bernard and his owner, now just yards away.

I take off, kicking at the little dog around my feet, leaving the scene behind, not looking back, but haring off with my rucksack, knowing that I've lost my cassette-corder and the evidence I needed for Emily's sake; knowing that I've failed; feeling, as I run, small reservoirs of blood begin to form in the fingertips of the Marigold.

CHAPTER TWENTY-ONE

By the time I get back to the tube station and make my way home, I'm beginning to feel weary again. The neon 'Need Coke' sign has gone off, only it's been replaced by one that says 'Need *More* Coke' (cocaine: the Panini sticker album of drugs. 'Want, want. Got. Want, want. Need') but the sign might as well say 'Need a Holiday on a Tropical Island' for all I can do about it. Black coffee's going to have to suffice – to help wake me up and see me through the writing of this feature; to take the edge off the alcohol. I hardly notice that the police have gone and the estate's back to normal as I walk home. I'm thinking instead about the wording of the feature, and whether I'll have time to knock it out before the deadline. It'll be tight – really tight – but I've had worse. What the hell, I'm always telling myself I work better under pressure anyway.

But there's pressure and there's pressure, and as I stick my key in the lock two men sidle up to me on either flank: Cooper's two cronies, RGB and Scart. It takes me a moment to click who they are; they've had a minor makeover. In place of baseball caps and Nike T-shirts, the pair of them now wear matching white short-sleeved shirts. They still wear the tracky bottoms, mind, but it's a step in the right direction. RGB is as big and pissed-off as ever, his Arsenal tattoo poking out from the sleeve of his smart white shirt; Scart continues to resemble the Before picture in an Oxy 10 commercial. 'Looks like someone got here before us,' says RGB, as the two of them stare with naked fascination at the bit of skin I'm currently passing off as a face.

I smile weakly, wondering whether my bruises make me look tougher, or just more vulnerable.

'Craig wants a word in the car,' says Scart with his hand on my front door. RGB's pointing behind us and I see a big black Mercedes parked over the road, but there's no sign of any car that might potentially belong to Cooper.

'Come on,' says Scart and we troop across the road, me feeling vaguely like I'm playing a part in a film, Scart and RGB staying close, making the most of their own roles. They open the back door of the Merc and motion me inside, where Cooper sits hugged by the beige leather interior, his little leggies about an inch from the floor.

'Awright, Greil,' he says. 'Like the wheels?' His tongue slithers around his bottom lip for a moment then retreats to his teeth.

'Yeah,' I say, getting in, frankly amazed at yet another evolutionary step for Cooper. Last I remember, his 'wheels' were a brown Vauxhall Chevette with a disabled sticker in the window that may or may not have been on the level. I check. There's no disabled sticker in the window of the Merc. Instead, RGB and Scart take their places obediently in the front and half-turn to face us in the back, their new smart-from-the-waist-up image seeming to promote them up the criminal sidekick ladder, from 'crony' to 'goon', maybe even to 'heavy'. The more I learn about Cooper, the more I think I'll end up shooting him before he can invade Poland.

'Greil, Greil, Orange Peel,' he sighs. 'Looks like you've been in the wars. What happened? You give somebody's band a bad review?'

'That's about the size of it, yeah.'

'What sort of band was it? Rhythm and Bruise?'

We all laugh.

His apparent levity worries me. The last time I heard Cooper make puns he was putting my hand up to Defrost, so I surreptitiously check for domestic appliances on the back seat. He must be reading my mind. 'We thought about bringing the waffle maker, Greil,' he says. 'Thought it would make an interesting pattern. You'd never be short of anywhere to play noughts and crosses, eh?'

We all laugh.

'Look, Craig,' I say, as our boyish guffaws die down. 'I know you said three days, and I know that you're probably thinking I've had three days . . .'

'Nice area this, isn't it?' says Cooper, cutting in. And the area's a shit-hole. Maybe an improvement on his native Plaistow, but still not the kind of place you'd call 'nice' unless you wanted to draw attention to something.

'I thought it would be useful to find out where you live,' he adds, with the same sinister look he used for tweaking the toaster's heating control. I get it, I think to myself. I get it.

'It's just that I've had to work on getting the cash, Craig,' I say quickly. 'In fact, mate, I've got something I'm working on this very minute. Soon as it's in the can, the money's mine, as in, yours. Paid in full.'

He slaps me.

I see red and lurch towards him but RGB's hand is in my chest, throwing me back against the door, and in an instant I'm calm again – more in shock than pain. Cooper remains unmoved on his side of the car and RGB's hand relaxes on my chest.

'Bet you've got a computer in the flat,' says Cooper. 'Probably worth a few bob.'

'You're not wrong,' I say, regaining my composure, 'but, Craig, please. I need that computer. Give me till tomorrow, then I can get you the money, in full. *In cash*. Come on, mate, it's only a grand,' and Christ knows why I add, 'for old time's sakes,' but I do, and I guess I deserve a second bitch-slap, which I get. This time he cracks me across a bruise so it really does hurt. I stare at him, one hand to my face.

'You've got until midday tomorrow,' he says. 'I want you at the house by then, with the money, or I'm going to be doing some cooking. You understand, Greil, Greil, Orange Peel?' For a second his face is pure hatred. Sitting there, all little and demonic in the back of the Merc, he looks like Chucky out of *Child's Play*. All that hatred, just for me.

'Yeah,' I say, quietly. 'I understand.'

'Good. Now get out. I don't want to stay in this shit-hole any longer than I have to.'

When I finally let myself into the flat, the first thing I do is find a drink to calm my rattled nerves. The vodka's finished. All I have is a bottle of foul green stuff two of George's PR twat friends brought back from holiday, 'as a joke'. Oh, how we laughed. But who's laughing now? Me. And even though I'd rather drink hemlock there's no hemlock available so I down enough foul green stuff to stop my hands shaking, cough, and ride the aftershock as my outraged taste buds are given scant consolation by the alcohol greedily absorbed by my bloodstream.

It occurs to me, on my sixth swig, that I've drunk too much of it, so I put the kettle on to make coffee, splash some tap water on to my face, then boot up the Mac. I nearly go for a quick look-see at All Fur Coat but decide against it. I'll see her tonight anyway, God willing. What I do is double-click on Microsoft Word and help myself to a blank page. On it I write:

//headline// Vegas

Not much of a headline, that: 'Vegas'. So I try to come up with a pun to add.

//headline// That lass, Vegas

Which is frankly rubbish. So instead I decide I'll think of something later, and go back to:

//headline// Vegas

Below that I write:

//stand-first//

And as the kettle clicks off in the kitchen, I lean back to consider my stand-first, and close my eyes to think harder . . .

Christ. I open my eyes with a cough, sitting up straight in my seat. Almost fell asleep there, I think. Not good. Not good at all. But then it dawns on me that the flat is dark, and in front of me my Mac has gone into screen saver mode, the mini-dancer jiving happily away. Feeling something like dread I activate the screen to see my word document which no longer says //headline// Vegas, then //stand-first//. Those two words of my 2000-word feature are gone. Now there is just a whole page of forward slashes, like a monochromatic optical illusion. One where, if you squint your eyes and relax, look *through* the picture rather than at it, an image will slowly appear. An image of a twat who's fallen asleep with his hand on the keyboard and typed, not just a single page of forward slashes, but 32 *pages* of forward slashes. And in the top right-hand corner of my screen, my trusty Mac tells me that it's 8.30 p.m.

I sit staring at the forward slashes. I sit for so long that the screen saver kicks back in, my happy lap dancer and her audience of one.

'That's torn it,' I tell her. She walks to the centre of the screen, turns and bends, placing a hand on her arse. 'That's really fucking torn it,' I add, rubbing my hangover-sore head. She blows a kiss at me and walks off the screen.

Somewhere in the deepest, darkest, untamed regions of my mind must lie a belief that this is all somehow *worth it*; that fucking up and feeling this way is a fair trade for all the fun stuff. Either that or the mind is an abusive parent to the body. Torturing it one moment, nurturing the next. I groan again. 'You fucking idiot.'

So I've missed my deadline. Sorry, Graham. I consider calling and leaving him a voicemail, but I reckon I can get the feature written overnight, and if he arrives to see it blinking from his email's in-box he might forgive me. In the meantime, I have to get to All Fur Coat, and to Heidi, who I need, now, more than ever.

*

'Hello? Hello?' The letterbox rattles impatiently. 'Hello?'

I creep to the hallway to see a shape at my door. The letterbox rattles again. 'I heard you screaming, love.' Whoever it is has a comforting Terry-sounding voice, but I say nothing, find that I'm unable to. My mouth is moving up and down, but no words will come out. When I put a hand to the wall to steady myself I feel it shake against the plaster.

'You don't have to open the door,' he calls. 'You don't have to open the door but I need to check you're all right, love. He's gone. The geezer's gone. My Bernard saw him off.' Then, 'Good dog, good dog, you killer,' to his dog.

Taking deep breaths, like someone trying to control a stammer, I manage at last to find my voice. 'Hello,' I call back, hearing my voice tremble, echoey in the hallway.

'For crying out loud, love, you tryin' to give me 'art attack or what? You okay, yeah?'

'Yes thank you, yes,' I reply. 'Are you sure he's gone?'

'Honest, he's gone. But the thing is, my dog – good dog, good Bernard – gave him a bit of a seeing-to. Well, not a seeing-to. A bit of a bite, like. This geezer was in a bad way when he went off, to tell the truth.'

'Yes?' I feel like I should be standing there clutching a bread knife. I feel like I've stepped out of my day and into someone else's. I pull my dressing gown tight around me.

'So, well, the last thing I want is some scumbag doing me for bodily harm, you know what I mean? So, thing is . . . I take it you've called the police, yeah?'

'Yes.'

'Right – good dog, you good boy – right, well I was wondering if you could just tell them you didn't see no one, you know what I mean? Or tell 'em it was a black geezer.'

I say nothing. But then – a delayed reaction or something, I don't know – I choose that moment to start crying, squeezing my eyes tight shut, trying to lock out the image of the man at my window. The rubber glove pulling at my hair.

'Not that I'm racist or nothing,' says the voice at the letterbox. 'A lot of my best mates are . . . Just to – you

241

know – just to throw 'em off the scent, like. Love? Are you all right in there, love?'

I put my hand to my mouth but a great, wracking sob escapes from behind it.

'Look, don't worry, you're going to be safe. I can hear the sirens now. I'm going to have to make tracks, but the police are on their way. You'll be in safe hands, all right?'

'Thank . . . Thank you,' I gasp, wanting to throw open the door and thank him properly, but not daring still, rooted to the spot in my hallway.

'It's this little one here we've got to thank – good dog, good little killer. Right, that's it. I'd best make myself scarce. Good luck, love.'

The letterbox clicks shut. I stay in the hallway, crying, hearing the siren as it approaches the estate then stops, a slamming of doors and hurried footsteps to my door before the letterbox rattles again.

'Police.'

I nearly throw myself at the policeman when I open the door. For a second or so he looks pleasantly taken aback then remembers who he is and holds up a finger. 'Is there anybody here?' he says. His posture says ready for action. He's already looking past me and into the flat, his hand at his waist. At his back stands another policeman, poised the same way. Both wearing bulletproof vests over short-sleeved shirts.

They relax when I say: 'I think he's gone. A dog chased him away,' still shamefully crying, but unable to stop.

'Right. Jim, do you want to have a quick look around the building, check it's secure. Miss, let's get you inside.' A look passes between the two. The second, Jim, raises his eyebrows slightly and gives his partner a look I recognise. It's the kind of look men give each other when they walk into the club.

'Perhaps we should call for back-up, just to be on the safe side,' he says, a nearly-smile sort of floating across his face.

'Er,' the first policeman looks at me, at my boobs. 'Yeah, Jim, good idea. Can I leave that to you?'

'There was a man,' I splutter suddenly, the words coming from God knows where, punctuated by sobs I wish I could stop. I want to be strong and not like a dumb blonde in distress, a bit of afternoon eye-candy, but I can't. 'There was a man at the window. He was at my bedroom window—'

The first policeman walks past me into the hallway, as big and out-of-place in the tiny flat as Peter. With his hand still at his waist, he says, 'Do you want to wait there a moment, miss? Let me just check the property's secure. It was the bedroom window, you say?'

He moves quickly around the flat. I hear him in the bedroom, opening the window and talking to Jim outside, their voices loud, then suddenly low. Then he comes back to the hall where I stand, still with tears streaming down my cheeks and my arms folded across my chest.

'Shall we go through to the lounge, miss?' He takes me by a shaking elbow. 'Get you sitting down, eh?'

Jim reappears, gets sent to make tea, then, at last, with a steaming mug in my hands, I tell my story. I tell them about the man at my window, and the struggle and the tape recorder. They fetch it from my bedroom, turning it over in their hands and passing it to one another. I tell them about the man with the dog who scared off the intruder. I say I never saw the man with the dog.

As I speak, gradually controlling my sobs, they listen and nod as if I'm telling them a story they've heard many times before. They ask me if I have jealous ex-boyfriends and I tell them no. Have I been receiving crank phone calls? None. What do I do for a living? I tell them, and a look passes between them. Have I ever given an, erm, 'client, no, sorry, not a client, a *customer*' my address or telephone number? No. Ever been followed home to my knowledge? No. They want to know if anything like this has happened before. I tell them no, and they exchange more glances. Knowing glances, saying, 'So this was an isolated incident?' as though that fact should comfort me.

'Have there ever been any signs of forced entry? Has anybody not sanctioned by you been in the flat?'

No, I tell them, but somebody posted chewing gum through my letterbox the other day.

Kids, probably, they say.

They ask if I had the curtains open and look doubtful when I tell them no. Do I often walk around in my bathrobe? Perhaps when other people could see in? And I reply no.

When my emotions spill out they try to console me. They say things like, 'You're safe now,' and 'It's no comfort, I know, miss, but these things are more common than you might think, and they almost never go any further than this. If I may say so, you're a very attractive young woman, and it's a sad fact of life that you'll occasionally be the subject of unwanted attention.'

'I was attacked,' I wail, needing them to take me seriously. I want to feel like they're on my side, not like I'm trying to tell them some tall, unfeasible story – about an alien living in my stomach, or the fact that all the teachers are werewolves.

'Attacked? Well, let's not be too hasty. From the sound of things he was trying to retrieve his tape recorder.'

'He was recording me,' I say imploringly.

'I'm afraid, miss, that offenders like this often – how can I put this – they like to take pictures and make recordings for, um, to, erm, you know, "relieve" themselves.'

'He probably can't afford the magazines,' adds Jim.

'He's dangerous,' I warn.

'He sounds *confused*, yes, but that's a very different thing. In cases like this a fright like he's had will probably be enough to keep him away for good. People like this man are cowards, miss. He may seem very scary to you now, but believe me, he was probably more terrified than you.' *I doubt that somehow*.

'He wore a single rubber glove,' I tell them, eyes wide with hopeful significance.

'Did he?' perks up Jim. 'Like a yellow washing-up glove?'

'Yes, yes! On one hand.'

'Aha!' he exclaims, like a mystery solved. 'It's just the fashion at the minute, miss. I've seen kids wearing it on the street.'

'It's not the fashion.'

'Honestly, you wouldn't believe what the kids wear these days.'

'Just the other day,' pipes up the other, 'we saw a group of schoolgirls, all wearing odd tights, every single one of them, like they'd all swapped.'

From outside comes the sound of a siren blast and Jim leaves the flat, returning moments later with another couple of officers who seem to do nothing but enter my lounge, look at me, exchange some words with their colleagues then leave. They adopt deadpan faces to jot down a description of the assailant, but I'm not fooled. Like I don't know what they want. Like I'm not a good-looking young woman, and it's a sad fact of life that I'll occasionally be the subject of unwanted attention.

They have a picture in their heads, and it is of a bumbling boy, sad and a bit confused. A bumbling pervy boy who saw a pretty young blonde in her dressing gown. Saw her through the curtains she'd unwisely left open (silly girl) and who decided to spy on her. Just a bumbling pervy boy (oh, and who also happens to be at the cutting edge of street fashion) who's probably learnt his lesson, and a poor hysterical blonde stunnah who's probably learnt hers. One more story to tell back in the canteen.

'But you didn't see his eyes,' I say, getting weary. My tears of shock have been replaced by tears of frustration, and are now gone altogether.

Then I become angry when I show them the face mark at my window.

'There! There!' I point out the mark.

But they make jokes about it, like, 'Um, maybe we should be on the lookout for a big-nosed window cleaner,' and,

'Can we dust for face, Jim? I'm not sure we can dust for face.'

We listen to the tape.

'Do you mind?' says the first policeman.

'If you think there might be anything on here you'd rather we know beforehand, now's the time,' smirks Jim.

'No,' I shake my head. 'Of course not. I want to hear.'

They rewind and place the tape machine on my coffee table. We listen to my half of my conversation with Peter. I keep a straight face and they watch me throughout. 'I talked to a friend,' I confirm, mentally fast-forwarding the tape, trying to remember what I said and cringing when I hear my voice on the tape saying, 'If that fucking drag queen has another go at me, you won't have to worry about the story coming out because there won't *be* any story to come out.'

They stop the tape.

'Do you want to tell us about this drag queen, miss.'

It's not really a drag queen, I say, it's Fortuna, a girl at work.

And she's not a drag queen, miss? they say. And I say no, she's not a drag queen, she just looks like a drag queen because, oh, she just does, and it wasn't Fortuna at my window, okay?

Next up is my talk with Helen, my voice plaintive and lost. I relive the confusion of the conversation before the unmistakeable sounds of the struggle begin. The tape had continued rolling throughout and everything is audible, especially my screams, which are so loud they have to adjust the volume on the machine. I stare at them accusingly, as if to say, Do you hear that? Do you hear how frightening that was for me? They look almost mollified until there's the sound of a faraway voice on the tape saying, 'Bernard! Kill!'

'Hey up, here comes the dog,' says Jim, and from then on they assume the look of two men listening to an exciting football match.

'Ooya bastard!' they chorus to the sound of Bernard jumping up at the intruder's arm and his accompanying yells.

'Ouch!' to Bernard's yelps.

'Gotcha!' as the intruder begins shouting at the dog.

Then it's over, just the sound of me calling the police. I reach across to stop the machine.

'I don't think you're taking this seriously enough,' I say. 'It's quite clear from listening to that tape that I have been the victim of an assault, and I think you're treating it like it's a big joke.'

Oh, they're good at looks these two. There's another exchange of glances, but this time I see guilt pass between them. Guilt, or more likely fear that I might make some kind of official complaint.

'Miss,' says the first. 'You're absolutely right, there's clear evidence here that an assault has taken place, and I must ask you, do you require medical attention for either physical wounds or shock?'

'No,' I say.

'That is our opinion also – you seem like a tough enough cookie. In that case, I must ask that you come down to the station sometime within the next two days to make a statement. Now, you've given us a very clear description of the attacker and we thank you very much for that. Do you have anything you'd like to add to that description?'

'No.'

'Right. Now, you've seen us pass that description on to our colleagues and we have units on the lookout for the suspect right now. If he's remained on the streets then we'll pick him up. In addition we'll alert hospitals in case someone should appear with a wound similar to the one you've described and matching the description you've given. Should we manage to apprehend this man, your testimony, plus the evidence on the tape we have here should be enough for a successful conviction, and I'd like to thank you for your assistance in this matter.'

'Look, you don't have to—'

'Just a moment, miss. If you'd allow me to finish. We've

also established that we don't think this man has any connection with yourself, so we have no clues as to the identity of the suspect. We've also established that this is the first occasion the suspect has tried to contact you, and that to the best of our knowledge, he has never tried to gain access to this property, which my colleague and I have ensured is secure.'

'Really, that's not what—'

'Now, I shall leave you my card, miss, and let me assure you I'll see to it that patrols in this area will be aware of what's happened here today. May I also recommend, in light of the incident, that you don't spend the evening alone tonight. Perhaps I might suggest you stay at a friend's. If you do stay here, you should keep all windows and doors locked and open the door only to persons known to you, and if you do see or hear anything suspicious, you must contact us immediately, either at the station – on the number on the card – or by dialling 999.'

He stands up and so does Jim, the pair of them putting on their caps. 'I'd like to assure you that we certainly *do* take matters like this very seriously, and if either me or my colleague's attitude has appeared to be at all light-hearted or jovial, then I must apologise. We were merely trying to put you at your ease following what must have been a very distressing experience and I can guarantee it was not at the expense of professionalism.'

They leave, all courteous and aggrieved, like two little boys told off for larking about, and when they're gone I spend a good five minutes trying to work out which experience was the worst. Either being attacked by a man with a tape recorder or being patronised by the two policemen. I know which one leaves the nastier taste.

They made it all sound so feasible, though. So much so that I begin to doubt it myself. The evil man with the staring eyes slowly becomes someone different. He morphs into the person they wanted me to see. A silly boy. A confused and immature youth. Scared and jumping at his own shadow. A kid frightened away by a tiny dog. Maybe they were right, I think, maybe I was just being blonde and hysterical.

I've almost convinced myself of all that. That my attacker wasn't evil, he was confused, and that he wasn't after me, he was just collecting material to masturbate over, and that after all he came off worse than I did, when I look in my handbag and realise that he has been in the flat after all, and that perhaps he's even been following me for days. Because in my bag is a bit of chewing gum, and folded around it is a travelcard. I can't say for certain, of course – they all look the same; but I check the date and time of issue, and I bet it's the travelcard I thought I'd lost two days ago.

I guess I start to lose it a bit then.

*

'Oh . . . Oh my God. Simon.'

I barge past Jill on my doorstep without saying a word, fiddling with my keys to gain access. For a second or so she stands there, startled, fluttering like a moth. But then she gathers her wits and moves to follow me and we struggle with the door as I try to keep her out but she wins, and I retreat to the middle of the studio, doubled over, breathless and dripping – dripping blood, sweat and tears.

'It's all gone wrong,' I manage.

'What's—What's gone wrong?' Jill's eyes bounce like a pinball: from my arm, bleeding, to my face, around the room and back again. She reaches out a trembling hand. 'What's gone wrong, Si? What happened to your arm? Why are you wearing that glove?'

I move away. 'It's hall, hall, hall, gone wu-rong,' I sob, hardly able to draw breath. Drip, drip, drip.

'Simon, please,' she says. 'Please try and hold it together. I don't know what's gone wrong, but you're bleeding all over the shop.' Her usual sardonic smile is absent. Concern is written across her face. She tries to control a nervous tremble in her voice, taking a step forward with one hand still outstretched, her perfume bottle now in the other. 'Please just try and relax, all right? Do you have a bandage in the house? We need to get that bandaged up and then we need to get you to a hospital. What is it? Is it a . . . bite?'

'It's hall, hall, hall, gone wu-rong,' I repeat, backing away, bent over, but with one drip-dripping arm held out to stop her coming nearer.

'Simon, Si, please. We need to get you to a hospital, mate.'

'Not going to the hospital,' I manage between racking breaths.

'Not *the* hospital. *A* hospital. Please don't worry about that. We just need to take care of your arm now.'

'It's hall, hall, hall, gone wu-rong,'

'I know, I know. Try and relax. You're overexciting yourself. Try and tell me what happened so I can take care of it for you.'

'Bitch. Dog.' I gasp.

'Bitch dog? A dog bit you!' She visibly relaxes at this news. Although we are some way apart our outstretched hands almost meet in the middle. 'Did a dog bite you?'

I nod an oxygen-starved yes.

'Okay, okay. Well done. Now why don't we take off the glove so I can look at your wound. We need to clean it up, do you understand? If a dog's bitten you we need to get that wound clean as quickly as possible. You'll need treatment.' She reaches to touch the tattered sleeve of the glove which I jerk away from her grasp, sending a spray of blood against the studio wall.

She flinches. Her eyes skitter and her voice regains its stammer, 'Okay, okay. We don't *have* to take off the glove. We don't *have* to do anything that's going to make you feel uncomfortable. Do you understand? Nobody is going to force you to do anything you don't want to do. I'm here to help you, is that clear?' I nod yes. She takes a deep breath. 'Okay. Now we've got that straight why don't you try and help me understand why you think the glove should stay on. What's with the glove, babe? Why is it so important to you?'

'Emily. Glove. Chewing gum,' I say, remembering with a distant horror that I haven't done my rounds.

She swallows. 'Who is Emily, Simon?'

I point to my right to where the triptych is but it's
broken
and ripped and
destroyed.

Holes and tears in each of the three parts, the upright frames pulled and snapped at right angles like shipwrecked masts; the painted canvases roiling, blood-drenched seas. Jill registers no surprise. She's seen it already. Did she?

Did she do it?

'Did you do that, Simon?' she says, eyes wide.

And through the fog of the pain in my arm I look for answers. I remember Jill being here. Her *trustandfriendship* smile so mendacious. I remember her phone call and the Voice Operated Recording facility of my cassette-corder which switched on, and the tape ('But listen, Roger, something else has cropped up. Yeah, I'm here now, actually . . .') which told me the truth about Jill and her part in the plot against Emily. 'Who is Emily, Simon?' Falsehoods spilling from her lips like filthy maggots now. This venal Jill, this Benstead courtesan. And yes, yes. That knowledge, that sudden, refulgent truth and the squirming, suppurating anger it brought to me. Yes, now I remember. I remember the triptych bending and snapping at my hands, the drumskin canvas breaking beneath my shoes. I remember now.

'You did it,' I say.

And she begins to back away.

CHAPTER TWENTY-TWO

'Fuckin' hell, Mr Sharkey, what happened to you?' says Karl, nudging the doorman next to him so he, too, can get a look at the elephant man who's just rolled up at the door. 'I am not an animal!' I want to shout at them.

It was George who introduced me to the wonders of Touche Eclat. For a man whose ideals had already been soaked in alcohol and incinerated beneath a sunbed, wearing a bit of blemish cover-up was hardly a radical next step. Even so, she was surprised how quickly I took to it. At first she applied it on me, keen to show how in Girl World they have a quick and easy reply to the stubborn spot shouting rudely on your forehead. What a revelation. I began to apply it myself – with her guidance, of course. Next I used it alone, without her supervision, and was duly scolded, reminded of the price and told not to use so much. Before I knew it I was being marched into Dickens & Jones and told to buy my own bloody make-up.

I don't use it in the heat – might as well try to creosote a waterfall. Nor, it turns out, is it particularly effective on more, shall we say, 'stubborn' blemishes, like the ones currently adorning the Sharkey boat race. It's night-time, so unless I want to fall down more stairs, sunglasses are not an option, and without the shades my cuts and bruises are horribly obvious: to the woman who turned and nearly objected to me gate-pushing at the tube; to the passengers who gave me a wide berth on the train; and to Karl and his mate, who clocked me the minute I sauntered up. I thought as much during my freshening-up routine, when I went tonto with the Touche Eclat, ignored the echo of George's voice saying, 'Don't use so much,' and looked in the mirror knowing I hadn't made a scrap of difference.

So: 'Fuckin' hell, Mr Sharkey, what happened to you?' And I'd hear one or two more variations on the same greeting during the night.

'Got attacked by a gang of kids,' I laugh, hiding in plain sight. As recommended by Sherlock Holmes.

'Don't tell me. I should see the state of them, right?' laughs Karl and I feel momentarily offended, as if Karl and his mate have forgotten the script, which calls for them to suddenly come over all serious before insinuating that they will 'take care' of the offenders for me.

'Well, they're a lot better off,' I reply, looking downcast, sowing seeds here. 'Took all my fucking money.'

'You sure it wasn't a gang of lap dancers?' says Karl, and he and his mate almost shit themselves laughing. Again, not quite the reaction I was looking for; again, I wanted 'take care' to feature somewhere in that reply.

A customer appears from the club on an errand for more money. 'Where's the cash machine, mate?' he says. Without looking Karl directs him to the Halifax two doors down, where a group of men in suits stand in a shuffling queue. I gaze enviously their way for a moment before moving to pass the two doormen who exchange a look, and with a sudden wave of shock I realise they're on the verge of refusing me entry.

'Oh, come on,' I say. 'It's just a few bruises. I'm still prettier than most of the blokes you get in here.'

'All right then, seeing as it's you,' says Karl, waving me through.

Shit. I hadn't even considered they might not let me in with my road-kill face. Thank God I am who I am. That thought is enough to give me a lift, at least for the two steps it takes me to reach the receptionist.

'Blimey, Mr Sharkey. What happened to you?' recoils Karen from behind her desk.

'Fell off the back of a lorry,' I reply, already bored with the question. 'You wouldn't let Terry know I'm on my way down, would you?'

I go downstairs, walk into the club, and not for the first time it occurs to me that if the most beautiful creature on the planet is the human female, then this is a wildlife park for the trousers. Still early by All Fur Coat standards, there are seemingly hundreds of women here, all cloaked in mankind's most revealing fabrics, like extras on the set of *Logan's Run*. As usual, I think 'mercenaries', but as usual I hardly care.

I hover for the expected arrival of Terry and look at the dancer on stage, most of the way through her act, on all fours and doing that stripper crawl: right knee, left hand; left knee, right hand. Then she rolls on to her back and arches herself so high her breasts are almost flat, but not so flat you'd mistake them for real, then slumps back down as the music finishes and I think, Crap DJ, for the umpteenth time as there's an almost interminable gap between the end of the track and calls for a big hand.

I scan the club for Heidi, sure my Charlton radar will pick her up almost immediately, but as I'm doing so, Terry arrives.

'Welcome to the land of hope, Mr Sharkey,' he grins, and I just have time to grasp the irony of what he's said before he sees the bruises on my face.

'Fuck me. What happened to you?' he says.

'Got mugged,' I say with my newly patented victim look.

'But I should see the state of them, right?' he laughs, but he's got an uncertain look in his eyes. My bruises make me not entirely welcome tonight, it seems. It's even clearer when he adds, 'Can I interest you in a seat at the bar?'

'That would be great. I'm not staying long. I just thought I'd pop in. Thought you could buy me that drink you promised me . . .'

'Did I promise you a drink?'

'Ha! You're not ducking out of it that easily, you old . . . bastard,' and I clap him heartily on the shoulder.

'If I said that, then that's what I said,' he replies and we move towards the bar, him gesturing at Paul the barman as I take my seat. 'But no trying to talk to Heidi though, eh?'

I look at him, remembering our conversation yesterday; Benstead suddenly vetoing my feature like that. I didn't know about the affair then, of course. Now it makes more sense. 'What's all this about not talking to Heidi, then?' I say. 'What's the big deal? I could get to speak to Madonna easier than this.'

'Orders,' says Terry. 'Mr B.'

'Yeah, but . . . Is it something to do with my review?'

And Terry's face is the picture of a man who's just been handed a great excuse. 'Yeah, mate, yeah. That review. Nasty business.'

But it's not my review, is it, Terry? I think. Because your – how-do-you-say – 'edict from on high' was issued before Benstead had the chance to see my review. No, it's not that. Benstead issued his edict because he doesn't want a journalist – any journalist, even a journalist who says he's doing a feature for a lads' mag – speaking to Heidi. And why not? Because your Mr B's worried about making the front pages of the papers. Which means I'm close, I think. I'm so close to you now.

'Come on,' I press Terry. 'Like, what if I was a regular punter?'

'But you're not, are you?'

'Okay, all right. Pretend I am. I'd like a dance with Heidi. You gonna say no to that?'

'I've got my orders, Mr Sharkey, and we don't want to break friends now, do we?' and as he says this he indicates the bruises on my face.

I discard an image of Terry giving me a shoeing and give up, take a seat, agreeing that no, we don't want to break friends and of course I won't try to talk to Heidi, my word is my bond, James Bond, and could I have a double vodka Martini, shaken, not stirred, please.

'Bloody hell,' says Paul the barman, after I've adjusted

my order to a more simple double vodka and tonic. 'What happened to you?'

'Cut myself shaving,' I reply with just the right measure of dark ambiguity, but I'm already turning my back to the bar and to the girl who's just ascended the stairs to the stage. I'm radar-scanning for Heidi. Scan, scan, scan, till my daddy takes the T-bird away, watching out for her, my eyes roaming the room: the girls, the tables full of laughing men, drink and money everywhere.

I don't belong here, I think, suddenly. Here, where we're ruled by the democracy of the suit. Where I'm surrounded by men who put one foot up on the baggage reclaim at airports, a hand on the head of the child at their feet, and wait for their family suitcase to arrive on the carousel; who smile at their wives as they skilfully squeeze the petrol pump to an even number. Sad, silly, deluded men buying into the gentrification of sleaze and paying with priapic hope; directed by doormen in dinner jackets to cash machine queues, production line workers at the money factory. It's not me, I think, forlornly – I co-wrote 'Gunpowder Plot', for Christ's sake.

I drink long and hard from my vodka and pray it'll slap away the blues, stop me turning tail and taking my hurt face home. But then I see her. An incandescent bleep on the radar, and she's walking in my direction, but with a man in tow. She's holding his hand and I feel a slap all right, something imperfectly balanced between jealously and hatred as I watch the two of them walk past me and to the back room where the private dances are held. His sheepish grin, a final look-back to friends who give a small cheer that I can't hear over the music – mouths open, thumbs up: '*G'wan, my son!*'

The back room. The beating heart of the club. Punters coming down the stairs get a glimpse inside and register the girls naked, each with their motionless audience of one. It's a club within a club, with its own velvet rope and door-man who unhooks it now, allowing Heidi and her customer through with a deferential nod of the head, positioned so he can see into the room and into the club, the keeper of rules.

I take another hit from the vodka to help wash the taste from my mouth. Make it last, I think. One vodka and tonic only. Make it last.

Watching the entrance to the back room like a hawk, I'm mentally calculating the length of a dance at the same time. I picture her dress, which she drops to the floor as her customer looks up from his seat and smiles (he hopes bashfully, but greedily really). Her hands run from her shoulders to the tops of her thighs and she looks down at herself, which invites him to do the same and he does so (he hopes sheepishly, but eagerly really). She turns and bends slightly and his eyes race up and down her body until she pivots around and off comes the bra. Her hands reach to the arms of his chair and she leans forward for presentation. Is that an impression of a nipple on his lips as her chest glides across his face? It's tempting to open his mouth and accept it, to flick out a tongue and taste her skin, but the bouncer sees all and the penalty is removal and humiliation so the tongue stays in and the hands remain at his sides. Not on her, or on his lap, but at his sides, because the rules state that a gentleman's hands stay by his sides.

And now she turns and wiggles again, because this is a dance after all. But when her back's turned his eyes betray her, and they roam the room to assess the level of service offered by the other girls, to gauge his value for money. Over the way he sees another dancer riding the lap of her customer, this one with the posture of a man making way on the tube, his hands fists by his sides, startled, almost, by the beautiful, naked creature writhing in his lap; hoping she won't leave a tell-tale smear on his Armani; hoping she will.

Then Heidi stops, because the meter's reached ten, and she smiles, 'Would you like another?', meaning another dance, another ten, and of course he agrees yes, because he hasn't seen what he came to see. So he digs deep in tented trousers and out comes another ten she puts he knows not where before continuing with her dance.

Two dances, I reckon. He's a two-dance-Tommy, and he'll drop his twenty quid with Heidi then return to his table with a thumbs-up for his mates. He'll leave the room with Heidi and I can be making my way to the toilet and waylay her. I look around for Terry, but see no sign. A girl and a customer come out of the back room, another girl, another customer go in. I take a sip of the vodka and stand up, maybe to pat my jacket for my fags, or maybe because I need to go to the toilet, all for the benefit of Bruno who stands over the way, and who nodded when Terry approached him earlier and whispered something I'd wager was along the lines of: 'Keep an eye on him.'

And then the doorman's hand is on the velvet rope – hook, unhook, all night – and Heidi and her customer emerge, her in front but no longer holding his hand. She says something to him and they both smile and he's fiddling with his jacket, doing it up even as I'm walking towards them, and catch Heidi's elbow.

'Heidi, isn't it?' I say, cheerfully.

There's something wrong with her. I might as well be shooting lightning from my fingertips the way she jumps when I touch her, and she turns, looking startled.

'Oh,' she says. 'Hello.'

For a second or so we simply stare at each other. Her eyes are saucer wide. She's spooked, no question, and I tear myself from her gaze to look at her customer – maybe I've missed something there? But he seems as happy as Larry, not a backward glance: a grin slashed across his face, complicated City trader handshakes as he reaches his table. Not quite the demeanour of someone who's just traumatised a lap dancer. So, what, then?

'It's okay,' I say instinctively. Suddenly, blissfully, paternal. 'It's okay. What's the matter? Are you all right?'

She seems to come to her senses, too. 'Sorry, yes. You gave me a shock.'

My hand goes to my face. 'The bruises.'

'What happened?'

'I was beaten up.'

'Oh,' she says. 'Sorry.'

'That's all right.'

Over her shoulder I see Bruno looking this way. Christ. He's on the move.

'Heidi,' I say quickly. Bruno near us now. 'Can we talk? Can we talk, later perhaps? After the club has closed?'

And she just has time to say yes before Bruno arrives: 'Bloody hell, Mr Sharkey,' he says, creating a sudden barrier between me and Heidi who takes herself back to the City trader table. 'What on earth happened to your *face*?'

Eyes meeting mine. 'I got hit by a cricket ball,' I reply, following the line of his arm which is leading the way back to my seat.

'Nasty, that,' says Bruno, escorting me back to the bar. 'You want to be careful, Mr Sharkey. You should be very careful.'

I sit. Look at him. 'Do you know *all* the lines in *Lock, Stock and Two Smoking Barrels*?' I say.

He stares back at me, in his eyes the dispassionate look of a cat with its prey. 'Perhaps you should just finish your *free* drink, then leave, Mr Sharkey. I expect we'll be more than happy to welcome you again when your face is healed, perhaps when you've bought some new clothes . . .' At this he flicks the collar of my Boateng then rubs his fingers together as if dirty. I sit rigid, fearful but rebellious somehow, a little of that old righteous anger returning. Fuck you, I think.

'Let's not break friends, Mr Sharkey,' he smiles, as though he's decided to play good cop *and* bad cop himself. Then he walks and whispers something to the barman – I'd lay money it's, 'No more drinks for that one over there.' Then he's walking away and I whisper 'Thatcherite' at his back as the song ends. The dumb DJ leaves a pause the size of London then says, 'Big hand, gentlemen, please, for the beautiful Aurora!'

Bruno resumes his post. He clasps his hands very deliberately in front of him and then he looks across the room at me. I don't want to get on his nerves any more than I already have, so I pick up my drink and pretend to glug, but really I just let the liquid caress my lips while I jerk my throat as though swallowing.

Now what do I do? Either I need a big fuck-off diversion or I need to camp out by the back door, wait for Heidi to appear and hope she hasn't got a chaperone, which, let's face it, she's bound to have. All I need is two seconds with her – enough time to ask her to call me, get her number, whatever. All I need is two seconds.

As I'm thinking about it she gets up from the City traders' table a second time and moves towards me, trailing a new recruit. Our eyes meet but I tear my gaze away. Bruno will be watching with Action Man eagle eyes, just waiting to swoop and pummel me to pork pie if I so much as look at her wrong. So I affect not to notice and my eyes travel upwards, looking instead for sprinklers because, hey, I've seen all those films too – the ones where the hero holds up his Zippo to the fire sensor and all hell breaks loose. I'm thinking that All Fur Coat must have sprinklers, and a trip to the toilet with my fag lighter might be enough to give me the diversion I need.

Just as I thought. I see the upturned flower of a sprinkler growing from the ceiling and finish my drink, making a play of collecting up my fags and lighter, looking over to Bruno who nods a goodbye at me. I doff an imaginary cap back, getting off my seat.

I never get as far as the toilets. I don't need to create my own diversion because God gives me one, right off the top of the pack. Or, at least, if it's not God, then it's the other fella. Because as I'm leaving All Fur Coat, about to make my way to the toilet, the music accompanying the stage act dies and the crap DJ leaves a huge pause, only the gap is filled, not by applause, but by the sound of someone screaming.

An agonised, terrified, high-pitched scream that comes from the back room.

And then all hell breaks loose.

THE LAST DAY

CHAPTER SIXTY THREE

CHAPTER TWENTY-THREE

He doesn't know I'm awake. At least I don't think so. As I watch he drinks from a miniature bottle of vodka or gin before disappearing into the bathroom. There's the sound of a tap running and he reappears, screwing the lid back on to the bottle, which he replaces in the mini-bar. He turns to me but I close my eyes before he sees me looking his way. I wish I knew what time it was, I think, doing an impression of a girl sleeping, but I don't want to move. I don't want him to know I'm awake yet.

Instead I screw my eyes shut and pretend to stir so I can make myself more comfortable. I try not to think about Paris and all that blood, and I do my best not to think about Fortuna in the dressing room.

But it's no good.

After the police left yesterday I sat listening to my home turning against me, like a best friend gone bad. The sounds that used to be comforting – the water heater gurgling, a tap dripping, people moving around upstairs – they all now belonged to the stranger with the glove.

He'd been in the flat before, left me a message to say so. I held it in my hand, the travelcard that I'd lost two days before; that he must have picked up and – what? – followed me, perhaps? Found out where I lived, certainly. Found out and broken into my flat to open my purse and return the card.

His message drowned out any reassurances the police had made, and when I looked out of my window there was no sign of extra patrols in the street outside, no indication that the manhunt they promised was under way. What did

I expect, roadblocks and machine guns? Either way, the sun burned regardless of my distress and the footballers carried on footballing. So I dressed, collected my stuff and left, locking the door and hurrying to the tube, checking behind me all the way. All the way from home to the tube, then all the way from the tube to All Fur Coat, where at last I began to feel safe once again.

'Where's Terry?' I said to Sandy, the house mum who was sitting behind Terry's desk when I knocked and entered.

'He's going to be a bit late, love,' she said, pulling out the cash box. 'You want to pay, yeah?' She regarded me with open distaste. I heard she used to be a stripper herself, and looking at her made me remember why I want to leave. In any other condition I might have rationally believed she treated all the girls with equal contempt, with the kind of mild disgust you think of a smelly kitchen bin. Today, though, it felt like she had a special hatred held in reserve just for me.

'Yes, but I also need to speak to Terry,' I said.

'You can speak to me. I'm the house mum,' she said, and with no other choice I decided to chance my arm, find out if there was a golden nugget of goodness in that jealous heart of hers.

'I think I'm being followed,' I said. 'Maybe a punter. He's been in my flat. The police came.'

She brightened up a bit. 'Oh, really? How awful for you,' she said. 'What happened, dear?'

'Perhaps I should speak to Terry,' I said, cowering in the gap between what she said and the way she said it. 'Perhaps I should wait and speak to him later.'

'What happened, dear?' she repeated, and despite myself, I told her.

'Chewing gum, eh?' she said. 'How *awful* for you. Chewing gum. And a *tape recorder*. No wonder you're terrified. Still, eh, whoever said there was no such thing as a satisfied customer.' She chuckled across the desk at me. Her mouth became a sneer. Age had turned her lips into a series of red-painted crevices.

I looked at her. 'Are you going to speak to Terry about it?' I said.

'As soon as it's convenient, yes. But, um, I'm not sure there's a lot we can do about it. After all, it's taken place outside club premises, and, you know, we do have strict instructions about giving out phone numbers and addresses—'

'I haven't given out my—'

She stopped me. 'And, you know, we do tend to discourage the girls using their real names as, I believe, you do, Heidi. It's all well and good making things easy for all those talent scouts you want to attract—'

'I don't—'

'But the other side of the coin is that you also make things easy for all those "talent scouts" you don't want to attract.' She curled her fingers into clever-clever speech marks and chuckled again, the laughing cow all of a sudden. Her spite said I was getting what I deserved, that unwanted attention is all part of the package.

'What do you mean by – "talent scouts"?' I said.

'Well, isn't that why you use your real name, Heidi? So you can be discovered, isn't it? You think you're too good for the likes of us.'

How does she know?

'I tell you what, Heidi,' she added after a pause. 'I'll have a word with Terry, okay? But in the meantime, why don't you see if you can stay with one of the girls, one of your "friends" at the club. I'm sure you'll find a whole dressing room full of volunteers.' Her crevices stretched into a sneer once again.

I wanted to kill her. Instead I settled for throwing the money across the table, but she chose not to notice, and with a final filthy look I left and headed for the dressing room. If the laughing cow had been issuing tidy-up orders lately they'd all been ignored – the place looked like a wardrobe had exploded. I noticed a gown hung strategically over the webcam and breathed a mental sigh of relief that the girls had found some kind of solution, however temporary. But elsewhere it was average All Fur Coatness, and for a moment or so I felt comforted by the room's weird, half-clothed normality: hip hop, cigarette smoke, girls, the smell of Impulse and a sticky mist of hairspray. I walked in on two girls loudly discussing what to do with tampon strings – one saying cut, the other saying tuck. Another girl came barging in behind me, breathlessly shouting to no one in particular: 'There's a guy out there, and he's either famous, or just really, really good-looking. Oh, hi, Heidi.'

'Hi,' I replied, turning to my locker and throwing a glance to where Fortuna sat, topless, just in case we'd all forgotten what big boobs she has, using a lip pencil to carefully outline her lips.

'Who's with him? Who's with the good-looking guy?'

'China.'

'China. That witch, man. She called me a player-hater.'

Fortuna coloured in her lips with – I thought – Rimmel. Something cheap, anyway. Then she picked up another pencil and began outlining again. She sat impervious to the noise and activity around her, radiating an air of command.

'Oh, Heidi,' she said, without looking away from the mirror, still pencilling. The conversation in the room died slightly, the way an audience hushes just before the main act comes on. The main act being me.

'Yeah?' I said, not looking at her, thinking, You took your name off a cigarette packet, you sad cow. Anything, really. Anything to try and diminish this hold she seemed to have over me and the rest of the room. Like a school bully.

'You'll never guess what?'

'What?'

'I've signed up to a model agency.' She said it with a mouthful of snide.

There was a barely disguised snigger in the room. I felt all eyes on me as I opened my locker door to see my portfolio inside. When I last left it, it was closed and on the top shelf, above the hanger. Now it was on the bottom one, open at a shot of me in a bikini. Of course, I thought: Sandy and her crack about talent scouts.

I reached for the portfolio, closed it and replaced it on the top shelf. The same snigger bubbled maliciously in the quiet room. 'Really?' I said.

'Yes. Sonia Jewel's agency.'

The room held its breath.

'Great,' I said.

'Yes, isn't it?' She dropped the lipliner and picked up a different lipstick. 'It was nice of Peter to put in a good word for me, wasn't it?' she said.

'Yes.'

'Because he and Sonia go way back. Way, *way* back. Peter's done Sonia a few favours in the past. She certainly owes him. But you'd know all about that, of course.'

But I wasn't listening. Fortuna had faded into the background. The roomful of silicone sniggers and spite melted away. Instead I was thinking – thinking about what she'd said: *'She certainly owes him.'* And that same little worm of paranoia writhed as it absorbed the information which had hit me like a thump, with more hurt than anything Fortuna could have said.

But she'd finished with me anyway. Her sport over, she'd said enough, and I changed in a kind of daze, aware of the silent looks passed around the room. A single enquiry, Was I okay? A glance back at Fortuna who sat making up and unconcerned.

Bless the job for one thing, at least. You can't do it with your mind on other things, whether you're worried about stalkers wearing gloves or the sudden feeling you're not the person in control of your life. With each customer you have to transform yourself into the centre of their world and you're competing against a club full of distractions: the girls dancing on stage, the other girls at tables, every one a beauty, maybe even more their type than you are.

'Would you like to buy me a drink?' I said to a young man who sat with a group of three friends, each of his colleagues already deep in conversation with a girl.

'Of course,' and he jumped up, about to go to the bar before I stopped him, signalling for a waitress instead.

'What's your name?' I said, giving him The Look, which goes from face to suit then back again, ending with a tiny smile, a fractional raising of the eyebrows. The Look pretends I've got the best catch in the club. Every dancer here has the best catch in the club.

He lapped it up. We talked. I learned he was a stockbroker and that he was engaged, and that, yes, his fiancée knew he was here, so we spoke about her for a while, and I wondered whether he'd tell her about me, tonight when he arrived home, drunk and tired, or in the morning when she'd ask probing questions disguised as gentle queries. Then he'd betray me. He'd lie to the memory of his eyes which roamed up and down my body, and his face which told me I'd won this particular competition. That with the right words and the right kind of eye contact, I'd taken her place for the evening. Had I touched a hand to his knee and asked him to leave her for me, he would have considered it for longer than he'd ever admit, even to himself.

So I gave it five minutes of honey-coated chat before I asked him if he'd like a dance and of course he said yes, throwing looks at his friends as I stood and took his hand, in charge now. In control here at least. Somewhere the Heidi part of me was having coffee and a bun, but in her place was the stripper, in control and barking commands like the captain of a netball team.

Moving towards the back room with my nervous charge in tow, I glimpsed the journalist. He sat at the bar, his back to the stage, and even in the half-dark I sensed him watching me. Heidi wondered about his magazine feature, mysteriously cancelled. Like the Debutarts job, mysteriously given to somebody else. The stripper wondered if he'd be good for a dance or two.

And then it happened.

No, not yet. Not on that dance. That one passed without incident. Well, almost. I left the room with the customer ahead of me when I felt a touch at my elbow that made me jump. Made the Heidi in me jump anyway, choking on her bun at the memory of the boy with the glove.

'Heidi, isn't it?' he said. It was the journalist. My second shock came at the state of his face. I hadn't noticed before but it was covered in bruises that he'd tried to cover up with foundation. Even in the dim light of the club I could tell he'd made a bad job of it. I almost told him: 'A rule of thumb: less is more. And use natural light wherever possible,' but instead I tried to concentrate on hiding my surprise.

'It's okay,' he said, his voice kind. 'It's okay. What's the matter? Are you all right?' He touched a hand to his face. 'The bruises.'

'What happened?'

'I was beaten up.'

'Oh,' I said. 'Sorry.'

'That's all right.'

He looked over my shoulder. 'Heidi,' he said, suddenly urgent. 'Can we talk? Can we talk later perhaps? After the club has closed?'

'Yes,' I said, and then Bruno was among us and my customer was taking his seat, 'please excuse me', and I went back to the table, joining the group and talking to a second stockbroker, making myself the focus of his world instead.

And that's when it happened.

I led the second stockbroker to the room, just behind Paris, who had a fat man with her, so drunk that Lee gave him a cautious look as he opened the rope and let us through. They took a place next to us, my stockbroker sitting to the left of the drunk fat man who slurred 'make it good and I'll make it worth your while' to Paris. The worst kind of customer, not

269

at all overawed, thinking his money put him on the pedestal, not the other way around.

She was hurrying, I could tell. My customer's eyes were being unfaithful to me, finding more attractive purchase with Paris, whose dress was already off while I was hardly into my act. 'Come on, babe,' the fat man said, and I saw sweating, pudgy hands reach out to her, naked now. She wiggled skilfully out of his grasp. I cast a glance at the doorway where Lee was looking out into the club.

'Come on, babe, this is supposed to be a fuckin' lap dance, innit?'

From the corner of my eye I saw Paris smiling at the fat man, trying to regain the upper hand. She turned to show her back and hide the discomfort I could sense pouring off her, her hands piling her hair up, then bending to show her bum. I locked eyes with my own customer and teased a shoulder strap of my dress down, trying to pull him back into my orbit.

I felt the commotion before I saw it. Sensed that the fat man's drunken frustration had pushed him over the edge, and he reached out to Paris as she turned back to face him, pulling her to his lap, bucking his hips into her, slurring 'that's better' at the same time. Paris tried to go with it. She tried to retrieve the situation by giving him a consolation grind but his hands had gone to her waist and he bucked, rubbing himself into her, pushing his face into her breasts even as she tried to pull free, her eyes finding mine, then searching for Lee at the doorway, Lee still unaware of her distress.

'Lee,' I called. My customer frowned.

She had her hands on his shoulders now, trying to lever herself away from his grip, wriggling at the same time, growing more desperate. His hips bucked.

'Lee!'

And I don't know how it happened. Something on his belt perhaps. Something down there that caught and linked and gripped and didn't let go, even as Paris with one final heave managed to pull herself from his lap and fell with a thump to the floor, the unmistakeable flowering of blood against her off-white bikini line.

'Oh God.' The fat man looked down at his lap and his face seemed to deflate at what he saw there. My eyes followed his and then went to Paris, and I understood what had happened.

It took her maybe half a second longer. Half a second for the pain and realisation to sink in. A half-second before the music died and the DJ, bless him, left the usual gap for applause, which never, ever came. And somewhere within that silence Paris knew her clitoris ring had been torn from her, and her body comprehended its agony, and she screamed.

At first the scream was high and loud like a horror film, and it tore open the silence. But then the scream dipped to become a howl. A long, low howl, like an old man's theatrical yawn; like an animal scissored by a metal trap. Her hands were at her crotch, covering herself the way footballers do, except blood was bubbling from between her fingers, and the colour seemed to leave her body as she grew pale before my eyes. She looked like the first woman having the first ever period – the full fury of nature tearing through her body.

And that moan . . .

Lee was wading into the room just as another girl was suddenly sick and bolting for the door. My customer stood with his own hand over his mouth, turning for the exit. The music began again. Lee's fist in slow motion slammed into the side of the fat man's head, who staggered before throwing a punch back, shouting in protest, the two fighting while Paris writhed below them and Bruno stormed into the room to join the battle.

I turned and fled, passing Terry and Karl who poured in, elbowing my way past customers suddenly aware of the commotion, craning to see into the back room. From inside I heard Terry shouting and Paris's agonised yowl. Sandy almost pushed me out of the way as she ran past, then darted back out, running to the office as Terry barked at her to get an ambulance. At the tables nearest the back room people stopped and stood. Further back others carried on as normal. And I ran straight into the journalist who all but ignored the horror behind us, looking concerned, not for the panic, but for me, the foundation on his face almost cute now, his hands reaching to me.

'Heidi?' he said.

CHAPTER TWENTY-FOUR

'Hello. You've reached the voicemail of Graham Stevenson. I'm either on the phone or away from my desk, so please leave a message after the tone and I'll get straight back to you.'

I check my watch: it's eight a.m. It's a bit rich to expect Graham to be at his desk, but he is the editor of a Sunday supplement, and the world of seasonal recipes, celebrity columnists and little graphs telling you what's 'in' and what's 'out' stops for no man, so you never know. I check my watch again. It's still eight a.m., and I figure I've got an hour to kill before Graham gets deskside. An hour that I'll no doubt spend in silent contemplation of the gorgeous creature in my hotel bed . . .

She almost ran straight into me. 'Heidi?' I said, as she came hurtling from the back room. Stopping in front of me she seemed to sway on her feet, like a game of Jenga about to end – pale as death beneath her navy cling-film dress. I went to steady her and my hands fitted around her waist, as though designed for that very purpose. Her knight in smelly Boateng.

Judging by the sudden surge of muscle to the back room, I assumed a punter had got drunk and out of hand. Didn't matter to me. All I knew was that I had the diversion I wanted, no having to hold up my lighter to detectors and no bouncers around to stop me speaking to Heidi. My head was a furious rehearsal room for a gentle, persuasive speech of I-have-a-dream importance. Good enough to talk her into coming with me; good enough, eventually, to talk her into giving up the details of her sordid night-time romps with Peter Benstead.

But then she pulled away from me and our twin trance was ended. I felt a tiny snag of my fingernail on her dress as she swished off, walk-running in the direction of the dressing room.

I shot a look towards the back room where it looked like happy hour at a bouncers' convention, then set off after her: 'Heidi, wait, we need to talk.'

She didn't slow down. I touched a hand to her arm but she pulled it away. 'Please just leave me alone,' she said.

She slalomed her way through tables, chairs, men and dancers, me at her heels. The dressing-room door loomed. 'It's about a story,' I said from behind her. She ground to a halt, swishing around to face me.

'Your magazine article?' she said, her eyes sharp. 'I was told it was cancelled. But don't tell me. That was nothing to do with you, was it?'

Puzzled, I said, 'No. No, it wasn't. What do you mean?'

It was barely more than a whisper: 'Bastard.' She started off again.

I caught up. 'Bastard? Why?'

She stopped. 'Not you. Him.'

'Who?'

'Peter.' She started off again.

I caught up. Perplexed, I said, 'It's Peter I need to speak to you about.'

'What about him?' Still going.

'Heidi, look, please. Please just stop and let me explain. There's going to be a story. Not the magazine story. Another story. About you and Peter.'

She stopped. 'No,' she said. 'No. Not yet. I haven't . . .' She tailed off.

Fucking confused now, I said, 'Yes. Now. I'm sorry, but this story's about to break. I'm really sorry. You need to come with me. I'm here to— I'm here to protect you.'

And when she looked at me next, her eyes were gleaming wet with tears and what I could have sworn was defeat. A look that shot yearning holes through my heart. 'Okay, then,' she said. Her eyes dropped away from mine. 'Okay.'

Within minutes we were meeting at the back entrance of the building where I was giving her my jacket and watching the club, half expecting to see Terry and a posse of doormen appear, carrying flaming torches and a noose.

'Where do you live?' I asked her, looking into the road for a taxi, furiously thinking, Objective one: to get the girl to come with me. Achieved. Objective two: to get her to talk about the affair. Still in the balance.

Once again, life lifted up a cheek and farted on my plans, but in the nicest possible way, as Heidi's face fell – the pain of a sudden memory – and she said, 'I can't. I can't go home.'

I stared at her for a moment or so. 'What? You want to go for a drink?' I said carefully, hardly daring to believe my ears. 'I know places we could . . .'

'I just can't go home,' she said, pulling my jacket around her shoulders and stamping her feet slightly. 'It's not safe for me there. You'll have to take me somewhere else.'

And with no further encouragement I was flagging down a taxi, talking to a duty news editor at the same time and repeating the hotel destination to a driver who looked straight over my shoulder at Heidi behind me, clutching a sports bag and wearing her evening gown and my jacket, staring off into space with the silent misery of a public schoolboy on his first day at school.

We sat hearing the diesel rattle of the cab's engine and watching the city slide by the windows. I was tucked into my corner of the taxi, as deliberately unthreatening as I could be; silent but trying to think of something to say that wouldn't break the spell. I half expected her to come to her senses and go, 'Just a minute. Who are you? What am I doing here?' I still couldn't fathom why getting this far had been so easy.

We passed Madame Tussaud's and I tried to dredge up some

waxwork-related trivia I could amaze her with. I didn't know any waxwork trivia.

'So,' I said at last. 'This is very, um, serendipitous, isn't it?'

She stirred as though woken, looking along the seat at me. 'Sorry?'

'Serendipitous. This. Us. You know – serendipity.'

'What about it?'

'It's your favourite word,' I said, but weakly, so it sounded like, 'It's your favourite *word*?'

'Is it?' she replied.

'That's what it says on the All Fur Coat website. That your favourite word is serendipity. It's a nice word.'

'How can you have a favourite word?' she said, turning again to stare out of the window. 'I'm sorry, but if this is serendipity then serendipity's not my favourite word.'

'Okay,' I said, feeling stupid and wishing I had some Baker Street trivia I could amaze her with. Whatever you do, keep it shallow and unthreatening, I thought: conversations about bird baths or the weather or how to dye shoes to match – good. Conversations about the Middle East, paedophilia or tabloid news stories about middle-aged club owners' five-times-a-night romps – bad.

'So is your favourite song "Always On My Mind" by the Pet Shop Boys?'

'No, it's "Clouds Across The Moon" by the Rah Band.' She slipped off her shoes, which dropped to the cab floor, and I watched her pull her feet on to the seat and wrap her arms around her knees, resting her chin on them, hugging herself into a tiny package.

'I don't think I know that one,' I managed.

'Really? I love it. It's about this woman, and she's making an intergalactic phone call to her lover who's off in space somewhere, at war. She can only call him once a year. It's kind of got this longing in it, because she really misses him, and she's trying not to cry, but there's her insecurity as well, because she wonders if there's someone else with him, and she's wondering how long she can cope by herself, and it's getting more and more difficult to keep rejecting offers at home because she's so lonely and she's got the children to look after. And when the song ends, even though it's perfectly obvious that she's head over heels in love with him, you kind of think that's probably the end for them, you know? So it's really sad. It's like a love that's failed to conquer all, the barriers are too high for them. It always makes me cry.'

A heartbreaking sadness fell across her face as she spoke. I wanted to reach over and take her in my arms, hold her little hugged-up package and tell her everything would be all right. Instead, I said, 'It sounds great. Available at all good record shops now, eh?' and she said nothing, lost in a world of sad songs, so I added, 'Do you like dance music?'

'Not especially, no. Not, like, "boff-boff-boff" dance music anyway, rave stuff.'

'Good.'

'Sorry?'

'Nothing. What about your favourite actor?'

She laughed and I felt the ice crack a little, just a little. 'What does the website say?'

'Paul Newman, because you like his eyes.' I was laughing now.

'I thought it was Robert Redford with the eyes.'

'I think they both have eyes.'

'Well, it's not Paul Newman. Or Robert Redford. If I had to pick anyone I'd pick Jean-Claude Van Damme.'

'Really?' I said. Then, 'So what happened? Some other girl got all your favourites?'

'I doubt it. They just make all that stuff up, don't they? That's okay, I suppose, to make stuff up. You've got to be what people want you to be, isn't that right?'

I briefly thought, Has she been drinking? It would explain a lot.

'What's your name again?' she said. She brushed some hair

back from her face as she said it; like everything about her, the gesture was as unique and exquisite as a snowflake. I sank a little further.

'It's, um, Greil. Greil Sharkey.'

'That's it. Well, I'm sorry about being sick on you the other night. I'd swallowed a bit of river water.'

'River water?'

'Yes, on a job. On a modelling assignment. I fell off a Sea Doo.'

'A Sea Doo? One of those wet bike things?'

She laughed. 'Yes.'

An ambulance rushed past in the opposite direction, all blues and twos; my mind went with it, back to All Fur Coat.

'What happened in the club?'

She told me. I crossed my legs. 'God. Must've been pretty horrific,' even though – and don't tell teacher – a tiny part of me offered thanks to Paris, her piercing mishap, her even more piercing scream, and the perfect diversion it had given me.

'It was. I hope she's all right. I mean, I don't really like her, but you wouldn't wish that on your worst enemy.'

'Was there something before that? Why isn't it safe for you to go home?'

'Oh, God.' She bit her lip. I nearly died of affection. 'Some-body's been following me. He's been into my flat. Today he attacked me.'

I checked an onrush of rage, 'Christ, are you all right? I'm not surprised you're . . .'

'I know, I'm really sorry.' She put her head into her hands, rubbing at her temples like an aromatherapist. 'I'm just tired and I've had an awful day, and I can't go home and I don't have anyone I can stay with. I'm sorry I've put you in a spot.'

My mind tried to jink and feint around a huge centre-back of a problem I was only just beginning to comprehend. From somewhere within a cloud of general trauma, Heidi thought I was her saviour; that I was taking her to sanctuary. 'I'm here to protect you,' I'd said in the club. Soon enough, though, she was going to start asking more probing questions, like, Protect me from what? And, Where are we going? And I felt certain the answer, 'To a hotel room so I can quiz you about your all-night shag-fests with Peter Benstead', might move me from the drawer marked 'my saviour' and into the one marked 'what a cunt'. I needed to get her trust pronto, or risk losing her.

'No, Heidi, I don't think you understand—' I began. But salvation knocked on the door, and it entered in the form of an Iggy Pop-like motherfucker with a strange line of work.

'He had a yellow washing-up glove on,' she said suddenly. 'Just one. A filthy washing-up glove.'

I nearly choked on my bile. Freak Boy, you little bastard. But thank you. 'Oh God. I know him,' I said, trying to paint my face into a picture six parts compassion, three parts horror and one part fireman-saving-baby-from-burning-home.

'You know him?' She turned to face me, a stunning combination of anger and fear.

'No, no, not *know* him. I know *of* him. He's . . . He's sort of the reason I came to collect you.'

She looked frightened, the first time she'd looked anything but mildly spaced out or annoyed since we'd got into the cab. 'Please explain,' she said. 'Before I ask the taxi driver to stop.' And she was already leaning forward, my jacket politely opening to show me the rise of her breast, which dazzled me for a moment or so.

'No, don't do that,' I said, recovering. 'This . . . This boy. He's a boy, yeah? About your height. Really skinny. I mean, a strange-looking boy. His name is Simon, and he's a bit demented. I don't think he's really dangerous, although . . . although he *might* be. Which is why I've come to collect you. Like I said, to protect you. To make sure you're safe.'

She still didn't look entirely satisfied.

'See, this Simon. He's besotted by Emily Benstead. Absolutely besotted with her. He wears the glove because he picks chewing gum off her posters on the tube—'

She groaned. 'Chewing gum.'

'Yes. He sees himself as her protector, you see. And he knows about . . .' and with a lurch of horror it occurred to me that I'd *never actually had* gold-plated confirmation of this fact . . . 'your affair with Peter Benstead.'

'Oh God,' she said. Which'll do, I thought.

'As I said, you see, there's . . . Well, there's going to be this story in the papers about your relationship with Peter . . .'

'And you're writing it, are you?' she said, and she said it with such a lack of emotion I could only assume her reserves of surprise had been completely drained for the day.

'Sort of.'

'I didn't expect it to be like this. I thought he'd warn me.'

'I'm not sure that he—'

'Your feature,' she interrupted. 'Your magazine feature you were going to do. They told you it was cancelled, didn't they?'

'They did, yes.'

'And they gave you this instead. What, as a consolation prize?'

'No, this is different. This is for a newspaper. Heidi, I'm not sure I—'

'He's been sabotaging my modelling work,' she said quickly, looking at me wide-eyed. 'He never wanted me to be a model. He tried to talk me out of it. He turned up in his car before my first casting. And now it's all fallen into place. There was your feature – they told me *you* cancelled it, not them; there was Sonia saying the Debutarts job had fallen to another girl, but telling Helen I was ill. Sonia, you see, owes him favours from way, way back. There was me thinking the game was fair when Peter had it rigged all along, pulling all the strings, manipulating me every step of the way. I thought I was in control. But it was him, he was in control.'

'Why has he been doing all this?' I asked cautiously.

'He doesn't want me to be a model.'

'Why?'

She snorted. 'Shouldn't you know? Because he wants to

hold me back. Everybody wants to hold me back. Have you ever had a dream?' I said I had. 'And did people try to stop you? Did they resent your dream? Did they make fun of it, probably because they knew their own dreams would amount to nothing, or even worse, they never had any?'

I agreed they had and we lapsed into silence while I tried to make sense of this latest turn of events. One thing I knew: if I'd been worried *why* Heidi might want to kiss and tell on Benstead, my worries were over. Here was a girl with an axe to grind, and in the shitty-gritty world of tabloid journalism, grinding axes equals spilling beans.

Once again it felt like things were at last beginning to go my way, and I allowed myself to relax a little, to hope the story might end happily, that my future might involve paid-off debts and journalistic glory and skipping over meadows with Heidi in one hand and a long glass of vodka and tonic in the other, just the one.

She interrupted my train of thought, saying sleepily, 'So we're we going to a hotel?'

'Yes. It's best. Because of Freak B— Simon, I mean. To make sure you're safe. And . . . And because once the story breaks the other papers will want to speak to you, and they'll make your life a misery. I've been assigned to make sure you're not hassled and the best way of doing that is to take you to a hotel for a day or so.'

'Are you going to pick chewing gum off my pictures as well, then?' she said, and then her eyelids fluttered closed. I thought, If needs be, and the city flashed by in a montage of shopfronts and street lights before the taxi pulled up to the hotel and I shook Heidi gently by the shoulder, saying, 'Heidi? Heidi? Do you have any money for the taxi . . . ?'

The triptych lay battered and smashed against the wall. Litter. I looked at Jill and said, 'You did it,' and she took a step backwards. The sudden upsurge of anger I felt disappeared almost as quickly as it had appeared. I felt myself reach a plateau beyond emotional involvement, forgetting my new-found hatred of Jill, knowing only that she needed to be stopped.

'Now hold on just a second, Simon,' she said. 'I haven't touched any painting, all right?' Her *trustandfriendship* smile had left for the day. Her face was darkened by confusion and concern. For a moment or so the only sound in the room was my blood, leaking to the floor from my dog-food arm.

I stepped forward and to my left. Behind Jill my studio door was ajar; a slice of the world outside was visible. In her hand was her bottle of perfume. She gripped it so hard her fist was a discoloured mess of blood-bleached pressure points. Her other hand was held out towards me, for comfort. Jill's two hands, like my own, were no longer equal partners, their functions too disparate and distinct. Her handbag was around her shoulder. In there, I guessed, was her mobile phone that she'd be dying to reach for, but knowing that to do so would be a transgressive act. That it might provide the trigger for violence that so far lingered only in potential. I was thinking like her now, my mind focused.

'Simon,' she said. 'Let's not get excited, okay . . . Okay, mate?' Unconsciously she mirrored my movement as she said it, taking a step to her own left, away from the door, unaware of its promise of safety becoming more faint.

Excited? I thought. Excited is what children get on Christmas morning, on trips to the fair and family holidays. I was not excited. I was calm. I took another step forward and again she moved in response. The only sound was the drip-drip of my blood to the floor.

'I'm not excited,' I said. 'I want you to listen to this, Jill.'

I reached to the stereo under Jill's gaze, pressing Play. From the speakers came the sound of the kitchen, a memory replayed from yesterday, and I watched Jill carefully, noting her confusion as the tape began and the familiar noises felt alien, until her own voice came on and wary comprehension fell across her face. I took a step away from the stereo and to my left, closing the gap on the door as Jill introduced herself to the man called Roger. The real Jill was thinking furiously before my eyes, wondering, I guessed, what she might have said during the phone call being played to her.

'That's all good, mate,' came her voice on the tape. 'But listen, Roger, something else has cropped up. Yeah, I'm here now, actually . . .' she laughed. 'No, more than usual. He tells me he's continuing with his medication but I'm almost sure he's stopped . . .'

'I don't need medication,' I said, taking a step.

'You do, Simon,' said Jill, making a corresponding move.

'. . . Well, that's the first thing,' said the tape Jill. 'The other thing is that he's been painting these weird paintings, nothing like he usually does . . . Oh, God knows, big blobs of red and yellow, nothing you can recognise. But he's been throwing huge bits of mushed-up paper on to them . . .'

She visibly winced at the brutality of her description and I lived the pain again. No amount of repetition had helped soothe it. Nothing could rub ointment on my wounds now. My pain had been absorbed into my purpose. I was crucifixion-exempt, my blood drip-dripping on the floor.

'I didn't mean—' said the real Jill, but her words fell off into silence.

'No, I'm in his flat now,' said the tape Jill. 'Sorry, his "studio". I'm in his "studio" now. He's skulking around outside at the moment, and I'm telling you, Roger, he's changed. He's . . . No, not at all, in fact, quite the reverse, it's almost as if he's calmer and more composed . . . Yes, I can see that, but in this instance I don't think it's a positive thing. Nah, I'm sorry, but I'm going to have to recommend he goes into Homerton for more evaluation . . . Well, no, not at all, there's never been any indication . . . Well, it's my intuition, Roger, what else can I rely on – a forked stick? If you're asking me if I think he represents a potential danger to himself and others, then I think the answer is, Not yet, but maybe, and definitely maybe if we don't bring him in . . .'

'I'm not going to the hospital,' I said, pleased at the command my voice carried.

'Simon,' said the real Jill. Her cheeks, always, it seemed, rosy-red in the heat, had lost their colour. She was quite pale now. 'I want to make it clear that I'm not – I mean, I wasn't – suggesting you *stay* anywhere. We all want you to stay here, and we're delighted at the progress you've made here, but remember the contract you signed? Remember that?'

I do remember the contract; we had a party to celebrate when I signed it. A party with jelly and coke that wasn't proper Coca-Cola but 'American-style Coke' and the three people present at 'my big party' gave me a little cheer when I put my name to the piece of paper that said 'Contract to Get Well' at the top.

I the undersigned (1) hereby agree to continue with the programme and good work instigated by the undersigned (2) to promote my continued well-being and good health.

But I had travelled beyond their place; Emily had helped me to do that. Jill still hoped to divert me with meaningless bits of paper; it was all she had left.

In accordance with the above statement, I, the undersigned (1), agree to take any and all medications as prescribed by the undersigned (2).

'We want you to get well,' she said. 'That's all we've ever wanted. Let us help fix you up.'

I also agree to regular visits and consultations with the undersigned (2) in order to verify that I continue to abide by the terms and conditions of this Contract To Get Well.

It was a stupid contract, the kind of thing you give a misbehaving primary-school child to sign.

'Roger,' said the tape Jill. 'This is a dangerous and confused kid. He blinded another pupil with a screwdriver—' The real Jill winced again at the weight of her words. I momentarily recalled the windy playing field and the Philips screwdriver. 'I'm so proud of you, Simon,' drawled my mum when the police arrived to take me away. 'Mummy's little hero.' She shouldn't have said it, of course. That, and other things she said to the police and psychiatrists – 'but he doesn't have to be one of our failures,' continued the tape Jill. 'Maybe all he needs is a little remedial work, some further evaluation. But I'm absolutely convinced that if we take no action now, he will only become worse. Please, Roger, let's look after this boy . . .'

'You see?' said the real Jill, her eyes wide. Both of us were now an equal distance from the studio door. 'You see? We're mates, aren't we? You and me? I care about you. We all care about you. We just want you to get well. And you signed the contract, you want to get well. Let's help each other.'

I closed the gap. Her hand gripping her perfume. 'You've come to take me away. You're one of them.'

'. . . Christ, "continued assessment"?' said tape Jill. 'What do you think I've been doing? I'm asked to make an evaluation based on my findings and that is what I'm presenting . . .'

'I haven't come to take you away, no,' said the real Jill. 'But I would like you to come with me. I don't think you're well, Simon. I think the fact that you've made this tape shows that. The fact that you've destroyed your work shows that. One of

285

who? Please, Simon . . .' A drop of sweat leaked from her hairline down the side of her face.

'. . . Is that really the best you can do? Well, don't come running to me when this boy is lost to us, when someone gets hurt . . .'

Thinking like her, reading her mind, one step ahead of the game now, I darted to the door. Two quick steps and it slammed shut beneath the heel of my hand, refusing the outside world entry. I snapped the Yale lock.

Jill was already reaching for her handbag, shoulders twisted as she felt for it, swinging it around as I ran and snatched it from her grasp.

'Simon!' she screeched, full of fear. I yanked the bag and she came with it, stumbling as the strap pulled her around like a ripcord. The bag came free – the sudden scent of handbag, of make-up and blackcurrant Tunes and cigarettes – and Jill was off balance. I pushed her as hard as I could, sending her running backwards on feet that scrabbled but moved too slowly for her body so she landed with a kindling crash in the centre of the wrecked triptych.

'Okay, Roger. All right. See you soon. Goodbye.'

The taped Jill had finished, her grave dug. The real Jill lay sprawled like a beggar in the centre of the paintings, splayed limbs and double chins, but eyes wide open and breathing heavily. Her left hand popped the lid off the bottle of perfume she held. She did it hoping I wouldn't notice, but I did. I knew that she would try to spray the perfume in my eyes, and that it wasn't perfume at all, but something they gave people like Jill to protect them from people like me, and it was now her only hope. I kept my distance. Her feet worked on the floor as she tried to stand up, dazed but needing to regain some composure.

To stop her getting to her feet I picked up a dictionary, still rightfully the property of a bookshop in Central London, full of soothing organisation, full of words like hurt and betrayal, and I heaved it at Jill's head as hard as I could.

She saw it coming and put out a hand to stop it, but it hit her in the face and I congratulated myself on a good throw before fishing my keys out of my jeans, locking the studio door's Chubb and moving to the kitchen to put the kettle on.

She lay still, watching me. Maybe trying to think like me. He's 'not well'. He's 'excited'. He's 'dangerous and confused', and he needs to go to Homerton for evaluation. And what do dangerous, excited, confused and unwell people think? Why do they put the kettle on? For a nice cup of tea?

I unplugged the toaster and took it back through to the studio where Jill had barely moved, lying in the paintings, trying to pull herself together. A trickle of blood ran from her nose and I looked at my own arm, caked in blood gone dark and crusty. The toaster was a Morphy Richards, a model with special 'cool' sides that don't get hot when the toaster's on. I held it up as if to throw it at her head and she pointed her secret agent's perfume weapon at me, shielding her face and firing it at the same time. *Pssst*, it said, a pathetic whisper. And though the spray went further than I expected, it was still not far enough to touch me, dissolving into useless mist a few precious feet away. Jill whimpered. I gauged the range and moved further forward, estimating that I was still out of sprayshot, but within a better distance for toaster throwing.

She held out the spray. Her other hand was up, ready to ward off the Morphy Richards with the cool sides. I moved it around and her hand followed it, like a cat chasing a torch beam. Up I moved the toaster. Her hand came up. To the side. Her hand moved in the same direction. I dummied a throw and she flinched, her eyes squeezed shut, the warding-off hand shaking in anticipation of the impact.

'Simon,' she said, a sob in her voice. 'Whatever you think you're doing, please don't do it. Whatever has happened, we can sort it out. Whatever is wrong we can solve. Please don't hurt me. I'm not like the boy at school. I don't want to hurt you, I don't hate you. I care very much for you.

Whoever "they" are, whoever Emily is, it doesn't matter – I can help you.'

I relaxed a little, but not a lot. 'You want to take me away.'

'I don't want to take you away.'

'You're with them. You're part of their plot.'

'I'm not with anyone. I'm not part of any plot. You must believe me.'

The kettle clicked off and I raised the toaster again as if to throw it at her head. As she flinched a second time, I dumped the toaster and scurried to the kitchen, returning with the kettle steaming in my hand.

'Stay there,' I said to her as she tried to get to her feet.

'What are you doing?' She held out the spray, ineffective as it was.

I hefted the kettle. 'I'm making a nice cup of tea,' I said, then poured the contents of the kettle into Jill's handbag, leaving the contents to stew and plopping the bag on the floor. Water began to leak from her bag, soaking the newspaper taped to the floor. It leaked a lot, and as I watched, it gradually dawned on me the bag wasn't watertight. All the hot water was escaping, not destroying the phone as I intended.

'Simon.' She tried to get up. I lifted the kettle as if to throw it at her. She shielded her eyes and stayed on the floor as I delved into her bag for the mobile phone. I found it, grabbed it. The plastic burnt my hands and the pain made me toss it into the air, but it fell with a satisfying crack, so I jumped on it, only for it to skid wetly from beneath my heel, sending me tumbling to the floor.

Jill saw her chance and tried to rise, but I was faster, jumping up and threatening her with the kettle a second time until she lay still, then using the kettle to hammer at the mobile phone until it broke. She sobbed and I remembered the phone in my studio, darting over and yanking it from the wall. The socket whipped out and caught Jill across the face and she screamed in pain as I began to hit the telephone with the kettle.

'Simon,' she screamed above the noise of the kettle smashing the phone. Bits of plastic casing broke and scooted across the room. 'Simon!' The telephone's innards cowered beneath. I carried on wielding the kettle like a pickaxe. 'Simon! You've been cut off! You were cut off months ago!'

But I didn't believe her so I didn't stop until the job was done. Until the phone was destroyed and all Jill's means of communication disabled, and I grabbed my rucksack and ran out of the studio, double-locking the door behind me.

CHAPTER TWENTY-SIX

'Graham,' I whisper into the phone, casting a look at where Heidi still sleeps. I take the phone as far away from her as the cord will permit, turning my back, keeping my voice low.

'Greil, hello,' he says, with the cheery air of a man who got laid last night. 'Congrats, you're my first call of the day. I haven't even had a chance to open my email, where, I suspect, I'll see your Vegas copy, am I right?'

Fuck. I squeeze my eyes shut and review a number of excuses that trip through my head, including Ma and her dodgy ticker again. In the end I opt for a wild card – the truth. 'Events have overtaken me, Graham,' I say. He starts to say something in return but I don't let him continue, hoping instead to wow him with my new developments. 'I managed to speak to the girl last night and we're at the hotel now, believe it or not. It's all on. I'm going to be interviewing her today.'

Graham says, 'That is fucking brilliant, mate. You star. Tell you what, you get cracking with the interview, I'll tell the news boys. Oh, and I'll get on to that cash, all right? It'll be yours within the hour.'

Except he doesn't say that. He says nothing. A big, fat *nada* of a dissatisfied pause, leaving me to fill the silence with, 'Isn't that great? I'll be able to get you her copy this afternoon, maybe even sooner. We should get photographic on to it, maybe get her shot by the end of the day. I'm telling you, mate, she's going to look fantastic. Front cover material, you know: "Peter Benstead's real-life Moll".' And still he says nothing. 'Graham? Did you hear what I said?'

'Oh, I heard you. And it's all good. Sure, I'll tell newsdesk. But there's one more thing.'

'Yes.'

'Where. Is. My. Fucking. Vegas. Interview?'

I gulp. 'Oh, that. Literally just tying up a few loose ends on that one, mate. I know I promised it to you first thing, but I wrote it overnight and there are a couple of bits I need to check out with her PR, just some fact-checking. After that it's all yours.'

'This morning, then?' he sighs, sounding – actually – fairly sedated. Yep, definitely a man who's had his oats.

'Absolutely,' I say, off the hook. 'Just as soon as the PR gets in and I've spoken to her.'

'All right, Greil, I'll look forward to it.'

'And the girl?'

'Like I say, I'll inform newsdesk and get one of them to call you. You do your interview before the excitement gives you a heart attack.'

'Will do,' I say, feeling like a proper journalist, the churning in my stomach a sensation I recognise – like going on stage for the first time, getting a new job, pulling off an exclusive. That feeling of outdoing yourself, of being better than you can be. One last thing, though . . .

'One last thing, though,' I say. 'The money. Now we're all clear could you authorise it? I was hoping you might even be able to sort it so I could get hold of the money today, like, this morning, even . . .'

'What money's that then?' he says, and my heart shrivels. There's a familiar and not-welcome tone to his voice, like this is his trump card, his ace in the hole, and I know what's coming ahead of time.

'The advance,' I say, 'on this story?'

'Ah, the advance. Sorry, you lost me there. Yeah, of course I'll authorise it—'

'That's brilliant, mate.'

'—when I get my Vegas copy.'

But I need the cash by midday, I almost say, but don't, because I'm skating on thin ice as it is, and because, of course, there's still time. There's not much of it – as deadlines go this is approaching my tightest ever – but the point is, if I can get home, get my laptop then get back here and bash out the Vegas interview, I should still be able to get Graham the copy in time for him to authorise the advance; for me to get to the cash window and then arrange the drop around midday.

So with time against me again I bid farewell to Graham, put down the phone, and I'm turning to the girl even as I'm pulling on my jacket.

'Heidi,' I say, kneeling before her and gently rocking her shoulder. 'Please wake up, I need to speak to you a moment.'

She stirs and her eyes open. 'Hello,' she says in a tiny voice, and for a second I consider not going anywhere, fucking off the laptop and the Vegas interview and the men who will hurt me if I don't pay them money, and just staying here with Heidi to swim in her eyes and listen to her say things like, Hello.

'Hello,' I say softly, wanting to brush away the blonde strands of hair from her eyes. 'Did you sleep well?'

'I felt safe,' she replies, sleepy. Then, 'What time is it?'

'Don't worry. Early. You carry on sleeping. You've had a tough time. Get some rest, recharge your batteries. We'll speak later.'

'I need to get some of my things if we're going to be here a while,' and of course she does. Her fear's driven her into a foreign country where she barely has a toothbrush to her name. My heart breaks for her, little girl lost.

'That's no problem,' I say, 'but can you manage for a while? There's something very important I've got to do first. Perhaps we could go over to your flat a bit later and pick up what you need. Do it together, yes? So you'll be safe?'

She blinks at me over the lip of the sheet. 'I've got some bits and bobs and a change of clothes in my bag,' she says. 'I'll be all right for a bit.'

'Great. That's great. Don't worry about anything now. You'll be safe here. I'll look after you, okay? I'll protect you.'

'Okay.'

'I've got to go out for a while,' I croak, somehow resisting the temptation to 'tuck her in' – to smooth the sheets around her body and fold them beneath her chin. 'Just an hour or so. Will you be okay here alone?' She nods a compliant yes, and I stand with a popping of knee joints. From the corner of my eye I spot just a mouthful of vodka calling to me from the desk and I really need it to maintain, so I down it quickly as I let myself out, hoping Heidi will think it's water.

There's a voicemail on my mobile, 'Greil, Greil, Orange Peel,' it says. 'Just thought I'd give you a call, make sure you haven't forgotten about . . .'

No, I think, I haven't, and I switch off my phone.

*

He downs the last of the drink I've seen him take from the mini-bar and goes, and I sit up in bed, wondering what to do.

I hate Peter for this. I hate the boy with the glove. I hate Holly, Sonia, the police and Fortuna for this. For making me feel as though I'm suddenly no longer in control of my life; confined, as though my choices have been taken away from me. The journalist? I don't hate him. He's doing his job, after all. He's part of the effect, not the cause.

I feel a tear I didn't even know was forming slip down my cheek and wipe it away, dragging myself from the bed and looking for my hold-all. Inside I have a change of clothes. Well, I have the clothes I was wearing yesterday, at least. Something to wear that's not my smoke-smelling dancer's gown from last night, that's more me, more Heidi.

As I'm rooting through the hold-all my phone rings, smothered at first, until I dig it out from beneath a pair of jeans and look warily at the name before answering anyway.

'Hello,' I say. 'Hello, Holly.'

'Heidi. Hello.'

There's a long pause. We're both of us thinking what to say, until at last she breaks the deadlock with, 'We need to talk.'

'Oh, too right we do,' I say. 'Let's see. Hmm. Maybe you could start by telling me why you've been messing up my castings. Let's start with what gave you the right to do that.'

'Heidi—'

'And. Hmm. What about why I'm here in a hotel with a journalist wanting to do this story and neither you nor Peter have said a word about it.'

'A hotel? Heidi, shut up a minute.'

'What—'

'Just listen. Just listen a second, will you? First things first. Can you tell me where you are?'

I feel a sudden coldness, a fright that passes through me. 'You don't know where I am?'

'No. No, Heidi, we don't. Now listen, I'm going to ask you a simple question, and I need you to answer just yes or no, okay?'

'Okay.'

'Right. Yes or no. Is the journalist – Greil – is he within earshot?'

'No.'

'Is he in the room?'

'No.'

'Okay. Do you know where he is?'

'No. He left a few minutes ago.'

'Did he say where he was going or how long he would be?'

'Look, what is this all about?'

'It's to do with the story, Heidi. There's been a misunderstanding. Did he tell you how long he would be?'

I'm panicking. *What misunderstanding?* 'About an hour. Am I safe?'

'Look, can you wait there. I'll be half an hour. Tell me the hotel name and your room number.'

I have to go and look to find out, confused, something about Holly's voice compelling me to do as she says.

*

It's not that sunny today, not as sunny as it has been. Which would be a good thing, except it's not, because instead of being sunny, it's close: thunderstorms-and-little-tiny-black-bugs close, and even more like Hades than usual on the street, where people wade grimly through the sauna temperature; where every tiny bit of cool, displaced air is like the breath of God.

I make good time, slinging my jacket over my shoulder and not giving a toss about the sweat patches that quickly form on my shirt as I rush to the tube. I get a kids' fare which I borrow from last night's taxi change and, like The Who song, I'm out of my brain on the train. Fighting tiredness, urging it to go faster, panting like a sick dog in the heat.

And worrying. Worrying that in my absence, Heidi's mind might change. That even now she's resolving to leave, getting her things together and walking out of the hotel-room door. I've still got that *GoodFellas* riff going round and round my head; the lucky hat is now this Vegas interview. Got to get the lucky hat.

Home is cool, at least, the curtains closed, and despite myself I stand in the lounge and get my breath back for a minute. The last thing I do before leaving is look in the bathroom mirror, and the prognosis is not good. Maybe my face has healed a little, but there's no trace of the Touche Eclat left. I look like a desperate, dishevelled man, hair matted flat with sweat, dark bags and bruises beneath my eyes. Somewhere there's a long drink and an even longer sleep with my name on it, but not yet.

I check my watch for the umpteenth time. Making good progress and should be back at the hotel within the hour, providing the trains are okay. Providing I don't get caught dodging the full fare. I sling the laptop bag over my shoulder and resign myself to the strip of sweat that immediately forms below the strap, lock the flat door behind me and head back to the tube.

*

It took Holly longer than she said, maybe three-quarters of an hour. I got myself together the best I could and sat on the bed with my hands in my lap, waiting and wondering, but when the knock came at the door I couldn't be certain whether it would be him or her.

Knock-knock. Who's there? 'Hello?'

Muffled from behind the door, standing in the heavily carpeted hallway, she says, 'Heidi? It's Holly. Are you still alone?'

I open up and Holly stands on the threshold of the room. She's well dressed in a loose-fitting linen suit. Not for the first time I notice she has good hair. Good nails, too, and a cute charm bracelet hanging from her wrist tinkles slightly as she reaches for me and we air-kiss, like two ladies who lunch, instead of two women in a strange hotel room, one of whom wants to know, 'What's going on? What did you mean, "misunderstanding"?'

She glances around the room like she's not convinced Greil isn't about to leap from a cupboard and clout her with a copy of the Gideon Bible. 'I'm sorry,' she says, 'but you're going to have to trust me.' She ignores the look I give her. 'The most important thing is that we get you out of here, and we do it before Greil gets back. Things could turn nasty.'

'Why?'

'Please, Heidi,' she says. 'Let's just get your things together. I can explain everything on the way out.'

Instead of protesting or demanding answers, I find myself doing as she says, half because of the force of her conviction, half because it seems easier, less wearing, to slip into the role of bewildered blonde. So I sigh and move to my hold-all, starting to pack my clothes.

'Anything in the bathroom, Heidi?'

'Toothbrush and make-up bag.'

'I'll fetch them.' And she hurries through to the bathroom, pulling the light-cord which automatically starts the extractor fan, which seems unusually loud in the room.

Which is perhaps why we don't hear the door at first. You'd never hear footsteps coming down the corridor anyway – the carpet's too thick, the walls too insulated and the place too posh for anything as common as noise. And the door takes one of those key cards. It's almost soundless. So the first thing either of us hears is the door closing behind Greil, who stands there looking first at me, packing my hold-all on the bed, and then to Holly as she emerges from the bathroom door, with my toothbrush in one hand and my make-up bag in the other.

A moment or so passes before he speaks, and when he does he addresses not me, but Holly.

'Hello, George,' he says.

CHAPTER TWENTY-SEVEN

Leaving the flat and Jill behind me, I drip-dripped breathlessly along the pavement, aware of passers-by herding their children from my path; aware, also, that I was an easy target, my energies depleted. So when I at last found a place to stop, I immediately lay down to sleep, like carrion.

They don't sleep, though. It's my first thought, hours later, when I awake on grass wet with dew, the canal calm beside me, hearing the sounds of the traffic from the road. There's another sound, too, from far away – a voice I recognise – slowly burrowing its way into my sleep-drugged head: 'Bernard! Where are you, good dog!'

I'm beneath a tree, my senses reassembling: Jill. Emily . . . But now—

Bernard, my former tormentor, has found me and snuffles at my body, lying in the shade and security of the canal bank tree. I hold my breath, hearing his owner's footsteps approach. Bernard stands panting in front of me and together we are two fugitives. I raise my finger to my lips and make a shush sound I'm not sure he understands. He regards me for a moment, tilting his head to one side the way dogs do, then he sniffs, first my face and then my arm. As if in response, the pain of my injury flares and I look at it, tattered and black with congealed blood, the Marigold grimy and torn. Bernard sniffs at the wound and discovers his DNA there, mingling with my own. Seized by an olfactory memory he takes an uncertain step backwards and sits on his hind legs. His eyes meet mine and narrow, watching my finger still at my lips, pleading for his silence.

'Bernard! Whatchoo doing?'

Through the branches I watch the owner's feet tramp along the towpath and draw level with my face, dirty white trainers and faded jeans. I resist closing my eyes and delay an outward-bound breath in my throat as a hand, letters tattooed across the knuckles, reaches down to scruff affectionately at Bernard's neck. Bernard, still watching me; still unsure whether to raise the alarm.

'You know what, Bernard?' says the owner, and Bernard's eyes narrow with pleasure at the rubbing on his neck. 'I love you, you good dog.'

Bernard smiles. His owner snaps a leaf from the tree and my hiding place shivers around me, and then he coughs, and I watch his dirty trainers and jeans walk away. 'Come on, then,' he says, and Bernard takes a final look at me, a salute of mutual respect, and trots off to fall in step behind his owner.

I relax back into the grass for a moment, waiting for them to go. I hear the squeak of the kissing gate as they depart, and when I'm sure the coast is clear I walk to the gate myself, easing out on to the pavement and looking left and right along the road. Two cars pass. One red, one silver. I check the contents of my rucksack; check to see if I have a spare Marigold, but I don't, and with senses keen I begin to walk, keeping an eye out for police cars, or cars that slow down, certain the authorities will be looking for me . . .

But I must have been followed. I walk straight into their trap.

'LONDON SWELTERS IN RECORD TEMPS!' says an *Evening Standard* A-board outside the shop, and I walk inside to see the newsagent serving a customer who turns to leave as I enter. By the door stand two men wearing suits, muttering to each other at a display of greetings cards. As I watch, one of them glances behind at the counter and puts a birthday card into his jacket. The customer walks past me to the exit, looking me up and down, and the shopkeeper sees me.

'Oh no you don't,' he says. He takes one look at the filthy, blood-coated person who's walked in and decides that alcoholics and junkies and women who are unkind to their children are suitable customers, but there is a line, and this person has fallen below it. I stop as if to stand my ground. Behind me the door closes on one of those spring things doors sometimes have. For a moment or so the shopkeeper and I look at one another. He assesses my physical and emotional state, auditing my appearance, making judgements about my temperament, perhaps my ability to defeat him in a fight. He should wear an apron and be ruddy of face. He should carry a cleaver, but this isn't a butcher's shop, it's a newsagent, and I realise dimly that newsagents don't usually have Marigold gloves for sale and curse my incompetence.

He lifts up the counter and steps through. I want to tell him that the evidence of his eyes is false; that I'm an artist, forced into this situation against my will.

Then one of the men in suits sees me, too. From the corner of my eye I register him do a double-take and nudge his friend. 'Fuckin'ell, Darren,' he says, 'dog shit.'

His friend looks down at his shiny black shoes and says, 'Where?' but his friend nudges him again. 'No, there. From school. It's Dog Shit.'

The shopkeeper frowns. He looks from me to the two men in suits.

'Fuckin'ell, it is as well,' says the other. 'It's the kid who blinded Jase.' He replaces a birthday card with a badge attached that says 'I Am 3' and turns away from the display.

'He's got a card in his jacket,' I tell the shopkeeper, who stands in the middle of the shop. 'I saw him put it there.'

'No I ain't,' he says, unconcerned. He and his friend take a step closer, a pair of nasty promises. 'What you wearing on your hand, Dog Shit?' says the other, staring at my glove.

'Still a dirty little fucker, then?' says the first.

The newsagent looks uncertain. Then, 'Just leave quietly,' he says, a nervy glance at the two men in suits. 'I don't want to have to call the police.'

'Yeah, come on, Dog Shit,' says the first man, the smaller

of the two. His face is spotty – too spotty even to work in a well-known electrical retailer. 'Let's go outside, yeah? We'll have a chat, yeah? Talk about school.' He moves forward and shoves at my shoulder, a taste of things to come. His face is twisted into a nasty, spotty shape, like a screwed-up flannel.

'Hey, we'll have none of that in here,' says the newsagent, nervous now. 'Just get out, all of you.'

I stand my ground, thinking, calculating the movement required to whirl around and yank open the shop door. Anticipating the resistance of the door-close. Thinking I must use my right arm, the good one. My left almost useless with the pain of Bernard's kiss.

'You heard the man, Dog Shit,' says the big one.

I feel the weight of my chest rising and falling. My eyes are locked on the two men in suits who look animated, as though electricity is being passed through them. They twitch, nerves in their faces jump in anticipation of the damage they will do to me.

(*'What you got in yer bag? Vaseline?'*)

The little one smiles.

'I don't want any trouble,' says the shopkeeper.

'There ain't gonna be any trouble,' says the small one. Then, to me, 'Until we get outside, eh, Dog Shit?'

They take another step towards me, crowding me backwards.

Behind me the door opens with a ping and a small boy scampers into the shop, his plimsolls slapping on the floor, heading straight for the sweet display below the counter. The shopkeeper walks back, 'Out!' he says to me, pointing, as he lifts up the counter to move through. The two men regard me, something like victory in their eyes, waiting for me to turn and leave so they can follow.

Behind me is more movement. 'Excuse me,' and I feel something nudging at the calves of my legs, turn to see a pushchair being angled into the shop by a young woman. 'S'all right. Don't bother to help, eh?'

Her child is staring at the sweets. In the pushchair is a small tree in a black plastic pot.

'Right,' sighs the big one, moving forward. 'Outside, Dog Shit,' and he moves in, his smiling little friend one step behind. But I'm fast. Faster than them. And as he goes to grab me I duck beneath his arm and make a move for the potted tree, whipping it from the pushchair and shoving it into his face.

For half a second he is a man kissing a tiny tree, his arms reaching around as if to smother it with a passionate hug. His face is obscured by leaves and branches and a sudden fountain of dirt which explodes from the pot and all over his face and shirt.

'Bowf!' he says. The small one is already reacting ('You little fucker'), the woman partway through an indignant screech, but I shoulder her aside, using the sudden foliage explosion as cover to duck around her pushchair, and with a final kick at the chair, shoving it right into the path of the small one, I get moving, out of the door and into the street, the pain in my arm flaring, my rucksack thumping at my back. Looking back I see the two of them come bundling from the doorway behind me – 'Oi!'

The big one is speckled with dirt, his face and shirt covered in it. The small one shouts but doesn't give chase because I'm too far away, dodging around cars to cross the road, barely able to contain my laughter so I don't. I bark it loud. Loud enough for all to hear, as Dog Shit makes his daring escape.

CHAPTER TWENTY-EIGHT

I open the door to the hotel room and walk in, but as it turns out I might as well have opened a portal to another time, another place: somewhere the world has moved on without me noticing.

'Hello, George,' I say.

Madly, the first thing I think is, Bollocks.

Like, bollocks that I look so, well, bollocks. You always imagine that the next time you bump into your ex you'll be looking your best, better than when you last saw them, at least. I'm thinner, that much I've got going for me – I've got Charlie Chang, the white weight-watcher, to thank for that. But otherwise I can safely say she won't be regretting her decision to leave me. If the bruised ghoul staring back at me from the bathroom mirror wasn't bad enough, I've added the trauma of the return journey on top of that. I look like a down-and-out who's found someone's dirty, discarded suit. Like a fashion shoot for *The Face*, only not fashionable. A far, far cry from how I would have chosen to look: great tan, perfect Shark-smile teeth, perhaps the diminutive pop princess Kylie on my arm. The whole package saying, 'Doing very well without you, thanks. Better, in fact. Oh, and can I have my Galaxie 500 album back . . .'

But I don't get George's marks out of ten for appearance. Instead she stands, stunned, in the doorway to the bathroom, her hands full and an expression on her face that slowly moves from shock, to resignation, then hardens. I'd wager her little voice is congratulating her – she looks great. From the chrysalis I lived with to the butterfly of today. She has the air of a woman in charge of her life and of those around her. What was I? The band? Practice mats for the George of today.

'What are you doing here?' I say into the silence that follows my greeting. A silence during which I resist looking at my watch, that deadline getting closer by the second.

She ignores the question. 'What happened to your face?' she says, in a way that suggests nothing has changed since we last met; that bashed-in faces were always par for the course and always will be. If you're me.

'Never mind my face,' I say. 'What. Are you. Doing. Here?'

'Greil, we need to talk,' she says, and she moves forward and very deliberately places what she's holding on to the bed, next to Heidi, who stands with her hands in her hold-all, looking for all the world like she's kneading the contents. She wears an odd, detached expression, as though she's watching events from behind glass. For the briefest second the two women are standing next to one another at the bed, both watching me, their arms touching. In that moment I think I might cry; actually feel my eyes misting, then stop myself.

'Go on, then,' I say. 'Kick off by telling me what you're doing in my room, and why you're helping Heidi to pack her bag.' I say this remarkably calmly, given the confusing turn of events; the way you do when you fear your temper might split its seams any moment. Perhaps a flicker of disquiet passes across her face.

'I'm very sorry, Greil. I really am. But there's been a mistake.'

'There has been if you think you're leaving with Heidi.'

'Don't make this harder than it already is, Greil. Why don't we let Heidi go down to reception while we talk about this between ourselves? I can explain everything to you.'

I feel my jaw tighten. 'Just explain now, please.'

She regards me. I'm blocking the door and she knows she has no choice. 'I have my own firm now. Public Nuisance PR,' she says.

'Great. Leave your card and I'll be in touch.'

'One of my clients is Peter Benstead.'

It clicks, and for a moment or so I feel sorry for her, at the same time trying to ignore a nasty glow of triumph in my stomach. Her, the newborn PR woman; me, the newborn hard-news journalist. Once we loved each other, but my disgust for her world of PR, for the endless schmoozing and small talk, was as much a part of our relationship as the booze. She'd kicked the booze, but the PR, it turned out, had let her down.

'You do Benstead's PR, then,' I say.

'That's right.'

'So you're here to try and gag the story.'

'It's not like that . . .' she starts.

'You're too late, George,' I interrupt. 'It's nothing personal. Really. I had no idea you were involved with Benstead. It's nothing to do with you and me, I promise. It's just bad luck, but the fact is—' Again she starts to say something, but I stop her. 'The fact is, you can't block this story. It's beyond your reach now.'

'It's not a story, Greil,' she says.

'Yes it is. Whether you like it or not, it is. Look, don't take it badly, it's hardly your fault. If he blames you then maybe you should tell him that the best publicity is not to sleep with his employees.'

At the bed, Heidi winces. Her head drops and I regret my words. George looks away, then at me, a renewed directness in her eyes. 'What if it's good publicity, Greil? Did you think of that?'

Maybe here I'm thinking of what the *NME* said vis-à-vis Sytemitis being about as effective as the Maginot Line, and how that publicity crapped all over our careers. But as for George, here and now, I say what she wants to hear, shrugging, 'All PR's good PR, isn't that it?'

'It can be, Greil,' she says, and there's a controlled, self-aware tone to her voice that unsettles me, like a teacher explaining a difficult maths equation. 'After all,' she continues,

'Peter and Emily have a multi-million-pound West End show to promote.'

'Great timing, then,' I say, aiming for sarcasm, but hearing a first note of uncertainty in my voice. The sense that this conversation is heading somewhere . . .

'Almost perfect,' she says, looking directly into my eyes: the George who managed Systemitis and got us on *Top of the Pops*; who kicked the booze; who washed that man right out of her hair then started her own company. A George who's never wrong.

There is a long pause.

'What are you saying, George?' I manage at last. And any trace of former confidence, or even sympathy, for poor old George has disappeared. Now in my voice all I hear is the beginning of panic.

'Please, can we talk about this alone?' she says. 'I don't think you're going to like what I've got to tell you.'

I stand my ground by the door, staring at George. Gorgeous, in-control George. I realise my bottom lip is quivering slightly. 'What are you saying?' I repeat. 'I don't understand.'

'It's not a story, Greil. It's PR.'

Now my head is shaking a slow-motion negative. George's eyes fall away from mine. Something like guilt, or sorrow, is pasted all over her face. Maybe it's pity.

'It's my story,' I offer quietly, redundantly.

'I'm sorry, but it's not.'

'It's mine.'

'No. Look, I don't know how this has happened, but this – this whole thing – is a set-up. It's a PR exercise.'

'What—'

'Black promotion, Greil. Stage-managed. Manufactured. We're putting it out ourselves in order to generate interest for the show.'

'No.' My voice is a pathetic, defeated croak. My world seems to fall away from me.

'I'm really sorry if you thought it was yours,' she adds.

'I really am, but it's not. It's ours and it's been promised elsewhere. I'll be telling your people just as soon as I leave.'

I think of Graham. Imagine his reaction. *That fuckwit.*

'Look,' she continues, seeing me deflate before her eyes, 'I'll make it clear you're not at fault here. It's just . . . It's an anomaly really . . .'

(*An anomaly.*)

'. . . We could never have anticipated that it might get out ahead of schedule. It's no reflection on you.'

'You can't stop a paper printing a story,' I say, without much conviction. 'If they want to run it, they can. They might still . . .'

She smiles the smile of a patient teacher. 'Of course they could. They could run a spoiler if they really wanted to. But is it worth their while? If they took that course of action we'd make it clear to them that our relationship would be over. Peter isn't our only client, Greil. They'd be cutting themselves out of the share of any future spoils. Trust me, they won't do that.'

I look over at Heidi. And I'm about to apologise to her, the second victim of George's 'black promotion', when I see the look of discomfort that passes across her face and know that I've made another mistake. Another misunderstanding. A fresh anomaly.

'It's good publicity for everybody involved, Greil,' says George, reading my mind. 'Including Heidi. She thought that this was it – that you were the journalist doing the story.'

She thought that I was the journalist doing the story.

Because of course it's better for Benstead if she's a dancer, rather than a model. His real-life *Moll.* The perfect story, I called it. And it would be, wouldn't it? It was the perfect story because that's how Holly orchestrated it. As Emily Benstead takes her debut role on the West End stage, a lap dancer lives the part for real in her husband's bed. Run it for two weeks, say. In week one, Heidi, with torrid tales of five-times-a-night sex; how Peter Benstead wined and dined her; how he was 'insatiable', the best she'd ever had. So let's all book tickets to go and see *Moll*, to revel in Emily Benstead's misfortune. It's event theatre. Like being a part of the news for the evening. It'll be a laugh. But, hey, doesn't she bear up well? That final number, what was it called? 'Never Gonna Cry For You'. The really defiant one. She didn't half belt that one out. Like she was actually singing it to Peter Benstead. Fair sent a shiver down the spine.

Then there's week two, when the grovelling really begins. Because we want a little contrition from our fallen heroes, right? So maybe some kind of photo opportunity, staged, of course, by George, the erstwhile Mrs H. Sharkey, reformed hellraiser and idealist. Made to look snatched. Some kind of kissing and making-up picture. Or a first-public-appearance-for-shamed-club-owner-and-his-wife shot. Headline: MOLL-IFIED! The perfect story. Everyone's a winner. *Moll*'s takings go up and Benstead gets to look like the country's biggest stud into the bargain; Emily Benstead plays the wronged wife to perfection and gains respect for her professionalism amid personal crisis; George gets a PR coup; Heidi gets the quick route to fame, or infamy, depending on how you look at it, probably a modelling contract to boot and no doubt a big pay-off. Nobody goes home empty-handed from this show.

Except me.

Unsteady legs take me to the bed where I almost buckle, bunching the sheet in a hot fist, taking deep breaths. 'You,' I say to Heidi. She's stayed in the same position the whole time. She doesn't meet my eye, her eyelids drooped, looking down at her hold-all. 'You told me he screwed you. That he was holding you back. You know why, don't you? They don't want you to be a model, because it's a better story if you're a lap dancer. It doesn't suit the plot if you're a model, Heidi.'

George looks uncomfortable. At the bed, buffeted by my words, Heidi stays still.

'I bet you never even slept with him, did you?' And as I say it, the final penny drops. Of course she hasn't slept with him. Why bother when it's so much easier to simply say you did?

Breezily fabricate all the stuff about how great in bed he was; make the fiction complete. That way Emily Benstead gets to tell her friends that she's not the victim at all, what a hoot – got the media in the palm of our hand.

From somewhere I dredge a shard of boozy indignation. 'How great are you going to say he was, Heidi? Are you on a sliding scale? What are you going to wear for the shoot, Heidi?'

'Leave it, Greil.' This from George, her hand going to Heidi's shoulder.

'Is it that important to you, Heidi? Is posing in your underwear really that important to you?' My voice rises a moment, full of self-righteousness.

'And what were you offering, Greil?' spits George with some of the old fire I remember. 'What exactly were you offering that was any different?'

She's right, but still I say, 'I thought you were special,' and believe it, my anger exhausted, replaced by ruin. They look at me together. George zips up Heidi's bag for her, and they move to leave, followed by my wet-eyed, pathetic gaze as they walk around the bed; skirting the broken man whose legs finally fold as he kneels to the floor, a fistful of bedding still in his hand.

'George?' I say.

'Yes, Greil.' She opens the door and they turn. George cannot meet my eyes, kneeling on the floor, slick-faced and broken before her. I want to say, Please don't leave me. Please don't go. Let it be different this time. I want to tell them I love them and ask them to save me, the only two people who can. But I can manage none of this, so instead I ask George for one final thing, 'Can you give me an hour?'

'I'm sorry?'

Because I can still do it. Maybe. 'Leave it an hour before you call the paper. Do that one thing. Please?' She looks as if she's about to ask why, then doesn't bother.

'I'll do that, Greil. Goodbye.' And she touches Heidi's shoulder, guiding her out of the door which closes silently behind them. Clunk. I don't even hear their footsteps from the other side as they leave, taking the last of my hope with them. In their wake I kneel on the floor and my hands go to my hurt face and come away wet. For some moments I remain like that, crumpled, the picture of a man who was born to fail alone. Then, slowly, I pick myself up from the floor, locate my bag and set up the laptop.

The ghosts of Heidi and George still linger in the room, but I ignore them, some long-neglected self-preservation gene kicking in. An hour now, I think. An hour to get this Vegas copy written, mail it to Graham and hope he can authorise my advance before he discovers there's no splash. If I can just make the payment. This one thing.

With the laptop on I pick up the dictaphone and find the tape I stole from Jenny's bag, which I look at for the first time. The tape is labelled 'Jen's Dope Shit Part I' on one side, and 'Jen's Dope Shit Part II' on the other, but I tell myself that's because it once had Jen's Dope Shit on it, a compilation tape she made one night, perhaps before a long train journey. Only she's decided the shit isn't so dope any more, so she's taped over it with my Vegas interview, and hasn't got around to Tippexing over Jen's Dope Shit and writing 'Vegas Interview' and the date.

That's it, isn't it?

It's impossible that when I put my tape into the dictaphone and press Play there won't be the sounds of Vegas, but music. And that when I fast forward it, there'll be more music. And even more music when I turn it over and fast forward the other side. All music. The whole tape. An entire cassette of Jen's Dope Shit.

CHAPTER TWENTY-NINE

'Are you okay, Heidi?' says Holly when we get to her car. I don't say anything because I'm trying not to cry, and I'm trying not to cry because I can't block out the picture of Greil on the floor of the hotel room, watching us leave. Holly starts the engine and waits for me to say that of course I'm okay, and how I'm used to seeing men make fools of themselves in front of me.

'Heidi? Are you all right?' she says again, and still I say nothing. She responds by switching off the engine, which goes abruptly silent with a last cough that echoes around the underground car park. She rests her hands across the top of the steering wheel and places her head on them, squeezing her eyes shut, and for a while we sit there. Me, a kid that's been naughty in the supermarket; her, a mum gathering her wits, wondering if she can cope. Her car's a four-by-four. Big. She's left the air conditioning on so all we can hear is that, making a low whooshing sound, keeping us cool.

'I'm sorry about all that,' she says. 'Nobody ever wanted something like that to happen.'

'He was right, though.'

'Right about what?'

I round on her. 'That all you cared about was me being a dancer. That you wanted to keep me down.'

'It's not like that.'

'Peter made calls to Sonia. Greil was going to do a feature with me and he stopped that, too. And he did it all to make his story better. He was using me. That was my *dream*, Holly.'

And suddenly Holly turns on me, her eyes shiny with tears. 'Your *dream*,' she mimics nastily. 'Oh, for God's sakes. Don't play the wide-eyed innocent with me. You came into this with your purse open. You were happy to take his money. All he wanted you to do was *wait*, for God's sakes. And you knew that. What about you, creeping around behind our backs, signing on with Sonia? All you had to do was wait, Heidi. After that he would have given you anything in his power to give. Yes, you're right, it was, it *is*, better for the story if you're a dancer. It *makes* the story if you're a dancer. It was never going to be the world's biggest story. It's hardly front-page material. But still, we need to control it as much as we can, and that becomes more difficult if you're plastered all over other magazines, and if you'd stopped to think for even a second, you might have realised that, and that it would have been beneficial for you in the long run to just *wait*, instead of running around bleating about your dreams like a fucking schoolgirl.'

There's the whoosh of the air-conditioning. On top of that, I realise, is the sound of me sobbing. I close my eyes and think about what she's said. Feel that feeling, like being told off, only worse. Like being told off for doing something wrong in a foreign country. After a long pause, she says, 'I'm sorry. I didn't mean to shout at you. That was as upsetting for me as it was for you. Greil and I, we were together once.'

'Oh, God, I'm sorry.'

'No, I'm sorry.' She starts the engine. 'Come on,' she says, 'let's go.'

I pull my seatbelt around. 'Will he be all right, do you think?'

She seems to consider. 'Greil? I think so. He's a survivor. I don't know what he's doing getting himself involved in news for anyway. He's too soft.'

*

I keep rewinding and fast-forwarding Jen's Dope Shit, just in case. Just in case somewhere, hidden between tracks, is my interview with Vegas. But of course it's not. It's just track after track of the very dopest shit Jen could find, and as a final indignity the last track I hear playing before I rip out the cassette and hurl it in the direction of the bathroom is 'Bug Powder Dust' by Bomb The Bass. You should've stayed around for that one, George, I think. Your favourite ever bass line.

And now, as Jenny might say, I'm *dans le* deep *merde*. Now I have zip. No splash story, no Vegas interview, and soon, courtesy of Cooper, a trolley dash at the torture shop.

Unless.

Unless . . .

Because, if I'm not mistaken, this is the very machine I used when I wrote . . . I click into the laptop's hard disk and yes, there it is: my interview with the Diminutive Pop Princess herself. A file nestled in a folder. 'Minogue Int'.

This they'll never teach you at journalism college. I double-click 'Minogue Int', which opens obediently, a souvenir from happier times. I go to the Edit menu – it's right there next to the File menu – and there under the Edit menu is the Find command.

The Find and Replace command.

Find: I type 'Kylie'. *Replace*: I type 'Vegas'. I gulp and hit Return.

'Word has completed its search of the document and made 40 replacements,' says a text box. Every instance of the word Kylie in my Kylie Minogue interview now says Vegas.

I do the same thing, swapping every appearance of the word Minogue with the word Vegas. Just four replacements made by Microsoft Word there. Next I tinker with the headline, which I change from '*//headline// headline to come*' to '*//headline// Vegas Nights!*'

And lastly I change the file name from 'Minogue Int' to 'Vegas Int'.

And then I email it to Graham.

'Graham!' I say, when he answers the phone. 'How's it going, mate?'

'On deadline. Your Vegas copy. Where is it?'

'Open your email,' I say with a vocal flourish. 'Should be with you now.' I'm grinning because I once read that you can hear a smile down the phone; that it projects an aura of relaxation and confidence. In reality I want to be sick. 'You got it, mate?' I smile. Grinning hurts my face. I hear the sound of a mouse clicking his end. My sphincter begins burrowing its way up between my buttocks.

'Yeah, it's here,' he says.

'Excellent,' I grin.

'Wait a sec.'

'What?' Grin.

'S'all right. I thought it was corrupted. No, it's opened fine. "Vegas Nights". Inspired headline, mate. Never would've thought of that. So, is it so good that I can send it straight over to subs?'

I'm banking on it. 'Absolutely. On my honour. No work needed.'

'Yeah, well, I haven't got time to read it anyway. Okay, Greil, nice one, we'll talk soon, eh?' And he seems about to put the phone down.

'Graham!'

'Yeah.'

'Um, the money.'

'Oh God, right. You got the dancer's interview done, then?'

'All sorted, mate. And seeing as that's in the bag and you've now got the Vegas interview, I was hoping you could authorise that advance, like now-ish?'

Graham's acting like this isn't his major priority of the day. As if he has better things to do. Get a magazine out, say.

'Jesus,' he sighs. 'Come on, I'm up against it here. It's going to have to wait till this afternoon, mate.'

'Please,' I say. 'What's it going to take? One phone call to accounts?'

He tuts. 'Christ, you're fucking breaking my balls here . . .'

'Come on, Graham,' I plead. 'One phone call.'

'All right, all right. I'll get a cheque issued for tonight.'

'That'd be great, mate,' I say. Then, 'Sorry, did you say *cheque*?'

'Yeah, cheque. Now listen, I've got to shoot.'

'Wait, wait,' I almost scream, and for a half-second I think he's put down the phone, and I'm thinking that a cheque is about as much use to me as trench foot, but then he's still there, going, 'What?', so pissed off with me.

'Sorry, yeah, the cheque thing,' I laugh. 'Great and all that, but could I get it in cash?'

'Cash?'

'Cash.'

'Well . . . yeah. I suppose. Don't see why not. You'd have to come here, though, collect it from the petty cash window.'

God, right into the lion's den, but still, 'That would be brilliant. I can come over now.'

'All right. All right,' he laughs. 'I'll make sure it's waiting for you. Jesus, is it really worth all this bother?'

Not to you, I think. Not to you. Saying, 'Thanks, Graham. I owe you a pint,' but knowing that he'll never want to collect on that pint. Not when he discovers, as he inevitably will, that I've just submitted a Kylie Minogue interview in place of Vegas. And even though time's already a monkey on my sweating back, the stakes have suddenly been raised a notch or two. He's banging his cymbals now. If a sub spots the switch before I collect my advance, Graham will nix the money. Simple as that.

So once again I heave the laptop over my shoulder, grab my jacket, filch a couple more miniatures from the mini-bar and I'm out of the room. The last thing to catch my eye as I close the door behind me is the impression of Heidi's head on the bed pillow. I fancy I can see strands of blonde hair catching the sunlight. I was wrong about her, I think, feeling the booze lay a maudlin arm around my shoulders. Always wrong.

Child's ticket. Suit soaking wet. Stares on the tube. Laptop weighing me down like a drowning man with his pockets full of rocks. Still, I make good time on the Underground and join the Docklands Light Railway at Bank, diving on the shuttle, which is half rollercoaster, half toy train, and making my way to Canary Wharf. I force myself to look at my watch. 11 a.m. The deal was money by midday. I won't make it dead-on, no way, but come on, five, maybe ten minutes behind schedule, and as long as I've got the cash that's got to be worth something. Got to be.

Security don't like the look of me but they let me through anyway. The laptop does it, I reckon. And then I'm negotiating lifts and ramps and finding my way into the bowels of the building where barely helpful signs eventually point me in the direction of petty cash. They don't make it easy for the paper's correspondents to collect the money due to them, I think ruefully, before remembering that the money's not due to me, and, in fact, when I think about it, I'm actually defrauding the company of the money since it's an advance on a story that doesn't exist, agreed in receipt of an interview I don't have. Using that logic they could put the petty cash window in Russia and I still wouldn't have cause to complain.

In the end it turns out to be somewhere near the earth's core. Only people needing to collect and deposit packages from the postroom have to go further. As I approach the window a motorcycle courier appears from the far end of the corridor, leathers creaking. 'All right, mate,' he says, with a wary look at my face.

'Press for attention' says a sign and I have to buzz the buzzer twice before the girl appears. In the late Seventies, probably in the Eighties, and maybe even for a little bit of the Nineties, we would have called her a punk. I would have seen the piercings and the multicoloured hair and the perma-scowl as a sign of disenfranchised creativity, assumed she probably ran a small pottery or made a living decorating leather jackets with ornate Cramps logos. Now she just looks like a girl who's too stupid to do anything but work in the dungeons of Canary Wharf, doling out pin money to staff.

Once upon a time she might have been a Systemitis fan. At the front, wetting her panties over the lead guitarist. Now she sees the sweating, dishevelled, bruised, half-drunk, desperate man standing on the other side of her petty cash window and she registers no emotion whatsoever apart from a slight curling of the lip.

'Hi,' I say, running an unnecessary hand through my hair. I rest my other hand on her windowsill.

She stares at me. Above me, floors and floors above me, I imagine the industrious hive of the supplement. Graham – what do they do now? – 'driving' his desk, maybe one of those green eyeshades. Over to his corner ambles a subeditor, speccy girl, like the speccy girl out of *Scooby-Doo*. 'Graham?' she says. 'Yeah,' he says. 'You know this Vegas feature?' she says. 'Yeah,' he says. 'Well, there's something a bit weird about it . . .'

'Yeah, hi,' I say to the metal-faced girl. 'Hi. My name's Greil Sharkey. I've come to collect some petty cash.'

'Authorised?'

'No, I thought I'd come on the off-chance.'

She stares, her lip curls some more.

'Yeah,' I say, 'of course it's authorised. By Graham Stevenson.'

'There isn't a Graham Stevenson in accounts.'

'That's because he's not in accounts.'

'Then it's not authorised.'

'Look,' I say, my fist clenching on the windowsill, 'Graham is, like, *above* accounts. There's God, the editor, then Graham, then accounts, then you, then me. And God authorises the editor to authorise Graham to authorise accounts to authorise you to give the money to me.'

She stares. 'Name?' she spits.

'I've just fucking told you.'

'I don't have to put up with language like that,' she snaps.

So do I. I snap too.

'Oh, don't come over the fucking Christian with me. Look at the fucking state of you,' I shout, but she's gone – 'fuck off' – gone.

I stand staring at the window. I can just about make out my own reflection in it. On the other side, the metal-faced girl has moved off to sit behind a desk in the furthest reaches of her cubbyhole. If I crane my head I can just see her, a little bit of postbox-red hair, an elbow and a Doc Marten. My reflection takes deep breaths. I pass another unnecessary hand through my hair and lean into the window frame, saying, 'Hello?'

She doesn't answer. I get the mad feeling I'm trying to make up after a lover's tiff, locked out of the house and calling through the letterbox. 'Look,' I say. 'I'm really sorry. I didn't mean to swear. I promise it won't happen again.'

'Piss off.'

I check my watch. 11 a.m. is a distant memory. Above me, Velma from *Scooby-Doo* gets up from her desk and wanders over to where Graham sits with his green eyeshade on. 'About this Vegas interview . . .'

'*Please*,' I say. 'I'm sorry. I really am.'

'Piss off or I'm calling security. And don't think I won't be telling Graham whatsisface about it either, cos I will be.'

I look at my laptop. A few years old, a bit scruffy, seen a lot of action. It would only fetch about £250 down Cash Converters and that's if I had the time to sell it, which I don't. So I'm about to heave it at the window, climb through, knock her senseless with it and steal all the money when I have a better idea.

'Hello?' I call. 'Look, I've got a laptop here. Now, I tell you what, you can *have* my laptop – to keep, no questions asked – if you'll just give me my money.'

She says nothing.

'It's a really good laptop, just a couple of years old. A Macintosh. Come on, you can't say fairer than that.' *You could sell it to buy drugs, perhaps*, I think, and maybe she thinks the same thing, because her chair scratches back and when I see her face there's a distinct gleam in her eye, although it might just be light reflecting off a piercing.

'Hold it up to the window,' she says.

I unzip the bag and fish out the laptop, offering it to the glass. She cranes her neck to see. 'I prefer the orange colour,' she says. Curse me for having blueberry.

'Still the same inside, though,' I say. 'And it's yours. All for . . .' *doing your fucking job* . . . 'just giving me my money. Or think of it as a sorry for swearing. Either way.'

She doesn't shift from her seat. I'm still holding up the laptop, like Lot 145 what-am-I-bid? Grinning stupidly over the top of it.

'All right,' she says without moving. 'Name?'

'Sharkey. Greil.'

She pulls herself back to her desk and I hear the tapping of a keyboard. 'Is Sharkey your first name?' she calls.

'No, my second name.'

'Ah.'

Pause.

'Okay, I've got you.'

My reflection in the window makes a YES! face. I hear something opening, then the unmistakable sound of money being counted, *fluk-fluk-fluk-fluk*, imagine fifty-pound notes flicking through Metal Face's brightly coloured fingernails. Then shuffling as notes are pushed into an envelope and now she's back at the window, a strange look on her face.

'It's definitely Greil Sharkey?' she says.

'Yes,' I say, the envelope so near I can virtually smell the cash. Just wanting to get the money now. Get away from here.

'*Graham, about this Vegas interview . . .*'

'And you're going to give me that computer in return for this envelope?'

'Yes.'

'First? Before I give you the money?' Still she has an odd

look on her face, the kind of look people have when they're half expecting a camera crew to appear from around the side of the house.

'Yes.'

'What's wrong with it?'

'Nothing. Nothing at all.'

'And it's yours to give away, is it?' Her eyes ramble across my bruises as she says this.

'Absolutely. Cross my bra.'

'Why don't you want it, then?'

'I'm a journalist. I've got tons. It'd just gather dust.'

'Oh, all right, then. Come to the door.' The door of her cubbyhole opens on to the corridor. She opens it a laptop-sized crack.

'What about my money?' I say, hesitating.

Her eyes regard me from around the door. 'Through the window. You'll have to sign for it. Give us it here, then, before someone sees.'

I hand her the laptop. All this for saying 'Fucking', I think. This has to be my most expensive fucking ever. She closes the door and I hear the bag being unzipped as she verifies there is indeed a blueberry-coloured iBook inside. Back at the window she's still regarding me as though I've recently arrived from the planet Moron, but after a shaky signature from me, she at last slides the envelope through a portal at the bottom of the window.

'Nice doing business with you,' she says, but she says it to my back because I'm already halfway down the corridor, the image of Velma in my mind. Graham picking up the phone to Petty Cash. Petty Cash picking up the phone to Security. 'Apprehend the sweaty man with the bruises.' But Security let me through and at last I step out into the sunshine, walk-running back towards the trains, not bothering to check my watch because I'm late, but I've got the money, and as I jog along, I rip open the envelope to check the cash inside.

I stop, the money in my hand. I leaf through the notes. I do it twice. With Canary Wharf towering way, way above me like a giant Ikea CD rack, I stare at the money in my hands, and then I count it again.

It comes to just £200.

A feeling like I've been suddenly hoisted into the air. Or like I'm going to be sick or fall over. But I ride it, reaching for my mobile with jittery fingers, thinking, This could be a very bad idea: Velma notwithstanding, what if George has been in touch? Yes, it could be a very bad idea indeed, but what choice have I got?

'Graham,' I say, when Graham answers the phone.

'Greil,' he groans. 'What *now*?'

So I'm safe for the time being. No Velma, no George. 'Well, it's about this advance on the splash, mate,' I say, grinning. 'I reckon . . . um, I think there must have been a bit of a clerical error.' I say the words 'clerical error' in a comedy robot voice because I know Graham likes that kind of thing.

'What do you mean? What sort of error?'

'Well, there's only two hundred quid here, mate.'

'Yeah?'

I do a sort of snorty laugh. 'Well, um, correct me if I'm wrong, but I don't think two hundred quid is the going rate on a splash. I was thinking more like . . . more like . . . a *grand*.'

Graham does a snorty laugh. 'Wait up, wait up. A grand, you say? A *splash* you say? Sorry if I've missed something here, but who said it was a splash?'

'You . . . did?'

'No I never. Not in this life is it a fucking splash. We're talking about the same story, right? The ex-footballer turned nightclub owner shagging a lap dancer. A consensual, legal, drug-free relationship between a lap dancer and an ex-footballer? A splash?'

'But—'

'No, Greil, no. Not even if Beckham fails to get his hair cut that week. No.'

'A good story, you said.'

'Yeah, a good story. But there's a world of difference between a good page-five story, some dollybird doing a kiss-and-tell thing, and the splash. You see what I'm saying here? Jesus, what century are you living in?'

The wrong one, I think, pennies dropping all around me.

'Wait a sec, Greil,' and I hear him off the phone talking to someone nearby. I hear the words 'Vegas interview', the words 'Jason Donovan', the words 'Michael Hutchence' and then Graham's coming back and I end the call as he's saying, 'Greil?'

*

Okay, let's think about this. A quick review of my current situation. I've just had two women I love walk out on me. Both at the same time. My face looks like a burst planet, I've just crapped on what little career I had, and I'm late for an appointment to pay a debt with money I don't have.

So I'm going to leave the country.

Drastic, yes, but I have a brother who lives in New York, and if I can get him to pay for my air fare over there, I've got a chance of making it. All I need to do is get to Heathrow.

That's all I need to do.

The idea is to get home, fetch my stuff and make my way to the airport. I'll worry about calling Tony when I get there. As long as I can reach Heathrow I should be okay. Fuck, even if he doesn't want to put me up he's bound to lend me the cash for a ticket somewhere. Systemitis were big in Australia. Maybe I could gauge the interest and release a compilation, perhaps get into music journalism out there. Point is, as long as they speak English wherever I go, I've got a shot at making a fresh start. A chance for redemption.

One silver lining: I can afford to buy a travelcard. I get home in about three-quarters of an hour, find the suitcase – an old weekend case of George's with a little trolley handle fit only for weak dwarfs – and chuck it on the bed before starting to pack. I say 'pack'. In fact what I do is burgle my own flat, pulling out drawers and emptying them into the case, throwing in random jeans and T-shirts, all with the names of bands on, all relics from my days with the *NME*. George and I always talked about having a 'special folder' for all our 'important' stuff but needless to say we never got round to it, so it takes me an age to find my passport. My mobile rings as I'm searching but I leave it.

Midday has long since gone.

I can't bring myself to leave without washing, though, so with my self-extradition kit ready I jump in the shower for what feels like the first time in decades.

I get out of the shower, pull on jeans and a T-shirt (The Fall. Apt), grab the suitcase and head for the door. I'll be back, when the dust has settled, hopefully, to collect the rest of my things before I jump island permanently. Not goodbye, I tell my flat, as I head for the door, just *au revoir*, and I pull open the door.

Perhaps they rang the bell while I was in the shower. Who knows, maybe they rang the bell and were waiting politely for me to answer the door. There they are, anyway, standing on my doorstep: the two cables, RGB and Scart.

It takes me a split-second to recognise them. Their makeover is complete. The tracky bottoms and trainers have gone, and they're now looking every inch the hired muscle. Sunglasses, smart trousers, jackets over white shirts and shiny black shoes. I just have time to notice that RGB's shirt seems to be speckled with dirt before he puts a hand to my chest and shoves me back so roughly I skitter and fall hard to the hallway carpet.

They hobble in and close the door behind them, both of them wincing slightly as they walk. There's a pause.

'New shoes?' I say, from the carpet.

'Yeah,' says RGB, and uses one of them to kick me in the stomach. I howl and writhe, tensing for a second kick which thankfully doesn't come. Instead Scart squats down and pushes his dot-to-dot face in mine. 'Missed your deadline,' he says.

'Hurg,' I say, in agony, and RGB reaches down and hauls me to my feet, thrusts his forearm across my windpipe and shoves me against the hallway of my flat.

I go, 'Ach,' but he ignores me. Doesn't even bother pinning my arms, just uses his weight to simultaneously pin and choke me. Scart does a quick recce of the flat, comes back, and for a moment the pair of them stare at me like *Planet of the Apes.* until Scart says, 'Craig played us one of your records. Fucking shite.'

'Ach,' I say against the forearm across my neck.

'Bring the car around,' says RGB to his mate, who smirks and leaves, then to me, 'Look at you. I've seen some sad fuckers, but you really are the daddy of the lot.'

'Ach,' I say.

He casts a look at my suitcase, which stands in the middle of the hallway, obediently waiting to be picked up and taken to New York. 'Where did you think you were going, then?' he says.

'Ach,' I say, and he releases his grip slightly.

'To you. To drop the money off,' I manage, catching my breath, trying hard to think what people in films do in situations like this. They usually rely on a deus ex machina – a plucky heroine or pet; a bottle of bleach left carelessly on a nearby table, the hero's fingers creeping towards it as he engages his attacker in witty banter.

'Bit of luck, then,' he says, looking up the hall at nothing in particular, wondering what's for tea. 'We'll save you the bus fare, eh?'

His grip on my throat has relaxed, and even though he's got the weight, height, fitness and probably countless spill-my-pint fights behind him, I've got motivation, and the minor relaxation of his arm on my throat gives me a whisper of hope in an otherwise silent day.

'What happened to your shirt?' I say, needing to keep him talking.

'Shut yer mouth,' he says.

'Did you fall over?' I say.

He looks at me like I've just asked him for a blow job. 'No. I did not *fucking* fall over,' he says. 'We ran into an old mate.'

'Good mate, then?' I say, still trying to keep him talking.

'Dog Shit?' he adds, looking away again. 'No. He was the school freak,' and I feel the little hairs on the back of my neck stand up: *Dog Shit*.

And I say, almost to myself, although it has the right effect, 'Not Dog Shit who wears the washing-up glove?'

He releases his grip. Steps away. Takes off his shades and says to me, 'How the fuck did you know that?'

And I use the opportunity to knee him as hard in the bollocks as I possibly can.

CHAPTER THIRTY

There is chewing gum to collect, the posters to patrol and, though I have failed to accumulate the evidence I need, there's nothing to stop me taking my gum to Emily and presenting it to her as an offering. A token. Material proof that I have been her protector and hero. I imagine appearing to her in her dressing room. I have made my way into the theatre, into its Byzantine depths, corridors like the tendrils of the tube map. I don't know where to find Emily's dressing room, but I'm somehow drawn there until I find myself standing before a door with her name and a large gold star upon it, knowing that she's inside.

I knock softly on the door, holding a bag of chewing gum in lieu of a bouquet.

'Come,' she says, with the soft serenity of stardom, and I enter, closing the door gently behind me and casting my eyes around the room. Admirers have filled it with flowers, the room is dark with them, the scent of them mingles with her perfume. Along one wall hang the gowns and costumes she wears for the production, ready for the evening's performance. She sits before a mirror with bulbs lining its edges. Her hand is to her mouth applying lipstick but she has paused and regards me in the reflection. Not her hero and protector, but somebody to be pitied. An injured, defeated man, one arm caked in blood, with a small plastic bag dangling from his fingers.

Yet when she turns demurely on her stool, tucking her robe carefully as she does so, her eyes brim with sympathy, and the image that greets her is not to be feared – her hand does not stray to her emergency call button, one press of which would bring security guards running; he is not a monster to be pitied.

Instead what she sees is the returning soldier, bloodied from battle, but proud.

With the light from the mirror behind her, she reaches out her hands and beckons him forward. Gently she takes the bag of gum from him and places it on her dressing table, knowing instinctively what it symbolises. For the moment she wants only to comfort him, and when she takes his hands and he winces with pain, she winces too, sharing. Soon she is asking him to take her seat and she brings a footstool forward, sitting on it to tend to his wounds. With the care and expertise of a nurse she removes the glove and winces again at the sight of the wound beneath, talking to him at the same time, gently telling him how proud of him she is, how brave he is: 'My hero. My hero.'

My hero . . .

And though the pain in my arm has become almost unbearable, and fatigue seems to have drained me of all energy, I manage to pull myself to the tube station, where I go into the bottle and begin my day's rounds . . .

*

RGB's on the floor and he's moaning with his hands cupping his injured bollocks, but he's not quite down for the count, and as I reach for the suitcase and make for the door, his hand hooks my trailing leg, sending me sprawling to the carpet. I kick out and scrabble away from his grasp, regain my feet and twirl to see him up on his haunches, ready to grab me a second time. His face works a picture of pain and anger. With one hand he steadies himself on the floor, with the other he reaches for me like a zombie, fingers clawed – *comin' to getcha*. He lurches forward, but I avoid him, and my shoe crunches into his eye. This time he falls flat to the carpet, yelping, a hand at his face. I kick him again – for luck – grab the suitcase and make it out of the door, whirling to pull it closed behind me, smothering his final, enraged roar.

How long does it take to fetch a car? Scart is nowhere to

be seen but I don't waste the seconds, hoisting the case and making for the pavement, glancing all ways and breaking into a run, needing to get out of sight, hearing something behind me which might be the door to my flat opening. I do a smart right into another street, offering up a silent prayer that I won't see Scart coming in the opposite direction. He isn't, and still at a trot I make my way to the canal.

The towpath gives me almost a clear run to the tube. It's not a route you'd take if you didn't have to. If the mud doesn't put you off in winter then the drunks and gangs of kids will do the trick in the summer. But keeping hidden is my main priority, so I find myself yomping along the sun-baked path, carrying my suitcase across my chest like a baby, huffing sweatily in the heat. All I hear is the sound of my own heavy breathing, the thump-thump of my footfalls. I picture the scene at my flat: the two cables, apoplectic with rage, piling into their Merc and laying rubber like an episode of *The Sweeney*, cruising along the road, scrutinising side streets, swearing, furious.

I reach the end of the towpath and lean into the kissing gate, trying to see into the road. The tube beckons. Four entrances, stairs and tunnels, like the arms and legs of a sleeping man. One sleeve outstretched in my direction, a dash across the road and two hundred yards away. Near. Very near.

I catch my stuttering breath, and think – put myself in their position. They're angry, but they have bugger all to go on. Okay, so the suitcase is a giveaway – they can be fairly certain I'm going *somewhere*. But for all they know I might own a car, I might have hurried for a bus. There's an overland station nearby, so I might have gone that way. In short, there are a ton of transport options, and how are they to know my preferred method of getting around? Plus, I had a head start. Plus, they're both wearing new shoes.

The odds, although hardly in my favour, aren't bad. They're a gambler's odds. Good enough to make it worth a punt.

So with a last look left and right for the Merc, I ease open the kissing gate and step out onto the pavement.

There is no noise of screeching brakes. No shout of discovery. Just the sound of the day and my own heavy breathing. So I hold the case, aiming to look as normal as possible and dart across the road, then begin the jog to the tube station.

I make it. Down the stairs and into the ticket hall, and there's still no sign of either of the cables. I allow myself the luxury of picturing them still cruising, banging the steering wheel in frustration, arguing over their options, falling out, then drawing guns and killing each other. It's a nice image. It warms the cockles as I manoeuvre my way through the gates and take the escalator underground.

On the platform I walk to the end and use the two minutes indicated by the timer to change my T-shirt. 'Let's get you out of these wet things,' I murmur to myself, peeling off my sweat-soaked Fall T-shirt and pulling another from my suitcase. This one says The Family Cat on the front, and on the back it says Make My Life Beautiful. Not much of a cunning disguise, but maybe just enough to fool the roving eye. Playing the odds now. If I get on the next train I'll be on the Piccadilly Line, so I've got a straight run to Heathrow, where the line ends and where planes take off. I'm not exactly home, but, I think, as I pull the T-shirt over my head, at least I'm dry.

And then I see them. As the train roars into the station, so do they, hobbling at a run on to the platform at the opposite end, looking frantically around them. I turn, pulling my suitcase in front of me to hide it, offering them my back and the logo that says Make My Life Beautiful, eyes squeezed tight shut and praying, Please don't let them see me. The train pulls to a stop and I steel myself against the sound of rapidly approaching feet, my heart in my mouth as the door opens and I shoulder past a woman to step inside.

I allow myself a look behind to check if they've got on, but see nothing, and I take a seat, hardly daring to breathe, hardly daring to believe they might have missed me.

They have. The doors close and no hand prevents them doing so at the last second. The train starts away and I find myself craning to look down the carriages again, half expecting to see them there, slowly making their way towards me, opening and closing the dividing doors like ticket inspectors on a mission. Still no sign, and the train begins to pick up speed, but not fast enough. Too slowly. Too fucking slowly. Come on, I think. *Come on.*

And with a sudden sick realisation I swivel to look out of the window in time to see RGB on the platform, level with me, half-limping, half-jogging alongside the train and banging at the glass as I turn to meet his eye. The good eye, at least. My kick has closed his other one. He has just enough time to draw his finger across his throat as the train enters the tunnel, Scart at his heels.

I turn back to quizzical looks from passengers, which I return with a never-met-the-fella shrug. I could care less. Instead I'm thinking furiously. They've clocked me on the tube. They know which way I'm heading. What will they do, board the next one? Possibly, but if I were them, I'd jump in the car and try and get on at a station further down the line. I know the routes, but I stand to check the tube map anyway, tracing my finger along the arteries of the different lines. I'm on the Piccadilly. All the way to Heathrow. It's the line I need to stay on; the problem is they know I'm on it. The next stop is Finsbury Park, but there's no way they'll make it there in time. Their best bet would be to go to either Arsenal or Holloway Road . . . in which case – my finger moves to another line – *my* best bet is to get off at Finsbury Park and get on the Victoria Line, bypass Arsenal and Holloway Road then get back on to the Piccadilly Line at King's Cross and continue to Heathrow.

If I can make it to King's Cross I'll be laughing – too many trains, too many people. If I can make it there I'll be in the clear. God grant me that. God let me win this one time. Please.

So I change at Finsbury Park. A quick dash across the platform. Ever-watching, like a spazmoid surveillance camera. I jump on the Victoria Line and grit my teeth for the two-stop journey to King's Cross. Meanwhile, the cables hobble to their car and race to Holloway Road, limping up and down the sides of trains as they pull in, failing to find me, arguing, drawing guns etc.

The train pulls in at King's Cross and I get off, wheeling my suitcase now, trying to blend in, using crowds of tourists to hide whenever possible. My heart's in my mouth all the way from the Victoria Line back to the Piccadilly, scanning the crowds, then scanning the platform extra carefully. When the train pulls in I hold back for as long as possible, keeping my options open until I'm sure there's no sign of them, and then, at last, I rejoin the Piccadilly, back on track now, en route for Heathrow, where the planes take off, where advertising hoardings promise sun in faraway places. Surely, now, I will have lost them.

The doors slide shut and I allow myself to relax a little, wiping the sweat from my brow, literally and metaphorically. I remain by the exit, half-sitting on my suitcase and trying to ignore a kid who looks like a foreign exchange student, and who clearly wants me to offer help because he's looking theatrically at a map. The train reaches Russell Square and Holborn without incident. Each time, I stand up from my perch on the suitcase and poke my head out of the open doors, scanning the platform for a glimpse of the cables, finding none then taking my seat again, counting the stops to Heathrow. Hoping. Hoping.

But this is me we're talking about here. Greil Sharkey: loser.

The train pulls in at Covent Garden and I stand, rubberneck out of the carriage and there he is: RGB. He's at the far end of the platform, walking painfully along the side of the carriage in my direction. He's peering in through the windows, wounded, angry, vigilant. Shit, he's unstoppable, I think. Like the fucking Terminator. Like Freddy, Jason and the geezer out of *Halloween* all rolled into one. For a second the sight of him freezes me until a high-pitched whistle brings me back to reality and I swivel round to see Scart at the other end of the platform, almost a mirror-image of RGB. He's seen me, whistled to get RGB's attention. Dimly I think, That was a good whistle. I never got the hang of that kind of whistle. Scart smiles and I jerk back but RGB has spotted me. Two sentinels at either end of the platform. They start to limp more quickly forward, closing in.

I grab the case and step outside the train, looking for the exit. But it's too far away, they'd reach it ahead of me. Passengers hurry on and off, and I'm on the platform as it suddenly dawns on me that my only hope is to get the two cables *inside* the train. I need to trick them inside and leave myself on the outside.

I place my suitcase. I put a foot on the step of the carriage, ready, like a gunslinger. The train bleeps three bleeps, the warning to say the doors are closing. The last of the passengers dive on.

'Mind the doors,' says an announcement. 'Mind the closing doors.'

The cables are, they're minding a door each. All three of us are standing on the platform now. Me in the middle, each of us by a door. RGB gets The Family Cat side of my T-shirt; Scart gets Make My Life Beautiful. They wait, ready for me to make my play. As if in slow motion the doors of the train begin to close and I see the cables tense. At the very last second I make a great show of flinging myself into the carriage and the final thing I see before I land back inside is Scart doing the same.

But I placed my suitcase carefully. I placed it so the doors of my carriage wouldn't close. So they'd hit the suitcase and leave a human-sized gap to leap through, back to the outside of the train. To safety.

And that's what would have happened if the foreign exchange student hadn't been so quick off the mark. If he hadn't spotted my dilemma and helpfully pulled my case out of harm's way, neatly avoiding the closing doors, saying, 'It can be confusing, yes?'

The train starts with a jolt which has me fighting to keep my balance, staring in disbelief at the doors, closed. Not half-open, with my suitcase in the way, but closed, with the foreign exchange student grinning at me, offering me the case.

'You stupid. Fucking. Cunt,' I say.

I look down the carriage. See RGB – what? maybe three carriages away – open a dividing door and limp through, his hunter's stare meeting mine, trapped and helpless. I whirl around and at the other end of the train Scart is doing the same thing. The two of them hobbling implacably towards me, piggy in the middle.

'Sorry? What is cunt?' says the student.

'Cunt is you!' I bawl back. And he looks shocked. 'Do you know what you've done? Do you know what you've fucking done?' I screech. He places my suitcase carefully to the floor and backs away, looking at me reproachfully then taking a seat.

But now I'm thinking. Actually, I'm counting. I'm remembering what Freak Boy told me: that Covent Garden to Leicester Square is the shortest distance between two stops on the underground and that the trip takes forty seconds, doors closed to doors open. Bearing in mind I've just spent roughly ten seconds calling the foreign exchange student a cunt, that leaves about thirty seconds. More to the point, it leaves them about thirty seconds to reach me, and they're more than thirty seconds away, making their way along the carriages, squeezing past the passengers, opening and closing the doors. More than thirty seconds. Got to be.

The passengers stare at me in the wake of my outburst, then go back to what they were doing. I heft the suitcase, ready, counting. From opposite directions, the cables continue to make their way towards me.

Twenty seconds. I try and recollect the layout of Leicester

Square. It'll be tight, but I'll have surprise and the cover of other passengers – and all those lovely tourists – to help me. If I can evade them on the platform then I can lose them in Leicester Square itself.

Ten seconds. I do a look left and right and they're still some distance away, perhaps not aware how short the journey is. New shoes slowing them down. Got that on my side. Thank God for Freak Boy. Thank God for new shoes.

And then the train stops . . .

*

Passers-by look nervously at my wounded arm as I take a seat on the platform at Leicester Square. My body is finally, blissfully, glad of some rest, but my mind does not accord. In my hand I hold an empty plastic bag, frustratingly empty. In front of me I see a piece of gum.

It rests on Emily's knee. How it appeared there, I don't know. Doubtless thrown from the platform, perhaps even left there by a tube worker, making his way along the track in the early hours of the morning when the tubes don't run. Either way, it sits there, mocking me. A symbol of my negligence, my failure. I feel my breathing, heavy. The pain in my arm threatens to overwhelm and then, despite my body crying out for more rest, I stand and walk to the edge of the platform. Passengers move around me, the station is busy, but I don't see them. They exist only on the periphery of my consciousness, which is focused now on the gum, a short distance way, across the tracks.

Then, suddenly, a train. It roars into the station before I'm even aware of it, almost brushing me, such is my proximity to the tracks. Momentarily it obscures the *Moll* poster and the offending piece of gum and I allow myself to believe, however briefly, that the train will wipe away the gum and that when it has discharged its passengers, and when the doors have closed and it draws off, the gum will have gone too.

It hasn't, of course, and as the train draws away I find myself dropping to my haunches, watching the carriages disappear, then dangling one foot over the edge. Somebody shouts something and it's aimed at me, I realise dimly. But it comes from a long way away, so far away I hardly hear it. All I hear is my own breathing.

And now my breathing is a roar in my ears, and my eyes are focused on the gum just a few feet away from me, so close. From somewhere there is another shout, but I ignore it, swinging my other leg and letting myself on to the tracks like a nervous swimmer, hearing nothing – not the shouts to stop, not the deafening scream of an oncoming train. Seeing only the gum and my outstretched hand, a yellow Marigold washing-up glove that grasps and pulls at the gum. Pulls it away from Emily's knee as she watches me from her seat on the poster.

'My hero,' she says.

*

It doesn't just stop the way trains normally stop, a slow-down and a last stagger as it reaches its destination and the doors open. It stops with a bang. A high-pitched shriek of brakes and then a bang, more quickly than you'd ever expect a speeding tube train to stop, even one on the system's shortest distance from station to station. 0.16 miles. Just forty seconds.

Those passengers standing are thrown as if pushed, grabbing at handrails to steady themselves, their faces wearing a sudden mask of panic instantly replaced by Londoner boredom. A book goes flying. My suitcase topples and I nearly fall over it. But then I'm on my feet, looking left and right to see Scart and RGB, still coming, both regaining their balance.

And now my back's to the carriage – Make My Life Beautiful – and my fingers have found the join where the doors meet and I'm pulling at them, even though there's nowhere to go but tunnel. I'm pulling at them because I half expect the train to suddenly lurch forward and complete the last few seconds of its journey, spilling me out on to the platform, the running man.

I hear the connecting doors. Everything else in the aftermath of the emergency stop is silent apart from the sound of footsteps towards me and, I realise, the sound of my own whimpering as my fingers claw uselessly at the train doors.

RGB thumps my face into the glass and spins me around. He's flanked by Scart, who looks up and down the carriage, warding off the stares of passengers with mean looks of his own. My eyes desperately scan the carriage over RGB's shoulder. He holds me in a depressingly familiar grip.

'You silly cunt,' he snarls, right up in my face, then headbutts me. When my vision returns I shout a help to the carriage, which pretends I'm not there. A fist thuds into my stomach, a knee into my bollocks. I drop to my own knees as hands grip my hair and a punch slams into the side of my face. My eyes meet the foreign student's and he seems to regard me for a moment before he looks away, just as a knee smashes into my nose which I hear shatter, my mouth suddenly full of blood.

TWO MONTHS AFTER THAT

Picking up the magazine, I wonder if I'll ever get used to this feeling, this thrill of seeing my name in print, knowing other people are reading it, too. People from the dim and distant past, all those people who wished me the worst; people from the not-so-distant past. Maybe I'll get used to it. Maybe. I haven't so far.

So you'll forgive me for making a bit of an event out of it. I've resisted sneaking a peek on the way back from the shop, and now I'm going to milk the moment; make myself a nice cup of tea; settle down and bask in my glory. It ends up being a good five minutes between arriving home with my booty and actually inspecting it – a cup of tea steaming in front of me.

I go to the contents and, because my piece is nice and prominent, I find the page number easily. Not all of the pages have page numbers at the bottom. It takes me a minute or so to locate the right one, and then – there it is. Not the 'Debutarts' section, for the rank beginners; not even 'Bap Idol' where readers get to vote the clothes off their favourite babe. No, I've got a whole feature all to myself.

What's he doing there? I think. They've added a comical touch to the page. Dean probably thought it up, knowing him: a tiny head and shoulders picture of Peter, a really old shot by the looks of things: he's got a Kevin Keegan perm and the old-style England strip on. In a speech bubble coming out of his mouth he's saying, 'I'm a lucky bastard.' But that's all from Peter. I assume he's mentioned in the text, but who's going to be reading the text when there are – and I count – seven pages crammed with pictures of me. Pictures of me in a bikini, in hot pants, in bed with the sheet artfully arranged around me. HEIDI, HI! says the headline, and below it, *It's Benstead's Porridge-Stirrer In All Her Glory*. I study the pictures carefully, realising with a thrill that they've removed a mole from my shoulder. In one shot I'm hugging my knees and I inspect my feet, which look good. To mark the occasion I had a professional manicure but the girl was dozy and I could have done better myself. I'd also been for a sunbed but Sonia reckons I should work on my tan a bit more, so it's lucky I'm going to Mauritius in a couple of days. After my shoot for the *Sun*, that is; after my afternoon shooting for the *Daily Star*'s MegaBabes website; after a morning filming my appearance on a documentary all about kiss-and-tell girls.

And after my appearance at a film premiere that Holly has organised, accompanying another of her clients, a young black footballer whose name I forget.

He's really quite fanciable, actually.

*

I buy two copies of the magazine I'm in. One for my records, for portfolio purposes; another just for show, to have it hanging around the place. So I don't read it straight away. I reserve that pleasure for later. Instead I use scissors to carefully excise the relevant pages from the magazine, and I place the pages into plastic folders for safekeeping, next clipping them into a ring binder. Safe there, I leave them. Not my first cuttings, obviously – hopefully not my last, either. And then I go to make a nice cup of tea before settling down to read my feature, *in situ*, as it were – in the correct context of the magazine. I find I still feel a frisson at seeing my name in print when I turn to the page and read the headline: A TROUBLED PAST. A MIRACLE ESCAPE. 'A TALENT TO DIE FOR'. Below that: HOW LONDON'S HIPPEST YOUNG ARTIST TURNED HIS LIFE INTO ART.

And there it is. The whole story of how I turned my life into art. How I was discovered by an agent following my escape from beneath an oncoming tube train. She followed the story and found I was an artist – saw a story of her own.

Not, as the article's author says, a 'miracle' escape. Actually, there was no divine intervention; everything was working as it should.

The suicide pit was first introduced to London Underground stations in the 1930s, a reaction to the high numbers of suicides during the depression. In fact, the pit was introduced to aid the clean-up operation following a 'one under' episode, as they are colloquially known, but an observational study printed in the *British Medical Journal* in 1999 found that their presence halved the mortality rate in instances of suicide attempts.

The Suicide Pit is the title of a painting forming part of my first exhibition, which opens at the Anthony Hoffman Gallery next month. It is a visualisation of what I saw that day, as I took my first steps across the tracks, reaching out for the piece of gum on Emily's knee, only to fall headlong into a metre-deep trench put there to collect falling human bodies. The piece uses oils and is textured to suggest the depth and darkness of the pit, its gloom lit by sparks, like fireworks above my head, as I lay there with blue fire raining down on me, the squeal of brakes – deafening – pitched so much higher than the screech more commonly heard on the Underground – the wheel flanges as a train rounds a curve. This was the scream of machinery in pain.

The driver was commended for stopping so quickly. Just half of his train had entered the station and I saw his ashen face as I climbed out from under the front of the train, clambered over the rails and plucked the piece of chewing gum from Emily's knee before placing it in my freezer bag. A witness to the event later said it was the most beautiful thing she had ever seen.

The Most Beautiful Thing She's Ever Seen is a video installation of CCTV footage of the event, and will also form part of my first show. Perhaps the article exaggerates when it compares the incident to Van Gogh severing his own ear, but it is certainly one of the most controversial exhibits appearing.

It joins several other pieces, some I'm currently working on: my Marigold glove, my journals, cassette-corder, and, of course, the triptych, since repaired. And if the story makes no mention of the artist assaulting his careworker, that's because following consultation it was agreed to overlook the matter on the basis that I sign a new Contract to Get Well, a fresh undertaking to continue with my medication, as well as agree to appear in a little article in a magazine for health workers: 'A Homerton Success Story.'

My Contract to Get Well will form part of my show, which opens at the Anthony Hoffman gallery next month. There will be many guests of honour, and a PR woman called Holly Foreman has confirmed Emily Benstead will also be attending.

I'm told she's looking forward to meeting me.

*

I have in my hand a piece of paper. It's in my good hand, naturally. Since Cooper and Co. came good on their promise to put me up to Defrost I've tended to favour my right. For a while I even had to wear a glove, and wasn't that just irony you can chew on. Me and Freak Boy, two sides of the same coin. But they let me off lightly as it goes. I still have to apply cream every day, and no amount of Touche Eclat is going to hide the damage, but I can use it, at least. I'm already working on a suitable anecdote – got it rescuing a baby from a burning building, a holiday chalet. The truth of your story lies in the details.

Which brings me to the piece of paper I'm holding in my hand. It was lying on the doormat when I arrived back from the shop armed with a packet of cigarettes and a magazine that caught my eye while I was in the newsagents. I'd be nosing through it right now if I wasn't basking in the glory of what's just landed in my hallway. Those magic words: Remittance Advice. Your ref. GS01. 'Feature "How my naughty piercing almost cost me my life" plus expenses'. And below that, a tear-off cheque for just under a thousand pounds. I detach it gingerly, careful not to rip it.

I had to embellish, of course. I gave Paris spouting geysers of blood coating the walls of the club; I took her much closer to death's door than she actually was, and I relocated her to Scotland for expenses purposes. Otherwise the meat and drink of the story was the same, and it turned out the style of writing, kind of ghoulish indignation, suits me well. Put it this way, I've already got plans for a few more stories along those lines: find someone willing to get their picture taken, who's also happy to confirm they were raped by their mother if they're ever asked, write it up, and it's another grand in the bag.

I owe it all to Cooper, of course, as in, I owe all the money to Cooper; but still, I sense a career move coming on.

And then I put my cheque to one side and I fetch a drink before opening the magazine . . .

ANDREW HOLMES

Sleb

Here's a top tip for the heavy drinker: never get drunk and force your way into the home of the country's biggest pop star, wielding a gun. It's bound to go off, big time.

Christopher Sewell is famous. He used to be an advertising sales executive with a wife, a drink problem and not much more. Now he's serving life for the murder of Felix Carter, who used to be a famous pop star with an acting career, a drink problem and the world at his feet. Only he's dead now. How and why Chris killed Felix is a mystery. Until, that is, he agrees to give a single interview from prison. Just the one interview, mind. You know what these celebrities are like . . .

'A thoughtful study, as well as a gripping psychological thriller' *Independent on Sunday*

'Ingenious twist . . . Holmes has a great line in drunken, rage-filled monologues that collapse into pathos. Very funny' *Literary Review*

'Holmes is a very funny storyteller' *The Times*

'Tragic, funny, touching . . . [Sleb] succeeds through brilliant characterisation and a cunningly devised plot. A talent to watch' *Big Issue in the North*

'Deliciously sharp celebrity satire' *Heat*

'A fascinating insight into the nature of celebrity and obsession' *Red*

'[Sleb] is not only a brilliant satire on the shallow times we live in, but also a moving portrait of the disintegration of one man's life' *Hello!*

'A funny and enjoyable book . . . Holmes's caustic perspective manages to hit the mark' *Express on Sunday*

SCEPTRE